happenstance

THE ORDER OF RAVENS AND WOLVES

T.L HODEL

T.L. HODEL
EMBRACE THE DARKNESS

Author Warning: This book is a dark romance and contains violence, profanity, non consensual and dubious consensual sexual scenes, anal intercourse, and alcohol, tobacco and drug use, racism, and homophobic slurs, rape. If you are a reader sensitive to such material, this might not be the book for you.

This book has m/m, m/m/f, pregnancy and forced proximity, tropes and scenes.

Happenstance is book 3 in The Order of Ravens and Wolves. Book two is Scartissue

Ashley you may get answers in this book

....

Then again, maybe not.

To EJ, Becky, Dylan, Ivy, Vivi, Heather and Drethi, with out you I never would've made it through this. Love you guys.

Playlist

"Don't Fear The Reaper' By Blue Oyster Cult
'Cake By the Ocean' By DNCE
'If Everyone Cared' By Nickelback
'Stack-O-Lee' By Samuel L. Jackson
'Sweet Child O' Mine' By Guns and Roses
'Mockingbird' By Eminem
'Girls Like You' By Maroon Five
'Kiss from a Rose' By Seal
'Hooked' By Dylan Scott
'I'll Take Everything' By James Blunt
'Tomorrow' By Madi Diaz
'Just Give Me A Reason' By Pink
'Girl' By Maren Morris
'Everything I wanted' By Billie Eilish
'IDGAF' By Dua Lipa
'Levitating' By Dua Lipa
'Undo It' By Carrie Underwood
'All Falls Down' By Alan Walker
'Forget to Forget' By Shy Martin
'Ready for it' By Taylor Swift

The Order Of Ravens And Wolves Titles

KINGS:
- Louis Kessler (King go Kings)
- Dean Whitley
- Sebastian Creswell
- Dr. Martin Creswell
- Ryker Hudson

KNIGHTS:
- Micha Kessler (Future king of kings)
- Mason Kessler
- Logan Hudson
- Parker Whitley
- Preston Whitley
- Silas Creswell
- Finn Creswell

Name Pronunciation

- Micha: Mike - ah
- Ryker: Rye - cur
- Silas: Sye - lass
- Riley: Rye - lee
- Paisley: Pase - lee
- Derek: Dare - ick
- Marnie: Mar - knee
- Trina: Tree - nah
- Logan: Low - gan
- Mason: Mase - on
- Preston: Press - ton
- Parker: Park - er
- Finn: Finn
- Junior: June - your
- Shelby: Shell - bee
- Naomi: Nay - oh - me (bitch)
- Chase: Chase
- Tanner: Tan - er
- Amy: A - me
- Ava: A - va
- Whitley: Witt - lee
- Kessler: Kess - ler
- Creswell: Cress - well
- Mathers: Ma - th - ers
- Grier: Gr - ear
- Harper: Har - per
- Louis: Lou - is
- Lana: La - na
- Sean: Sha - awn

Prologue.

Parker

Pain.

The deep-seated agony tearing across someone's nerves could make the strongest fucker bend. It didn't take much. The right poke or prod, hell, even just the threat, had the power to make someone act completely out of character.

What fascinated me was the sound that came with it. Not quite loud enough to give a sense of urgency, but enough to let others know something was wrong. It didn't matter how big someone was, or how much experience they had.

They all made that sound.

A low drowning growl somewhere between a scream and a groan. The same muffled noise the prick I had on the ground was making now. The left side of his face was already starting to swell, and blood trickled from his nose. Pretty sure I broke it. Still, the prick wouldn't give.

He threw his fists up in my ribs and grumbled, "Fuck you."

At this point, I was driven more by adrenaline than anger and answered his strike with one of my own. He wasn't a small guy–I definitely felt his hit–but mine was followed by a loud crunch. The split in my lip reopened as my mouth curled. He was making that sound again, only this time it was louder.

There was no mistaking the agony etched across his face. Broken bone hurt like a bitch. One quick snap sent more pain rushing through a human body than any burn or cut. I'd had my fair share of injuries–part of the job description of being a football player–and still nothing compared to that type of anguish.

The prick on the ground mumbled something incoherent and shifted under me. He was done. About fucking time.

Hurting someone like this probably should bother me. It would bother other people. Micha would say my brother and sister made me numb to it. Preston started torturing people before his preteen years, and Ava… I loved my sister, but she was all kinds of crazy.

The truth was, this shit never really bothered me. Preston stabbed one of our nannies when we were kids, and all I could remember thinking was, 'why is she screaming like that?' Everyone knew my siblings were fucked up, I just hid it better.

My opponent looked up at me and muttered, "Pussy."

I cocked my brow. Guess he had some fight left in him after all. If he wanted to go another round, I was game. I tipped my head down at him, smirked, and dropped my fist into his face.

My knuckles grazed his teeth as his head twisted to the side. That seemed to shut him up. He coughed and spit out a mouthful of blood, but remained silent. I smiled and tapped his cheek.

Good boy.

If he didn't come strolling in here with his friends, running their mouths, he could've avoided all of this. What the fuck did they think would happen? Probably thought they were big shots, coming from one of my mother's rallies. She had a way of manipulating people, winding them up.

I'd seen it a hundred times. A seemingly docile crowd turned violent with a few words from Lillianna Whitley. These fuckers obviously didn't do their homework.

Preston was not my mother's ally. He'd take them out for just knowing her name. My brother didn't give a shit about our parents. They were nothing but annoying obstacles in the cogs that he couldn't just get rid of because Ava and I were in the way. Ava was a daddy's girl through and through, and I cared about our parents.

Would I call it love? Probably not. If they died, I'd feel the loss, sure, but I had no urge to protect them. Hell, I felt more loyal to Micha and his brother than I did to them. There was only one person on this earth I'd die to protect.

I glared down at the prick trying to push me away and slapped him across the face. He'd put his hands on her. Dared to taint her with his touch.

I knew guys like this. Strolling into a town like they owned it, because as far as they were concerned, they were better than everyone else. Except this was Ashen Springs. Our town. And unlike them, we didn't think we were better…

We knew we were.

Was this prick going to cry? Wouldn't be the first time. Though usually it was Preston making some poor sap cry for mercy. This guy should consider himself lucky. I'd just fuck him up a little. His friends, however…

I could feel warm drops of blood hitting my back from Logan's swinging fists. He was behind me, on top of the big one. Logan had that look in his eyes. The one he got when he'd completely lost control.

Not sure what that guy did to piss him off, but there wouldn't be much of his face left when Logan was done. Then again, no one walked away from a fight with Logan without at least one scar. He'd marked us all in one way or another. Preston's foot, my arm, and Micha's leg. Mase was the only one he took it easy on. Never did understand why.

"Come on, pussy." Micha reached out and bitch slapped the guy he was squaring off with. "Is that all you got?"

He only had a few bruises and a couple cuts. No more than Micha himself. Knowing our illustrious leader, he was probably just toying with the fucker. Micha's thrill didn't come from the beat down. It came from the mindfuck.

And then there was my brother.

I glanced over at the guy curled up in the fetal position, blubbering like a little girl. Preston stood calmly over him and lit a smoke. Logan and Preston were lethal. No one liked squaring off with them, but at least with Logan you could see it coming. He'd get this feral look in his eyes.

With Preston, there was nothing. That was the scary part. I grew up with the asshole. I knew what he took in his coffee, who he lost his virginity to, and how he liked his steak. And even I couldn't read him.

Preston took a long pull off his smoke and flicked the ashes down on his victim. "Got anything else smart to say?"

"I'm sorry, man." The guy started crying harder when my brother crouched down and grabbed his chin. "I won't fucking say it again."

"I know you won't." Preston stood up, grabbed his ankle, and dragged him away. "You won't be saying much of anything when I'm done with you."

I'd say the smell of piss was coming from that one.

The fight was dying down. Micha had finished playing with his guy and had him down on the ground, Preston was doing God knows what out of sight, and Logan jumped up off the beaten mess he left behind.

"I need a fucking drink," he said, swiping the blood off his face.

Great fucking idea.

I stretched my arms over my head, enjoying the breeze cooling my skin. When Logan called me and told me to bring a keg, I'd thought we were going to one of our usual spots.

The last place I expected to end up was some broken down stone bridge in the middle of a field. I kind of liked it though. It was a cozy set up. Little couch and firepit, with a bunch of graffiti on the stone walls.

Apparently this was where Riley and her friends hung out. The Causegrove. Stupid fucking name, but honestly, I never even knew this place existed. Might've taken a look around, if it wasn't for a certain someone showing up.

Once Lana arrived, I couldn't take my eyes off her. Or those tight jeans she was wearing. An ass never looked so good.

Then again, she always looked good. Whether her hair was straight, or wild and curly. I didn't give a fuck. I'd stare at her covered in mud and grass. She'd look real fucking good rolling around in the mud...

With me on top of her, legs wrapped around my waist as I plowed into her.

I had to stop thinking about her. As desperate as I was to dive between that girl's legs, it wasn't worth what my mother would do to her. My dick, however, disagreed.

I bet she's as sweet as fucking honey.

God damnit.

I stood up and adjusted myself.

"Don't get any ideas," the prick on the ground twisted his neck and spat. "Fag."

My brow arched. Yeah, I liked dick, and I liked pussy. I was a greedy motherfucker and wanted it all. What really got me off was making guys like this realize how much fun a deep dicking could be. Sexual preferences didn't matter when their prostate was hit the right way. Couldn't stop that shit.

"Stop looking at me like that."

I snickered and slid my gaze down to the bulge in his jeans. *I'd seen better.* "You think I can't see your hard on?"

His jaw clenched, making me smirk. Stupid fuck. Logan wandered over and dropped his arm on my shoulder.

"You want me to hold him for you?" He took a drink from the red solo cup in his hand and cocked his head down at the guy whose eyes were now wide with worry. "Should be easy. I don't think he's got much fight left in him."

"Don't fucking touch me!" he growled back up at us.

"Oh, but you want me to touch you." I crouched down and cupped his dick. Sure enough, he was hard. "See?"

Logan's lips tipped up. "Think his friends know cock turns him on?"

There it was. That glimmer of self hatred. I loved that look. It wasn't me that was turning the prick on, though. It was the adrenaline rushing through his system. Was I going to tell him that? Fuck no. Let him spend the rest of his pathetic life confused.

"Listen," he said in a quiet voice, "You don't... I'm not..."

Aw, poor thing didn't want his friends to know.

"You're not what?" Logan taunted, "A fag?"

"No."

"You like pussy."

"That's right."

"Huh?" Logan turned his gaze my way. "What do you think?"

I squeezed the prick's dick just enough to make it jump. "I think he's pretty hard for a pussy lover."

Now the guy was really getting scared. His arms swung out to push me away. Logan was ready for that. He pounced, grabbing his wrists and holding him down.

"How much time do you need?"

Based on how hard he was, I'd say this guy was ready to blow. "It won't take much." Two or three pumps and he'd be done.

"Listen man, I'm fucking sorry, okay?" the prick cried out desperately. "I won't say shit about you anymore."

"I don't give a fuck what you say about me." I leaned in and softly growled in his ear, "You touched *her*."

This motherfucker put his hands on Lana. He dared to touch the girl I'd been dreaming about for years, and now, he was going to pay.

Chapter 1
Parker

The first time I saw Lana Crawford it was her first day of kindergarten. Micha, Logan and I were showing Mason and Silas around, because having been there the year before, we obviously ruled the place. And then I saw her.

This girl standing perfectly in a ray of sunlight, as if the heavens themselves were pointing her out to me. She looked like an angel, wearing a blue dress, red sneakers, and a sparkly purple bow in her wild, curly hair. I was entranced by her magnificence. The way her big hazel eyes and bronze complexion seemed to glow.

I stood there staring at this beautifully weird girl, jealous of the people she smiled at. Every time she stopped to talk to someone, my fists would ball. Why was she wasting her time with these people? A unicorn shouldn't talk to a frog.

I wanted to hurt all the kids that played with her. Beat them down until they bowed at her feet, like I was ready to do. But she was a goddess, and I was just a boy.

How could someone like me approach her? So, I stayed in the background. Watching with complete contempt as other people got her attention. Later that day, I found her bow on the playground and carefully picked it up like some treasured item to take home.

My intent was to return it to her the next day. Get down on one knee and present the lost item like one of those knights in the stories my mother read to me. Before I could ask for the princess's hand, I had to prove myself. That's what all those stories had taught me. A bow might not be as good as slaying a dragon, but it was a start.

My grand adventure came to a crashing halt when we were all sitting down to dinner. My mother started talking about the 'colored girl' they let into our school. She said 'Mansworth should be evaluating applicants better, because those people are taking over America.'

At first, I was mad. Why weren't we doing more to stop these people? How could they let someone come in and take over our country? And then I thought, maybe these people were my dragon? I could slay them and really have a reason to ask for the princess's hand. Then I realized exactly who my mother was talking about.

That was the first time I remember hating her.

"Heads up, Whitley!"

All I saw before I was knocked off my feet was Sean running at me, head down, and shoulder at the ready. My lungs deflated, exhaling all my air as I went flying back.

I managed to hook my fingers in Sean's shoulder pads and drag the prick down with me. While I was shaking off the ache rushing through my shoulder blades, Sean wrapped his fingers around my face mask and shook my helmet.

"That's three, Whitley." He crashed his facemask into mine, "Get your fucking head in the game."

I gritted my teeth and growled back, "Go fuck yourself, Callaghan."

Prick was enjoying this way too much.

Football was a rough sport, and as much as I hated to admit it, Sean was a great team captain. Most Quarterbacks avoided tackles during practice. Hell, they avoided tackles period. Sean not only embraced them, he was the first to go after the slacker. Today, that was apparently me.

Sean jumped to his feet, shot me a smirk, and held out his hand.

He was definitely enjoying this too much.

I stared at the outstretched arm for a second before accepting. With a grunt, he pulled me up and slapped my shoulder.

"You gonna go for four?"

He might not find this shit so fun if he knew why I was distracted. How happy would the smug fucker be if he knew I'd knocked up little sis's best friend?

"Piss off, Callaghan," I grumbled, shoving his shoulder. "Shouldn't you be practicing your throws?"

His eyes narrowed, which made my lips curl. Last Friday he missed a pass, costing us the game. This time I got to watch Callaghan march away with a scowl.

The second he was gone, the pit in my stomach came back, followed by the words that had been swimming around my head for over a week. *I'm going to be a dad'.* Me. Parker Easton Whitley. The supposed golden boy of Ashen Springs had knocked someone up. I was oddly proud of that.

Not because my baby was getting ready to come into the world, but because *she* was carrying it.

The girl I once wanted to slay a dragon for. Even if she could be persuaded to get rid of the problem, I didn't want her to. When I was balls deep in some chick, or stroked my cock at night, it was Lana I thought about. Now that image had morphed into looking into that baby's eyes, while having my arms wrapped around her.

My girl and my baby. A family.

How fucking unreal was that? I was still trying to wrap my head around it. How it happened was no mystery. I didn't put on a condom–which I always do. I was too excited. The only thing I could think about was getting my dick in her. Didn't even ask if she was on birth control.

Honestly, the thought never occurred to me. Why would it? I had the girl I'd been dreaming about most of my life wrapped around me. Who the fuck cared about anything else?

Maybe some part of me wanted to knock her up? Logan and Micha were always talking about claiming their women. As if it was a competition or some shit. Micha preferred the 'if you look at her I'll kill you' approach, while Logan liked to physically mark Shelby.

There was always something on that girl. A bite, a scratch, or some shit to let everyone know who she belonged to. Looks like I won that contest. What better way to mark a chick than to knock her up?

My thoughts got cut off when a football came sailing through the air and clacked off the side of my helmet.

Fuck sakes.

"Jesus fucking Christ, Whitley!" Coach yelled, waving his hands through the air, "We're not here to fucking daydream!"

"Sorry Coach, I've got something on my mind."

"I don't care if you have a goddamn log shoved up your ass. Get the fuck…"

Coach Keegan continued to scream at me while I watched his face get redder with every word. I cocked my head at his swinging arms, fisting in the air. I'd seen him go off like this before. Sometimes it seemed like hours before he calmed down.

I glanced over at the track coach and his assistant. While coach Bantam had the same red look in his face as my coach, the new assistant was calmly helping Shelby stretch. He pulled her leg up and leaned in, smiling down at her. Logan was definitely going to kill that guy.

"You better not stand around with your thumb up your ass on Sunday…"

"Yes, Coach." At this point, I was pretty sure he didn't need oxygen to live.

"Get your ass out there…"

I nodded. "Yes, Coach."

"Run the goddamn ball!"

"Got it, Coach."

This time when the ball came at me, I caught it and rushed down the field.

It'd been almost two weeks now, since I found out I was going to be a dad. In front of every-fucking-one. Logan found a pregnancy test and thought Shelby was pregnant, and could he announce that in private? Of course not. *Prick.*

Lana still wouldn't talk to me. It wasn't just her. The girls had banded together. Every time I'd try to talk to her, Shelby or Riley would intervene. Harper just ran away, Shelby called me a jerk, and Riley hit me. For a tiny thing, she sure packed a punch. At least she didn't crush my nuts like she did Silas. Poor fucker couldn't walk straight for a week.

At this point, I'd say it was a safe bet that Lana told them what I did. Especially considering the pimp comments Logan kept throwing my way. Who'd have thought giving a chick money was a bad thing?

Of course I handled it in a bad way, but I did it on purpose. Had to do something to chase her away. She was staring at me all doe eyed, which I really liked, but if my mother found out…

Ava once came home with a Cuban guy. He was okay, I guess. I didn't want to kill him. Which was huge, considering he was fucking my sister. He lasted an hour with my mother. Longer than most. Ava was heartbroken, and our mother had him deported the next day.

"Heads up, Whitley."

I turned to see Sean barreling at me.

Aw fuck.

I SWEPT the water off my face and glanced over at Logan, who was leaning against my locker. "Do you mind?"

"Not at all."

"Unless you want to suck my dick dry, I suggest you move."

Logan tipped his head and smirked. "I think that's more Mase's department."

"You're never gonna let that go, are you?" Mase grumbled from the bench next to him.

I pushed Logan out of the way, opened my locker, and pointed at Mase. "You were the one that opened your big mouth."

"He's got you there," Logan winked.

Why Mase decided to say shit, to Logan of all people, I didn't get. We all knew the fucker couldn't keep a secret. Though I think it was more by choice.

Bastard liked to throw everyone off. Including Micha, who I had a rather awkward conversation with after that little outburst. And by conversation, I mean me explaining that I didn't completely defile his little brother while dodging his fists.

"Seem extra grumpy today." Logan's hand landed on my shoulder with a resounding smack. *Fucker.* "Lana still not talking to you?"

Chris, our wide receiver, gave me a sideways glance. Sean made it very clear to the whole team that Harper and Lana were off limits. Unfortunately for Sean, I didn't give a fuck what he thought. I went along with it because it kept all these other horny fuckers away from her.

"No," I said, giving Chris a look that said 'try me', "And your girl isn't helping."

"Hey, I claim no responsibility for what Cherry Pie does." Logan crossed his arms and leaned back. "It's kind of hot watching her give you a hard time though."

I snorted. *Prick.*

Rummaging through my bag, I shook my head and pulled my clothes out. "It'd be easier to talk to her if her friends didn't get in the way."

"Micha's on board with you there," Mase added. "He was yelling at Riley yesterday for getting involved."

I actually saw Micha smile the other day. The last thing I wanted was to cause problems between them.

"Go to her house," Logan suggested.

"Tried that."

"Did you try kicking in the door?"

Was he serious? Of course he was. Logan would burn the whole world down to get to his girl. Though I had to admit, he might have a point. Maybe it was time to take a page from his book.

Mason leaned forward on the bench and rested his elbows on his knees. "You could always choose the other route."

"What other route?" Seemed pretty black and white to me. Either I hunted Lana down, or she kept avoiding me.

"Make her come to you."

Both Logan and I stopped and cocked our heads at him.

"I gotta say, Lana doesn't seem like the chasing dick type," Logan pointed out.

"Exactly," I nodded at Logan. "She won't even talk to me. How am I supposed to get her to chase me?"

Mason's green eyes sparkled as they rolled up to meet mine. "You tell everyone."

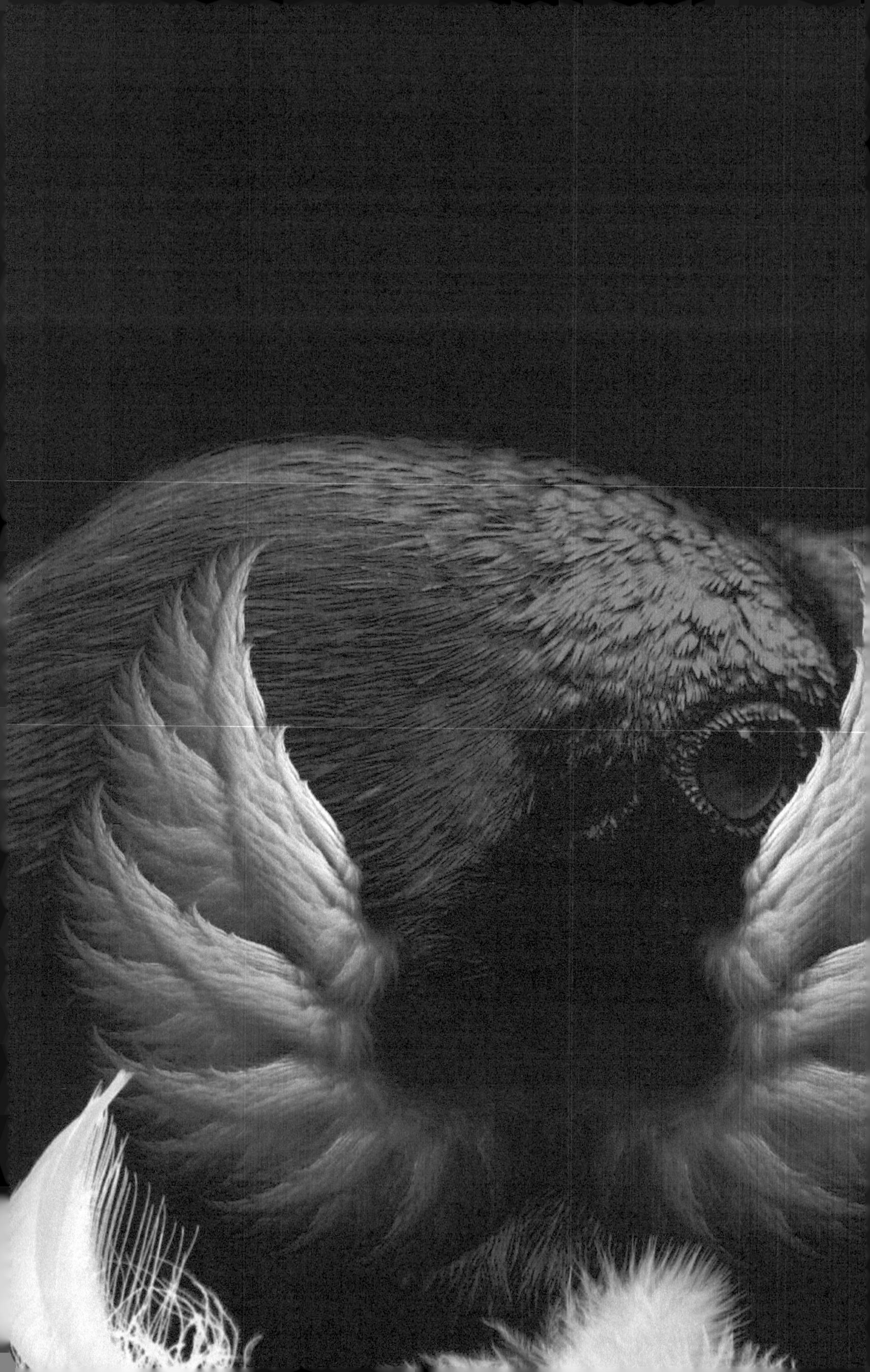

Chapter 2
Lana

"Have a good day, my sweet girl."

I smiled at Nan and begrudgingly got out of the car. Sweet girl. Would she still call me that if she knew? I should've been smarter.

I wasn't one of those bobble-headed girls that got stupid over a guy. I wanted to be a doctor, for Christ's sake. A pediatrician. All my life, I've watched girls fall for the crap guys said, and swore I wouldn't be one of them.

Then again, I was always a little stupid when it came to Parker Whitley. Honestly, I wasn't surprised that I fell down that hole, or about the way he treated me after. Parker was one of the Knights. Of course he was an asshole.

It was something else that brought tears to my eyes. Memories of another voice whispering in my ear, while hands roughly held me down, and I stared at the moon, praying for it to end. That was the night my soul was shattered. Torn apart by someone I trusted.

"Bye Nan." I managed to give her a small wave, "Love you."

Nan gave me her *'go get em'* smile and blew me a kiss. "Love you too."

I rolled my eyes at the girls that had their noses turned up. Apparently our little beat down car didn't meet their high standards. Brushing it off my shoulders, I sauntered past them. From a young age, I knew I was different from the other kids. I didn't know why or how, just that they had something I didn't.

In this school, there was a lot that the other kids had that I didn't. Money, staff, prestige. But none of that caused the heaviness I felt in my chest. I didn't realize what that was until I showed up for parent teacher interviews with my Nan. All the other kids were there with their moms and dads. They had parents. I had Nan and Henry, our goat.

That was the first time I noticed Parker Whitley. I saw him on the playground when Nan and I were leaving, beating up one of the kids that made fun of me. His little fists flew through the air, raining his fury down on the other boy.

I used to tell myself he was protecting me. I knew better now. Parker Whitley wasn't a fairy tale knight, seeking to defend the maiden's honor. He was the thing in my closet. The creature that made children scream in the middle of the night. They all were.

Micha was the devil. Preston death, Logan war, Mason pestilence, and Parker famine. Which was exactly why no one could find out what happened. I couldn't subject someone I loved to Ashworth's apocalypse squad. No matter what he did to me.

Speaking of squads...

Naomi and her minions were standing by the front door. Hips cocked, while they rolled their eyes at people passing by. If Parker and his friends were the apocalypse squad, then these girls were Ashen Springs version of sirens. Lulling men to their deaths with sweet songs.

I walked up the steps and smiled back at Amy. I didn't mind her. She might be a member of the slut squad–as Riley called them–but she had sweet moments. Lately I'd seen her talking to other people. Most of whom were on Naomi's hit list.

Maybe she was getting tired of Naomi's crap? I know I was glad the queen and her minions would be gone next year. If only Mason could graduate, then my senior year might not be so bad. Except for the baby I'd be raising, of course.

"Jasmine," my gaze rolled over one minion in particular, "Showing a little extra skin today, I see."

Naomi's light eyes locked on mine. "Why are you talking to us?"

"Aw," Jasmine's lips twisted in a mocking frown, "Is little orphan Annie lonely?"

I snickered out a scoff. Little orphan Annie. How original. Mason was the genius behind that one. It still hurt though. I knew it wasn't my parents fault they died, but sometimes it felt like it was.

"Still full of quick wit, I see."

"Careful, Annie," Naomi leaned back and continued filing her nails. "You wouldn't want someone questioning your choice in wardrobe."

Jasmine rolled her eyes judgingly over me. "A word of advice, honey, that sweater isn't hiding anything."

I faltered. Took a step back, and pulled the hem of my sweater down. Did they know? No, I told myself, shaking it off. There's no way they could. I didn't tell anyone, and I was pretty sure no one else was talking about it. Not any of my friends, anyway. Taking a deep breath, I pushed my way into Ashworth.

The change in the air was so thick, it was palatable. It rolled through the hall in heavy waves, crashing through my anxious heartbeat. The whispers and sideways glances were unnerving.

So much so, that I looked down to make sure my bump wasn't visible. Something I tried not to do, because it would draw attention. It wasn't that I was trying to hide my pregnancy. Then again, maybe I was?

Parker Whitley not only destroyed my idealized teenage fantasy of him, he crushed it under his overpriced boot. Still, there was a small part of me that couldn't let go of what I'd seen.

That was the problem. I wanted to hate him. Wanted to curse the very ground he walked on. But I couldn't, because for a few hours, three months before, I saw the real Parker Whitley.

I could still feel his hands on me. Touching me with the same feral need I felt for him. And it all started with one simple question...

"Why did you stick up for me?"

Parker cocked his head and stared at me with his beautiful grey eyes. The way they sparkled, happy and full of life, drew me in. Day after day, I got lost in those eyes, wishing that just once they'd look at me. And now that they were, I couldn't breathe.

"No one should be treated that way."

I moved my gaze up to his soft blond locks. That didn't help much either. All I could think about was running my fingers through it. Maybe tug on his hair a little? Would he like that? Maybe he'd groan. I'd really like to hear him groan.

Okay Lana, breathe. Parker's just being nice. That's all.

He turned away to drop my keys on the dresser and it felt like air suddenly came flying back in the room. This was my moment. I'd say something smart and witty, and Parker Whitley would finally see me.

"Would your mother agree?" And just like that, the oxygen was gone again.

Way to go, Lana. Total genius move.

"Just because she's my mother," Parker's back straightened as he glared over his shoulder, "Doesn't mean I agree with her."

Glared! Great, now I'd made him mad.

Everyone knew about Lillianna Whitley. Nan kept an eye on her. Considering Lillianna's entire view on life demanded that people like Nan, myself, and even Riley, be sent off somewhere else, I didn't blame her. Though there were rumors that she'd done more than send them off.

How involved was Parker with his mother's organization? He didn't fit her vision of a perfect America either. Then again...

"Does she know?"

Could I internally facepalm, because a slap might knock some sense into me.

My heart started pounding when the corner of Parker's mouth curled and he took a couple steps closer. "Does she know what?"

Judging by the gleam in his eye, I'd say he wanted me to say it. No. That couldn't be right? Seriously, what would Parker Whitley get out of hearing me say he liked dick too? Either way, I wasn't going to say it.

No way, José.

"That your bat swings both ways."

Fuck.

Parker belted out a laugh, making my pulse flutter more. He had the sexiest chuckle. Sometimes, that's all I'd need to make my day better. Admittedly, I may have sought him out a couple times.

Not like I went up to him or anything, I mean, come on, he was Parker Whitley. But if he happened to be right around the corner talking to someone, it would be rude to interrupt. I wasn't eavesdropping. I was being polite.

Oh god, I'm so pathetic. Stalker much, Lana?

Parker's grey eyes slowly raked down my body, making me wish I'd had time to put on more than a t-shirt and panties. Unfortunately, I was kind of stuck with what Riley could find for me to sleep in. Which happened to be one of Logan's shirts. So, in other words, I smelled like a man whore. Better than Mason, I guess. Then I'd smell like tears and misery.

"Do you tell your Nan about your sexual proclivities?"

While my internal-self was screaming, 'Parker Whitley knows you call her Nan', my outer-self was struggling to remain calm.

Wait... is he still coming towards me?

"Well, Angel," Parker's deep tone purred through the air, vibrating up my spine, "Do you?"

Oh my God, he called me Angel. Angel!!

"Do I what?"

"Talk to your Nan about who you fuck."

I didn't have to look to know I was probably as red as a tomato. I could feel it burning in my cheeks. I'd only been kissed once, by Brandon, so there was no fucking to talk about. And Nan knew all about that.

"Nan will always support me."

Parker stepped up to me and cocked his head. He smelled good. All powerful and manly. I really wanted to touch him. Would he let me touch him? It wouldn't take much. Just lift my arm...

"Always?"

"Yes." I nodded my head, "Always. She'd never stop me from going after something I really wanted."

That was true. Nan wasn't high on me getting so close to Harper, or spending time at Logan Hudson's house, but she trusted my judgment.

"She'd never stop you?" he said, leaning in so his hot breath brushed my skin. "What if it's something you shouldn't have?"

This must be what heaven felt like. I couldn't think of anything better than being able to feel the heat coming off Parker Whitley's body. I hummed and leaned in a little closer, almost running my nose up his neck, before stopping myself.

Jesus Lana, have some self control.

"No one should make you feel like you don't deserve what you want."

That was something Nan preached daily. I thought it was good advice, but Parker didn't respond. Probably because he thought I was some kind of creeper. Who leans in to smell someone? A creeper, that's who.

When I looked up at him, that was not the vibe I got. His grey eyes had darkened, and if I didn't know better, I'd say there was desire sparking in his gaze.

Parker stepped in, pressing his hard body against mine. I couldn't move. Couldn't breathe. I just stood there staring at his chest like an idiot. He was so... hard.

"What if you want a girl you have no business being with?"

My eyes snapped up to his. Did he mean...

That's when I saw it. The loneliness and want etched across his face. His hand twitched at his side as his brows furrowed.

"What if she doesn't agree?" I said.

He leaned in and grazed his lips across the shell of my ear, making me shiver. "Then she's stupid."

"Or she's brave," I breathed out quietly.

Was it hot in here? It suddenly felt really hot in here.

"Bravery is just another word for stupid."

I tipped my chin up and studied him. I mean, really studied him. Parker Whitley was the team's star running back, on the honor roll, and had his choice of scholarships to choose from. He was what every parent wanted their son to be. Ashen Springs' golden boy. And not once had it occurred to me that he didn't want any of it.

"What are you so afraid of, Parker? That you'll disappoint them," I stepped in, pressing my body against his, "Or yourself?"

"It's not always that simple, Angel."

My brows furrowed as I looked up at him. "Yes it is."

"Is it?"

I licked my lips, swallowing my nerves, and nodded my head.

"Prove it." He bent down and softly growled in my ear, "Take your shirt off."...

.   .   .

IT WAS THAT MAN, the brief glimpse I got into Parker Whitley, that I prayed was the father of my child. Because the other option was too much to bare.

My brows furrowed at a couple of students pointing at me and staring with wide eyes.

Something was definitely up.

The only time people in Ashworth paid any attention to me was when Mason Kessler decided to torment Harper. Since I wasn't about to let him push my best friend around, I'd also become a target of the youngest Kessler.

When we were kids, I thought Mason was sweet, until he showed his true colors. Maybe all men lied about who they were? Even the ones you trusted the most.

I wiped the tear off my cheek before anyone could see, and rounded the corner. Harper and Shelby were waiting for me by my locker. Normal for Harper, but Shelby was usually with Riley.

More concerning was the look on their faces. Somewhere between worry and sympathy. I forced the lump of guilt down into my gut and focused on Shelby. Her light brown eyes didn't make my skin crawl.

In the short time I'd known her, I'd learned two things. Shelby had a huge heart–she once spent an hour chasing down a fly so it could be released safely outside–and she was completely insane. Anyone that loved Logan Hudson as much as she did had to have a screw loose. That boy was not right in the head.

"Did someone die?" I was only teasing, but then they both flinched.

"Depends if Riley finds them," Harper grumbled under her breath.

That didn't explain much. Someone was always on Riley's shit list. Mainly Micha. He seemed to occupy the top spot ninety percent of the time. Why those two were together, I had no idea. They argued more than Nan and our goat.

I don't know how many times Nan had come charging into the house muttering that Henry was about to find himself at the slaughterhouse.

"Hey," Shelby's pretty face scrunched up as her hand swept down my back, "How are you doing?"

The girls had been super sweet about this whole thing. I loved them for that, but I still shied away from Shelby's touch.

"Are you okay?" Shelby stared down at me, eyes glimmering with unshed tears. "Is there anything you need?"

"Alright." I spun around, dodging Shelby's comforting hand, "What's going on?"

Right then, Jasmine decided to walk by with Naomi's other minions. She flicked her dark hair over her shoulder and muttered, "Orphan Annie moving up to Mommy," as she sauntered past.

I swallowed and glanced down at my belly. Was I busted? Of course I was. There was only so much Ashworth's sweater could hide, and my bump was definitely starting to show.

"Knew I shouldn't have changed in the locker room," I grumbled under my breath.

Harper's worried gaze darted around as she leaned in and whispered, "It wasn't that."

"My idiot boyfriend and his friends decided to inform every-one," Shelby explained, with an exaggerated eye roll.

Of course they did.

"Rye's currently hunting them down."

Was it wrong that I hoped she found them? Riley was a tiny thing, but the girl had bite. This was her first year at Ashworth, and she'd managed to do something I never could. Get Mason to leave Harper alone. When she was around, anyway.

"Let me guess," I released a loud sigh and glanced at Shelby, "Micha's leading the charge?"

Every time I went to see Riley, Micha made it quite clear how he felt about me avoiding Parker. The last time he called me a selfish bitch. Trust me, I would love nothing more than to be able to talk to Parker, because the other option made me sick.

Shelby shook her head. "That would be Parker."

I snorted. Parker Whitley didn't lead shit. "I think it's more likely it was your boyfriend." This crap screamed Logan.

Harper added in a quiet voice, "Sean said Mason told him."

Sean knew?

I swallowed the bile rising in my throat, and quickly turned my attention back to my locker.

Hoots and hollers came from down the hall as Logan pranced towards us, with Riley over his shoulder. She beat her fists off his back and kicked her feet, which of course didn't detour Logan any. He continued on his way with a big smile on his face.

Shelby's boyfriend wasn't someone I'd associate with relief, but when she dropped her face in her hands, I'd never been more thankful to see the charming asshole. I'd take any distraction I could get. Even if it was in the form of Logan Hudson.

"Oh my God." Shelby's blonde hair swayed as she shook her head. "Lord take me now."

"Logan," Riley's screech echoed off the walls. "Put me down, right now!"

"No can do, Sis," Logan shot Shelby a wink. "You started this shit."

I could see the rage building in Riley's face. She was not happy, which usually meant bad things for the person that pissed her off. She was like a tiny feral kitten. Fluffy and cute to look at, but if you tried to touch it, it'd scratch your face off. Mind you, Logan was the type to poke the feral kitten. Like I said, the boy was not right in the head.

"*You* started this shit! Running your mouth around the whole damn school," Riley growled. "I'm so gonna kick your ass."

"Sorry, Sis," Logan chuckled, green eyes sparkling, "I'm the one in control of asses here."

To reiterate his point, he swung his arm up, palm landing with a resounding smack on her butt.

The thing that got to me was how not one person questioned what was happening. I shouldn't be surprised. Even if Logan wasn't one of the infamous Knights, he was *that guy*. Blessed with looks and impossible charm. The guy that nobody could hate.

Nobody except me, because I truly did hate Logan Hudson. Loathed the very ground he walked on. Not because of anything he did to me. Until recently, I don't think he even knew I existed. Harper, on the other hand…

My lip curled as he strutted over and leaned in to kiss Shelby. I don't know what she saw in him. Shelby could give Naomi a run for her money, and unlike Ashworth's queen bee, she wasn't a complete bitch.

"Uh huh," Shelby held up her hand, cutting off his kiss. "You think I'm gonna kiss you after this crap?"

Logan let out a long groan and stood up. "But, baby…"

"Don't 'but baby' me."

Gotta say, I liked the snide look Shelby shot him. It made me like her a little more. Not many girls turned down Logan Hudson. None, actually. In fact, I could see three in the hall right now, waiting to swoop in and pick up the pieces of his broken heart.

But did all that female attention bother Shelby? Nope. She was utterly confident in Logan's devotion to her.

"You see that, Sis," Logan sighed and rolled his eyes back to a fuming Riley. "Now you're fucking with my pussy."

"Good," she snarled. "Don't you give in to him, Shell."

"That's it," he smirked at me, *asshole*, and sauntered down the hall, "I'm taking you to your boyfriend. Maybe he can control your crazy ass."

Riley lifted her head, looking back at us, and held up her fist, "Stay strong."

Shelby gave her own reaffirming fist bump and draped her arm over my shoulder. I bit my lip and forced myself to accept her comfort. For some reason, these two girls had my back.

I'd never done anything to deserve it, yet they were standing up to their boyfriends for me. I quickly swept away the tear running down my cheek and sniffed back my sob.

Stupid hormones

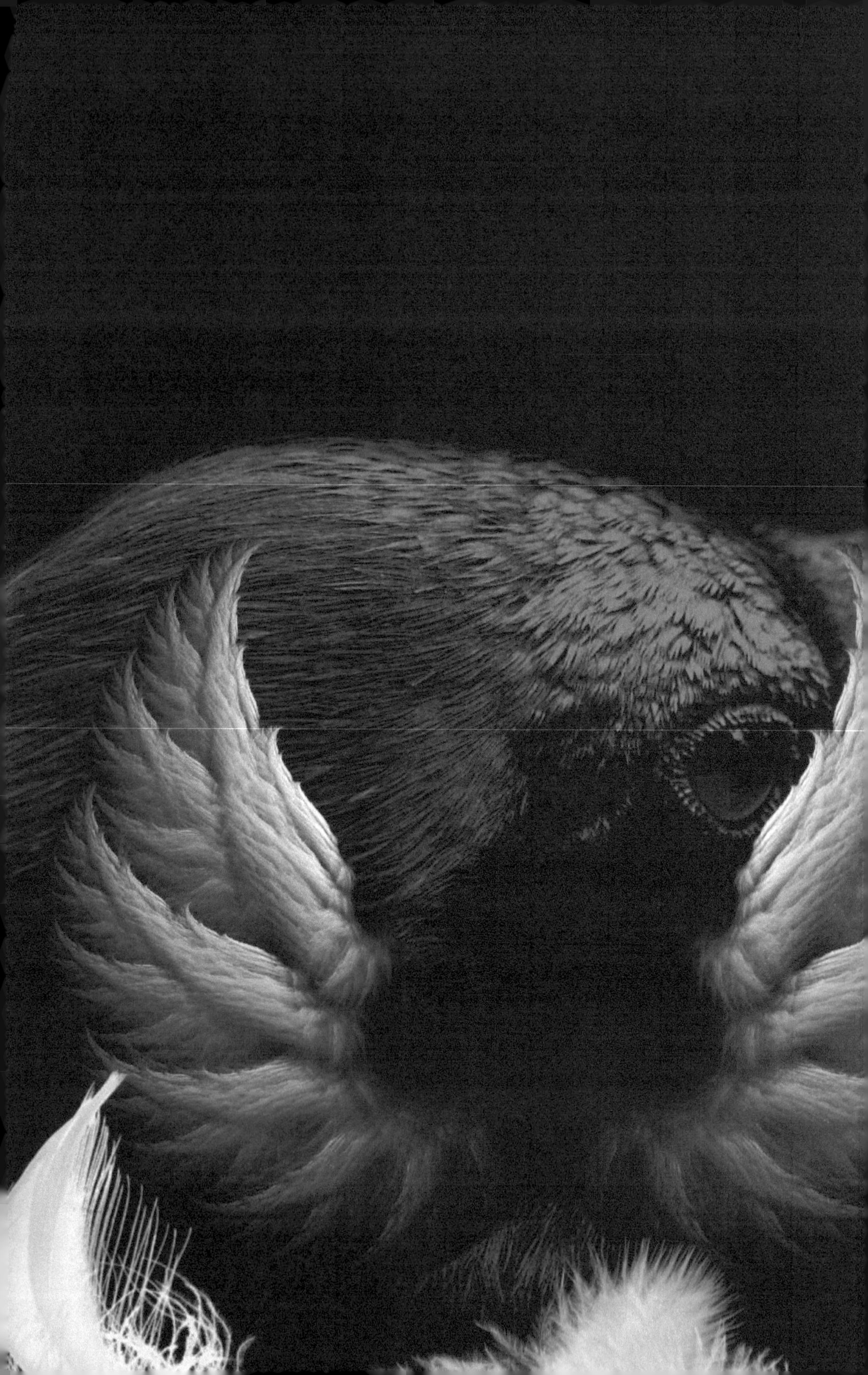

I could feel eyes on me all morning. Rooms would suddenly get quiet when I entered, and despite what my friends said, I could hear them whispering. My friends had my back. Riley made that quite apparent when she punched a guy in English class for calling me a slut. I couldn't talk to the one person I wanted to, though.

From the time we were in diapers, it was Harper and I against the world. She was my best friend. My confidant. The girl who knew all my secrets. And now, the person I dreaded seeing every day.

I couldn't talk to her, couldn't even look at her, because there were only two people she had in this world, and if she found out what happened, she'd lose them both. I'd never felt more alone in my life.

I wove my way through the rows of desks to take my seat, trying to ignore all the sideways glances. Was it wrong that I was relieved to be in a class without my best friend? That for an hour, I didn't have to see her face, or tell her everything was okay, when it wasn't. Nothing would ever be okay again.

"Slut," someone in the room coughed, making me wish that Riley wasn't stuck in the office waiting for reprimand.

These people would like nothing more than to see me run out of the room in tears. As far as they were concerned, I didn't belong. I didn't have a trust fund, or powerful parents, and I was proud of that. I could hold my head high knowing that everything I had, I earned. How many of them could say that?

So, no, I wasn't going to run out of the room. I'd never give them the satisfaction. A few rumors weren't going to chase me away. I belonged here, just as much as they did, and I wasn't about to be bullied out of a spot I rightfully earned.

Speaking of bullied...

Mason Kessler strutted in and loudly announced, "I know you all missed me, but you don't need to cry anymore. I'm back."

Was I surprised by Mason Kessler's grand entrance? No. Quiet wasn't his style. Hence Harper's hyper terrified state. The only time I wished I had influence was when Mason Kessler was around.

I'd like nothing more than to wipe that stupid smile off his face. Of course, influence in this town didn't matter much when it came to the Kesslers. You couldn't out-power someone who had it all.

"Hey, Lana banana." Mason dropped down into the desk next to me and shot me a grin. "Miss me?"

"Hardly," I muttered, while pulling my books out of my bag.

I'd come to the conclusion long ago that arrogance must be a Kessler trait. Even their father walked around like his shit didn't stink. If I had to guess, I'd say Louis Kessler had more skeletons in his closet than anyone else. It was nice to see him humbled, even if I was just a little.

Shelby's mom insisted on things like family dinners. I knew

this, because Micha was constantly complaining about it. And no, he didn't go to any of her required family functions. Not unless Riley made him.

The teacher came in and started class. Not that that mattered much to Mason. While I was trying to pay attention, he kept poking me. Quietly calling my name, and flicking little balls of paper my way.

As much as I tried to ignore him, my frustration built up until I finally snapped, "What!" in a growled whisper.

"What'd Parker do to piss you off?"

I glanced down at the book open on my desk. *The Scarlet Letter*. Fate sure had a sense of humor. Studying a book about a woman being dubbed a whore, when that's exactly how Parker made me feel. Throwing money at me the next morning!

"None of your business."

"That bad, huh?" Mason sat back and hummed.

I'd seen that look before. The dark glint in his bright eyes was unmistakable. Whatever he was thinking, it wasn't good.

"Well, whatever it is, you better get over it quick."

He had no idea what I had to get over. Was I mad at Parker, yes. I hated him for how he treated me. But that wasn't what weighed me down everyday.

"You belong to him now."

My glare snapped his way. "Says who?"

"Says that." He tipped his chin to the bump I was trying to hide, making me blink back the tears threatening to burst forth.

This baby didn't prove anything, because I didn't know who put this baby in me. The man who filled my dreams with tender words and gentle kisses. Or the one who haunted my nightmares.

I hated Mason for reminding me of that. For making me once again wonder if I could love the child I was carrying. Would I hate it for being a living reminder of the worst night of my life?

"I'm curious, Mason, why didn't daddy cover up your stint in rehab?" I twisted my neck and gave a small frown. "Has he finally given up on his youngest son? It's got to be hard, living in your brother's shadow."

The tick in his jaw brought a satisfied grin to my lips. Unfortunately, I forgot the number one rule when it came to dealing with Mason Kessler. Never underestimate him.

"Lana," he pronounced loudly, "That is so inappropriate."

Suddenly everyone's eyes were on me.

"Mr. Kessler," our teacher, Mr. Hanes, said, "Is there a reason you're interrupting my class?"

"I'm sorry sir, it's really hard to concentrate when someone keeps propositioning me." Mason paused to slide his gaze my way. "I keep telling her I'm not interested, but she won't leave me alone."

This son of a...

"I did no such thing!" I shrieked.

"Look, I'm sure there are plenty of guys you can find into butt stuff."

Snickers filled the room as my jaw dropped. He did not just say that.

"Miss Crawford, kindly leave Mr. Kessler alone."

I stared at the teacher, shocked. "But I wasn't–"

"You heard the man," Mason interrupted me.

I spent the rest of class plotting Mason Kessler's death. Even had the tombstone picked out. A nice wooden cross. Blessed in holy water to keep his evil spirit in the ground.

BY THE TIME LUNCH CAME, I was more than ready for this day to be over. Thanks to Mason, I wasn't just the school slut, I was the girl that liked butt stuff. On the upside, I had about twenty detailed plans on how to rid the world of the youngest Kessler. I just needed to get my hands on a hive of bees, and a woodchipper.

I sat back and closed my eyes, enjoying the gentle breeze toying with my hair. Out here, it was just me, the fresh air, and the sun. Peaceful solitude. The only thing I missed was Harper.

I could've brought her out here with me, but then I ran the risk of the football team starting a search. I understood why. The last time Harper didn't show up for lunch, it was because Mason had trapped a claustrophobic Harper in a locker.

Guilt welled up in my gut as I thought of my friend sitting in the cafeteria, with no one to protect her. Yes, Riley and Shelby were there, but Harper wasn't comfortable around them. Riley scared her. Heck, Riley scared me sometimes, and Shelby was too touchy feely.

They were both incredibly loyal and sweet in their own ways. That wasn't the problem. The only person Harper was comfortable around was me. And now, I wasn't comfortable around her. I sniffed and wiped away the tear rolling down my cheek. It felt like I had lost my parents all over again.

"Well, this is a first."

I jumped back and turned my head to see the new assistant coach, Luke Lannister. I didn't personally know him, but Shelby said he was nice. Which Logan was not impressed about. That boy gave jealousy a new name. He once went after a guy just because he talked to Shelby.

Mr. Lannister tipped his chin at my bag. "Don't you guys usually eat in the cafeteria?"

"I'm sorry," I sat up and started collecting my things. "I'll go."

Should've known someone would have a problem with me eating out here. Ashworth was a strictly by the books school. Students belonged in desks, and food in the cafeteria.

"No, no. You're fine." I couldn't help but notice the way his light eyes sparkled when he leaned in and whispered, "I won't tell anyone."

That made me eye him. Ashworth was all about image. An orphaned scholarship kid didn't exactly help their reputation. They'd like nothing more than to kick me out. Yet another reason to hide my current predicament. Last year, Krissy Smythe got pregnant and was sent to a more *appropriate* school, and she *was* from a prominent family.

I guess Mr. Lannister sensed my apprehension, because he quickly added, "It's kind of nice to have someone normal to talk to."

"What do you mean normal?"

"No offense to the staff here," he sighed and propped his elbow up on the bleachers, "But I doubt any of them has had to live off peanut butter."

I couldn't help but snicker. *Okay, maybe he wasn't as bad as the rest.* "You can't forget the jam."

"I'm more of a honey guy, myself."

"No thanks," my nose scrunched up, "Too sweet for me."

"Ah, you're more of the salty snack type?"

"Give me a bag of chips over a chocolate bar any day."

My heart fluttered a bit when he smiled. He was probably only a couple years older than me, and definitely handsome, with his thick chestnut hair and bright blue eyes, but so not someone I would go for. Not to mention that he was technically a teacher, and I had enough rumors floating around about me. It was still flattering, though.

He looked up, squinting against the bright sun. "Can I ask you a question?"

I shrugged.

"Does the reason you're out here," his face took on a more serious expression as he shifted his gaze to my belly, "Have anything to do with that?"

Shifting in my seat, I quickly yanked my sweater down. "I don't want to talk about it."

"Don't worry," his lips tipped in a frown, "I won't tell anyone."

"Thanks, but I can't hide it forever."

"No. You can't. But you can fight them."

I stared back at him, not sure what to say. It wasn't entirely out of the realm of possibility for Mason to tell people Parker was the father. The guy did announce to the world that I liked butt stuff. A claim that was so far from reality, it wasn't even funny. There were only two guys I'd been with, and only one of those was by choice.

"Don't let the stuffy snobs that run this place win."

Easy for him to say.

"Isn't that kind of like fighting city hall?"

Carrie Simone had fought against the gender biased uniforms. Organized a rally and everything. She didn't go to this school anymore.

"Maybe." He pushed off the bleachers and brushed his hands on his jeans, "But someone had to fight them. Otherwise, women wouldn't have the right to vote."

I watched him walk away, wondering why he'd bother to try and help. Shelby seemed to trust him, but as I learned recently, trust wasn't necessarily a solid foundation to build things on. One action was all it took to snap that bond. If I couldn't have faith in the one man I should, why should I trust anything Luke Lannister said?

Shaking away the memories threatening to surface, I stood up. It was ridiculous to think anyone would help me. Let alone Mr. Lannister. He worked at Ashworth. No one was going to stick up for me. It was better if I was on my own, and much safer for everyone involved.

I trudged my way down the bleachers, dreading the looks I'd get once I was inside. Since the day I took that test, I'd been avoiding facing the reality of my situation. It was easier to pretend everything was normal. The illusion started to shatter when Logan announced to the entire room I was pregnant.

There was a baby growing inside me! An actual living, breathing, human being that would rely on me for everything. It was too much. How was a seventeen year old supposed to handle that? There were options, that I knew. I couldn't picture myself 'getting rid of it' or handing my child over to strangers.

If it was *his*, would I be able to move past that horrific night? Could I love a child that was conceived in such a violent way? Or would I see *his* face every time I looked in my baby's eyes? I could find out easily enough.

One trip to the doctors, and I'd know the conception date. My night with Parker, and the assault, were weeks apart. Problem was, I was utterly terrified I wouldn't get the result I wanted.

I rounded the corner to the back of the bleachers and stopped dead in my tracks. A pair of sparkling green eyes were glaring down at me.

"Hey Lana banana. I've been looking for you."

"Get out of my way, Mason." So not in the mood for this, I attempted to shoulder past him. But he grabbed my arm and yanked me into the dark space under the metal benches.

Dark and alone, with a man...

My pulse started to pick up, as a wave of panic threatened to wrack my body.

"We need to talk," Micha said, stepping out of the shadows to join us.

Not again! Get away! Get away now!

I yanked my arm out of Mason's grip and took a step back. It gave me some relief to have his hands off me, but that didn't mean I was going to take my eyes off either one. I'd learned that lesson.

"*We* have nothing to talk about," I snarled in Micha's direction.

Mason's gaze narrowed in on me. "We're just here to give you a friendly warning."

Yeah, sure. Friendly, my ass!

"Give me your warning then," I crossed my arms, using the only thing I had as a shield, "So I can leave."

Micha stepped forward. "You're going to talk to Parker by the end of tomorrow."

"Am I now?" Micha and his goon squad couldn't make me do shit. At least, that's what I told myself, while my pulse thundered in my ears.

"Do you know what you do in rehab?"

My heart dropped when Mason smiled.

"You think." The rage burning in his green eyes reminded me of something.

Big doe like eyes filled with malice and lust.

"Fuck, you feel good."

"So you see, I've had a lot of time to think about ways to destroy your friend."

Mason's threat pulled me back, making my fists ball. "You leave Harper alone!"

"No." He cocked his head and smirked, "But if you stop ignoring Parker, I won't concentrate *all* my efforts on her."

"If you do anything…"

"You can count on me doing something." He took a step forward, causing me to take one back.

Leave Lana, leave now. It's happening again.

"How bad it is, all depends on you."

"You have other things to worry about," Micha added.

I turned my glare on him and snarled, "Such as?"

"The DNA of the baby you're carrying."

I stopped. That was exactly what I was worried about.

Dim moonlight...

Sweaty, heavy grunts...

"I-I'm not afraid of Parker."

"But you should be afraid of big brother."

And just like that, my heart went from thundering in my chest, to stopping altogether. Anyone who wasn't afraid of Preston Whitley was just plain stupid. Thinking about that cold, dead stare was enough to make my blood run cold.

"What do you think he's more likely to do? Play happy little match maker and help you two patch things up?" Micha stepped into a beam of sunlight streaming through the bleachers above, and smirked. "Or wait until he can cut that baby out of you and toss your body off a cliff?"

I licked my lips and forced the lump of nervousness down my throat. What would the master of death do if he found out? What would happen to me? My eyes snapped up to Micha as I sucked in a shocked breath.

What would happen to him?

He was so drunk that night, he didn't remember doing it. It would kill him if he did, not to mention what the Knights would do to him. Which was precisely why I hadn't talked to Parker. If this baby wasn't his... Let's just say, I had good reason to believe the rumors I heard.

"Parker is the only thing standing between you and death. You really want to give up that lifeline?"

Staring back at Micha Kessler's dark eyes, I could feel the inevitable march of Death, riding in on his pale horse. If this got out, there was only one conclusion. None of which were good for Sean.

Chapter 4
Parker

Lana didn't show up for lunch, so Sean sent the team out to find her. He wasn't taking the rumors well. I suppose I wouldn't either, if the supposed pregnant girl was Ava. In fact, I'd probably string the motherfucker up. That wasn't something I had to worry about with my sister, Ryker took that ability away from her.

If I could string him up, I would. Lana wasn't Sean's sister, but she may as well be. Honestly, I was kind of jealous of the fucker. He got to take her to daddy-daughter dances, and the spring luncheon, when we were in middle school.

Normally when he started barking orders, I'd have told him to go fuck himself. Just because I was on the team, didn't mean I was his lackey. Besides, Harper made her own bed. Not my fault her brother had a problem with her lying in it. Since this was Lana, and I was done with this avoiding me shit, I was more than happy to play along.

And then I found her.

Sitting on the bleachers, talking to the new assistant coach. I watched him smile up at her with a fucking twinkle in his eye, and had to hold myself back. What the fuck was he doing flirting with a student anyways? Letting her bright hazel eyes sparkle back at him. Fucking prick.

I stood there, watching them, feeling the red bleed into my vision. Until all I could see were thick red drops falling from my fingers as I held the bastard's still beating heart in my hand. It was so vivid, I could smell a coppery tint in the air.

Wouldn't be the first time I took care of some asshole. Everyone around here thought Mark Stevens died in an electrical fire. It was one of those tragic accidents that called for a candlelight vigil.

If he hadn't made the wrong person cry, then he might've spent another birthday with his family. Instead, they had flowers delivered to his grave. I warned him to stay away from Lana. Not my fault he didn't listen. Right now though, there was another corpse I wanted to smile over.

My hands fisted, and I tried to push the image down as he walked away. The prick actually grinned and winked at me. As if he was saying, 'she'll talk to me, asshole.' I might've gone off to plot Shelby's new coach's demise, if something else hadn't caught my attention.

Mainly, what the fuck Micha and Mason were up to. They pulled Lana under the bleachers, and a few minutes later, she darted back into the school like the devil himself was chasing her.

Fucking Kesslers.

I leaned against the flagpole. One word to Logan about Shelby's stretching session should take care of the coach problem. Micha and Mason, however…

My gaze narrowed on the two Kesslers walking my way. The second Mase saw me, the corner of his mouth tipped up in a smirk. *Prick.* Micha, on the other hand, returned my glare. Mase and Logan, I just wanted to slap, but Micha I respected more than I did anyone else. He didn't take shit from anyone, including my brother.

Considering what Preston called extracurricular activities, that took balls. Even I was afraid of my brother. The only thing on this planet that shouldn't be was Timothy. His damn turtle.

"Hey buddy," Mase sang, "Decided to get some fresh air?"

I crossed my arms and let out a huff. "What did you two do?"

"Reminded your girl about the repercussions of her choices," Micha grumbled.

Of course he did. Micha was all about consequences and repercussions. That wasn't what pissed me off.

"This is my situation to handle."

Micha snorted as he walked past me. He didn't have to say anything, I could hear the words swimming through his mind. *'You're doing a great job so far.'* Wouldn't be the first time one of them said something like that. In all honesty, they'd be right.

We all grew up in the Order, and none of them were afraid to get their hands dirty. I wasn't either, but they wouldn't know that, since I was never called in on the harder jobs.

"Do me a favor, Micha," I spun around and marched after our illustrious leader, "Stay the fuck out of my business."

"Why?" his cold glare rolled over his shoulder, "You gonna suddenly sac up?"

I threw my finger up in his face, "You don't know shit about me."

And he didn't. None of them did. I was only one thing to the people in this town. Ashen Springs' golden boy. Whatever. Worked for me. No one suspected the prized pig.

"Why the fuck should I expect you to handle shit now?"

Most guys would back away from a guy my size. Not Micha. He grew up with Mase, and Mase liked to punch fuckers out for fun. Prick hit me a couple times, and when Mase hit you, you fucking knew it.

"Tell me, Parker," Micha stepped right up and got in my face, "Where the fuck were you, when shit was going down?"

Leader or not, I wasn't about to back down. I pushed back the urge to tear his throat out and followed Micha's lead. Pressing my puffed out chest against his. "You never fucking asked me."

"That's the point," he shook his head and walked away. "I shouldn't have to."

I stood there with my mouth open. Was that the reason I was never called in for backup? Why the hell hadn't this occurred to me sooner? Unlike my brother, I tried to fit in with the innocent citizens of Ashen Springs.

The best way to do that was to pretend I was normal, even though I knew I wasn't. I wasn't as far gone as my brother, but I wasn't like everyone else either.

That's what I did for most of my life. Hid the darker parts of myself behind a wave, or a smile. The simple things people did that I had to constantly remind myself to mimic. Like pretending to care, when I couldn't give two fucks. It was exhausting, and something I thought I had to do. But maybe I didn't? Did my friends really think I couldn't handle my own shit?

"No offence, buddy," Mase threw his arm over my shoulder, "But you've been letting her ignore you for weeks."

Shit. He was right. I'd been letting Lana run all over me. None of them would allow that crap to happen. Logan got right in Shelby's face when she tried to blow him off, and I wouldn't be surprised if Riley murdered Micha in his sleep.

That didn't deter him. He laid down in that bed with her every night. Even Mase, who fucking hated Harper, was constantly reminding her he was there. Don't get me wrong, she deserved everything he did, but I kind of agreed with Logan. Mase should just get it over with and hate fuck the bitch.

"That shit stops now," I growled, and stormed across the field.

I'd be damned if I was going to be another Mason Kessler. Denying myself the girl I desperately wanted. There were benefits to being in the Order. This was one of them. If I wanted Lana, she was mine, and there wasn't a goddamn thing anybody could do about it.

Mase skipped up behind me with a giddy smile on his face. "What do you have in mind?"

My lips curled in a crooked smirk. I could play dirty too.

MY FATHER'S car was parked outside when I pulled up to the house. Unlike my friends' parents, mine preferred to be involved in our upbringing. I grew up with nannies, but my mother was the one to tuck me in at night, and my father taught me how to ride a bike. Maybe it was because of my brother?

Safety wasn't a factor associated with Preston. The only other one of my friends that had parental involvement to the same degree were Micha and Mase. Lou was so embedded in their lives, it bordered on the obsessive.

I walked into the house, hung my keys on the hook by the door, and headed for the parlor, where I knew my father would be. Another difference between my friends and I was the place I called home.

Yes, we lived in a gated community where I could look outside and see my neighbors. It wasn't that we couldn't afford the grand estates that everyone else had. This was my father's choice. He believed extravagance rotted the brain.

Mike Brady didn't have shit on my dad. Dean Whitley had a saying for everything. If I fell off my bike, he'd tell me to get back on and keep trying. Never let the world defeat me.

When Preston killed my dog, it was the everything has a season speech. And when I lost my first game, he said I could never understand the value of winning, if I'd never lost. I skipped down the steps to the parlor, wondering what he'd say about this situation.

I found him sitting in one of the wingback chairs, reading today's newspaper. He looked up long enough to nod at me and set his glass of brandy down on the table beside him.

"How was school, son?"

Rage still boiled through my veins. All I could think about was how my hands would look coated in Luke Lannister's blood. Logically, I knew he was probably just talking to Lana. That's what teachers did. They found the lonely student and tried to encourage them to participate.

What I couldn't shake was the way his eyes sparkled up at her. I knew that look. Fuck sakes, Logan perfected that look. Sly prick had it so perfected that chicks didn't even know he was flirting with them until it was too late.

"School was fine," I muttered, while sauntering over to the bar to down a shot of scotch. It wasn't Luke Lannister's blood, but it might dull my craving for it.

"Buck up, son, everyone has bad games."

I stopped and glanced back at my father, bothered by the fact that he could tell something was wrong. Huh? Bringing the shot glass up to my lips, I tipped my head back and let the alcohol burn a path down my throat.

Lana's little games were making me slip. I didn't slip. Even fucking Lou, the esteemed psychologist, thought I was a regular chip off the old block. Now that shit took talent.

"You need to just move on." My father looked up from his newspaper and raised his fist in that 'go get 'em' way he did. "That's what makes a man."

I leaned against the bar and forced my tense muscles to relax. "That's what makes a man, is it?"

"That's right." He nodded and picked up the glass beside him. "It'll only get you down if you let it. Just pull up your pants and move forward."

Yeah, I'd heard that one before too. Though it was oddly fitting for this situation.

"I got someone pregnant."

Brandy went flying everywhere as my father hunched over in a coughing fit.

"Kinda too late to pull up my pants now, Dad."

After managing to catch his breath, my father sprang out of the chair and began pacing around the room. I rested my elbow on the bar behind me and patiently waited for him to stop muttering under his breath.

This was pretty much the same thing he did when Preston knocked someone up two years ago. Right down to the curses he was grumbling. That girl was given a choice; get rid of it, or free fall off the bluffs. The second Lana let me touch her, she lost all freedom to choose.

"Okay," he finally stopped pacing and looked at me. "We can take care of this."

"I don't want to take care of it."

There was the shock again. "You're saying you want to keep it."

"Yes."

He cocked a brow at me. "And the girl?"

"Her too," I nodded.

The strange thing was how quickly the unease on his face morphed into a smile. That, I did not expect.

"Alright. We're going to need a few things. But first things first, we have to get you a contract, my boy."

"That's gonna be a problem." The contracts with the Order

required the signature of the male head of house. In Lana's case, there was none. "She doesn't have a father."

"That's fine. We can go to her uncle, brother, or grandfather if we have to."

I shook my head. "She doesn't have any of those either."

"There's always someone," his finger waved through the air, "You just have to know where to look. What's the girl's name?"

"Lana Crawford."

"Lana Crawford?" His brow rose. "The girl that lives on the edge of town with her grandmother?"

"That's the one."

"Your mother is not going to be happy about this."

No shit, Sherlock.

"Is that going to be a problem?"

I could handle my mother. Hell, Preston had been waiting for a reason to take her out of this world, but it'd be easier if I didn't have to. She was still my mother. Besides, Ava was pretty close with her, and while I cared about my mother, I loved my sister.

"If it is, I'll take care of it." The next words he spoke removed any doubt I had about that statement. "Your mother might be my wife, but she's not my blood."

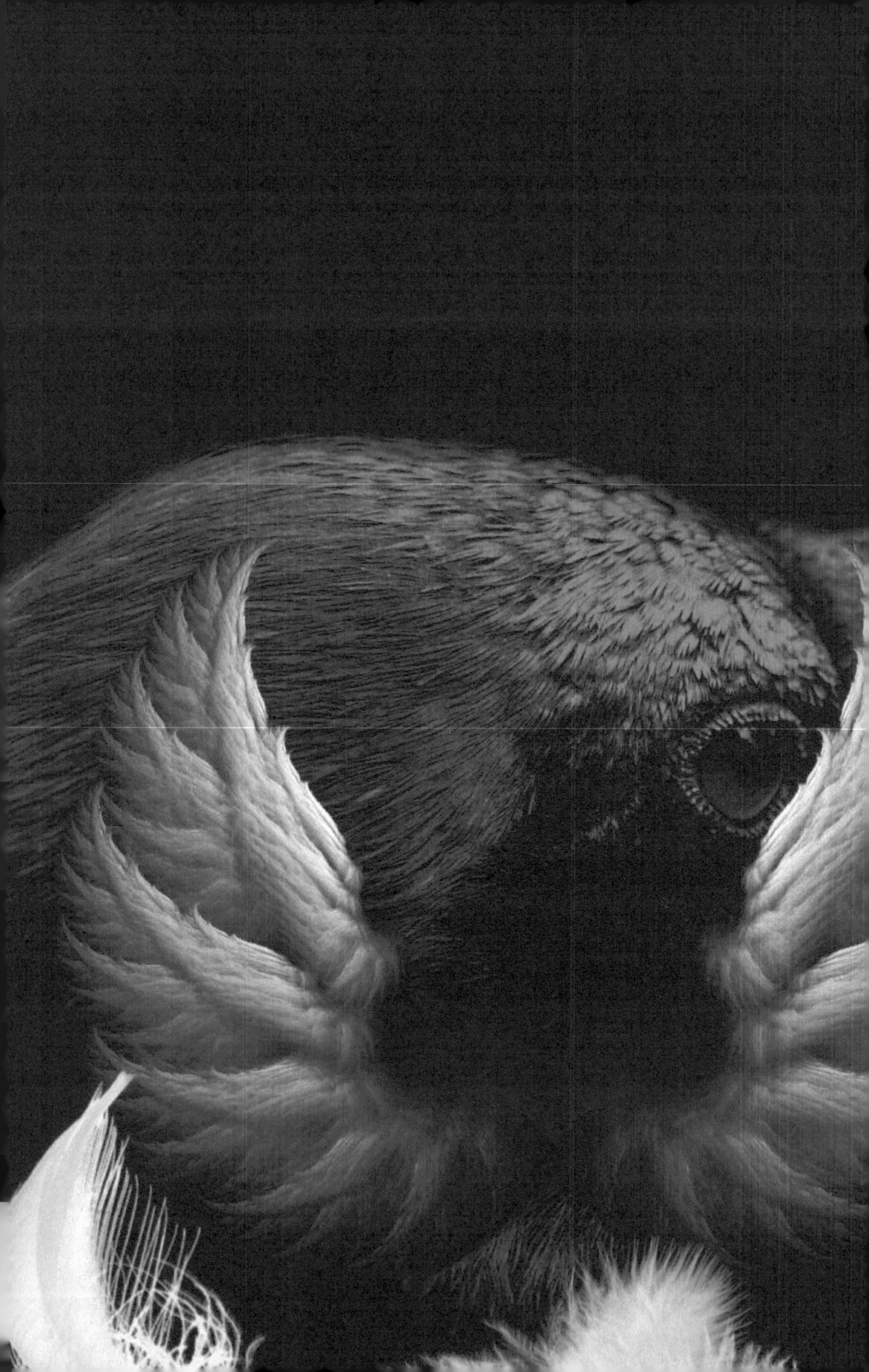

Chapter 5
Lana

I was seeing Preston everywhere. Hiding in the shadows. Staring at me from the corner of every room I entered, and in the mirror's reflection. When I closed my eyes, there he was, with a sick smile on his face and a blade in his hand.

It was the reality behind Micha's words that got to me. Preston would shoot someone on main street during rush hour and not blink. Why was I so sure of this? Because he'd actually done it, and he didn't spend a day in jail.

I was more worried about Sean than I was myself. The next day when he saw me at school and I jerked away from him, I saw the hurt in his eyes. He didn't understand. That's when I knew, he didn't remember. It was a bit of a relief, honestly, because the same guy that bandaged my knee when I fell off the swings would never hurt me.

He'd kill anyone that did. Exactly why he could never find out what happened that night. It would not only destroy him, but

Harper as well. They both carried so many crosses for me. It was my turn to shoulder pain for them.

So I told myself that the man who held me down and forced himself inside me wasn't Sean. He just wore his body. Did it help? Not really. It was still his eyes that haunted my nightmares.

His raspy grunts I heard wafting through my ears. And his spicy scent that made me want to throw up. Every time I heard his voice, I was brought back to that moment, and the way the moon shone down on us.

The only thing that chased away the nightmares was thinking about another night. The way someone else touched me, and the words they whispered in my ear. Parker Whitley should not be my saviour. I hated him for the way he treated me. Paying me off like a whore. But that didn't stop my mind from seeking him out as a refuge from my fear.

I hugged the toilet and wretched out the last of my breakfast. *Morning sickness, indeed.* Every morning this month, I spent at least an hour praying to the porcelain gods. The easy way out of this situation would be to take care of the problem.

Girls did it all the time. But every time I thought about walking into that clinic, I felt more sick than I was right now. This baby was innocent. It didn't ask for any of this, or choose to be made. However its inception came to be, it wasn't this child's fault. And it was a part of me.

Knowing what I was going to do, I sighed and glanced down at my stomach. It was time to tell Nan.

"Lana, honey," Nan knocked on the door, "Are you okay?"

Sometimes that woman seriously scared me. It was like she could sense my thoughts.

"I'm fine." *I was so not fine.* "I'll be out in a minute."

"Okay, hurry up. We have to leave in fifteen minutes."

"Okay, Nan."

Using the sink, I pulled myself up and rinsed my mouth out.

The minty mouthwash cut through the bitter taste of vomit, but did nothing to dull my guilt. No amount of toothpaste or mouthwash could take that away.

No matter what I did, Nan was always there. She didn't get mad if I screwed up or failed a test. She helped me fix the situation. One time, she stayed up all night helping me study for a make-up exam. So why was I afraid to go to her now, when I needed her the most?

Because you don't want to disappoint her.

We didn't have much, and what we did have, Nan busted her butt to get. I dreaded telling her when I needed something for school. Mostly because she'd just smile and say, 'we'll figure it out.' And she did. Even if that meant eating instant noodles for a week.

That's why I tried so hard at school. She was so happy when I got the scholarship, her entire face beamed with pride. I just wanted to make her proud. Not make things harder, with another mouth to feed.

I looked up, studying the girl in the mirror. She looked the same. Black hair, pink lips and bronze complexion, but her eyes were different. The hazel color glimmering in the sunlight wasn't as bright. There was no spark or glint. They simply stared back, dull and empty.

Tears burned in my eyes as I opened the door to our small bathroom and stepped out into the hall. Instead of letting myself be drawn to the kitchen by the mouth-watering aroma, I slipped into my room. Burying my face in my pillow and crying for a few minutes seemed like a better option, then facing Nan.

"Alright, child," I jumped at the sudden sound of Nan's voice. She might be on in age, but the woman was sly as a fox. "I've had enough of this."

Nan was sitting on my bed with her hands folded in her lap, and her eyebrow cocked. I knew the look well. It was her, *'keep pushing me kid and you'll get the wooden spoon'* look. She was like a ninja with that thing. Once she hit me from across the room, and I swear the damn spoon ricocheted right back into her palm.

I blinked back the tears in my eyes and forced a smile on my face. "Hi, Nan."

"Don't you 'hi Nan' me, Missy." We were getting dangerously close to spoon talk here. "You are going to sit your butt down and stop lying to me."

Staring into her deep brown eyes, I broke. All the emotions I'd been holding back came bursting out at once. My chin started to quiver as hot tears flowed down my face.

"I'm sorry, Nan," I blubbered and glanced down at my belly, "I didn't mean for it to happen."

"Good lord, child, is that what you're so worked up about?" She released a relieved breath and waved her hand through the air. "I know about that. A baby is a blessing, Lana."

I stared at her for a second with wet streaks rolling down my cheeks. "You knew?"

"Of course I knew."

All I could say was, "How?"

"I do have some experience." Nan cocked her brow again. "Do you think your mother just appeared out of thin air? Because let me tell you, that woman came into being through twenty-seven hours of hard labor and a lot of cussing. I was beginning to think you were going to wait until that baby came out before you told me."

With just a few words, Nan managed to do what Harper never could. She shut me up. For the first time in my life, I was speechless. My mouth kept opening, but nothing came out. She knew all this time and didn't say anything. I wasn't sure if I should be mad, or relieved.

"Have been to see the doctor yet?"

I shook my head. That was the one thing I couldn't do. The

second I found out the conception date, the happy illusion I was hiding behind might shatter. I wasn't ready to let that go.

"Well," Nan stood up and smoothed her skirt down, "I'll make an appointment tomorrow."

I couldn't let her take me to the doctor. "Doctors cost money, Nan."

"So do babies, child." She opened the door and looked over her shoulder at me. "The father can help with that. Now get your stuff. It's time for school."

"I can't–"

"A baby changes nothing. If I have to raise that baby myself, you will get an education, Lana." Her serious gaze locked with mine, "Do you understand me?"

I licked my lips and nodded. It wasn't my education I was worried about.

FOR THE FIRST time in years, I hated walking through the halls of Ashworth. Don't get me wrong, things were never great. Harper and I were prime targets for the popular crowd. The only part of that that bothered me, was the cruel treatment my best friend lived through every day.

The names and stupid pranks that Naomi and Mason played on me were just that, stupid. Naomi's idea of taunting was reminding me of the labels on my clothes and my unattached status. Neither of which I particularly cared about. Would I argue a Gucci dress? No. Did I need it? Also no.

Besides, I had other things on my mind. Like the appointment Nan already had booked in the ten minutes it took me to get out to the car. Why did she have to be so efficient? Not only that, but she had a meeting arranged with the principal next week, to discuss my situation. Or, as Nan put it, "They are not kicking my baby girl out."

Ashworth wasn't prepared for my Nan. Last year, when Severson said something about the elderly needing assistance in his store, she decided to show him just how capable a woman her age was. Ten minutes later, the entire senior's center, and her church group, were swarming his store.

It didn't matter what the issue was, Nan would stand up for it. Even the ones she didn't agree with. Homosexuality was a prime example of that. She called it ungodly love, yet she was the first to fight for some guy's right to suck dick.

She even took on Lillianna Whitley and her Nationalist group. With the whole five other African American families in town. There used to be seven, but Parker's mother chased the other two away.

There was a heavy Latin population in Ashen Springs, all of whom were more than happy to back Nan when it came to the Whitley witch. It was kind of ironic that I hoped the baby I was carrying had the same last name as the woman Nan had been fighting for years.

I tried to put her latest call to arms out of my head, and spent the first part of my morning focusing on my classes. It worked, for the most part. I was actually enjoying the conversation I was having with Harper. It was nice to feel normal again.

"Mr. Saddler wants to pair us up for our history project."

I didn't need to look at Harper to see her apprehension. History was one of the few classes we didn't have together, and Harper didn't do well with people. Sometimes she didn't do well with me.

"Ask Shelby to partner with you," I suggested.

"The project requires a female and male point of view."

Shit. Normally I'd tell her to ask Brandon, but with stuff like this, Mr. Saddler often assigned partners in alphabetical order. It helped avoid boys or girls picking someone for the wrong reasons.

Last year, Logan had ten girls in the class fighting to be his partner. Literally fighting. I saw more broken fingernails, hair and bleeding noses that day than I had thought possible.

"So, that means…"

"Silas," she whispered in a shaky voice.

Of course. Creswell and Callaghan. Silas himself wasn't so bad. That wasn't what had Harper shaking like a leaf. If you hung around Silas, there was one person you were guaranteed to run into. Mason.

"Don't worry, Harper." I wanted to wrap my arms around her, but all I could see were her eyes. The same eyes I saw staring down at me in my nightmares. Instead of comforting her, I took a step back. "Mason won't screw with you. Silas is all about getting the work done."

And he was. Strictly by the books Silas, I called him.

Harper dropped her head. I could still see the tears glimmering in her eyes, though. I moved to get closer and comfort her, but stopped when I saw someone storming down the hall. Someone who looked pissed as hell.

With a hard swallow, I readied myself for the wrath openly portrayed on Sean's face. I could do this. I could keep my cool and pretend everything was normal. Sean probably heard about Harper having to work with the enemy and was coming to reassure her.

I didn't realize I was moving, until my back hit my locker. *Get it together, Lana. It's just Sean mad about something. Nothing new. Except for what he did to you.*

My heart stopped dead in my chest when he stormed right past Harper and grabbed my elbow.

"Come here," he growled in that big brother voice I'd come to know so well.

Only this time, that sense of familiarity didn't help calm my nerves. It shot them right up to high alert.

"Sean," I snarled, trying to sound angry instead of scared. "What the hell is wrong with you? You can't just drag me away like that."

"The hell I can't." He pulled me into an empty room and pushed me back against the wall.

No matter how many times I told myself that this was just Sean being Sean, I couldn't suck in enough oxygen. The air in the room got thinner with each breath.

"I've been hearing some rumors."

My eyes darted around, looking for a way to escape. "They're just rumors."

"Tell me you're still a virgin?"

That's when I got angry. I wasn't a virgin. He would know that if he didn't drink so much. If he could control himself. Why didn't he remember? I did, and I had some to drink that night too. "That's none of your business."

Sean's light eyes darkened and that vein in his forehead began to throb. The same vein I saw that day. Hovering over me, throbbing in the sweat coating his forehead.

"Who touched you?"

You did.

The image shifted to the smiling little boy smoothing a bandage on my bleeding skin. The warm eyes gazing down at me while we swayed on the dance floor. I could hear his voice whispering reassurances in my ear.

"Don't pay attention to them. You don't need a dad, you have me, and I'll protect you."

This was Sean, the same little boy that beat kids up for making fun of me. He wouldn't hurt me. He loved me.

"I'm not having this conversation with you." I turned to leave, but Sean's arm shot out, cutting me off.

"You sure as fuck are." He leaned in and slowly rolled his gaze down me. I felt sick. I needed to get out of here. "You wanna tell me why you're wearing sweaters all the time?"

The next thing I knew, his hands were on my sweater, trying to pull it up. That's when I lost it. Screaming, "Don't touch me!" and, "get away from me!" as I swung my hands through the air, violently striking him anywhere I could.

"Jesus Christ, Lana," he fought to contain my arms, but that only made me swing them harder. "Calm down. I'm not going to hurt you."

The words left my mouth before I could stop them. "You already did."

"What?"

I stopped and stared at the confusion on his face. My mouth opened, prepared to take back my statement, but nothing came out. Because he had hurt me. In the worst possible way. And no matter how much I wanted to tell him he didn't, I couldn't force the words to come out. They sat there, lodged in my throat, filling my mouth with a bitter taste.

His brows knit as he took a step closer. "When did I hurt you?"

Guilt settled deep in my gut at the concerned way he reached out for me. It was killing him to think that he might've hurt me. Sean could never know the truth. I had to bare this pain for both of us, but I couldn't stop the tears either. So, I did the only thing I could.

I ran.

Burst out of the room, and wrapped my arms around the first thing that gave me a sense of safety.

Chapter 6

Parker

The last thing I expected when I turned the corner was to find myself standing in the hall with Lana tightly clinging to me. Don't get me wrong, I wasn't complaining. In fact, it took less than a second for me to wrap my arms around her and pull her tightly into me.

I was just a little shocked. She'd spent the last few weeks avoiding me, and now she was using me for... protection, maybe? Fuck it. I'd take it. If Lana wanted me to strip naked and dive into a pit of snakes, I'd do it. As long as I could feel her soft body afterwards, I'd do whatever the fuck she wanted.

The way her body was shaking had me seeing red. My little angel was scared, and not just scared, but fucking terrified. I was about to ask her why, when Callaghan came out of a room. The same room Lana was in a few seconds ago.

This motherfucker.

"What the fuck did you do to her?"

Sean's lip curled at my question. "I didn't do anything to her."

"Bullshit!"

I don't know what the fuck went down in that room, but whatever it was had me tempted to slap the shit out of this asshole. Self appointed brother or not. No one made my Lana cry.

"I don't need to explain myself to you, Whitley. Come on, Lana." When he reached out for her, she buried her face in my chest.

I smiled internally and tightened my grip on her. *She picked me, prick.* "Looks like she doesn't want to go with you."

"Too fucking bad."

This prick didn't give up. He kept trying to pull her away from me, and that shit wasn't happening.

"Eat shit, Callaghan," I growled, and twisted so he'd have to reach around me to get her. "You can have her when you pry her out of my cold, dead hands."

I wasn't kidding. Didn't give a shit if people were watching. Lana Crawford was mine, and it was time everyone knew that.

"This doesn't involve you, Whitley."

"The fuck it doesn't. She's pregnant with my kid."

Silence. Complete and utter shocked quiet fell down the hall. Sean wasn't the only one staring at me with his mouth open in shock. Fuck, even Lana twitched in my arms. And what did I do? I smiled. A big, wide, toothy grin. *That's right, motherfuckers, this one's mine.*

"You've got to be kidding me!" Sean cried out, "Him? I thought you were smarter than that, Lana."

The only thing that stopped me from charging forward and smashing in his damn skull was Lana pulling away from me. Guess what she was scared of didn't matter anymore, because the tears streaming down her cheeks were with filled with anger. It was kind of hot, actually. I loved the way her nose scrunched up, while fire waged war in her eyes.

"You guys are unbelievable."

Sean grumbled, "She's the one whose pregnant, and I'm getting shit."

I chose to take it another way and puffed my chest up, saying, "Thank you."

Her bright hazel eyes rolled at my words. "That was not a compliment."

She was so cute right now. Black hair swaying behind her while her hip popped out, and she shot me attitude. Her hair was straight today. I think I preferred it curly and wild. Then again, I could always have fun giving her the wild look myself.

"You can't just talk about me like I'm not here." Her hand swung between me and Sean, "You two don't get to make decisions for me."

Sean frowned and crossed his arms. "No one's trying to make decisions for you, Lana."

"Don't worry," I told him, "It's probably just hormones. She'll calm down once I get her moved into my place."

"She is not moving in with you," Sean declared.

At the same time Lana objected, "I'm not moving in with you."

"Uh, yes you are."

"No," they both said in unison.

Great, I had a couple of parrots on my hands. I let out a long sigh. Honestly, I'd hoped this would be easier. At least she was talking to me. That was an improvement.

"You're carrying my kid. Henceforth, your ass belongs in my bed."

Her arms folded across her chest, pushing her breasts up. My eyes fell down to the small bump in her belly. The bump I put there. My dick hardened at the thought. I never wanted to fuck anyone as much as I wanted to fuck her right now.

"What if it wasn't your kid?" she shot back. "Would you leave me alone?"

I stopped and thought for a minute. Though it would piss me off to no end knowing someone else touched her, it wouldn't make a difference. Lana was mine. Plain and simple.

"No, it wouldn't matter." I shook my head. "You're mine. Period."

Apparently, she wasn't expecting that answer, because her jaw dropped. Sean grumbled something, but I didn't really give a fuck what he was saying. My eyes were stuck on the beauty in front of me, and the way the light bounced off her plump pink lips.

Get your head in the game, Parker.

"I'm giving you the easy way out here, Lana." I paused long enough to arch my brow, "I'd take it, if I were you."

She scoffed, "Right, because you've been so nice to me this far."

"Trust me, baby, I'll be real nice to you." *Every night, in our bed.*

"Go fuck yourself, Parker."

That was about what I expected. Most chicks liked getting money. My mother was a gold digging whore. The only reason she married my father was because her family was going broke. Arranged marriages had their advantages. For instance, my dad could care less who my mother fucked, and vice versa.

That wouldn't be the case with my girl. The only other guy she'd be fucking, would be someone I decided to bring in and fuck as well. Just thinking about that shit got me hard. Some prick all hard for my woman, taking it up the ass while I fucked them both…

No time to fantasize now.

"Have it your way, Angel." I held out a piece of paper for her. "Don't say I didn't warn you."

Lana snatched the paper out of my hand and glared down at it. The smile on my face widened with the shock in her eyes.

"You're suing me for custody!"

I tipped my head and slowly raked my gaze over her curves. "Should've taken the easy way."

"You know what you can do with your easy way?" She stepped in, bringing her narrowed glare close enough that I could smell the vanilla scent of her perfume. "You can shove it up your ass."

If she wanted to play hardball, that was fine with me, but she wasn't going to like the outcome.

Her angry glare rolled onto Sean next, as she snarled, "And you, go find someone else to brother," before storming down the hall.

"What did I do?" Sean muttered from beside me.

I shrugged. "Women."

Lana was barely out of view before Sean's fist cracked off my jaw. It was on after that.

THIRTY MINUTES later and I was still sitting in the office next to Mase. I didn't bother to ask why he was here. If Mase had a second home, it was the red chair he was currently seated in. I'd never been in trouble before, but I got the soul sucking comments Riley made about the receptionist now.

Mrs. Grier sat behind the counter, giving us the evil eye. Well, mostly Mase. He'd of course smile back at her, flashing his teeth in a charming way. Fucker even blew her a couple of kisses.

"She just smiled at me," I whispered to Mase when Mrs. Grier gave me the tiniest smirk and returned to her work. "Should I be concerned?"

Mase's green eyes went wide, "Fuck off. She did not smile."

"Language, Mr. Kessler."

Even her voice was creepy.

"You like it when I talk dirty." He puckered his lips out and shot her a wink. "I bet you're wearing lacy little panties right now."

Oh god, why was he talking about her panties? I was never going to get that image out of my head.

"My undergarments are none of your concern, Mr. Kessler."

I couldn't agree more with that statement.

"It's so fucking hot the way you say undergarments."

This was the worst foreplay I had ever witnessed. "I think my dick just died."

"There will be no talking about genitals in this office, Mr. Whitley."

But undergarments that were going to haunt my dreams were okay?

"Sorry, Ma'am."

"Pussy," Mason snorted.

I hoped my dad got here soon. At this point, I'd even take my mother. Anything was better than listening to this shit.

"Parker?"

Correction, almost anything was better than this shit.

I closed my eyes, praying I didn't hear who I thought I did. That dream died the second my gaze landed on the blonde with her hand on her hip. My head fell back as I let out a long sigh.

My sister was the last person I expected Ashworth to call. In her first year here, Ava burnt half the school down because someone stole her pencil. And it wasn't a special pencil or anything like that. It was your run of the mill stick of wood with lead.

"Holy shit, Ava," Mase sang. For some reason, the stupid bastard liked my sister, "How the fuck have you been?"

"Language, Mr. Kessler."

Both Ava and Mase shot the receptionist a look, which she more than happily returned. The fucking terrifying part was that Mase wasn't the only one to back away from the stare down. My sister did too. Ava's light eyes turned away from the receptionist and rolled back to me. Maybe Mrs. Grier really was a soul sucking demon?

"Called to the office for fighting?" Her chest puffed up as her smile widened. "I'm proud of you, baby brother."

Of course she was.

"Calm down, I didn't start it."

"But did you finish it?"

I guess that depended on what she meant by 'finish it.' Did I beat Sean down? Yeah, but he beat me down too. We both had bruises, cuts and scrapes, but we pulled apart before it could go beyond that.

"You should've seen him." Mase slapped me on the back.

I scowled at Mase. What the hell was he talking about? He wasn't there.

"He finally sacked up and claimed his girl."

Ava cocked her head. "He has a girl."

Fucking big mouth.

"Fuck yeah, he has a girl." Mrs. Grier once again reprimanded Mason on his choice of words. "Knocked her up and everything."

My face dropped into my palm. I could literally hear Ava's eyes light up as she excitedly squealed, "A baby?"

Fuck my life.

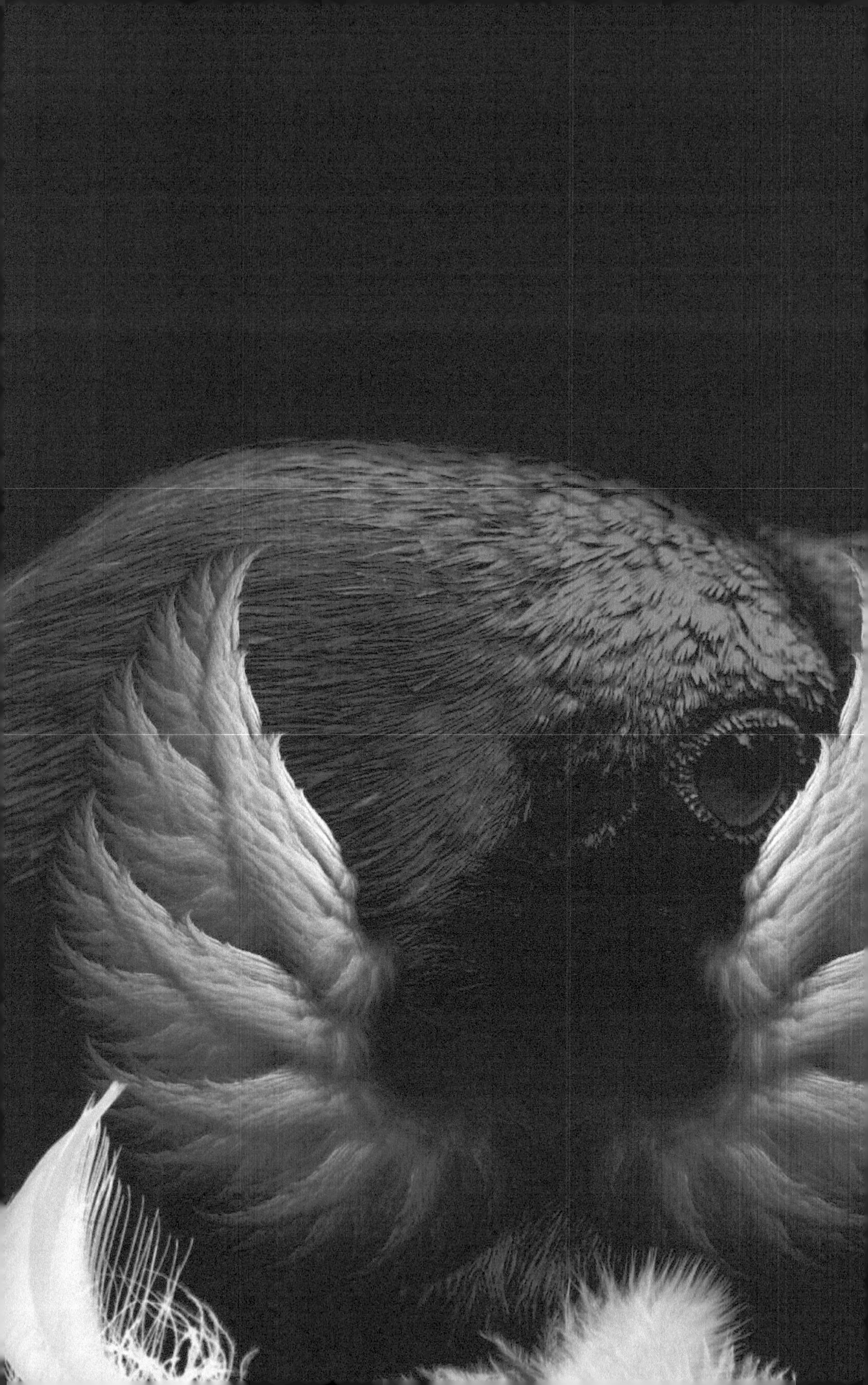

Chapter 7
Lana

Heat. That's all I could feel. Everywhere I went, hot slices of fire erupted across my skin.

I stumbled outside seeking the relief of fresh air and smacked my dry lips together. My body was covered in a fine coat of moisture, while my mouth had none. Even the air flowing down my parched throat felt like sandpaper.

Water, that's what I needed. A lot of cool, clean water. Harper had a pool, or was that Riley?

My brows furrowed as I searched the foggy landscape for a shimmering patch of liquid. There was a lot of green and red. Roses, I think. Harper's mother planted them before she left. Or were they carnations? That's what Paisley liked.

I glanced around. Was I at Riley's? Maybe I was at home? Where was Henry? That grumpy little bastard had the softest fur. I wanted to run my fingers through it. But the grass looked so cool. I fell down to my knees and slid my hands across the ground.

Dampness trickled down my skin from the tiny green blades, making me sigh in relief. The coolness felt so good. I needed to feel it everywhere. Dropping down, I rolled onto my back and groaned as I dug myself further into the cold ground. Was grass always this soft? Maybe it wasn't grass?

"You're looking a little under the weather, Doll."

I smiled at the brown eyes gazing down at me. Sean. He'd help me. He always helped me.

"I want to go home," I whined, "It's too hot here."

"Maybe you should take your clothes off?"

That was a good idea. Wait... what did he say? I turned away and pressed my cheek into the grass, nuzzling into its coolness. God that felt good.

"Don't worry, Doll, I'll help you feel good."

I frowned. Why was his voice so deep? Was he mad at me? Harper and I only had one drink.

Suddenly there were hands tugging on my shirt. Rough and mean hands, shredding the cloth off my skin. I didn't like it. I tried to crawl away, escape the coarse hair abrading the skin on my neck, but I couldn't. Something heavy was on me, grunting hot breaths in my ear.

I dug my fingers into the ground. Help me, grass. Hide me from the ogre. But the grass didn't help. It didn't do anything when I was flipped over, or when my legs were pried apart. I shook my head and swung my arms, trying to avoid the hooded brown eyes staring down at me.

And then the eyes morphed. Lightening in color, vividly lit up with lust.

"You're so beautiful, Angel." Parker's hot tongue slid along the column of my neck, "And you taste fucking delicious."

I moaned and arched my back, silently begging him for more. He smelled so good, I couldn't get enough of it. I buried my fingers in his soft sandy locks, and pulled him in closer. The solid planes of his chest pressed against my breasts, weighing me down in the most delightful way...

Weight, heavy and grunting.

I couldn't breath. Couldn't push it off. Couldn't escape the smell of sweat, or sound of horrid grunts that turned my stomach. I stared up at the moon, shining brightly in the night sky.

Except it wasn't the moon, it was the soft glow of a lamp. The ogre was gone. It wasn't him on top of me. It was my grey eyed knight with his strong hands and tempting mouth. He chased the ogre away. Took me to a safe place where love wasn't dirty or wrong.

"You're mine, Angel."

"Parker," I moaned, wrapping my arms around him. My knight. My protector. My safe place. But even he couldn't chase the ogre's voice away.

"Remember to keep your mouth shut, Doll." The ogre smiled down at me, moonlight glinting off his gold tooth. "No one would believe you anyway."

...

I shot up in my bed, fighting to catch my breath. It was just a dream. Sean wasn't here. I was safe in my bed, with Nan in the next room. That didn't stop my skin from crawling when I pictured that gold tooth. My brows knit as I searched the shadows.

Sean didn't have a gold tooth. He didn't have facial hair, either. But it had to be him. I'd never forget those eyes. Brown with gold flecks, just like Harper's. They were his eyes. I knew they were.

But were they?

I could still feel his hands on me. Maybe I was crazy. I mean, it was Sean. He wouldn't do that to me, right? All thought fled my mind when the soft flick of a lighter rang through the air. My heart stopped.

The small flame across the room lit up a face worse than any childhood monster or boogeyman. I would've preferred the ogre from my dream, because the face I was looking at now was the face of pure evil. A man that had no morals.

Death himself.

"Hello, Lana." Preston's cold eyes rolled my way.

I wanted to crawl away. Or run for the door and never look back. But fear had me trapped in its icy grip. He sauntered slowly closer and all I could do was watch as the words on my gravestone slowly became visible.

Step.

Here lies Lana.

Stride.

She was stupid and didn't run.

Preston's shoulders glided under his jean jacket. Smooth and graceful. Like a cat getting ready to pounce on a mouse. In this situation, I was the mouse. By the time he stopped at the foot of the bed, all I could hear was my own blood pumping loudly in my ears.

When his fingers curled around the top of my footboard, my mind snapped out of its terrified state. I sprang back, opening my mouth and sucking in a deep breath, but he cut me off.

"Before you do something stupid, like scream, I want you to think about what I'll do to your beloved grandmother if she comes through that door."

I froze, sucking my scream back, and quickly shifted my gaze to the door. Though it was easier to stare at a plank of wood than the cold gaze of death, Preston wasn't the kind of guy one took their eyes off.

I stared back at him, searching for some semblance of life or humanity. I found none. No blue sparks in his glare, like his brother, or hint of emotion on his face. He was void of anything.

Dark…

Empty…

And black…

The words that eventually came out of my mouth, I could only chalk up to pure shocked stupidity. "Do you have a gun?"

"Do you think I need one?" He cocked a brow and I suppressed my shiver.

No, he didn't.

Preston having a gun would be a blessing. At least then things would be over quickly. Kent Drews wasn't that lucky. I don't know what he did, but he was last seen with Preston. Kent now called Northwood Sanitarium home.

"What do you want?"

There was no need to irritate the man. I wasn't suicidal. Besides, no one told Preston Whitley what to do. Earlier this year, I'd overheard Logan and Micha talking about some girl that got in his face. I felt sorry for whoever she was.

"You're supposed to care about your family." He shot me a look, and then stalked his way across my room. "Love them, obey your parents, look out for your siblings." His hand twirled through the air as he spoke.

"At least that's what I'm told. Honestly, I wouldn't give a fuck if my parents died. Hell, I'd slit their throats myself. There is one person I care about, and you're carrying his child." He stopped, turned around, leaning back against my dresser. "So, my question for you, Lana, is how many people am I going to have to hurt, to make sure my brother gets what he wants?"

What if it wasn't Parker's? My mind instantly went back to the gold tooth and facial hair. For the first time in my life, I hoped I was crazy. That my foggy mind had created something that never happened. Because if it had, Sean wouldn't be the only one lying in a grave.

"Does your hesitation have something to do with Sean Callaghan?"

My eyes shot up to his.

"You think I didn't notice how my brother isn't the only person you're avoiding? Difference is," he plucked a letter opener off my dresser and twirled it in his hand, "You're not scared of my brother."

I licked my lips and forced the lump down my dry throat.

"Is Sean going to be a problem?"

I shook my head. Even if I wasn't crazy, and Sean did do something to me, I wouldn't want him hurt. I may never trust him again, but he was the closest thing I had to a brother. Eventually, I'd forgive him. I hoped.

If there was something to forgive.

Attempting to turn the conversation around, I said, "If you knew what Parker did..."

"I don't give a fuck what he did." Preston glared at me, but all I could see was the moonlight glinting off the sharp edge of the letter opener in his hand. "When you go to that meeting tomorrow, you're going to come to an amicable solution with my brother. One that involves both you, and his child."

"And if I refuse?"

"Then I'll cut my way through everyone you care about."

The flatness of his statement was terrifying. Still, I opened my mouth to argue, "If you think you can bully me–" Once again he cut me off.

"Let's get one thing straight." His hand slammed down, stabbing the letter opener into the top of my dresser, "I don't bully. I don't make threats, and I don't taunt people on the playground. Before you decide to play this game with me, I want you to remember one thing,"

Preston walked over to my bedroom door and placed his hand on the doorknob, "Death isn't the worst thing that can happen to someone."

And then he was gone, just as quickly as he had appeared.

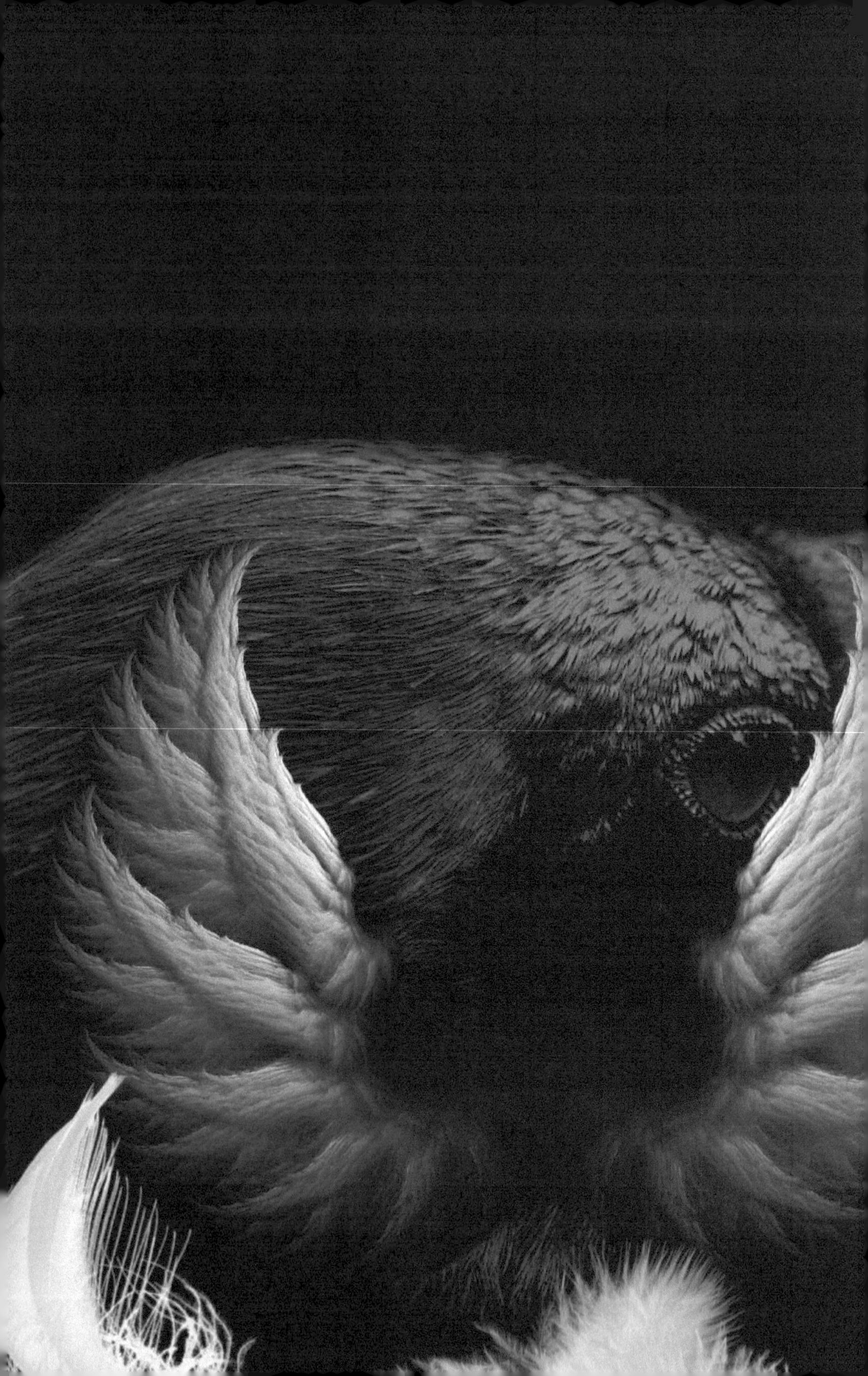

Chapter 8
Lana

My mind was a raging storm of thoughts the next day. The summons Parker gave me–which I still had to tell Nan about– was going to be *fun*. Nan didn't like Lillianna Whitley on a good day, and now, thanks to me, she was going to be linked to her forever. Sean would definitely be a better choice in Nan's eyes.

She wasn't fond of Ned Callaghan, but she could at least tolerate him. I was with her on that one. Harper's dad was way too strict, in my opinion. With Harper at least. Sean had a lot more freedom. He was allowed to come and go as he pleased. Harper needed permission to cross the street.

Half the time Ned was at home, he spent arguing with Sean, who felt his sister had the right to her own life. Which once again made me wonder if I was crazy?

I was so sure Sean had attacked me, and was just too drunk to remember. I'd seen him so trashed he'd forgotten where he was. So, I mean, it was possible. But then again, maybe I was the one that was too drunk?

It felt like I was going in circles. So much so, that the world around me spun with my thoughts. Honestly, I was amazed I made it to breakfast without falling down. The second I saw Nan's smiling face, something else flooded my thoughts. Coffins, dead bodies and funerals.

Preston wasn't the kind of guy that made idle threats. When he said if I didn't come to an amicable agreement with Parker, that the people I cared about would pay the price, he meant it. And by agreement, he meant whatever made Parker happy. Because I could guarantee Preston didn't give a shit what I wanted.

God forbid I wasn't crazy, and this baby wasn't Parker's. We'd all be dead if that were the case. Either way, there was no good outcome here. Not that I could see. I was well and truly fucked.

"We have an appointment with the doctor at four, so I'll pick you up after school."

Shit. Well, here goes nothing.

"Actually, we have to rebook that."

I carefully slid the summons across the table and gave Nan a nervous smile. Her brow tipped up in her 'what are you up to' look as she picked up the paper. I remained quiet and just watched her read it.

The instant she came across the last name Whitley, I knew. Her face morphed from suspicion, to shock, and settled on the most unimpressed glare I'd ever seen on a human being.

Holding my breath, I waited for the inevitable lecture. Nan always told me not to hate people. That it was an ugly emotion not worthy of the time and energy. Except when it came to Lillianna Whitley.

I could feel the ugly waves of contempt that filled the room. It weighed me down more than the possibility of my baby's DNA. I could either make Nan mad, or Sean dead.

When Nan quietly got up and began digging through one of the drawers, I thought for sure I was getting the wooden spoon. I used to bury them in the backyard when I was a kid, hoping that would alleviate my punishments.

It didn't. Nan just went out and bought some more. Something that never occurred to my naive childhood mind. Apparently not much had changed over the years. I did sleep with Parker Whitley, after all. How smart was that choice?

Instead of a wooden spoon, Nan held up a business card. Which made my brows rise. Why wasn't she yelling at me?

"Nan?" I called out as she picked up the phone.

She didn't even look at me when she answered. Just said, "Yes, Lana?" while she typed in a number.

I think we were the only house in Ashen Springs to still have a landline. And not the cordless type, either, because that would be too much technology for Nan to handle. For at least a month after I finally convinced her to let me get a cellphone, she was suspicious of it.

She'd whisper whenever I was around, in case someone could hear us. Despite how much I told her otherwise, she was convinced it worked like a walkie talkie. She still stared at it suspiciously.

"What are you doing, Nan?"

"Calling Mr. Craig."

"The funeral home guy?" That really made my brows rise. "Why?"

"Because you, child, are going to land me in an early grave."

Oh my God.

Nan always did have a flare for the dramatic. "Nan, it's not the end of the world."

"You tell me that when that witch does something horrible to my great-grandchild."

"She won't do anything. It's her grandchild too." *Hopefully.*

Nan hung up the phone and rolled her eyes my way. "Do you think that matters to a woman like her?"

"Well, yeah. Family should matter to everyone."

Preston's words swam through my mind. *'You're supposed to care about family, that's what I'm told.'* Okay, maybe not everyone. But surely a grandmother would care about her grandchild. Lillianna might be a real piece of work, but she seemed to love her kids. Even Preston, who, personally, I think she should've been terrified of.

"You're overreacting, Nan." I picked up my plate and took it to the sink. Wasn't really hungry today. "Everything will be fine."

I could feel her watching me as I plucked my keys off the hook by the back door.

"Where are you going?"

"Do you mind if I drive myself to school?" There was something I had to do, and I needed to do it alone. "We can meet at the Whitley's after school."

I didn't wait for her answer before I left. We might not be able to take on the Whitley family in court–though I'm sure Nan would try–but I could at least find out if we needed to. Or if we should pack our bags and run.

Though I doubted there was anywhere we could go that Preston wouldn't find us. I could give us a head start. More importantly, give Sean a head start.

ASHEN SPRINGS free clinic was attached to the hospital in the middle of town. Early in the morning should've been a good time to go. Most people were just starting their days.

Apparently, it was the same time half the town decided they needed to see a doctor. I had to wait for two hours before I was called back, and another hour to see a doctor. On the upside, I'd conquered two cities, a town, and started building my keep in the game on my phone.

After the quickest sonogram in history, where I wasn't permitted to look at the image, I sat on the bed waiting for the doctor to come back and give me the results. Though the nurse smiled at me, she obviously wasn't impressed by my age. Not sure what she had to be upset about. It wasn't like she had to do her senior year of high school while raising a child.

Thankfully, I didn't have to wait too long for the doctor to come back. I'd already talked to the school twice to explain my absence.

If I didn't show up for afternoon classes, they'd probably call Nan. The only bad thing about that would be explaining to Nan why I came to the free clinic, instead of waiting for an appointment.

A man in a white coat walked in and pushed his glasses up his nose. "Miss Crawford," my heart picked up its pace as his eyes swung my way, "What brings you in today?"

How many times was I going to have to explain this to people? Didn't they talk to each other? He had a file in his hand. Was it that hard to make a simple note?

"I took a home pregnancy test a couple weeks ago…"

"Yes," he said, not letting me finish. "You are, in fact, pregnant. Thirteen weeks."

I released a relieved breath as he flipped a page in my file. Thirteen weeks meant it was Parker's. Thank God. At least I didn't have to worry about that.

"Was there something you were worried about? Because the babies look healthy."

"No, I'm not worried about anything." *Except my sanity.*

"Alright." He turned and walked away, but not before adding, "If you have to come back, please make an appointment. We're very busy."

I cocked a brow at his retreating form. Riley was right. The free clinic was staffed by dicks. I scooped up my bag and sauntered out.

While I was relieved that Parker was indeed my child's father, I was overcome with guilt. All this time I'd been scared of Sean, thinking he did something horrible. I was so sure of it. I could feel his hands on me, and smell the tequila on his breath.

Something must have happened, right? But maybe he didn't do anything? This was the same guy that used to take Harper and I for ice cream. He even had tea parties with us. Would he really hurt me?

My thoughts were interrupted by a deep voice.

"Lana?"

I looked up into a pair of dark eyes. Mr. Kessler. Great. Just what I needed.

"Does Parker know you're here?"

Seriously? He asked if Parker knew. As if I belonged to him or something. Can't say I was too surprised. I mean, he was the almighty king of Ashen Springs. And no matter what Harper said,

I had my suspicions that he ran The Order of Ravens and Wolves. I'd met some girl named Marnie at that Causegrove place Riley had told me to come to. What a night that was. Had an encounter with some racist pricks, met a fellow conspiracy theorist, and got pregnant.

If I could go back in time, Marnie was the one thing I wouldn't change. At one point, we slipped off to chat, and let me just say, that girl knew her facts. If there was one person in this town that could take on the Order, it was her. Kind of wished she was here right now.

Louis folded his arms. "Is something wrong with the baby?"

I was a little shocked he knew about the baby. Then again, his knowledge only confirmed my suspicions about the society. Why else would he know? Other than their kids, the Whitleys and the Kesslers didn't hang out together. Not that I'd seen, anyway.

"The baby's fine."

I might not be, though.

I cocked my hip and eyed Mr. Kessler's black suit. He was a psychiatrist, and a well respected one at that. Still…

"Do you want to ask me something, Lana?"

No.

Yes.

Maybe.

"I don't know." Could I trust him? Of course I couldn't trust him.

"Why don't you come with me to my office," he placed his hand on my back and steered me down the hall, "Where we can speak in private."

What I should've done was leave. Thank him for his time and just go. Instead, I found myself following him. Apparently my fear of possible insanity outweighed my desire for self preservation. I needed to know if I had blamed a man I considered a brother for something truly horrific, when he had, in fact, done nothing.

Louis Kessler's office was about what I expected, and not at all something one would find in a hospital. I could smell the luxury when I entered the room. Dark bookshelves, filled with more books than one person should have, lined the walls. On either side of the door sat a black leather wingback chair, that matched two in front of a desk made of the same wood as the bookshelves.

Even the beige carpet in this room was luxurious. My feet sunk into the plush flooring like they would sand on a beach.

Mr. Kessler headed across the room and walked around the desk to the chair behind it. His seat didn't look like the other four. It was black, but taller, with big arms and a cushy back.

A throne fit for a king. I listened to the leather creak as he sat down, and ran my hand over the back of one of the chairs by the door.

What are you doing here, Lana?

"Why don't you tell me what's on your mind."

What was on my mind. The question itself was comical. Was I raped? Did the man I trusted most in this world betray me in the worst possible way, or had I lost what was left of my sanity? All answers I wasn't going to just freely give. And certainly not to Louis Kessler.

"What makes you think there's something on my mind?"

"I'm a psychiatrist, my dear," he chuckled and leaned back in his chair, folding his hands in his lap. "My job is the mind."

Fair enough. Didn't mean I was going to say anything to him. Even if I really wanted to.

I guessed he sensed my reluctance, because the next words he spoke were, "I am a professional, Lana. Whatever you say to me in confidence, will remain in confidence. I take my oath very seriously."

The question was, which oath was he referring to? I might not have any proof that secret society existed, but I also didn't have any proof that it didn't either.

Sure, there was doctor-patient confidentiality, but did that really matter to a man like Louis Kessler? Even if he did break his so called code, what was I going to do? Sue him? No one in this town went against the Kesslers.

"I should go."

Mr. Kessler nodded. "If that's what you want."

Why wasn't he trying to stop me? My eyes narrowed on his

calm expression. Maybe he really did just want to help? Would it really hurt to ask?

Deciding that it couldn't hurt if he didn't know exactly what happened, or who it pertained to, I asked, "Is it possible for someone to think something happened, when it really didn't?"

"I suppose," he tipped his head in a questioning way. "It would depend on what, exactly, they think happened, and the circumstances under which said incident occurred."

Touché, Mr. Kessler. But I was too smart to fall for that.

"There may have been alcohol involved."

He nodded as if he understood. Given Mason's recent stint in rehab, I suppose he did. "Alcohol can fog the mind."

"But it was only one drink," I pointed out.

"Was there anything else in the drink?"

I shook my head.

He retaliated with, "How sure are you?"

I was with Harper at her house, so, "One hundred percent."

"I see." He rested his elbows on the desk and steepled his fingers. "How long ago was this?"

"Why does that matter?"

"Time can have an effect on your mind. For example, if you stubbed your toe last year, and then again today, which memory do you think would be clearer?"

That made sense, but this wasn't last year. "It's only been about a month."

"So earlier in February, when Parker was at football camp."

I froze. How did I forget about that? Sean wasn't even in town that week. He couldn't have done anything. So I *was* crazy. That was oddly relieving. The breath I let out felt like it'd been sitting in the back of my throat for over a month.

"Was it something I said?"

Mr. Kessler was now leaning back in his chair, looking like the cat who caught the canary. I really needed to get out of here.

"I should go." I spun around and opened the door. "I've missed enough school."

"Very well," he said. "I'm here if you ever need to talk, my dear."

Unease settled in my stomach as I hurried my way out of the hospital. For some reason, it felt like I'd just handed the enemy the keys to the kingdom.

Lou called. I guess Lana felt the need to go to the free clinic. Why did she go to that skeezy cesspool of second rate doctors; who fucking knows? Lou sure as hell didn't. As far as he could tell, there was nothing wrong with her, or the baby.

Physically, anyways. All he could tell me was that she was asking all these weird questions. Some shit about thinking something happened, when it didn't. Which got me thinking.

Lana hadn't been herself lately. No sparkly bracelets or pretty hair clips I could steal for my collection. She walked around the halls quiet as a mouse, which in itself was wrong.

My Angel couldn't shut her mouth if her life depended on it. And she was avoiding her friends. I could understand Riley, that girl had serious anger issues. I could even understand Shelby. But Harper?

There were three things I could count on every day. That

Logan, Mason, or both, would say something that'd make me want to punch them. That some groupie floozy bitch would be trying to suck my dick–football chicks were the worst–and that if I saw Harper, Lana wouldn't be far behind.

I'd lost count how many times I'd smacked Mason because Lana got caught in his Harper vendetta crossfire. Because of this, he was probably the only one of my friends who knew how I actually felt about the girl. Until I knocked her up, that is.

We had a quiet understanding. I didn't give him shit about fucking countless chicks to rid his mind of the one pussy he really wanted. And he didn't say shit about Lana. It worked. We could both watch them walk around every day without the other saying shit about it.

If he hadn't had to do a stint in rehab, maybe he would've noticed my Angel's odd behaviour. I should've fucking noticed it, but I was too busy trying to push her away from me. It was kind of fun, though. I liked seeing her nose scrunch up when she got all mad. It was cute as fuck. But my head wasn't in the sand anymore, and something was up with my Angel.

"Something on your mind, baby brother?" Preston leaned back against the kitchen counter and rolled his eyes my way.

I fucking hated when he called me that. Prick knew it, too. "Nothing that concerns you."

"That's where you're wrong." He popped a cigarette in his mouth and flipped open the zippo I gave him last year for his birthday. "What kind of brother would I be if I didn't help you out?"

"What the fuck is that supposed to mean?"

He lifted his chin and exhaled a stream of smoke. "Let's just say your girlfriend should be much more compliant."

"What the fuck did you do?" If he hurt Lana…

"Relax," he sighed, "I didn't touch her. Just added to the nightmare she was having."

What? Lana had a nightmare?

"Did she say anything?"

"Nothing useful," Preston shook his head. "But if I were you, I'd talk to Callaghan. She got pretty jumpy when I mentioned his name."

My mind went back to the other day, when Lana came rushing out of that room she'd been in with Sean. She wasn't pissed off; she was afraid. I didn't know why she'd be afraid of a guy who was her brother in every way but blood, but I intended to find out.

The trick was beating the King of Kings to the information. He was already sniffing around, and Louis Kessler had his nose so far up everyone's ass, he could taste what they'd had for breakfast.

He was even in my brother's shit. A place that no one on this planet wanted to be. Preston didn't take too kindly to people getting in his shit. I used to follow my brother around. Know what that got me? A broken arm, and a dead fucking dog. But somehow, the King of Kings eluded my brother's repercussions.

Despite knowing what Preston really was. Then again, my brother didn't give a shit. I, however, did, and had so far avoided the illustrious Dr. Kessler diagnosis. As far as he was concerned, I was the good one. Fuck sakes, I once heard him tell Mase he should be more like me. If only he knew.

Which was precisely why I didn't want him digging around. If he got too close, he might find out what was really going on in my head. While the look on his face when he realized he'd missed something so close would be priceless, I didn't need him to shrink me. Besides, there was something to be said about fooling the keeper of the secrets. Who else could've pulled that shit off?

My parents walked into the room. My mother had her 'woman of the house' look on her face, while my dad curled his lip at the smoke wafting out of my brother's mouth.

"Preston, put that shit out."

"Blow me."

"There is no smoking in this house." Our mother placed her hand on her hip and glared at my brother. "How many times do I have to tell you that?"

Preston's response was to look her dead in the eyes, while flicking his ash on the floor.

Lillianna Whitley wasn't one to back down. She stood there, daring Preston to push her with her eyes. Other children might've backed down from that look, but they didn't have the matricidal fantasies my brother did. Not only did he return her glare, but the fucker went so far as to pull a letter opener out of his pocket and twirl it in his hand.

At that point, she turned her attention to me. "Where is this girl?"

I couldn't help but snicker at her subtle change in subject. No one could accuse Lillianna Whitley of being stupid. One of the many reasons I'd tried to avoid this whole situation in the first place. Lana was fearless and smart. Not once did she back down from Mason, but my mother wasn't Mase. She was cunning, and coldly cruel.

"Are you sure you want to do this, sweetheart?"

"Yes," I answered flatly.

"Parker, she can't even show up on time," my mother sighed. "How are you supposed to have a child with her?"

"She'll be here."

"Let's hope so, son." My father glanced down at his watch, "If she's not here in fifteen minutes, I'm sending Mr. Weinstein out to get her."

Mr. Weinstein was one of our lawyers, a former private eye, and a member of the Order. One of the few who wasn't blood bound. The Order of Ravens and Wolves wasn't a huge society.

We didn't recruit on college campuses like the movies would have one believe, but if someone was exceptional, or useful in some way, such as a politician, we offered them the chance at induction. Only one person had turned us down. He currently resided in the forest next to Manning Keep.

More specifically, six feet under the forest floor.

"You sure you want this cunt involved in your kid's life?"

"Preston," my dad snarled, "That's your mother."

"So?"

As much as I'd like to argue with my brother–sometimes I disagreed with Preston, just to disagree with him–in this case, he had a point. When our mother found out her baby boy knocked someone up, she came rushing back.

When she found out who was having my baby, she insisted on fixing the situation. Even had the gall to tell me it was okay to slum it with someone lesser, but not breed with them. She called my baby a mistake. *My baby!* If my father hadn't stepped in, I might've helped Preston live out his matricide fantasy.

Completely ignoring my brother's comment, my mother placed her hand on my cheek and gave me the same fake smile she gave her white nationalist groupies. "Parker, honey, this girl is just trying to trap you."

My hands fisted at her sparkling blue eyes. Red started to bleed into my vision. I could almost feel her warm blood trickling through my fingers.

She's your mother, Parker. You can't kill her.

"Lillianna, we had this conversation." My father's brow rose, "I expect you to be nice to this girl. She's carrying our grandchild."

Last night, my father explained how things were. Their marriage was more of a business arrangement. Her family was going broke, and he bailed them out. A lifeline he threatened to take away. But if there was one thing Lillianna Whitely was used to getting, it was her own way.

"Your grandchild," she hissed back at him, "Not mine."

Preston brought the argument to a grinding halt. "I used to hold a knife to your throat."

"Preston!" My dad barked, while my mother's hand flew to her chest in a mock hint of surprise.

I snorted. *Please bitch, you're not that good of an actress.*

"When I was a kid, I used to sneak into your room and hold a knife to your throat." He stared down at the letter opener held tightly in his grip. "The night I decided to slit your throat, the damn dog bit me."

My gaze zeroed in on the light glinting off the clean metal edge. Where the fuck did he get that? It looked oddly familiar.

"Is that why you killed Max?"

Preston shrugged. "It got in my way."

It, not he. I'd loved that fucking dog. Max was just doing his job and protecting the family. My eyes once again fell to the sharp point of the letter opener. It wouldn't take much to shove that thing in his throat. Stain that nice shiny metal red with his blood.

"Go ahead, brother, do it," Preston dared with a smirk. "You know you want to."

I did. I really fucking did. Wanted it so bad my skin was crawling.

"Leave your brother alone." My mother smiled at me. *I could slap her around instead.* "He's a good boy."

Preston snorted. "I doubt Mark Stevens would agree."

How the hell did he know about that? No one knew about that. I'd made sure of it. He had to be bluffing.

I straightened up and stretched my neck. "I'm gonna go wait for Lana."

I had to get out of there before the urge to hurt someone became too strong. Last time that happened, I didn't come to until I was elbow deep in a gutted corpse. That took a long fucking time to clean up. Almost called my brother for back up. Funny thing is, I can't remember what the prick did to piss me off.

I spun around and headed for the entryway. Besides blood, there was only one thing that could dull the itch for violence rushing through my veins. I smiled at the old blue Ford Taurus pulling up in front of the house. *And here she is now.*

My perfect, sweet little angel. The first person in this world to call me on my shit.

"What are you so afraid of, Parker? That you'll disappoint them, or yourself?"

I COULD STILL FEEL her perky nipples pressing against my chest. Her breath cooling my heated skin. How could I not touch her? She was right there, looking at me with need in those beautiful hazel eyes. My Angel. The girl I thought about when I jerked myself.

"It's not always that simple, Angel."

Her breathy words flowed through my ears and straight down to my dick. "Yes, it is."

"Is it?"

I'D TASTED the forbidden fruit, and now I couldn't let her go. Or the memory of that night…

My dick was already hard as fuck, but when her whole body shuddered against mine, I couldn't take it anymore. I had to push her away before it was too late. "Prove it." *I leaned in and inhaled the only part of her I could touch, the sweet vanilla scent of her perfume.* "Take your shirt off."

I hoped my demand would make her back off, maybe even slap me. Instead, a flush of heat flooded her cheeks. Before I knew it, my hand was under her chin, thumb running over her plump bottom lip, as I tipped her gaze back up to mine.

"Well, what's it going to be, Angel? You going to take your shirt off? Or am I going to leave?"

It took everything I had to hold back when her lust filled gaze met mine. I should've stepped away then. Should've turned around and left her alone. But I was trapped by the softness of her skin warming my hand. And then, she opened her mouth.

"Shouldn't you kiss me first?"

I snapped. Speared my fingers through her hair and slammed my lips down on hers. One taste. That was all it took to dissolve my years of control. The second her tongue touched mine and her sweet taste exploded in my mouth, I was done. Fuck the consequences, tonight Lana Crawford was mine.

With a growl, I picked her up and slammed us up against the wall. A second later, her shirt was gone, ripped apart like tissue paper.

"Parker."

Her breathy objection didn't penetrate my lust addled brain. All I heard were the soft moans that escaped her parted lips when my mouth latched on to her rosebud nipple. I'm not sure who took off whose clothes, or how we got on the bed, but I didn't care.

The only thing I needed more than to taste every inch of this woman's body, was to be inside her. Buried so deep, she'd never forget the way I felt.

I ran my fingers through her folds, groaning at her wetness. I wanted to lick her there. Bury my head between her thighs and lap up all that sweet honey, but my dick couldn't take any more. Lana gasped against my mouth when I lined up with her opening.

"Parker, wait. I've never..."

I pushed in, growling at the way her walls gripped my shaft. She was so fucking tight. If I didn't know any better, I'd say she was a... I stopped and stared down at the grimace on her face.

My mouth curled as I snapped my hips forward and felt myself tear *through a resistance. She was a virgin. I might not be able to keep her, but Lana's innocence would always be mine.*

"Shh," I hushed, while gently kissing away her tears. "Just relax."

Her fingers dug into my shoulders. "It hurts."

"I know, baby. It'll get better."

I took my time, soothing her with my mouth. If I'd have known she was a virgin, I'd have done this slower. Ah fuck, who was I kidding? There was no slow when it came to my Angel, but I could ease her into it. I fluttered kisses over her eyelids and down to her neck, pausing long enough to enjoy her thundering pulse. Once I felt her muscles relax, I began to move.

Slowly at first, which was torture. I was balls deep in the most perfect pussy on the planet and all I wanted to do was pound into her. The instant her hips snapped up to meet my thrust, that's exactly what I did. Pounded into her so hard, she had to bite down on my shoulder to muffle her screams...

HER TEETH HAD DUG SO hard into my flesh that I'd had a mark on my shoulder for weeks. A mark I wore proudly. No one knew who gave it to me, but I showed it off every chance I got. Especially when she was around. That really pissed her off.

I watched her get out of the car and smooth down her shirt. She was wearing blue today. The same light blue she'd had on when I first saw her. Did she go home to change, or was that one of the many outfits she had stashed at school? It didn't matter; I liked that color on her.

It highlighted the natural tan of her complexion, and made her hazel eyes shine brighter. I liked it so much, I briefly thought about taking it from her, like I took the panties from her locker last week.

She let out a huff of air and ran her hand through her dark hair. My gaze honed in on her fingers moving through her silky black locks. I could feel them wrapped around my fingers, softly flowing over my skin as I tugged on her scalp.

She liked it when I did that. When I was rough and took what I wanted, her cunt squeezed tightly around me. I went easy on her the first time. Next time, I'd give her what she really wanted. Long, deep, hard strokes, while I controlled her with my hands and body.

"Fuck," I grunted, and adjusted myself.

Lana was coming. I had to get my game face on. I could play later.

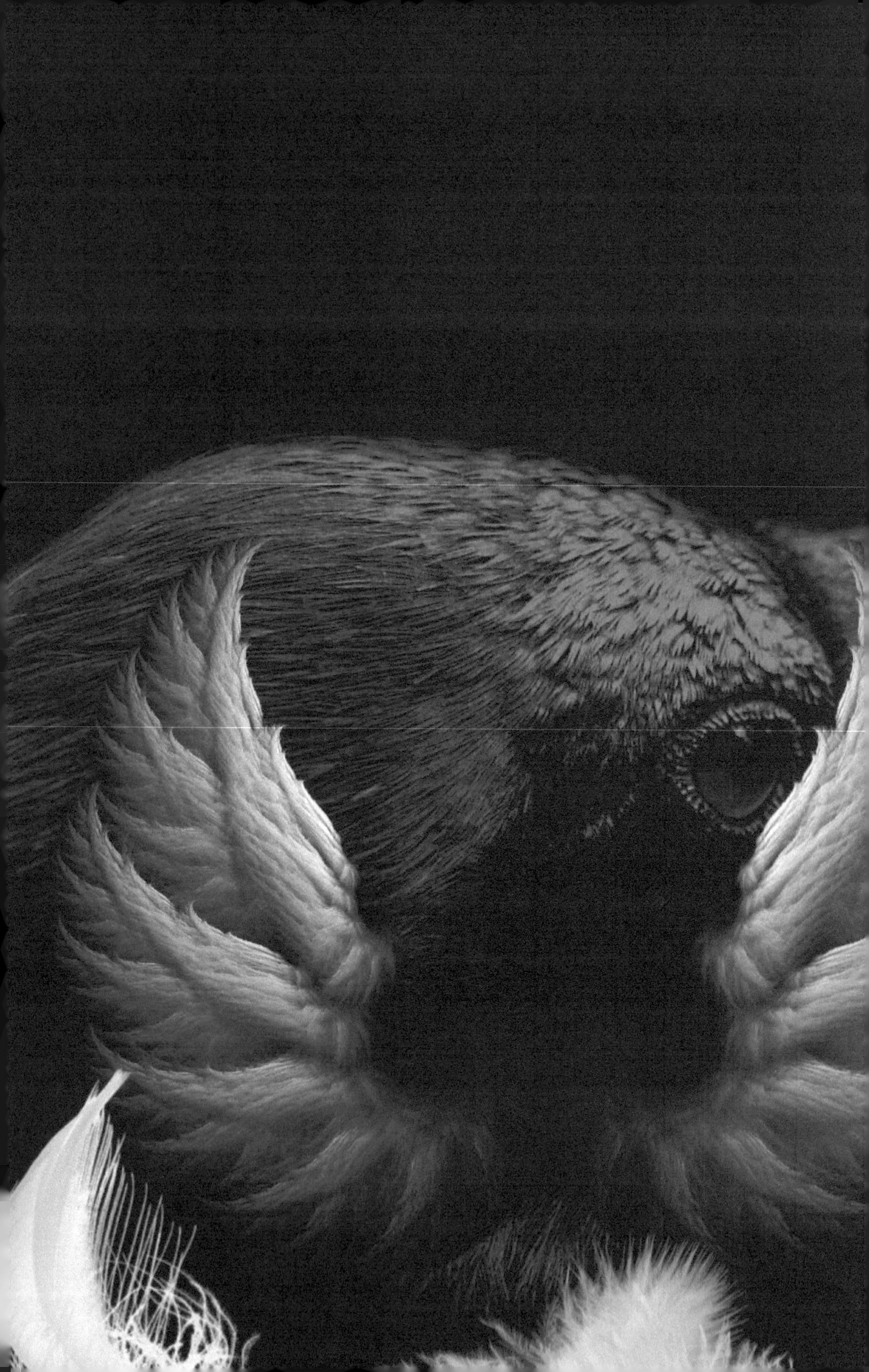

Chapter 10
Lana

I stared at the Whitley house, big and grand compared to the place Nan and I called home. There wasn't a fountain or grand garden of opulence, like at Logan's, but it was just as intimidating.

Mainly because of the people inside. Death on his pale horse, and the woman Nan called the Dragon Lady, were the least of my worries. Parker was the one who had my stomach flipping.

Gramps used to take me for walks. We'd wander through the forest studying the various plants. One time, we came upon a clutch of daisies. All of them stood tall and perfect, except one.

It was crooked, bent a little to the left, with two oversized petals. I remember how it stood, beautiful, flawed and proud, despite the perfect flowers around it stealing all the sun's attention.

That's how Parker Whitley made me feel. One night, thirteen weeks ago, I was special and unique. Until he plucked me out of the ground and tossed me in the dirt. Another discarded flower that used to be loved. Standing there under the hot afternoon sun, I couldn't help but wonder what happened to all those bouquets when people went back for them?

Knowing Sean was still the guy I thought he was should've made me feel better. Given me some sort of peace. And it did, for a bit. Until Parker kindly reminded me of our appointment.

After that, all I could see was Preston's cold, dead stare. I kept going through possible scenarios, hoping I'd come across one where I came out on top. Should've been easy for someone who managed to stay in the top five percent of her class. Guess how many plans I came up with? None.

Zip.

Zilch.

Zero.

Which was the extent of my loved ones' survival if I didn't make Preston's brother 'happy,' as he put it. So I decided to do the one thing I could. Self-sacrifice. I mean, it wasn't all bad, right? Parker had a sweet side. At least he did that night. And my child would have both parents. Who knows, maybe we'd turn out to be a real family after all.

I raised my hand to knock, but the door flew open before I could.

"Glad you could make it, Angel."

I looked up at the gleam in Parker's eyes.

Happy family indeed. Keep kidding yourself, Lana.

I sighed and said, "Can we talk?" May as well get this over with.

His brows rose. "What do you want to talk about?"

Here goes nothing.

I sucked in a deep breath and spit the words out before I lost my nerve. "Is the easy way still on the table?"

The asshole actually smiled. "Could be. I have stipulations though."

Of course he did.

"Whatever," I muttered. "Can you give me your *stipulations* inside, or is there some kind of passcode to enter?"

Parker stepped to the side and waved me in. I sauntered past, trying to ignore the way his cocky smirk made my stomach flip. After everything he did, Parker Whitley still had the power to make my knees weak. One look at his sandy-blond locks and shimmering grey eyes and my body was ready to submit.

Even worse was the fact that I knew what was under his shirt and jeans. I'd seen his chiselled form. Felt the power in his broad shoulders, smelled the intoxicating blend of our sweat mingling in the air. Sometimes, when I closed my eyes, I could still hear his voice purring in my ear.

"We should talk about this privately." Parker led me around a corner.

"What do you mean privately?"

Did he have a crowd waiting to weigh in their judgment or something? I could see Parker having his own personal jury. Who wouldn't back the towns the golden boy?

"This way." He waved his hand at a small flight of stairs. "Unless you want my parents and lawyer involved in this conversation?"

I snorted. Yeah, not likely. I didn't want to be involved in this conversation, but what choice did I have?

He placed his hand on my back and urged me forward. "Does your sudden willingness to discuss an arrangement have anything to do with my brother?"

Arrangement? Nice choice of words.

"No," I lied, as we entered a room that I could only describe as a living room/library.

There was comfortable looking beige furniture, and book-shelves lining the walls. What was it with rich people and books? Logan had rooms like this too, and I'd bet my left arm, he hadn't read a single book on those overpriced shelves.

"Parker…" I spun around, prepared to give Parker a piece of my mind, but was cut off by the solid chest inches from my nose.

"You're not a very good liar, Angel."

I happened to think I was pretty good at the art of deception. Not that I lied a lot, but there'd be a lot more wooden spoons buried in my backyard if I hadn't at least mastered it somewhat. I wasn't under the strict house that Harper was.

Nan didn't have many rules. The ones she did set out though, she was firm on. One of which was no spending the night with boys in the house. I pretty much obliterated that one. The baby in my belly was proof of that.

"Can we just get this over with?"

"Are you that anxious to hear my stipulations?"

Goddamn him and his deep voice. The way it thrummed through my body made me forget, for just a second, how badly I didn't want to be here. Giving myself some space, I nodded and took a step back. Space was a good thing. I couldn't breathe when his stupid clean smell was overwhelming my senses.

"I only have one." The corner of Parker's mouth lifted as strode forward, closing the gap I'd made.

I used to get jealous of the girls he'd give that seductive smirk to. Now, it just reminded me of that discarded flower. I swallowed, forcing my nerves down and continued my retreat. By the time I managed to cough out the words, "What's that?" my back bounced off a bar I hadn't noticed until that moment.

I could hear Riley's voice in the back of my head, *'Get your head out of your ass, Lana. Grab a fork and stab him in the nuts.'*

I don't know what her obsession with forks was, but right now, I was tempted to get her a nice, shiny, well sharpened set. Better for her to stab Parker with, and probably Micha. No, definitely Micha. I wondered if he'd be mad at me for arming his girlfriend, or pissed at her for actually carrying through with her threat?

My daydream was cut off when Parker moved in and gracefully

placed his hands on the bar behind me. Forgetting the bar was behind me, I tried to back up more. When that didn't work, I darted my gaze around for somewhere else to go, but I was trapped between his solid forearms. I really needed to start listening to my inner Riley.

Parker bent forward and sucked in a deep breath. "You smell fucking great."

I gulped back my gasp and said, "Just tell me what you want, Parker."

"You, Lana." His grey eyes locked on mine, blue flecks twinkling with dark desire. "I want you."

The air grew heavy. My mouth couldn't spit out the words I wanted to say, and my chest shook, struggling to suck in a full breath. When my lips finally parted, all that came out was a shuddered hiss. Where the hell was my inner Riley now?

We stood there for what felt like forever, in the luxury of Parker's house. I'd never felt more out of place with him staring down at me, while I attempted to ignore the intense sparks wisping through the air. The steady rise and fall of his chest rang out. Deep, echoing breaths, that enhanced the blood pulsing in my ears.

My fingers twitched, palm aching to reach out and feel the power behind his firm muscles once more. Thankfully, my voice came back before that happened.

"I agreed to your easy way," I pointed out, though right now, it seemed more like a quicker way to damn myself than a temporary solution. "Isn't that enough?"

"No."

I was barely hanging on, and didn't have anything left to give. "What more do you want from me, Parker?"

"I want it all, Angel." He caressed me with his eyes, slowly dipping his gaze down. Over the swell of my breasts, along the curves of my hip, and back up. "In my bed, sleeping in my arms, bouncing off my cock."

Without laying so much as a finger on me, Parker made my entire body shiver. One look, and every fiber of my being wanted to purr and stretch against him, like a cat in heat.

When his arm lifted and he splayed his palm across my belly, I jumped. I don't know if it was instinct, fear, or something else, but whatever it was held power over me. Parker Whitley was a fantasy I never should've indulged in. The kryptonite to my Superman, and sooner or later, he'd weaken me.

He was the perfect flower in a clutch of daisies.

"Have you felt it move yet?" Parker's gaze dropped down to my stomach, and the hand he had laid across it.

All I could do was shake my head in response. The way he was staring at me, with this revered adoration, had me completely stunned. Parker didn't just want this baby, he already loved it.

I was too afraid of who had put this child in me, that I couldn't even bring myself to touch my stomach, and he was ready to give everything he had for it. What kind of person did that make me?

I swallowed and guiltily whispered, "I almost got rid of it."

The appointment was made. I was at the clinic, sitting on the exam table, dressed in one of their gowns, and I left. I still don't know what made me walk out. Maybe it was the hurt and anger I expected to see when Parker's gaze snapped up to mine. But that's not what I got. All I saw when I looked into his eyes, was compassion.

"It's okay, baby, you were probably scared." He tipped his head and grazed the pad of his thumb over my bottom lip. "But you don't have to be scared anymore. You're mine now. I got you."

"I'm not yours," I snarled, shoving him back.

Admittedly my reaction might've been a little overkill, but I didn't like what he was saying, or how it made me feel. All tingly and terrified at the same time.

Within a second, the energy in the room shifted. Parker flattened his hard body against mine, and glared down at me with darkness in his eyes.

"Lie to yourself all you want, Angel, but you're mine."

This time, when my body twitched, it wasn't because of some tempting desire. It was because of the coldness of his stare. A dark, violent glint, just like Preston.

"You remember what that feels like, to be mine, don't you, Angel?" his voice grated his chosen pet name, making it sound anything but divine. And then, just like that, it was gone, and something else filled his eyes. "The way your tight little pussy stretched around my cock, and how hard you screamed my name into that pillow."

I clenched my thighs together. How could I forget? That night was all I thought about for weeks. It was the comfort I used when my crazy mind thought something horrible had happened.

"Because I do," he growled, sliding his tongue up my neck. "I jerk myself to your hot little cunt every night."

Oh my god.

In an effort to regain control, I said, "I'm not sleeping with you, Parker."

"Sorry, baby," he chuckled and backed off a bit. "That's part of the deal. I get to fuck you whenever I want. Like I said, you're mine."

My hands tightly balled at my sides. So that's what he wanted. A whore. Parker made me feel cheap and used once before. Never again. He took a memory I should've cherished for the rest of my life, and ruined it by throwing money at me the next morning.

"Are you going to pay me this time, too?"

Bastard had the gall to roll his eyes.

"I should've fucking known you'd bring that shit up."

"Oh, I'm sorry. Should I give you my rates beforehand?" I lifted up on my tip toes and got right in his face, "Or do you just want to pay me based on my performance again?"

"I know you don't believe me, but I did that for your benefit."

"Let me guess, you thought I could use some new shoes?" I'd get some shoes alright. Stilettos I could stab him with.

He blew out a puff of frustrated air. "Jesus Christ, Lana. I was trying to protect you."

I stopped and eyed him. Protect me? Well, I'd give him points for originality. That was not the excuse I was expecting.

"You're right," I said, "I don't believe you."

"It doesn't matter. You're mine now. You always were."

Sure I was. "Uh huh?"

"I mean it, Lana. You're mine to protect, mine to take care of." His fingers speared in my hair and he yanked my head back, forcing me to meet his gaze, "And mine to fuck."

I almost laughed. Seriously? He wanted to go there right now? "No."

"No?" Parker's brow arched. "You sure about that, Angel?"

Parker Whitley wasn't god. "Absolutely."

"Alright," he shrugged, "Guess we better get up to the meeting then."

The pit in my stomach churned as I watched him walk towards the stairs. Preston was up there. I knew it. I could feel him judging me, waiting for me to fuck us, so he could carry through with his threat.

"Wait," I called out, stopping Parker.

He looked over his shoulder and cocked a brow my way. Micha's words replayed in the back of my head. *You really want to give up that life line?'*

"Fine," I grumbled, crossing my arms. "I agree."

"Come again?"

"You heard me." *Asshole.*

"Be very clear, Lana," Parker's voice carried through the air, each word growing in intensity as he stalked slowly across the room. "What exactly are you agreeing to?"

I looked for somewhere else to go. A place where I could avoid his closeness, because I needed to keep my wits about me. I eyed one of the chairs in the corner. There was a small space behind it, and a chair was a good barrier. Might be a possible means of escape?

"I don't hear an answer, Angel."

My glare snapped back to Parker as I snarled, "I agree to your terms."

The smirk on his face made me seriously rethink the chair. Parker wasn't a small guy, *dick*. He could easily move a couch, let alone a chair. I'd probably just end trapping myself in a tighter more confined space.

"You agree to sleeping in my bed?"

I huffed out a sigh. "Yes."

"Laying in my arms?" He tipped his head, causing a lock of his sandy hair to flop over his forehead.

"Yes," I hissed in response.

Why couldn't I have gotten knocked up by someone like Brandon? He didn't have that stupid, sexy smoulder.

He stopped in front of me and reached out to scoop a lock of my hair in his fingers. I stood motionless as he leaned forward and inhaled deeply. The groan he released after had me squeezing my thighs together.

"Bouncing on my cock?"

I didn't trust my body to say what I wanted it to, which was mainly where he could shove said appendage. So, instead, I just bit my lip and nodded.

My knees trembled as I stood there waiting with bated breath for him to say something. I agreed to his stupid stipulations, that should be the end of it, right?

Wrong.

Parker dropped his hand, letting my hair slip out of his fingers. "Why should I believe you?"

"What choice do you have?" I challenged back.

That was a mistake.

"Oh Angel," he snickered and stepped in, forcing me back against the bar, "In this situation, I have all the choices. For instance, I could walk up those stairs and start custody proceedings right now…"

I tried to shy away from his breath warming my skin, but there was nowhere to go. "Or?"

"Or, you could give me a reason to believe you."

"What?"

Seriously, 'give me a reason to believe you?' What kind of crap was that? How do you make someone believe you? It's not like they have a cream for that. How cool would that be though? *Excuse me sir, just let me pull out my instant trust cream.*

That definitely would've come in handy a couple times with Nan. I'd package it in pinky sparkly containers so no guys would dare use it. Well, except for Logan. I don't think the sparkles would detour him any. Not that that prick needed miracle trust cream. He already had a miracle trust smile.

Parker's voice pulled me out of my daydream. "So, what's it going to be, Angel?"

"Huh?"

"Are you going to give me a reason to believe you?"

Oh, right, that.

There had to be a way to make him believe me. I just had to figure out what it was. Preston was the obvious choice. Telling Parker about his brother's visit would probably do it, but something told me Preston wouldn't be too happy if I said anything. And I'd take an unsure Parker, over a pissed off Preston any day.

"What do you want me to do, Parker?" I blew out a frustrated sigh and slapped my hands down on my thighs. "It's not like I have miracle trust cream."

Brought to you by Crawford Corp.

"Oh, for fuck sakes," he grumbled, "Were you always this naive?"

"Well, *excuse me,* Mr. High and Mighty." I didn't ask to be here, that was all him. And now he wanted to play games. Screw him. "Maybe if you didn't beat around the bush, the rest of us peasants wouldn't have to–"

His mouth crashed down on mine, swallowing the rest of my words. I was too stunned to pull away. At least, that's what I told myself. It was easier than facing the truth, which my body was more than happy to portray for me.

Parker's mouth moved against mine, easily coaxing my lips to part. The instant his tongue touched mine, the lies I told myself fell away. I couldn't stop myself from melting into his arms, as I rose up on my toes, seeking more.

He growled and slammed me back against the bar. The wood digging into my tailbone didn't even bother me. As long as he kept kissing me, I didn't care what he did.

And then, he was gone.

I blinked my eyes open, clearing the hazy fog that was clouding my mind, and found myself staring up into Parker's sparkling gaze. A very satisfied, pleased with himself, look was written across his stupid face.

"That wasn't so hard now, was it?"

Son of a bitch. I just fell for his shit again, didn't I?

"Screw you, Parker! You can't just toy with people's emotions."

Tears started to drip down my face at an uncontrollable rate. I tried to suck them back in, but I couldn't. They kept coming in waves of crushing despair.

"Great, now I'm crying. See what you did." I cried out, slapping him in the chest. "You made me cry!"

Honestly, I didn't know why I was crying. I just was. Big, fat, ugly tears of I don't know what kept rolling down my skin. I was definitely losing my mind.

First, thinking Sean would ever do something like that, and now I was balling my eyes out because Parker had kissed me. They should lock me up. That was kind of what I expected Parker to say. After all, what kind of girl loses her shit because a guy kissed her?

A crazy one, that's who.

Parker didn't say a single thing. He simply wrapped his arms around me and held me close while I sobbed into his chest. Instead of calling me crazy, or telling me to stop my incessant crying, he kissed the top of my head and stroked my hair until whatever insane fit I was going through had passed.

"I'm sorry," I muttered, wiping the tears off my face while shrugging out of his embrace. "I don't know what's wrong with me."

I was so embarrassed, I couldn't even look at him.

"You're pregnant," Parker said, pulling me back into his arms. "Emotional outbursts are normal. Your hormones are going crazy."

"How would you know?" Did I miss the part where he had a uterus?

"Research, baby," he explained. "If I'm gonna take care of you, I have to know what I'm doing."

I snorted. *Yeah, sure, take care of me.*

"You going to pay me to stop crying too?"

"Fuck sakes." His head flopped back with a loud groan. "I told you, I had reasons for doing that."

I pushed myself away from his chest and snarled, "What possible reason could you have to treat someone like a whore?"

"Parker," a woman's voice wafted down the stairs, "There's an old black woman standing in our driveway."

"You're about to find out," he muttered.

Preston once told me, the more you suffer, the more it shows you really care. Of course, it was right after he killed my dog, so it was more of a 'deal with it' than some rare piece of insightful advice. But as I led Lana up those stairs, that's all I could think about.

My mother's views pissed a lot of people off. That wasn't why I hated my mother. Honestly, I could care less what other people thought, my friends included. The girl I was leading through my house however…

I looked down at Lana and wished my mother would be able to keep her mouth shut for once in her damn life.

The first voice I heard wasn't my mothers'.

"Where is my granddaughter?" Lana's Nan did not sound happy. Then again, she was in a room with my mother. "I know you did something to her."

"If you took better care of your offspring, we wouldn't be in this situation in the first place."

I rolled my eyes at my mother's response, though when it came to her, I supposed that was tactful.

"Are you saying this is my Lana's fault?"

"Well, it certainly isn't Parker's. My boy would never go near your granddaughter. She must've seduced him."

Sorry to burst your bubble, Mom, but I've been dreaming about this girl for years. The only reason I stayed away was because of you.

I remember the first day my dick got hard. It was after football practice, and Lana came skipping out in her uniform. Every time she jumped up, I got a glimpse of her white and pink striped panties.

I'm not sure which was worse, the how to avoid pitching a tent speech from my dad? Or the jerk off lesson from my brother?

"My Lana is innocent in all this. You leave her alone."

Gotta say, I kind of liked Lana's Nan. There wasn't much to her. Fuck sakes, the woman made Harper look tall, but she had big brass fucking balls. This wasn't the first time she'd taken on the great Lillianna Whitley.

"Parker is the innocent one here." I didn't have to be in the room to see the scowl on my mother's face. I could even picture her hand waving through the air. "At least he was, until your offspring sunk her claws into him."

I watched Lana's throat move with a heavy swallow. Though I really wanted to see her throat move like that for a completely different reason, she needed me right now. I grabbed her hand, entwining my fingers in hers, and gave her a reassuring smile.

You're not alone, baby. I got you.

"Actually, Mother," I said, pulling Lana in the room and cutting my mother off before she could spew more shit, "I seduced her."

The look on her face was priceless. A deep embedded scowl

that didn't match the proper attire of her black pencil skirt and blouse.

"Are you saying you wanted to have relations with this…" her lip curled as she rolled her eyes over my girl, "This girl?"

My dad slapped his hand down on the table, warning my mother. But he wasn't who I was staring at as I pulled Lana further into the kitchen. My brother was the one I stared at.

More specifically, the letter opener in his hand. One word, and all my problems would be solved. Preston would lunge across the room and shove that thing so deep in our mother's throat, she wouldn't have time to think about what happened. So, why didn't I?

"Just so you know, Mother, I wanted to fuck this girl. Dreamt about her pussy for so long, my balls ached when she walked in a room."

My little angel didn't like my bluntness. She twitched at my side, and tried to pull her hand out of my grasp.

Sorry, baby, you're not going anywhere.

"I still want to fuck this girl." Now that I'd finally told my mother how I felt, I couldn't stop. That, and her expression was the most satisfying thing I'd ever seen. Besides my girl screaming my name, that is. "I'll put twelve more babies in her, if she'll let me."

Pretty sure Lana's Nan was two seconds away from stabbing me with the first sharp instrument she could find, but I didn't care. Hell, I was getting off on the silent conflict. Because like it or not…

"Lana's mine." I wrapped my arm around Lana's shoulder, and pulled her in as close as I could. "If you don't like it, you can leave."

And by you, I meant both of them.

Neither one said a word. We stood there staring at each other. My mother's venomous glare trained on Lana, while her Nan's was trained on me. Everyone else in the room remained tensely quiet. Well, except for my brother and I.

We didn't give a shit how this turned out. The result would be the same regardless. Lana already agreed to my terms. I couldn't help but smirk just a bit at the angry glint in Greta Crawford's brown eyes.

The heaviness in the air lifted a little when my mother spun around and sauntered away.

"By the way, Mother," I called out, making her pause before she could leave, "I also suck dick."

The gasp Lana sucked in made me smirk. My amusement was short lived though, because Lana's Nan's hand flew through the air, smacking me in the back of the head.

"Don't talk to your mother that way."

Red.

Deep dark crimson drops, thickly sliding across my hands.

That's all I could see. Greta's dead eyes staring up at me as I dug through her corpse. Luckily, my mother spoke up, distracting me before I could act out my murderous fantasies.

"Did you just hit my son?"

"Yes, I did." Greta's little chest puffed out. "You should teach your son more respect."

"Alright, that's enough," my dad interrupted. "We have more important things to discuss."

Yes we did.

I couldn't wait to make things official. I wanted Lana to be mine as soon as possible.

Mr. Weinstein threw a briefcase up on the table and popped it open. "We're here for the custody matter of the unborn Whitley baby…"

"Actually," I glanced down at Lana, "Miss Crawford and I have come to an agreement." She sneered back at me, which made me smile and add in, "Isn't that right, Angel?"

Lana's lips thinned as she clamped her mouth shut. She wanted to say something smart, I could see it. Tell me off, or storm out, but she couldn't. Not without raising Grandma's suspicions. Kind of hard to get someone to agree to something if they think you don't want to do it.

"Did she forget how to speak?"

Fucking Preston.

My eyes rolled over to my brother. "Why are you talking?"

"Why aren't you?" he challenged back.

"No one asked for your opinion."

"It wasn't an opinion," he leaned back and eyed me, "It was a statement."

Smug prick.

"You know what…"

"That's right," I called out, interrupting our brotherly argument, "We came to an agreement."

I cocked a brow down at her and resisted the urge to smile. Look at my Angel, stopping us before it got to the fist rounds, which it usually did. Preston and I had kicked the crap out of each other more times then I could count. She was going to be such a good mom.

"What kind of agreement?"

Like my mother, Lana's Nan's brow was raised. Except hers was out of impatient confusion. It was an interesting expression, and not one I'd seen very often. I tipped my head and studied the lines in her face. Crinkles in the forehead, with the mouth tipped down at the corner. Could I mimic that? Would I ever have to?

"So, she's agreed to move in with you."

Her eyes morphed to shock, deepening the lines etched across her face, while smoothing out others. *Interesting.*

I tore my gaze away from Greta, glanced over at my dad, and nodded. "Yes."

"Fantastic," he clapped his hands. "We'll be needing contract B then, Richard."

I thought that was it. We'd sign the contract and it would be done. Greta had other plans.

"My granddaughter is not living here," she barked out. "That woman you call a wife…"

"Won't be a problem," my dad stepped in, stopping the impending disagreement, and quite possibly Greta Crawford's early demise. "Besides, they'll only be here for a couple of weeks, before they can move into the house Parker bought."

This time it was Lana who looked at me with big round eyes. Her shocked expression was different from her Nan's. She didn't have the same deep lines. Maybe that came with age?

"That's very kind of you, *sir*," she said to my dad, "But *you* didn't have to do that."

Getting the hidden meaning behind her words, I chuckled. "He didn't do anything. I bought the house."

I don't need daddy's money, Angel.

She gritted her teeth at me.

I stared back at her.

"Yes," my dad piped in, "Parker was granted early access to his trust, so you will be well provided for, as will the baby. Considering all the advantages that your child will be getting, a trust, first spots in the best schools, and of course, the finest tutors money can buy, it's only fair you give this relationship a chance, don't you think?"

I couldn't agree more.

"If it's a boy, you mean?" Lana pointed out.

"You seem to have forgotten, Lana, I have a daughter as well. And she has all the same things the boys do."

Their voices faded out as my gaze zeroed in on the old woman on the other side of the table. Whatever anger or distaste she had with the situation was gone. The only thing I could see on her face now was fear. Complete, and utter, pale faced terror.

"A boy, I didn't think of that." She spoke so softly, I was probably the only one who heard it. Something sparked across her brown eyes. Guilt, maybe, or worry? "The sooner Lana moves in, the better."

My brow rose.

Well, this is an interesting turn of events.

"Nan?" Lana cried out. "What the hell?"

"Lana, honey," a stern look washed over her face as she placed her hand on Lana's. "Your child deserves both its parents. You can't do this on your own."

You can't do this on your own? My gaze narrowed. Something definitely wasn't right here. I'd watched Lana grow up. I'd seen the way her grandmother supported her. Heard all the times she told her she could do it. This woman, speaking to my angel right now, was not the Greta Crawford I knew.

She was hiding something.

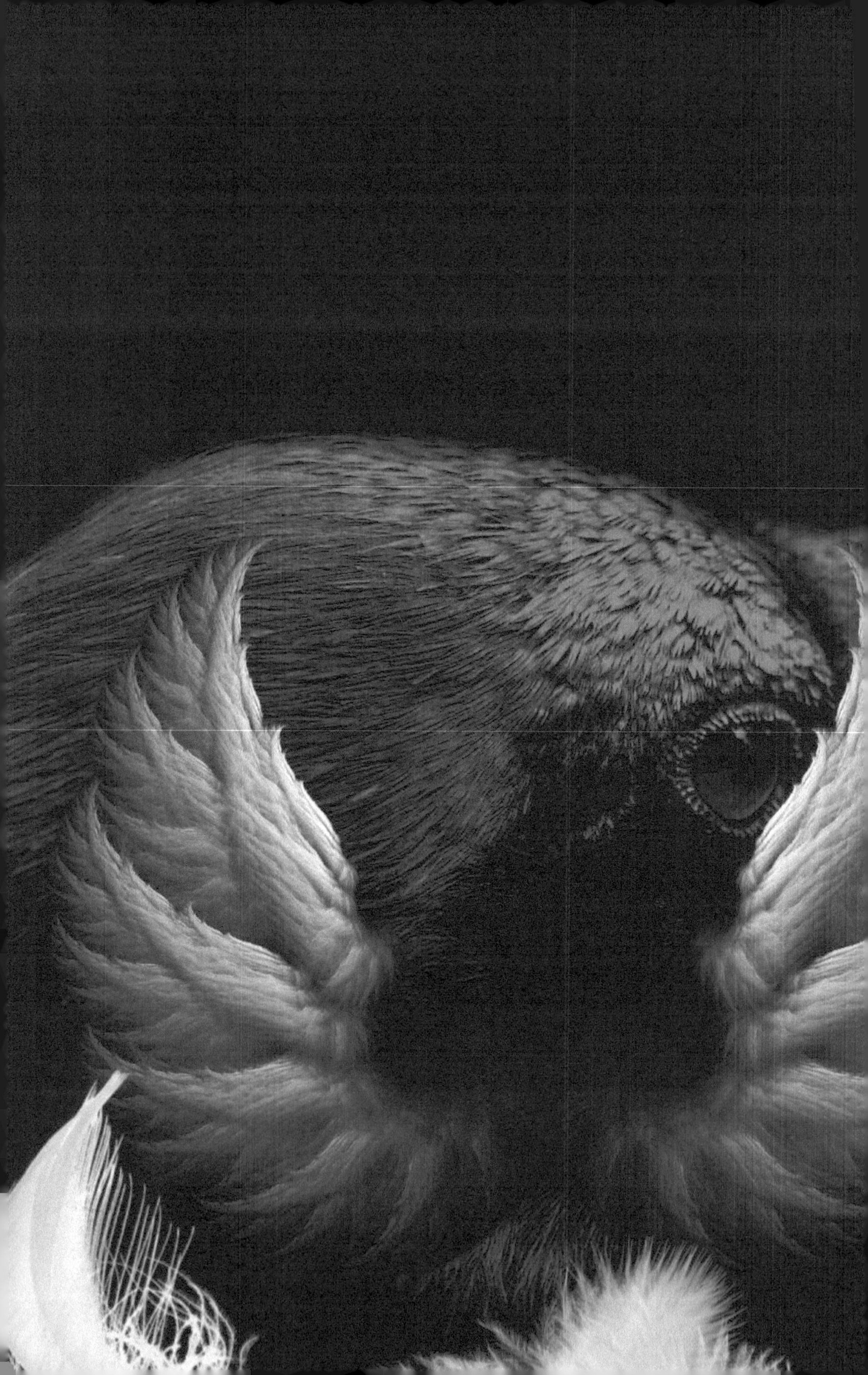

"*A*re you okay?"

I used my hand to shield my eyes from the sun and gave Harper a small smile. "I'm good."

It was incredibly sweet that she was worried. Though if it was up to me, she wouldn't have a reason to worry about me. Unfortunately, Parker had other ideas. He'd proudly announced that we'd be moving in together the day after Nan and I signed the contract.

Trying to explain to my friends why I was suddenly shacking up with the guy I'd been bitching about was incredibly exhausting.

Riley was utterly convinced something shady was going on, and spent the last two weeks on the warpath. She was right, not that I was going to tell her that. The girl was a force to be reckoned with, but even she was scared of Preston.

"Callaghan!"

I looked over at where the football team was practicing. The coach was yelling at Sean again, which probably had something to do with Parker picking himself off the ground. Needless to say, Sean was less than impressed when he heard the news. He was never a fan of the Knights. Now, though...

He'd started three fist fights with Mason, threatened Micha, and openly hit on Shelby in front of Logan. Part of the reason I'd agreed to this whole thing was to protect him, and he was diving head first into the pit. This was the fourth time today the coach was giving him crap for tackling Parker.

"Your brother is going to get himself hurt."

Harper lifted her head and squinted. "He chose to play the stupid game."

I wasn't talking about football.

"Today's the day, isn't it?" Shelby tore open a pastry, I swear she could eat whatever she wanted and not gain a pound. She was a good match for Logan. in that regard. He was always stuffing his face.

"Tomorrow," I corrected her.

The timing of the move was one of the conditions Nan insisted on. She'd refused to sign anything that would make me reside with Parker's mother. So, I didn't have to move in with Parker until he took possession of the house, which he did today.

Nan was always looking out for me, but I wasn't sure if being alone in a house with Parker was any better. There was safety in numbers, even if one of those numbers was Lillianna Whitley.

Not that I was worried Parker would hurt me. If anything, he was kinda sweet. It was other things I was worried about. Like how good he looked all sweaty in his football uniform. Parker ripped his helmet off and pushed his fingers through his sandy hair. My gaze fell on his parted lips. Soft, moist, and plump.

What would he taste like right now?

"Aww," Shelby sang, nudging me with her elbow, "Look at you all thirsty for your man."

"What? I am not." I wouldn't mind running my hands across his chest though. All firm and chiselled. I could run my finger over each dip and curve.

Snap out of it, Lana!

"Girl, it's okay. Football players are hot."

Riley grumbled and rolled her eyes. "Stop gawking at the football players."

"There's nothing wrong with looking."

"Tell that to your barbarian boyfriend."

I couldn't help but nod in agreement. "Riley has a point."

As far as Logan was concerned, looking was as bad as touching. And it wasn't Shelby's fault, it was the guy's fault for getting her attention.

"Ugh, you guys are no fun." Shelby flicked her blonde hair over her shoulder. "Since when do you care if I look at other guys?"

"Since I don't feel like consoling a crazy pregnant woman when her son goes to jail for murder. No offense," Riley added, shooting me a look.

I shrugged. "None taken."

Crazy was a nice way of putting it. So far this week, I'd cried because I couldn't find my shoe, stared at the wall trying to remember the word bush, and gotten in a fight with Henry our goat over a carrot. I didn't even like carrots. At least I wasn't as bad as Paisley. Riley spent an hour comforting her last night, because she'd broken a nail.

The whole Sean thing, well, that was different. I was still having nightmares, and even though I knew he didn't do anything, a chill ran up my back every time I looked into his or Harper's eyes. It was messed up.

No matter what I did, I couldn't shake it. Even went back to see Mr. Kessler. I didn't give any specific information, but I did tell him I was the one remembering crap that didn't happen.

He said that pregnancy psychosis was incredibly rare, but could occur, and set up monthly appointments so he could keep track of my mental well being. I tried to tell him I didn't need to keep seeing him. Ever try to tell a Kessler no? It doesn't work out so well. I ended up walking out with biweekly appointments instead.

"Speaking of you and Parker," Shelby's big cinnamon eyes glimmered with excitement, "Tell me everything."

"Not much to tell." I liked gossip as much as the next girl–okay, maybe more than the next girl– but this topic wasn't one I wanted to talk about.

Shelby grumbled out a sigh. "Does no one respect the girl code anymore? Friend's are supposed to share the dirty details. I tell Riley everything."

"I know," Riley frowned. "Please stop."

"Sorry," Shelby shook her head and took a bite out of her pastry, "It's part of the best friend package."

"If graphic details of anal are part of the best friend package, I'd like to apply for a new position."

"Oh, that reminds me." Shelby sat up a little straighter, "Logan had me tied up the other day, and do you know what that bastard did? He came out with a unicorn costume on, and not one of those full coverage deals either. I'm talking white furry buttless chaps, and matching vest, with a horn strapped to his head, which he promptly stroked and asked if I'd like to suck his horn."

Eww.

"That's an image I didn't need."

"Me either," Harper grumbled in agreement.

"At least you only have the image." Shelby's eyes shifted my way. "I had to see it. I think he's taking this unicorn thing too far."

"Don't you like unicorns?" I thought she did. Almost everything Logan gave her was a unicorn. It was kind of disturbing how much unicorn stuff there was.

"I used to," Shelby muttered.

Harper let out a huff of air and quietly said, "I used to like a lot of things."

I swallowed my pang of guilt at Harper's words. It wasn't me that tormented her, or made her too scared to do the things she loved, like dancing. But I should've been able to protect her. I'd always believed in the Order and should've known that under that sweet little boy, Mason Kessler was just another asshole.

Harper's big doe eyes stared at the half eaten sandwich in her hand. She used to smile all the time, before Mason decided to show his true colors. I still remember seeing her that day in the hospital, beaten black and blue. We were only ten. Just children. I shouldn't have had to visit my friend in that place. Harper's dad insisted that Mason be arrested.

He wasn't, of course. The sheriff said there wasn't enough evidence. Funny thing is, the day before, Sean, Mason, Harper and I had spent the afternoon playing and having fun.

I remember thinking how nice it was to see Sean and her smile. Their mother had left two weeks before, and I thought Mason wanted to cheer them up like I did. Guess I was wrong.

Things got better when Riley showed up at school. No one at Ashworth wanted to mess with her, or her boyfriend. Therefore, most people left Harper alone. And now I'd put her back in the Knight's path. Well, Preston's path anyway. Which was pretty much the same as putting a gun to her head. The only thing I could do was make sure said gun was never loaded.

"Don't worry about your project," I said, brushing a strand of Harper's hair behind her ear, "I'll be there."

Harper was terrified that Mason would show up at her house with Silas tomorrow. Not that I blamed her. Since he came back, the youngest Kessler wouldn't leave her alone. It was like the asshole was making up for lost time.

Right now, he was standing by the school, talking to one of the cheerleaders. There was no reason for him to be out here. Parker, Micha and Logan all had practice. He should be in the cafeteria with Silas.

My eyes narrowed in on him. He was up to something. My suspicions were confirmed when Mason noticed me glaring at him. He looked at Harper, and them back at me, and smiled. Naturally, I flipped him off. That didn't do much other than make his green eyes sparkle as he shot me a wink.

Bring it on, Kessler.

As if Mason could hear my thoughts, his lips rounded in a mischievous O. I could practically hear him saying, *'Oo, I'm game. Let's play.'* For half a second I thought he was going to come over, until the expression on his face fell away and his eyes shifted to something else.

"I see you girls out here so much, I'm starting to question the cafeteria food."

"Hi, Mr. Lannister," Shelby sang at the same time I turned to see her assistant coach's big smile.

"Now Shelby," Mr. Lannister said, dropping down on the ground beside me, "I told you to call me Luke."

Out of all the staff at Ashworth, Mr. Lannister was the only one that seemed real. He didn't go to the stuffy colleges the rest did, and didn't have a rich background. If he did, he didn't show it off. The car he drove was as beat up as mine was, and every day I saw him eating a bagged lunch. I enjoyed talking to him. He was funny and nice. Who else could I debate jam versus honey debate with?

"How are you doing, Lana? I hope you haven't had any problems?"

He was referring to Ashworth using my situation to relocate me. Which he was very adamant I didn't let them get away with. So far, no one had said anything. Mind you, I wasn't sure the staff even knew I was pregnant.

"I'm good," I whispered, and turned my face away before he could see the heat I felt filling my cheeks.

Did I mention he was also really cute? The attention he gave me was kind of flattering, considering half the girls in school gossiped about him. He didn't talk to them though, he talked to me. We did have more in common. Mr. Lannister grew up in foster care. Meaning he didn't have any parental memories either.

He flashed his perfect white teeth and shoulder bumped me.

God, he smelled good, and those lips…

I tipped my head, eyeing the contours of his mouth, before shaking myself out of it. What was wrong with me lately? Every guy I saw had some hot feature. Even Mason's damn green eyes mesmerized me. He did have really big forearms though.

I bet he could toss me around like a rag doll. Throw me on the bed and…

No Lana! Stop it.

I closed my eyes and took a deep, relaxing breath. When I started fantasizing about Mason Kessler, something was seriously wrong. How low have I sunk?

"Don't worry, Mr. Lannister," Shelby said, pulling my attention back to reality. "We got Lana's back."

"Yes you do," I nodded.

Their blind loyalty both warmed my hear, and terrified me. It'd been Harper and I for so long, it was hard to let anyone else in. Or even trust them, for that matter.

"I keep telling Harper she should try out for the team." Shelby's eyes fell on my best friend. "What do you think?"

"Absolutely." Mr. Lannister smiled at Harper.

It was cute how quickly she ducked her head and shuffled my way. I saw the flush in her cheeks. Harper thought he was cute too.

"We're always looking for good runners."

"Harper's a good runner." Side effect from spending years hiding from Mason, "But she's not really a crowd person."

"She'll be fine," Shelby reached over and swept Harper's red hair off her shoulder. "It's not that–"

"What the fuck is that!"

We all froze and eyed Riley. Except for Shelby, who didn't seem phased at all by Riley's scowl. Her dark blue eyes were locked solely on Harper.

"Ugh," Shelby groaned, "What's up your ass now?"

"That," Riley snarled, throwing her finger up at Harper.

Shelby gave her an 'are you stupid' look, complete with lip curl. "What the hell are you talking about?"

I hadn't seen Harper shake this bad in… well, ever. It looked like she was going to pass out. I would've pulled her into my protective arms, but Riley beat me to it. She sprang over to Harper, and scooped her hair up on the top of her head.

"That," she growled, pointing at the back of Harper's neck.

Call me curious, but I had to look. Riley was fiercely protective of Harper. She didn't get mad at her. Along with Shelby and Mr. Lannister, who was also apparently curious, I leaned over and studied the three stars on the back of my best friend's neck.

Huh? How did I not notice those before?

"So she has a cute tattoo," Shelby sang. "Calm down, tattoo police. It's not the end of the world."

Riley's arm dropped, allowing Harper's hair to tumble down her back. I was ready when she slid over and tucked herself in my embrace. My arms wrapped around her, shielding her from the other two.

"You don't have one?" Riley asked Shelby.

"Please," she rolled her eyes in response, "My mother would kill me if I got a tattoo."

So what if Harper had a tattoo? Big deal. I guess Riley didn't see it that way. She was pissed as hell. Her fists were so tightly balled at her sides, I thought they might get stuck that way. Maybe there was some tattoo artist code about stars or something?

"Who did this to you? Never mind. You don't need to answer that." Riley stood up and locked her glare on Mason.

His brow arched back at her.

"She died, did she?" Riley snarled at Mase.

I swear a spark of surprise flashed across his eyes before he narrowed his gaze angrily on Harper. Fuck him. I hoped Riley kicked his ass. Which was apparently exactly what Riley had in mind.

She yelled, "Mason Kessler, you're a dead man!" and took off across the grass with so much speed and fury that I thought she should be the one to try out for the track team.

Mason wasn't an idiot, he slid through the door and slipped inside before she could reach him.

"What was that all about?" Mr. Lannister said as we all watched Riley follow.

"I have no idea."

And I really didn't. But I couldn't think about that right now. Parker was coming my way, and he did not look happy.

"Come on, Angel," he said, shooting Mr. Lannister a glare. "Time to go."

Mr. Lannister flattened his palms on the grass behind him and leaned back, while Shelby argued, "We still have fifteen minutes."

Parker completely ignored her. Didn't say a word, or even look at Shelby, as he typed something into his phone. A minute later the door to the school flew open and Logan came bursting out, dripping wet, with only pants on.

"Oh crap," Shelby muttered and sprang up, rushing over to him.

"Time to go," Parker repeated.

I looked over at the murderous snarl on Logan's face as Shelby fought to hold him back, and then back at Parker's cocked brow. *Yup, definitely time to go.*

I swallowed and pulled Harper up with me, saying, "Bye, Mr. Lannister," as I headed for the school.

"See you around, Lana," he sang back.

Parker grabbed my elbow and muttered, "No, you fucking won't."

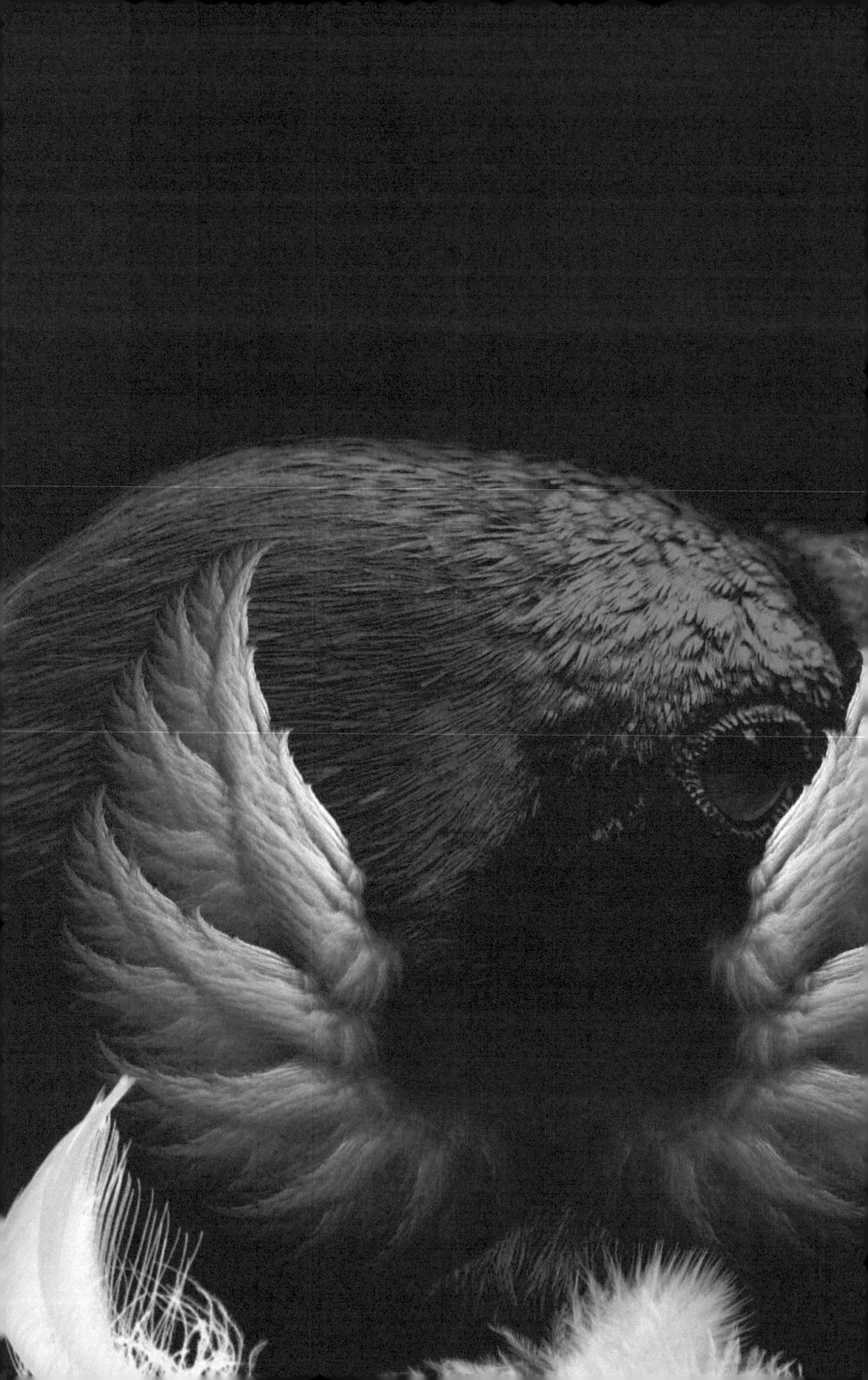

Chapter 13
Lana

I blew out a puff of air at the building I could see through the windshield. The hair on the troll dolls on my dash danced around in the breeze. I watched the different colors sway back and forth, as if my precious dolls were as confused as I was. Parker had set up an appointment with Dr. Creswell, who was the best doctor in town. And Silas's dad.

Hence, my conundrum. I'd get top of the line medical care, but at what cost? If Louis Kessler was in the Order, then so was Martin. And what did that mean for me? Would I be able to voice my opinion, or would Parker have final say?

It wasn't like I had any solid evidence to go on, but I was pretty sure that's how things worked. The men ran the show. I mean, I'd never heard of a girl in the Order. Ava Whitley didn't walk around school with a title. Other than crazy, that is.

Naomi was just bitch. Some people called her cunt, and Riley called her Barbie. They all fit. Was there a bitch, cunt, Barbie?

Maybe I should email the Barbie people. Heck, I even had the perfect model for them.

My phone went off. It was Parker again, telling me he was almost here.

I patted Gavin, my favorite doll. Gramps gave him to me. Every time I saw his green hair and cute little freckles, I felt better. Comfort was something I was in dire need of right now.

Everyone's strange behavior this afternoon had me on edge. Parker's fingers dug into my arm as he steered me into the school. Don't know what his problem was. I was just having lunch with my friends when he came barreling in like a bull in a china shop.

And now I was here. Parked outside doctor Creswell's office, missing the free clinic.

Well, no time like the present.

Begrudgingly, I got out of the car and headed into the building, which was not at all what I expected. I thought it would be another boring white walled interior, with a single lonely plant in the corner. There was a plant in the corner. Along with two by the door, three around the security desk, and a small garden next to a fountain.

Naturally, there was a fountain. What office building didn't have a fountain? Then again, what did I know? My usual doctor had a small space above a hair salon downtown. It was the only one Nan could find that directly billed the insurance company.

I stepped into the elevator and pressed the button for the top floor. As the doors closed, I couldn't help but wonder if this was why rich people always looked so good? If their doctor put this much effort into his building, I could just imagine what kind of effort he put into his patients. Maybe they did have miracle trust cream? Or some super secret anti-aging formula that was made from goat placenta or something.

Wash the years off your face with goat spread.

Even the elevator mocked my simple clothes. Some classic song played overhead as the girl in the shiny mirrored wall stared at me judgingly. Pointing out all my imperfections. *Those jeans have a hole in the knee. The mess in your bun isn't right. Did you forget to put on makeup this morning?*

I'd never been so happy to get off an elevator in my life. Until I stepped into the doctor's office.

The prim and proper receptionist looked over her magazine at me. Her eyes wandered across my frame as her lip curled. "Do you have an appointment?"

Was it wrong that I wanted to stuff her fashion magazine in her mouth?

"Um, yes," I stammered, while cursing myself for not being braver. "Lana Crawford."

"The girl Mr. Whitley made an appointment for?" Her brow rose. "Does he owe you a favor?"

How was I supposed to respond to that? *Considering he put this baby in my belly, I'd say he owes me a lot more than a favor.* Somehow, I didn't think pissing off the receptionist at my first appointment was the best way to go. Lucky for me, I didn't have to think about it too long. The elevator door dinged and Parker stepped out.

"Hello Karen." He wrapped his arm around my shoulders, something I was kind of getting used to. At least I wasn't on his lap again. "Did you get my girl checked in?"

I didn't have any issues with Karen after that. She got me checked in, and before I knew it, I was being led back to an exam room. Parker in tow, of course. Though I'd like nothing more than to slap him, I was kind of amazed at how quickly he got things done.

Sometimes Nan and I would sit in the waiting room for an hour before we got to see the doctor. Which usually turned out to be a simple five minute appointment.

Speaking of which...

I looked back and searched the waiting room for her warm brown eyes. "Nan isn't here."

"I know," Parker said, urging me forward. "I asked her not to come."

"What!? Why would you do that?"

What right did he have to tell my Nan to stay home? I needed her more than him.

"Because it's our baby, and I'd like the first time we see it, for it to just be you and me."

I could already feel my chin quivering. "But I need her."

"I know Baby, and I swear she can come to every other appointment." He leaned over and laid a gentle kiss on the top of my head. "Just not this one."

Tears were burning in my eyes, blurring my vision as I walked down the hall. I didn't know if they were there out of anger, or something else. While Parker had absolutely no right to do what he did, a part of me found what he said kind of sweet.

Stupid hormones.

That was the last thing I should be thinking. Parker was forcing me to move in with him. Tomorrow night, I had to sleep in his bed, and did he care if I wanted to or not? No. He didn't give two shits. But he cared enough to want a special private moment with me? How much sense did that make?

It was awfully hard to hate someone when they were being nice to you. Even if they were doing it in a jerkish way. Like right now. Not letting my Nan come, total jerk move. Yet his palm warming the small of my back as he gently steered me was a tender gesture.

If he slipped his hand a little lower, he could grab my butt. Firm fingers digging into my backside. Or better yet, slapping me. How good would it feel to be spanked right now?

Damnit. What the hell is wrong with me? I need to watch some porn or something.

Karen took us to a room and shoved a bundle of cloth in my

arms. "Change into this, nothing underneath, and get on the table. The doctor will be in shortly."

I sneered at her as she waltzed away. *Screw you too, Karen.*

As soon as I turned around, Miss Snotty two-shoes was forgotten. My eyes wandered over all the equipment and the large padded table. This was the exam room? Everything was so… clean.

Nan and I used to fight over the one chair, because neither of us wanted to sit on the doctor's old dirty table. Christ, my bedroom was smaller than this. Bedroom, huh? This would make a good bedroom.

I'd put the bed by that nice big window so I could fall asleep to the sounds of the ocean. Maybe a comfy chair would be better? That'd be a good place to read. Curl up with a warm blanket while the stars twinkled in the sky…

"Do you need help?"

I cocked a brow at Parker. He was standing there, staring at me expectantly. "With what?"

"The doctor will be here any minute," he said, nodding at my arms.

That's when I remembered the gown I was holding. *Oh crap.*

I started to pull my shirt off, but stopped to glare at Parker. "You can leave."

"Not gonna happen, Angel."

Jerk two, nice one.

"I'm not changing in front of you."

"Well," he leaned against the door and looked at me. "I'm not leaving."

"The doctor's going to be mad if I'm not ready," I pointed out.

Parker crossed his arms. "He won't be mad at me."

I stared back at him. Seriously? He was going to go there? Like I cared who the doctor would be mad at. I did, but that was beside the point. That's when an idea came to me.

"Alright, you win."

A smirk spread across Parker's face, as if he was saying, *'of course I do.'*

Don't count your chickens before they hatch, Mr. Whitley.

Obviously, he'd never played this game with a girl before. We had a natural talent for changing without being seen. Harper and I used to make a game of it. 'Let's see who can put their bathing suits on the fastest without getting caught by her brother.' I was the reigning champ. Although, we hadn't played since Mason Kessler made her terrified of her own shadow.

It wasn't too hard to pull off. I removed the arms of my shirt through the ones on the gown, while shimmying the cloth over my head. Once that was gone, I unclipped my bra, and tied up the back of the gown. The rest was easy. Pants and underwear came off in one slip. All done, without exposing an inch of unnecessary skin.

Parker was not impressed.

I, however, smiled brightly back at him, before skipping over to the table.

Yup, still got it.

The doctor came in just as I was sitting on the oddly comfortable table. It was so soft, I had to look down and make sure it was an exam table. Man, high priced doctors sure had their benefits.

"Good afternoon, Lana"

This wasn't the first time I'd seen Martin Creswell. Silas was his son, so he'd been at parent teacher interviews and stuff. Those times I was just the little girl in his kid's class and nothing more.

Now, I had to actually talk to him. One of the most powerful men in Ashen Springs was going to see my naughty bits. Not exactly a comforting thought.

He flipped through my file and clicked a pen. "How are you feeling today?"

Huh? Okay, I got where Strictly By the Books Silas got his right down to business attitude.

"I'm fine."

Except for the fact that I was talking to a possible murderer. I'd heard the rumors, and untimely death wasn't the worst one attached to the esteemed Martin Creswell. His appetite for young teenage girls was talked about the most.

That was one of the few things, I didn't put much stock in. The man had a famous wife, who was absolutely gorgeous. Why would he screw around with some dumb high school girl?

"Any morning sickness?"

"A little." Thank god that had died down.

I sat there studying Dr. Creswell's white coat as he continued to ask me questions. He seemed normal, a little uptight, but normal. I don't know why, but I'd thought I'd find more. A monstrous voice, or some scar that showed he was really a bad guy. Maybe I was looking for something else? A sign that the Order existed.

Was he going to go back and tell all the other members my business? Would they get detailed descriptions of my girly parts? For all I knew, they had a special file just for that. I could see it now.

A big filing cabinet with various drawers. People of Ashen Springs, secrets and other stuff, and at the very bottom a single white sticker saying: *The Order of Ravens and Wolves pussy information.*

"How's your mental state?"

My eyes narrowed. Why would he say that? The only person who knew about my appointments with Mr. Kessler, was Mr. Kessler.

"I mean no offense," he explained. "Pregnancy can be difficult on a young girl such as yourself."

Uh huh?

"Is there anything I should watch for?" Parker asked.

"There are a few things," Doctor Creswell passed him a pamphlet. "Mood swings, aggressive behavior..."

Their voices drowned out as he continued explaining possible pregnancy symptoms and the things Parker could do. I was paying more attention to the pamphlet titled, 'Pregnancy, everything you should know.' Why didn't I get a pamphlet?

"And of course, increased sexual appetite."

What?

That caught Parker's attention too. "So I can fuck her?"

"Absolutely."

This is so not what we came here for.

"Sexual intercourse is encouraged."

No, no it's not.

"It can help with the birthing process."

I call bullshit.

"Especially with someone so inexperienced."

Hey!!

"I have experience," I argued.

"Having sex one time is not what I call experienced."

How did he know that?

"Alright, we're going to do a sonogram now, Lana." He wandered over to something that looked an awful lot like a computer. "Lie down, please."

My gaze narrowed as I laid back and eyed the doctor pulling the machine across the room. The wheels quietly rolled along, making me wonder what kind of doctor had nice shiny hardwood floors. *A sketchy one in a secret society, that's who.*

"It's okay, Angel." Parker sat down in the chair beside me and held my hand in between his palms. "Don't be scared."

"I'm not scared."

I'm suspicious. There's a difference.

"And just so you know," I whispered, so the doctor wouldn't hear, "I'm not having sex with you."

"Bouncing on my cock? Or did you forget that part of the deal?"

I glared at him. "You can't force me."

"I won't have to." His eyes burned a path down my body. "You want my dick as much as I want to give it to you."

I pressed my tongue up to the roof of my mouth and forced back a swallow. My thighs clenched together and I turned away, telling myself to just ignore him.

Kind of hard to do, when he was all I could smell. His earthy masculine scent seeped into my pores, making my blood run hot. It wasn't fair. I should be smelling gross, chemical sterility, not tempting man-musk.

I snickered. Man-musk. What a horrible name. That cologne would not fly off the shelves.

Parker's grip on my hand tightened as Dr. Creswell placed a blanket over my hips and carefully lifted my gown, baring my belly. Was he scared? I rolled my head and looked up into his light eyes. It wasn't fear I saw there. It was anger. What the hell did he have to be so angry about? I was the one on a table being prodded.

Dr. Creswell squirted some cold crap on my stomach, that made my breath hitch. The sleeve of his coat had ridden up with his reach, exposing a small raven tattoo on his inner wrist. My inner-self screamed, *I knew it!* Which made it really hard to keep my outer-self quiet. Every fiber of my being wanted to jump up on the table and yell, *ah ha!*

All those years of Harper calling me a conspiracy theorist, and here was the proof. A little black bird staring me right in the eyes. I wondered if that girl I'd met at Riley's party knew about it?

She seemed to know her shit. Even claimed to have some evidence, though she wouldn't tell me what it was. What was her name? Mary? Marnie? Maxine? I'd have to ask Riley. I was curious to find out if she knew about this tattoo. My eyes swung Parker's way.

Does he have one?

My thoughts were cut off when a light thumping sound filled

the room. One look at the screen and I forgot about everything else. What I was seeing was much more shocking than any secret society revelations. I had to blink twice, just to make sure what I thought was there… was really there.

"Both heartbeats are strong."

My wide eyes flew to the doctor, and then back at the monitor, where two babies were displayed. Not one baby with two arms and legs, but two! Four tiny little hands and feet moving around and stretching. I felt it then. The jab coming from inside. A small little kick from one of the two children I was carrying. Not one, but two.

Two!

With my mouth hung open, I looked up at Parker, hoping he'd offer some comforting words. This was what he said he would do. That I was his to protect. Well, he needed to protect me. Like, right now.

"Parker?"

His face was all lit up with a gigantic smile. "It's twins, baby."

Yeah, I know, I can see that. Fix it!

"Congratulations," Doctor Creswell said.

Congratulations? Really? That's all he had to say? I couldn't breathe. My heart was pounding so hard in my chest that I couldn't make my lungs work. Two babies. Two! How was I supposed to take care of two babies, when I was terrified of raising one. I couldn't do this.

That's it, I quit. Where's the tap out button? I need a redo.

Mr. Creswell looked back at the screen and asked, "Would you like to know the sexes?"

I didn't get a chance to answer, because the black that started to bleed into my vision, won.

Chapter 14
Parker

$\mathcal{I}$ was too excited to sleep last night. Today my family is set to move in. I spent all day yesterday setting up the house. Got the furniture moved in, (blue, Lana's favorite color,) and set our bedroom up.

The nurseries would have to wait. Or, should I say, I was informed they would have to wait by my sister. I think Ava was happier than I was when I told her my angel was having twins. A boy and a girl. One of each.

Logan called me an overachiever, what could I say? I knew how to get shit done. First try and I got one of each. While Preston couldn't care less, my dad was ecstatic. Like Ava, he was currently out shopping. He wanted to find something to welcome Lana to the family.

As far as he was concerned, that's what she was now. What did my mother think? Didn't really care. I hadn't even told her about the twins, because fuck her. Today I was getting everything I'd ever wanted. Not even Lilliana Whitley could ruin my mood.

The only thing I was worried about was my girl. Lana passed out yesterday. Went limp, right there in the doctor's office. As I watched her eyes roll to the back of her head, I felt my heart stop. I'd never been so scared in my life.

Silas's dad assured me that she was fine. She simply fainted from the shock. Didn't stop me from babying her like some pussy whipped motherfucker for hours after. I took her out for her favorite burger at Mae's, and refused to leave her side until she was tucked safely in her bed.

If my friends had seen that shit, I'd never live it down. The weird part was, I'd do it again. I'd pamper my perfect little angel in front of the whole world. Rub her shoulders, stroke her hair, or wash her feet. Whatever the fuck she wanted, and everyone else could suck a dick. I loved taking care of her.

I steered my truck down the bumpy road that led to my angel's house. Tonight I'd get to take care of some of her other needs. I couldn't wait to feel her pussy again. Walls tightly squeezing my shaft. Grunting, I shifted my hard on. My dick had been in a permanent rock like state for weeks now.

I hadn't fucked anyone since the night I'd fucked her. Didn't see a point in it. No one could live up to her, so why bother with the disappointment? Well, I hadn't fucked any girls. Bent a couple guys over, but those pricks were asking for it.

"Here we are," I said, parking my truck in front of the little yellow house.

They didn't have much in the way of money, but I had to hand it to Lana's Nan. She took great care of the place. The yard was neatly cut, with a small vegetable garden on the side, and red flowers planted around the deck. Simple, but pretty.

I stepped out and stared at a tire swing hanging off a nearby tree. I used to hide in the bushes and watch Lana sway back and forth through the air. Hair trailing in a black wave behind her. Now we could watch our little girl swing on it.

Her grandpa caught me once. It was just after she'd gotten my dick hard for the first time. I was about eleven. Thought the old fucker was going to tan my ass. Instead, he took me for a walk and explained how he carefully tended his garden.

How important it was to pluck out the weeds and make sure the flowers had enough nutrients to grow. Though I didn't get his meaning at the time, that conversation always stuck with me.

Time to get my flower.

One step was all I made before an old goat came running around the corner, and bashed his head into my nuts. My insides twisted as I clutched my aching ball sac and dropped to my knees.

"Motherfucker."

"Bah!" the goat spat back at me.

Holy fuck, that goat could hit! Pretty sure if I coughed too hard, I'd taste my own spunk. Mental note, goat head beats knee.

The goat's ears twitched as a brown hoof scratched the ground.

"Don't even think about it," my hand shot up, "Or I'll be having goat meat tonight."

I swear the snarky son of a bitch curled his lip at me, before barking out another bah and taking off around the house. After taking a minute to pry my nuts out of my throat, I rose to my feet. Much more aware of my surroundings this time as I made my way to the front door. I couldn't see where the fucker went, but I knew he was out there.

Leaning over, I checked the sides of the house, and then knocked on the door. Greta answered almost immediately. I stared down at the older woman. Even a stranger could tell this was Lana's grandma. She wore the same hard expression Lana did when she ran her mouth. Greta was much shorter though, with greying hair and fierce brown eyes.

"Well, are you just going to stand there and stare, or can you speak?"

Same sharp tongue as her granddaughter, too.

"You know why I'm here."

"Don't think I'm not watching you, boy." Her eyes narrowed. "Just because you got my Lana pregnant, doesn't mean I trust you."

Well, she wasn't stupid.

"And you still signed on the dotted line." I leaned against the doorframe and crossed my arms. "If you ask me, I'd say you're the one that shouldn't be trusted."

"You didn't give my Lana a choice."

"Neither did you," I argued back. Although I was curious as to exactly how much Lana told her grandmother, or if Greta had come to this conclusion on her own.

"I had my reasons."

"My point exactly." I shouldered past her and waltzed into the house. "What are you hiding, Greta?"

She moved quick for someone her age. Her hand shot up and whacked me in the back of the head before I could spin around and look at her.

"Don't talk back to me, boy."

"Jesus Christ," I grumbled, rubbing my head, "What the…"

I was cut off by another quick slap. "Do not use the Lord's name in vain."

"Shit lady…"

Another slap.

"There's no cussing in this house."

"Fuck sakes…"

Once again her arm flew through the air. "I said no cussing."

"Jesus Christ…"

That one got me hit harder.

"Will you stop doing that!" I barked out, quickly shutting my mouth before I said what I really wanted to. At this rate, I'd be braindead before I got Lana out the door.

Lana's grandma didn't seem to care. Her little hands flew through the air, striking me on the back of the arm and leg. I suddenly understood how my old dog must've felt when my mom went after him with a newspaper.

"You get my girl pregnant," she hit me in the stomach and then swung up to get my head again, "And then take her away…"

"Shit," I growled, ducking under my arms, "You fucking gave her to me."

The assault stopped and everything got suddenly quiet. Which kind of made me more scared. When I dared to come out from the protection of my arms and take a peek, the old woman was staring at me with wide eyes.

"You can protect her, can't you?"

"Of course I can," I snarled, still pissed from the assault. *Wait…* "What do I need to protect her from?"

"Nothing."

My brow rose. "But you just said–"

"I know what I said." She placed her hands on her hips and tipped her chin. "Do you think I don't know what I said? Oh look, it's the crazy old lady that remembers her own thoughts. I'm not senile."

I huffed out a sigh as she continued her rant. This was getting me nowhere. "Is Lana ready or not?"

She slapped me in the face. "It's rude to interrupt people."

Motherfucker!

I rubbed my cheek and watched her calmly walk into the kitchen.

"Lana, sweetheart," she sang, "Can you come here?"

My angel's sweet voice echoed down the hall. "Jesus, what do you want now? I'm trying to get ready."

Her Nan cocked her head down the hall and smacked her lips together, while picking up a wooden spoon.

Oh shit. This can't be good.

Didn't really think a wooden spoon could be threatening. I was wrong.

Lana sauntered around the corner, and I'd never seen the color drain so fast from someone's face. She froze and stared at me like a deer caught in headlights. Kind of made me smirk a bit. Especially when her grandma snuck behind her and raised the wooden spoon.

"Talk back to me!" The spoon came down, smacking off Lana's ass with a thwack that made me cringe internally.

"Nan–"

Smack!

Oh shit!

That time I visibly grimaced.

"Stop it!" Lana loudly cried out.

Smack!

Goddamn, the old woman was vicious with that thing.

"You're still in my house, little girl." A snicker escaped my lips until she pointed the spoon at me, "Don't you smile, boy."

The smirk dropped off my face and I shook my head.

"You will be respectful in my house."

I nodded. "Yes ma'am. I never–"

"Don't talk back to me."

"No ma'am."

Wasn't stupid enough to head down that road. Not after the whipping Lana just got. Besides, I doubted killing her Nan would win me any favors.

Lana's lips twisted as she mockingly shook her head and grumbled, "No ma'am."

Smack!!

Damn, I felt that one.

Should I help her?

"You don't get to be selfish anymore." This time she smacked Lana so hard the force of her hit propelled her forward.

Fuck that. She made her bed, let her lie in it.

I couldn't help but snicker as Lana grumbled and rubbed her ass.

"You ready to go, Angel?"

Her lip curled. "No."

"Well, you better hurry up. The boys will be here in ten minutes."

Her pretty pink lips twisted in a frown. "The boys?"

"That's right," I nodded, "Logan and Preston are going to help."

I couldn't think of two better people to remind Lana of what was at stake, should she decide to change her mind last minute. And judging by the look on her face, my assumption was one hundred percent accurate.

There's no backing out now, baby.

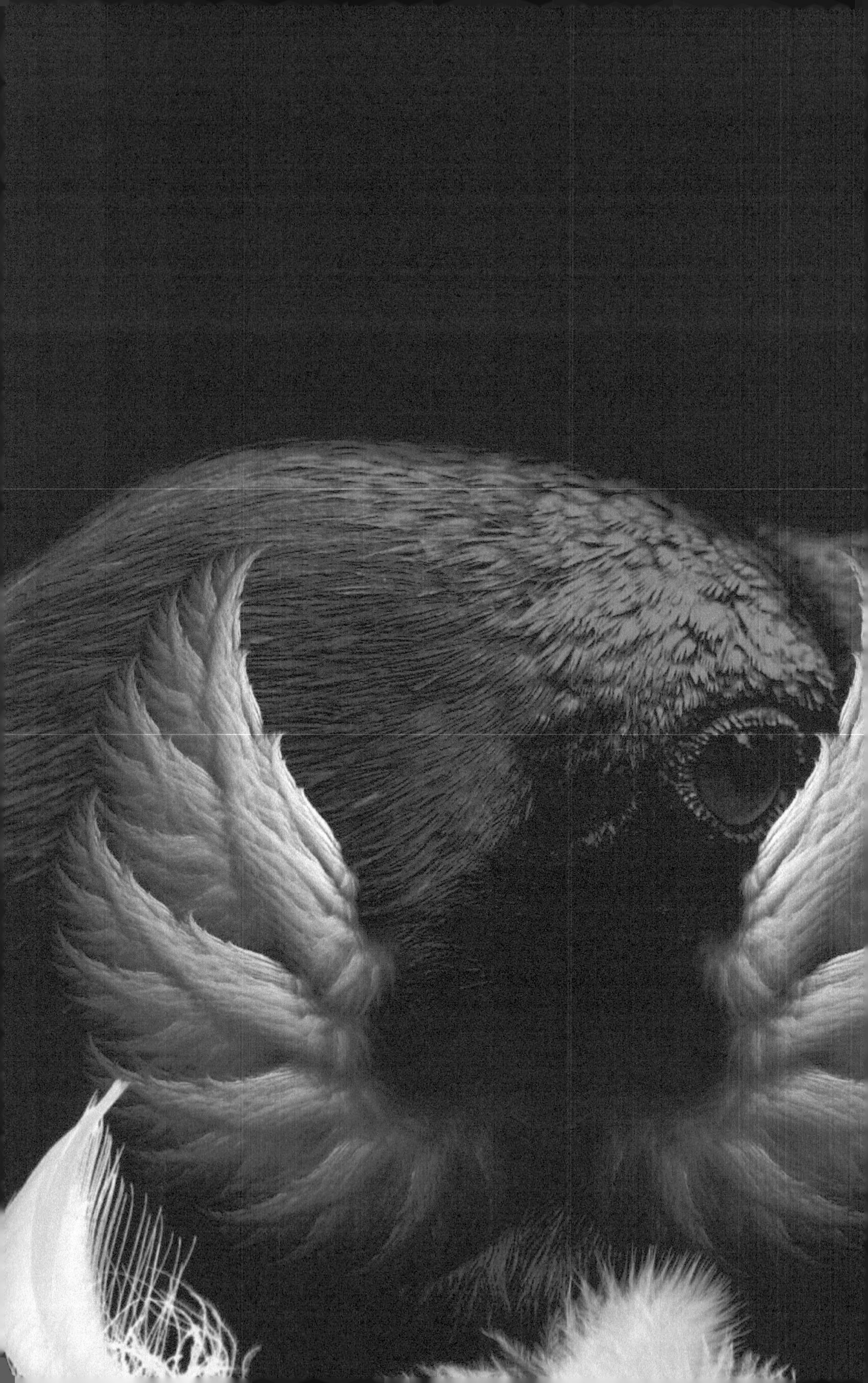

Chapter 15
Lana

I managed to convince Parker that his friends didn't need to come and help. Nothing I had was heavy, and most of the boxes were already in my car. Knowing Nan wouldn't have to meet Preston allowed me to breathe. Until Parker announced they'd meet us at the house. The same house Nan insisted on coming to.

She wanted to make sure it was up to her standards, or so she said. Considering the Whitley's weren't lacking in financial means, I doubted she'd find anything wrong with the place. Though I don't think that was why she was currently sitting in the passenger seat of my car.

She was coming to suss out how well the Whitley's would treat me, plain and simple. Exactly why I didn't want her to come. If Nan got one whiff that something sketchy was going on, she'd be on the war path. I had enough trouble with Sean poking the sharks in the water. I didn't need to add her to that list.

"My baby," Nan said as we drove through security at Meadow Springs.

Meadow Springs was neatly tucked into one of the forests at the top of the bluffs. It was the kind of place where you couldn't see your neighbor and everyone had staff, bodyguards, or both. Out of the two gated communities in Ashen Springs, I knew this one best.

Harper lived here, as did Silas. It was the place the rich set up residence, and where the Whitley family should've lived. Parker's dad, Dean, was the only powerful man I knew that didn't flaunt his money. I liked that about him.

Following Parker's truck, I turned down a long driveway. Apparently he didn't follow the same philosophy as his dad. The white house I was staring at was so massive I began to wonder if house was the proper term. Large marble pillars stood proud on the deck, wrapping around the side, holding up a balcony on the second floor.

My eyes skimmed over the largest windows I'd ever seen, to the pretty little flowers in black pots by the dark blue double doors. The big red bow both warmed my heart and terrified me. It was marking this grand place as if it were a present. A much too big and way too extravagant present.

"You're moving up in the world, baby girl."

The look on Nan's face wasn't helping any. I couldn't tell if she was being sarcastic, or serious. I guess most parents would be happy to see their child taken care of like this, but Nan wasn't most parents.

We lived by the philosophy of love, because that was all someone needed to make a place a home. That warm environment was what I wanted for my children. I placed my hand on my stomach, wondering if that was possible.

Would my babies have a place they could feel safe and loved, or would this be one of those horrible mistakes that would mess them up for life?

Ever since I'd felt them kick, that was all I could think about. What would be best for my children? Last night I kept rolling over everything I'd done. How hard I tried to deny that they were there. Would they know that? Could they sense my hesitation to bond with them?

I didn't even start taking maternity vitamins until I went to the free clinic. What if that caused problems? Would they come out malnourished and broken?

Nan said these were normal concerns for a new mother, but their father didn't have that problem. He loved them from the start. I was their mother, and I couldn't bring myself to touch them. Guilt clawed away at my insides as I watched Parker get out of his truck to greet Logan and Preston. I didn't deserve these babies.

"Come on, Angel," Parker called over to me. "Come see your house."

My house. My babies. My family. All truly terrifying thoughts.

"I know you're scared, my sweet girl," Nan grabbed my hand and gazed deep into my eyes, "But you got this. This is your life, and you need to take those reigns and steer that horse."

Tears dripped down my cheek, splashing in tiny wet dots on my jeans. "I can't, Nan."

"Yes you can, child."

I shook my head. No, I couldn't.

"My sweet girl, you have no idea how strong you are." Nan placed her hands on the sides of my face and rested her forehead on mine. "Your mother would be so proud of you."

"Would she?"

I didn't remember much of my parents, but the memories I did have were of a strong, confident, beautiful woman. My mother grew up in the same house I did and she became the first woman of color to earn a spot on the hospital board. Dr. Marian Crawford was one of the leading orthopedic surgeons in the country. How could I ever live up to that?

"She would be so proud," Nan assured me, while wiping the wet streaks off my face. "Now," she nodded towards Parker, Logan, and Preston, "Let's go show those boys how much power us women have."

I let out a sigh, feeding off Nan's strength and stepped out of the car. I could do this. Logan's face immediately lit up.

"Look at you, Lana Banana, getting all fat and shit."

"I am not fat!" I shrieked, glancing down at my belly. *Was I?*

"Fuck yeah you are." He sauntered over, threw his arm around me and added, "You should see Ma. It looks like she swallowed a fucking beach ball."

I'd have hit him, but Nan beat me to it.

"Young man, watch your mouth around my granddaughter."

Cocky bastard didn't seem at all phased by the smack to the back of his head. He tipped his brow at my Nan and smirked.

"Now how am I supposed to do that?" he asked." Have you ever tried to watch your own mouth? Your nose and shit is in the way. I guess I could make a duck face, but who the fuck wants to talk to someone when they're doing stupid shit like that?"

I'll admit it, I rolled my eyes down to my mouth, testing his theory.

Nan's hand flew through the air again. "No cussing."

"Okay old lady, I'm sensing we got off on the wrong foot."

The wrath in Nan's eyes when he said 'old lady' was strong enough to make me take a step back.

"No cussing you say, but where do you draw the line. Fuck?"

Smack.

"Shit?"

Smack.

"Asshole?"

Smack.

"Motherfucker?"

Smack.

"Damn?"

This time Nan didn't hit him, though I'm not sure if she was giving up, or trying to think of a harsher punishment. My answer came with the next words she spoke.

"I'm getting the wooden spoon."

"You don't want to use that. The handle is skinny and fragile. A few good swipes and that shit will break. What you want to use is a flipper." He took his arm off me and made a whipping motion in the air. "It has a nice wide surface to displace the force."

Nan and I both stared at him for a second before Nan pointed and said, "There's something wrong with you, boy."

"So I've been told," Logan shrugged, while strutting away.

We stood there watching the boys gather in front of the house. Nan had this look on her face, eyes scrunched together and mouth pursed. I'd seen it before when she played bridge with Mrs. Granger and she thought she was cheating. It wasn't the worst face she could've made. She did just meet Logan Hudson after.

"Is there something wrong with that one too?" she asked, nodding at Preston.

"That's Preston. He's... umm..." *Terrifying, scary, possibly the antichrist or death incarnate,* "Different."

"Uh huh." Nan shot the boys one more glare. "Well, let's go see your house, child."

Nan and Preston were not two people I ever wanted in the same room, or even on the same planet for that matter, but thankfully neither one said a word as we walked up to the front door.

Preston didn't even spare my Nan a glance. He leaned back

against his red BMW and lit a smoke, leaving us to do our thing. Relieving as that was, I couldn't help but feel like he was watching me. I wasn't going to glance back to find out though. Preston Whitley was better left alone.

I stared at the matching envelope hanging off the red bow decorating the door. Once again, tears welled up in my eyes. Written on the front was: *Welcome home, my sweet Angel.*

"Open it," Parker whispered in my ear.

My gaze shifted over my shoulder to his smiling face and then back to the envelope. Why did he have to be so sweet? Then again, I could just be crying for the sake of crying. I seemed to do that a lot lately. I gingerly reached out and plucked the envelope off the door. Inside was a beautiful card with a green haired, freckled troll doll saying 'my baby is having a baby.'

When I opened the card, the tears really started to fall. There was a sonogram picture with the words, *'family is everything. I can't wait to start mine with you.'* Along with a set of keys. It was all so sweet. The only thing that confused me was the poem tucked in the envelope behind the card:

Sing a song of sixpence,
Hear the baby cry,
Four and seven order members cooked up a lie,
When the lie was forgotten,
The ravens ceased to sing,
Gutted by the bastard of the king of kings.

It was signed The Piper.

"Parker, what is–"

The paper was torn out of my hand before I could finish speaking. Unease settled in my stomach as the dark glint in Parker's glare grew.

"Is something wrong?"

He smiled down at me and passed the poem to Logan. "No baby, everything's fine."

"Uh huh," I grumbled, eyeing the shocked expression on Logan's face.

The fact that Preston walked up behind him was enough to tell me, everything was not fine. The poem mentioned ravens and the Order. Was it a threat? Was I in danger? Because Parker didn't look happy. Although he was trying hard to convince me otherwise.

My suspicion took a backseat when Parker pushed me through the door.

"Welcome home!"

I jumped back at the loud declaration. Standing in the most beautiful entryway, were Parker's dad, his sister Ava, and his mother. Above them, hanging off a balcony attached to a spiral staircase, was a banner, saying 'Welcome Home Lana.'

I couldn't believe it. This was not something I was expecting. The whole Whitley family was here to welcome me. Well, except for Mrs. Whitley, who stood there with a scowl on her face, sipping from what looked like wine.

I wasn't about to let one sour puss ruin the mood, so I smiled at all of them and said, "Thank you. You didn't have to do this."

"You are family now, my dear," Mr. Whitley proclaimed, "And we like to go above and beyond for people in this family."

"It's fucking annoying," Preston grumbled from behind me.

My heart seized in my chest as I spun around, ready to grab Nan, but it was too late. I watched her hand whack off the back of Preston's head in slow motion.

The strike rang out like the chimes of a doomsday clock. His icy cold glare locked onto my Nan, sending a shiver down my spine. Next to come out was his gun.

"Hit me again," he cocked the hammer back. "I dare you."

The room went so quiet, I could hear my own blood pumping. Nan didn't back down. She stood strong where she was, straightened her shoulders, and stepped in closer. Squaring off with death himself. My chest heaved with my unreleased breath.

The only thing that broke the tense situation was the sound of Ava's voice. "Heads up, little brother."

Parker barley pulled me out of the way as a knife sailed through the air and dug into the door. What the hell?

Preston looked over at the blade, and then at his sister, while holstering his gun. "Stop calling me that."

"But you are my little brother," Ava argued with a smile.

"Three minutes hardly constitutes as little."

"I'm still three minutes older."

Preston muttered under his breath and pushed his way past us. I buried myself further in Parker's arms, wondering if I'd just embedded myself in the Manson family, as Parker lost his shit on his sister.

"What the fuck, Ava!" he yelled, "You could've stabbed her."

"Oh calm down, she's fine."

Parker's dad joined in the yelling. Honestly, I wasn't surprised. Ava Whitley gave crazy a new definition. If aliens invaded the planet, they'd take one look at Ava coming down the street with a smile on her face and a can opener in her hand, and turn around and leave. I say this because I'd seen what she could do with a can opener. Poor Bobby Tompkins. I bet he missed his ball.

"Come on, child." Nan wrapped her arm around my shoulders and steered me away from the squabbling family. "Let's explore your new house."

I glanced back at the Whitley's hands flying through the air, and locked eyes with Lillianna. The matriarchal head of household wasn't paying attention to the others, she was too busy glaring her hatred at me.

Welcome home, Lana Crawford. The hellfire rains at ten.

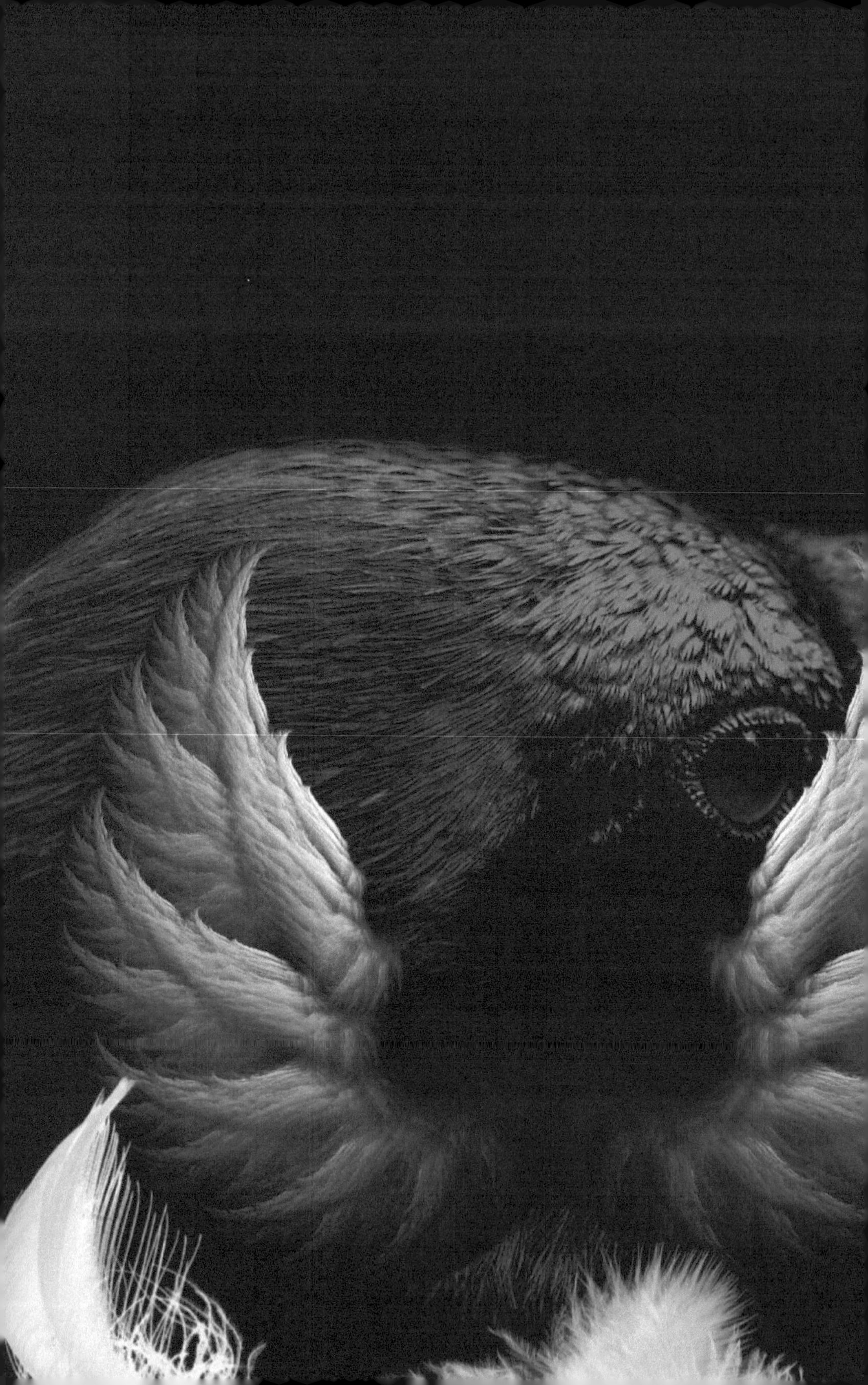

Chapter 16

Lana

Nan and I spent what felt like hours wandering the house, and I still don't think we saw everything. The kitchen alone took forever to explore. Each room was furnished with top of the line furniture and fancy little decorations. I couldn't help but notice the care Parker took in decorating.

The paintings on the wall were of my favorite flowers, orchids, or of places on my dream vacation list. There was at least one troll doll in every room we entered, and the color scheme was made up of my favorites, Royal blue and lavender.

What really caught my attention was the large portrait hung up in what I assumed would be the nursery. It was the only empty room in the house and was right next to the master bedroom, which was almost as big as Nan's house. Nan and I stood there, staring at the warm brown eyes we hadn't seen in five years. Gramps was the best man I knew. I missed him everyday.

Nan brushed a tear off her cheek. "How did he get this?"

My fingers grazed over his smile. I didn't care how Parker got the picture. None of the bad mattered anymore, because the man I loved most in the world was back. I didn't care about anything else. Gramps' smiling face would be the first thing my children saw every morning. That was the only thing that mattered.

"There you are." Parker walked over and placed his hand on my shoulder. "Everybody's leaving."

I turned my teary face up to him, smiled, and kissed his cheek. "I better go say goodbye then."

Nan didn't join us for awhile, and I wasn't going to interrupt her. She deserved her time alone with her husband. By the time everyone left, I was utterly exhausted. Mostly from dealing with Ava. She'd be almost out the door and turn around to talk to my belly. Telling the babies that Auntie Ava couldn't wait to meet them.

She was more excited than anyone else. Every time her palm flattened on my stomach, her eyes lit up. She'd already booked a company to come in and baby-proof the house, as well as marked down all the best places to shop for baby stuff.

While it was kind of sweet how much she loved her future niece and nephew, getting cozy with Ava Whitley was not high on my list of things to do. A couple hours ago, the girl threw a knife at me, and that wasn't the worst thing I could imagine her doing. Hell, I think Preston would be a better option to chum it up with.

Once we were left alone, I couldn't help but think how easy this all seemed to be. I was worried about the move. Thought I'd be a lot more stressed out than I was, but the Whitley's made me feel oddly comfortable. And then I walked into the bedroom.

I told myself that nothing was going to happen between us. Parker and I would be more like roommates raising our children. Parker, apparently, had other ideas. He was sprawled across the bed with his hands behind his head.

My eyes immediately fell to his exposed chest. Following each dip and curve embedded in his tanned skin, down to the V dipping into his pants. Grey sweatpants, to be specific. Women's kryptonite.

"Alone at last." He smirked up at me.

Alone. That word did not sound good right now. I looked everywhere but at the half naked man. Studied the swirling carvings in the cherrywood posts on the bed. Sturdy posts that a girl could be tied to. Tied and used hard… *okay, don't look at those.*

My eyes fell down to the dark carpet under my feet. Thick and soft flooring that would cradle my knees… *alright, carpet is a bad idea too.* So was the furniture, which could easily support my weight, and the eggshell walls Parker could press me up against.

Everything in the room sent my mind somewhere else. Decorations and pictures falling on the floor. Navy bedspread tangled up with the silky sheet underneath. I couldn't pull my mind out of the gutter. I decided my best option was to escape to the bathroom with a big comfy pair of flannel pajamas. Which I had to get from the dresser that was a perfect height to prop me up on.

Thankfully Parker didn't argue when I slipped into the bathroom. He just shot me a cocky smirk as I shut the door. He knew I wasn't going anywhere. How pathetic was it that a small part of me was grateful he allowed me privacy to change? My eyes wandered around the opulent bathroom.

Beautiful dark blue tiles were laid across the far wall, depicting a waterfall scene. Next to that was a stand alone shower, jacuzzi tub, and his and her sinks. Other girls might've admired the extravagance. Maybe even been flattered that Parker obviously spared no expense. Not me.

This big house with the grand expenditures only reminded me of one thing. The morning after the best night of my life. Parker threw money at me then, just like he was doing now. This place, with all the furniture and welcome home party, was only another way for him to buy me.

I picked up one of the bottles on the counter, studying the label. Giorgio Armani, Nars, and Kevyn. All brand names I'd normally be squealing over. Except right now. All they looked like to me, were high priced bottles of bribery. I didn't want them. I didn't want any of this. All I wanted was my small bed and the one person who loved me beyond reproach. My Nan.

I pushed back the tears threatening to break free and changed into my pajamas. They weren't any of the high priced designer label stuff hanging in the closet. This red plaid fabric used to be Gramps.

They were big and comfy and safe. Something I really needed to feel right now. I hugged my waist and rubbed my hands over my belly. The babies were kicking up a storm. Could they feel my anxiety?

"Shhh," I whispered, "It's okay. Your daddy loves you."

That I never questioned. Every time Parker put his hand on my stomach, I could see it in his eyes. So much love and adoration that I couldn't help but picture him holding our babies. It was that image that gave me the strength to walk back out into the bedroom.

I opened the door and stepped through, telling myself that I was doing the right thing. Everything would be fine. I might've been able to hang on to that, if Parker wasn't standing outside the door.

"I was about to come in after you."

I licked my lips and forced the lump down my throat. His chest was eye level. Expanding and contracting, bringing back memories of how he felt on top of me. *Remember the bottles, Lana. You can't be bought.*

"I'm tired..."

"And I'm hard." He grabbed my hand and pressed my palm against his dick.

My thighs immediately clenched together. Yes, yes he was. Very hard, very big, and very hot. Somewhere in the back of my head, I wondered how it even fit the first time? Thankfully, my mouth still had it's senses.

"No."

"No? Are you saying you don't want me?"

I tipped my chin and looked up into his eyes. "That's right."

He pushed me back against the wall, leaned in and whispered, "Then why is your hand still on my dick?"

Not only were my fingers still wrapped around him, but his hand wasn't holding mine there anymore. I quickly tore my arm back, but I could still feel him there. His hard length still twitching in my grasp. My body ached, wanting to feel him in other places. Have his breath warm my skin as he pumped into me.

You're not his whore, Lana.

"I'm going to bed, Parker." My hands fisted at my sides. "Be glad I'm sticking to our arrangement and sleeping in the same one as you."

I thought he'd stop me and remind me of the bouncing on his dick clause. He didn't. Parker let me storm past him and crawl into bed. Gotta say, out of all the places I'd slept, this was by far the most comfortable. The mattress wrapped around me in a silky cocoon, cradling my body.

"If you want to play this game, Angel, that's fine," Parker chuckled and joined me. I barely had time to enjoy the comfort before he pulled me into him and softly growled in my ear, "But you'll lose."

As the warmth of his body seeped into my bones, the pit in my stomach fell deeper and deeper down. Because the man rubbing my back, lulling me into a relaxed slumber, was the same one from that night. The Parker Whitley that made me fall in love with him and broke my heart in the span of twelve hours.

*M*Y BODY WAS ON FIRE, *I needed something, but I didn't know what.*

"That's it, baby," a husky voice growled in my ear.

Parker! He could give me what I needed.

"Yes." I moaned and arched back, loving the feel of his hard body against mine.

My mind honed in on his fingertips smoothing across my fevered skin. Slowly dipping lower and lower, closer to the aching apex between my thighs. I reached back, burrowing my fingers in his soft hair, silently begging for something my voice couldn't articulate. But Parker knew what I wanted. He knew how to answer my body's desperation.

A long groan escaped my mouth as his lips latched onto me. His tongue worked a hot, wet trail up the side of my neck, but he still wasn't giving me what I needed. His hand toyed with the waistband of my pajamas, refusing to dip inside and relieve the need throbbing through my clit.

"Please," I whimpered, arching my hips and grinding my ass against his erection.

Parker released a masculine groan that had my blood boiling. "Tell me what you want, baby."

His hand slipped under my pants, stealing my ability to think. All I could do in response was fold myself back against him and moan, "More."

"More what?" His breath wafted over the shell of my ear, sending shivers of anticipation down my spine.

Why was he teasing me? "I need it."

"What do you need?" His fingers gripped my hip, pressing my ass back into his hard cock, "My dick?"

Yes, yes, give me that.

But his hand let me go. My lips curled in a frown as a pathetic sound of desperation slipped past my parted lips. Parker forced his hand between my clenched thighs and slid his finger through my folds. "Or do you want my fingers?"

He pressed down on my clit, making me call out a desperate, "Yes!"

"You're so fucking beautiful."

The growl he released in response vibrated through my very soul. He worked me expertly, pinching and swirling my aching bundle of nerves, applying the pressure my body craved.

"I'm gonna make you come so hard, Angel. But you have to be a good girl for me." His hand wrapped around my neck, holding me firmly against him. "Can you do that for me?"

I nodded. Parker could do whatever he wanted. Hold me, bite me, choke me, as long as he kept doing what he was doing.

"That's right, baby, give in." His finger pushed in my opening, hitting a spot that made me scream his name.

That's when he really finger-fucked me. Thrusting roughly in and out, hitting that sinful spot, over and over and over again. White hot sparks of ecstasy exploded behind my closed lids as a wave of pure pleasure stole my breath.

I clung to him, riding out the most intense orgasm I'd ever had. My inner walls clenched tightly to his fingers as an extreme gush of wetness soaked through my pants. That's when I realized I couldn't just feel him, I could smell him.

I wasn't dreaming!

"Fuck," Parker grunted in a deeply masculine tone, "I knew you were a squirter. I can't wait to feel you soak my cock."

While my body was completely and utterly satisfied, my mind was stunned. *What just happened?*

"I-I-I-I," I stammered, staring up at his grey eyes, filled with dark desire.

His fingers were still in my pussy, slowly stroking my wet walls, and I was too hazed from my orgasm to push him away. I knew I should, but it felt so good, and it'd been so long since I felt this way. Loved and cared about in the most intimate way. I liked it.

You shouldn't.

I couldn't move, couldn't do anything but watch as Parker pulled his hand out of my pants, smeared my juices over my lips and gave me a breath stealing kiss. It was so powerful that I actually sank into it, letting him control me with his mouth. Until I tasted something else. Something sweet, with a musky undertone.

Me! My senses hit me like a freight train, knocking me back into harsh reality.

I tore my lips away from Parker's hot mouth and growled, "I'm not your whore, Parker."

"No, you're my wife."

"What?! No I'm not!" As if I'd marry Parker Whitley!

"Do you know all it takes to be legally married, is a signed marriage certificate?" My heart stopped at the way his lips curled. "You should really read what you sign."

He wouldn't. I could tell myself that all I wanted, but deep down, I knew, he would.

"I'm not old enough to sign a legal document." I was only seventeen. Still a minor in the eyes of the law. "Anything I signed wouldn't be legal."

"Unless your guardian signed it too."

Shit, Nan signed the contract too. But she would've noticed something like that, right? I thought back to that day and how the lawyer helped Nan and I understand the legal jargon so we wouldn't have to read through pages and pages.

Oh.

My.

God.

"Time to get up," Parker smiled down at the shock on my face. "We have school today, Mrs. Whitley."

Some days it feels like the universe is on your side. That God, or the fates, or whatever you want to call it, is on your side. I didn't believe in any of that crap. Actually I thought faith was a gigantic waste of time.

Why should I spend every Sunday praying to some mystical being when there were so many other things I could be doing. I had read up on religion though. Lana and her Nan were regulars in their church, and I wanted to know everything there was to know about my Angel's beliefs.

I'd never knock her faith or try and stop her from practicing it. I was fully prepared to stand next to her in that pew and fake my way through prayer. Believing in some all loving being up in the sky wasn't hurting anyone. Besides, religion instilled good morals. Who would my Angel be if she didn't grow up thinking there was good in humanity?

Hiding the ugly parts of the world from her was my job. She

might hate me now, and think I was forcing her into a life she never wanted, but I was only giving her what she needed. Protection, security, and love.

In time she'd see that no one could take care of her like I could. Because Lana Crawford was, and always had been, mine. Apparently that was a lesson I had to teach someone else.

I glanced down at the note Lana found yesterday.

"He could've arranged to have it sent before." Logan pointed at Micha sitting across the table, and popped a fry in his mouth. "You know how prepared my old man liked to be."

Ryker had been dead for months now, this time for sure. Preston and Lou made sure of that. Or so they said.

Micha's brow rose. "And how did he know Parker would buy a house? Let alone that the idiot would knock her up?"

"Smooth move on that one." Mase rolled his green eyes my way, "Didn't your dad tell you to wrap your shit?"

"Maybe I knocked her up on purpose. Ever think of that, jackass?"

The table went quiet as Micha, Mase and Logan all stared at me. Silas was the only one who didn't look shocked, though that could have something to do with the dark circles under his eyes. These days he spent most nights calming Finn down.

The shit Ryker did to him gave him nightmares. Kid couldn't cope without Junior. Micha offered to swap out, have Junior spend a week at Silas's, and then Finn the next week at his. The esteemed Dr. Creswell was dead set against it. He said Finn needed to learn to deal with his shit. Prick.

"Damn man," Mase slapped Silas on the shoulder and then waved his hand at me, "You were right."

Silas shrugged. "Told you."

That made my brow rise. How the fuck did Silas know anything? It wasn't like I planned this shit. I didn't do it on purpose, but I didn't take any precautions either. Didn't even stop to ask Lana if she was on birth control. Honestly, I didn't care. I needed to pump her full of my cum. So I may as well have done it on purpose.

"It doesn't matter," Micha growled, "We need to find this asshole. None of our girls are safe until we do."

"Looks like this grumpy fuck and I are the only smart ones here." Mase threw a wink at Silas, who flipped him off. "We don't have girls."

"First off, this prick," Logan threw his thumb in Silas's direction, "Doesn't have one because they're all afraid of his shit. And do I need to remind you of a particular redhead?"

Mase's face dropped. "I don't give a shit what happens to her."

We all snorted at that. Mase might fucking hate Harper, but nobody else better touch her. She was his to torment, and God help the fucker that decided to try and get a piece.

"And yet, you still have the contract," Micha added.

Mase glared at his brother, but didn't say anything. They all thought they knew the youngest Kessler. They didn't know shit. Mase was going through with the arrangement for one reason. To make her life a living hell. Harper couldn't go near other guys if she was married to him. She'd never feel wanted or loved.

I had to hand it to him, Mase's long term plan for the girl was the ultimate fuck you. Preston couldn't have come up with something better. And how did I know this? There was a lot of things a guy would tell you when you had his dick in your hand.

We sat for a few more minutes, discussing what to do. By the time I had to leave for practice, Micha had a plan laid out. Each of us was given a job. Logan and Preston were going to look deeper into the note. See if they could match handwriting and check security cameras around my house. Mase was sent to check out the office files, in case the fucker was hiding in Ashworth. Which I'm sure Mrs. Grier would love.

Silas was going to pull on his family's political strings and see if he could uncover adoption records, and Micha said he had a few places to check for information. What places? He didn't say and no one asked. Louis Kessler was the keeper of secrets. There was probably a bunch of places we didn't know about that Micha could utilize.

As for me, I was to watch my girl and see if anyone was getting oddly close to her. There were a few people on my list, but my Angel was a friendly girl. People naturally liked her, except for Naomi.

I don't think Ashworth's queen bee liked anyone though. I'd have to keep a closer eye on my girl. Look for someone paying a little too much attention. Not that I hadn't been doing that already, but this guy was with Ryker, and Logan's dad was one hell of a sneaky fucker.

I snorted out a chuckle as I walked into the locker room. The Piper. Logan assumed that came from shit his dad used to say. I knew different.

When I was a kid, Ryker played 'games' with me. His favorite was 'let's see how quick we can break your brother'. Preston would be forced to watch as Ryker and his sick friend Ned ran a pipeline on me.

The day my brother finally broke, he shoved a lead pipe up Nash's ass. When Ryker pulled him away, Preston shoved the shitty end in his mouth and yelled, *'Who's the piper now, fucker.'*

The nickname wasn't some sick way for him to taunt his son. It was a fuck you to the one kid that dared to stand up to him.

None of this made sense. Especially for a guy like Ryker. That bastard planned everything. He didn't fuck with us when we were kids because he was some sick kiddie diddler. Every twisted thing he did brought him closer to the throne, because he who controlled the Order of Ravens and Wolves, had all the power.

He'd spent years terrorizing the next generation of Kings. Kind of smart, if you thought about it. Fear was a great motivator. None of us would've stopped him from taking the crown. He would've succeeded, too, if it wasn't for two people.

Micha and Preston.

Though in time, I'm sure he would've gotten to the king of kings' heir. My brother, however... How do you convince someone incapable of feeling fear, that you're the boogeyman? That was the fatal flaw in his plan. Preston was the voice whispering in our ears and arming us with flashlights to fight the darkness.

There was fuck all Ryker could do to intimidate my brother. Including using Ava and I against him. The final nail in his coffin was my brother, and he knew it.

So why go after Riley and Shelby? What purpose did that serve? Micha was wrath personified. If he could bring his mother back to life just to kill her again, he would. And Logan... yeah, he was his son, but he already fucking hated the prick. Why take his girl at all? That didn't include Junior and Finn. Ryker had to know the second he touched Finn, we'd all band against him. None of it made sense.

That's what was bugging me, because when it came to Ryker Hudson, there was always an end game. He wouldn't have left a protégé behind without a plan. The last person in this town that plan should include was my angel.

If anything, Micha's illegitimate brother–which is who we assumed this asshole was–should be targeting that mousy little church girl Preston was stalking around town. Then again, who the fuck knew what the prick's agenda was?

"You gonna have your head in the game today, Whitley?"

I strapped on my shoulder pads and rolled my eyes Sean's way. "Go fuck yourself, Callaghan."

Sean walked past, crashing his shoulder into mine and jarring me forward. Asshole had been gunning for me since he found out I knocked up little sister's best friend.

"See you on the field," he muttered.

"Hey Callaghan," I called out, and shot him a smirk, 'Guess who slept in my bed last night?"

Sean stopped and tipped his glare my way. "You a sucker for punishment, Whitley?"

"Just figured you should know whose dick she'll be swallowing tonight." I popped my helmet on my head and slapped his back, "Don't worry, I'll take real good care of her. Though personally, if I were you, I'd be more worried about your sister. She's sixteen now, right?"

Mason had a contract, and if it was anything like Micha's, Harper was fucked.

"What the fuck is that supposed to mean?" Sean growled back.

"Ask your old man." I shrugged and sauntered out onto the field.

Sean had other things to worry about. Lana was mine now, and I couldn't wait to show her that.

I BLEW out a huff of air, striped my uniform off, and pushed my fingers through my hair. Coach made me run laps after practice. Sean should've been running them with me. It wasn't my fault the prick couldn't take what he dished out. But he was the quarterback, and quarterback's always got special treatment. Despite how many touchdowns I scored.

"Fucking prick," I grumbled while snatching my towel out of my locker.

I needed to calm down before I took my Angel home, or the first time I fucked my wife, it'd be rough and hard. The first time I took her, I was too consumed by carnal desire to give Lana the attention she deserved.

I should've made her first time more special. A mistake I planned on rectifying tonight. If I couldn't get rid of this rage boiling through my veins, that wasn't going to happen.

Fucking Callaghan.

I stormed into the showers and stopped. There was only one reason Brady would still be here. Our wide receiver was a fan of the closet. At parties he played the pussy parade like everyone else, but he was really a cock fan. He'd begged for mine on several occasions.

I cocked my head and followed the bulging ridges of his arm braced up against the tiled wall. Brady was a good looking guy. Dark hair, tanned skin, and firm ass. Under the water he looked even better. Hard body, slick and wet.

My dick was ready to go before I stepped under the warm spray. My mind, however, was not. I'd never betray my angel by touching someone else. My dick belonged to Lana and no one else.

Brady rolled his forehead against the wall, turning his light eyes my way. "Hey."

I nodded back at him and went about my shower. Should've known ignoring him wouldn't do anything. Brady stood there watching me, gaze following my hand's movements as they slid over my body, washing away the grime from practice. Three steps later and he was in front of me, breath cooling my face.

"You know," he licked his lips and dropped his stare down to my hard cock, "I could help you with that?"

His words weren't what made my dick jump. It was the small gasp twitching in my ears. Lana was pressed up against the wall, trying to hide behind some lockers. Maybe my angel wanted a show? Her curious hazel eyes locked with mine as I reached forward and grabbed the back of Brady's neck.

"You want him to suck my dick?"

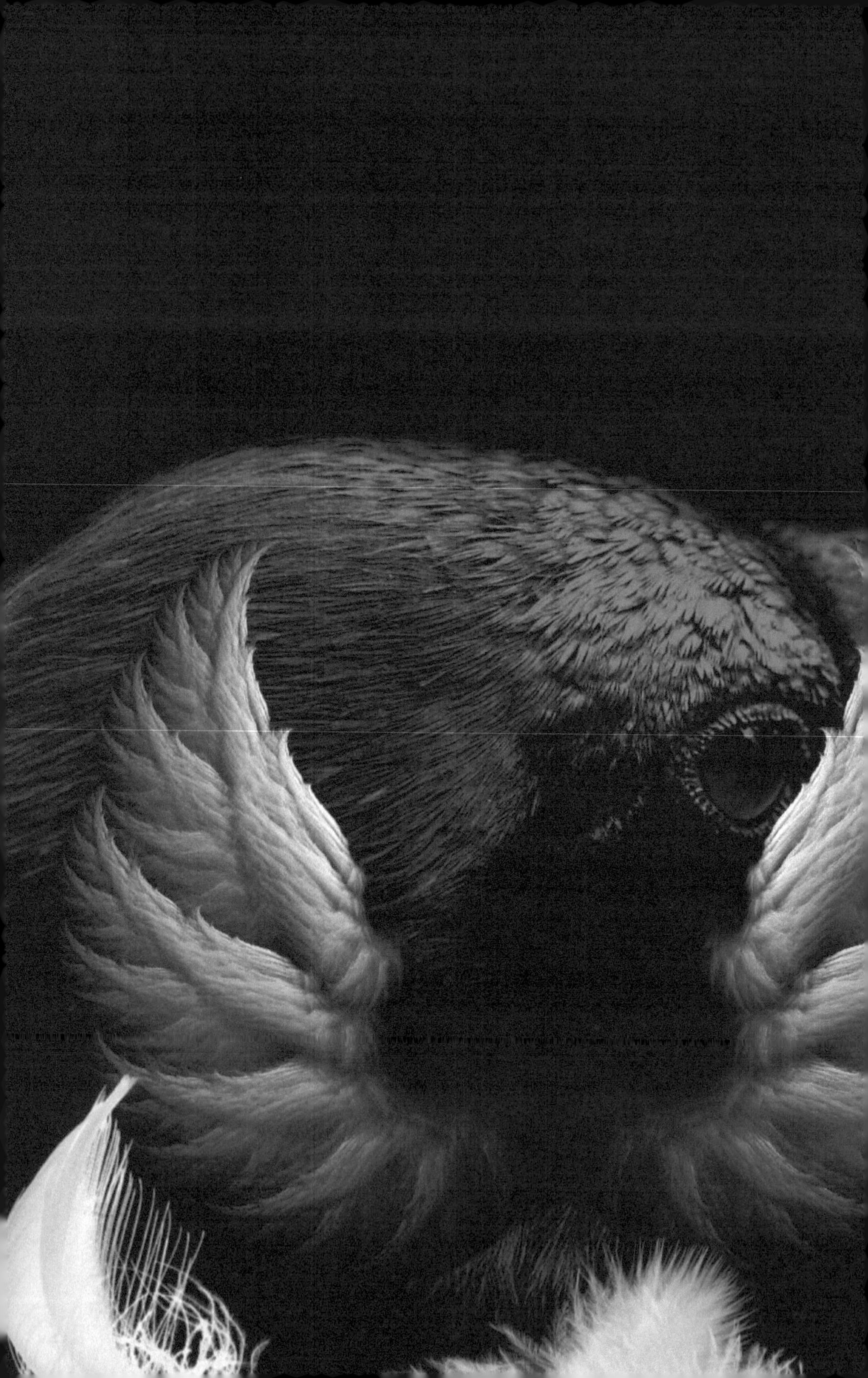

Chapter 18
Lana

It was surprisingly difficult to find things to do after school was done. Not like I had a choice. Parker wouldn't let me drive myself, so I had to wait until he was done with practice.

I'd heard football players' girlfriends complain about having to wait around, but didn't get it until today. I didn't even have Harper to hang out with. She had an appointment or something, so her dad picked her up after school.

I talked to Mr. Lannister for a bit while Shelby practiced, and then moved onto the library, but Naomi and her minions were in there, planning stuff for prom. Even though it was still months away, the queen bee insisted on starting this year's committee early.

God forbid Naomi's prom was anything but perfect. She'd even started campaigning for her tiara. Which was kind of a moot point, as far as I was concerned. Naomi Prescott was born to be prom queen. King was a different matter. It would either be Micha Kessler, or Logan Hudson, none of whom seemed to give a shit about the title.

By the time football practice was done, I was more than ready to go. I didn't even care that I'd have to go home with Parker. Heck, I was looking forward to seeing something other than Ashworth's white walls. But of course, Parker had to stay longer. Thanks to Sean. I made sure to give him a piece of my mind before he left. My so-called husband was next on my list.

This whole day sucked. I spent most of it plotting ways to become a widow. The stupid thing was that I was more upset about not having a wedding, than I was about being tricked into marriage. Something I pointed out on the way to school. Parker said we'd have a wedding. As big and fancy as I wanted. Which only felt like a new way for him to pay me off.

I didn't have a dream wedding, or perfect gown picked out. The only thing I imagined as a little girl was the perfect husband. A charming, handsome guy that would treat me well.

We could get married at the courthouse for all I cared, as long as he loved me. It wasn't the ceremony that mattered. It was the marriage. The strong relationship I should have. Not this fucked up, fake bullshit I was forced into.

Fuck Parker Whitley.

I charged into the locker room, prepared to rip my *husband* a new asshole. When I was done with him, Parker would be a sniveling baby, crying on the floor. At least, that was my plan. That went out the window the second I saw Brady inches away from Parker. Both were very naked, and very hard.

My eyes skimmed over Parker's chiseled chest and down to the other man's firm ass. Everybody knew Parker's bat swung both ways, but Brady was a well known player. This couldn't be what I thought it was. I mean, football players showered together all the time. That's just what teams did.

"You know," Brady said in a husky tone, "I could help you with that?"

Oh my god.

I gasped and pressed myself against the wall. It was what I thought it was. I should leave. Problem was, I couldn't stop watching them. Somewhere in the back of my mind, I prayed one would touch the other. My core tingled just thinking about it. Parker's eyes locked on mine, making my stomach flip. Would he be mad that I was spying?

Would he stop?

Parker's fingers curled around the back of Brady's neck, and I held my breath as he pulled him closer.

"Do you want him to suck my dick?"

Shit, he was talking to me. I prepared myself to bolt out of the room, but Brady didn't seem to notice they were being watched. His lips parted as he purred up at Parker, "Yes, please."

Parker didn't answer him. He kept his gaze trained on me, while holding the other man firmly in place. He was waiting for my answer. Or permission, maybe? I looked at the desperation on Brady's face, pondering what I wanted. If I said no, would Parker stop?

Did I want him to?

I licked my lips and slowly nodded.

Parker's mouth curled as he leaned in and growled in Brady's ear, "You know what I like."

A second later, Brady was on his knees, sucking Parker's hard length down his throat. It was the hottest thing I'd ever seen. The way Brady's lips wrapped around his shaft. How his throat bobbed with each swallow, and the masculine grunts coming from Parker's mouth.

The entire time Brady bobbed on his cock, Parker maintained eye contact with me. Not only could I see the pleasure on his face, I could feel it in my veins. Rushing along with my singing blood, rising to an uncomfortable heat. I didn't even realize my hand was dipping inside my skirt until Parker shook his head.

"You don't come until I say."

Brady whimpered along with me. Desire was so thick in the air, I could taste it with each breath I heaved into my lungs. My mouth opened to whisper the same plea Brady called out. "Please."

In a flash, Parker pulled the other man up and had him face first against the shower wall. His fingers wrapped around Brady's shaft, slowly stroking him from root to tip.

"Is this what you want?" he whispered in Brady's ear.

Brady muttered out a breathy, "More."

But he wasn't talking to Brady. Parker was talking to me. My eyes fell down to his hard length pressing against Brady's ass. This was so wrong. I shouldn't want to see this.

Thinking about Parker controlling the other man while plowing into him, shouldn't be turning me on, but it was. I didn't just want to see more, I needed it. Needed to quench the desire aching through my body. I didn't have to tell him that, though. Parker already knew. One look, and he gave me what I was too afraid to admit I wanted.

"I assume you brought a condom?" Parker said to Brady when my eyes met his.

Brady nodded and passed him a foil packet.

My thighs clenched in anticipation as Parker tore open the condom and sheathed himself. He pressed Brady's face harder into the tiled wall and lined his cock up. I sucked back an anticipatory gasp and slapped my hand over my mouth. With his eyes still locked on mine, Parker's lips twisted and he thrust in.

He fucked Brady without mercy. Shoving his hand in his mouth to muffle his cries while pumping furiously into his back hole. I couldn't look away. It was depraved and wrong in the most glorious way. The sweat dripping off their brows, mingling with the water beating down on them.

I could feel their heat. Taste each echoing groan vibrating through the room. When Brady's fingers tightened on the wall and his cock throbbed, spraying his release, my only regret was that I wasn't over there, enjoying the moment with them. That was the terrifying part.

I not only got off on watching Parker fuck another man, I wanted to do it with him. That was what made me turn and bolt. I wasn't running from Parker. I was running from the dark voice whispering debaucheries in the back of my mind.

PARKER DIDN'T SAY a word on the way home, and neither did I. I could barely look at him without shame burning in my cheeks. How could I have watched, and why couldn't I stop thinking about it? That was the most uncomfortable car ride of my life. On the upside, I never noticed all the pretty plants around the town before. I even got a few ideas for our house.

Ugh. I needed to stop thinking about it that way.

I was supposed to be mad at Parker, and here he had me all twisted up. Thinking about things I shouldn't be thinking about. Yet when I looked at him, all I could do was squirm in my seat and turn away, hoping he didn't sense my embarrassed state. If there was a jail for pushovers, I'd get the biggest cell. Tours would stop outside my door to gawk at the epic failure.

"This one didn't do a thing to fight against her forced marriage, and she enjoyed watching her husband with another man."

Shocked gasps followed by shaking heads of disapproval.

Sighing, I flopped back in my seat. Who thought I'd be happy to spend time with Lillianna Whitley? Her car was parking in front of the house when we got home. Parker seemed less enthusiastic about it than I was. To me, she was the perfect excuse to escape my so-called husband. How sad was that? I opted to spend time with Ashen Springs dragon lady, over facing Parker.

"I hope you're feeling okay," Lillianna's hand swirled through the air as she spoke. "Preston and Ava were the worst. I was sick all the time. But not my baby boy." She smiled at Parker as he rolled his eyes and walked out of the kitchen. "My Parker was a breeze."

Her Parker? She didn't talk about her elder children like that. Nor did she look at them with the same loving shine in her eyes.

Then again, Ava was crazy, and Preston... Well, I doubted he loved her either. But she did seem to genuinely care about Parker. Perhaps she wasn't as bad as Nan thought? Someone who cared that much for her child had to have a heart somewhere, right?

"Of course, pregnancy might be different for you."

Okay, maybe she only had half a heart.

"Other than some nausea in the morning, I feel fine."

That was a bold faced lie. I yacked my guts out almost every morning for at least an hour, but she was being nice to me, so...

"I have something to help with that." Lillianna walked around the island and opened the fridge. "It's an old family recipe."

"Okay." I didn't really know what else to say.

This was the same woman that judged me by the color of my skin, but who was also the grandmother to my children. That earned her some credit. Gramps used to say some people were by-products of their upbringing.

Ignorance begets ignorance and I shouldn't hold what someone was taught against them. My acceptance might be the thing that made them open their eyes. When it came to Parker's mother, Nan didn't agree.

My nose crinkled at some of the things Lillianna was dumping in the blender. She put a raw egg in there? Eww. I didn't want to be rude though, so I turned away and looked out the window.

Better to study the flowers in the garden than to throw up all over this nice shiny floor. And it was nice and shiny. Black tiles sparkling in the sunlight. Didn't think I'd like a black floor, but it suited the room. The entire house was pretty. New appliances, and fully stocked rooms. I'd never seen a fridge so full in my life.

Then again, the only other fridge I'd seen that big was at Harper's, or Riley's.

A glass of what I could only describe as thick pinkish-grey sludge was placed in front of me.

"Here you go." Lillianna beamed down at me. "This will cure your nausea."

I looked down at the cup, studying the chunks floating inside. What the hell was that? Strawberries, or some kind of raw meat? God, it smelled like feet. I gave Lillianna a small smile and picked up the glass. Scratch that, it smelled like ass. This crap was suppose to cure my stomach issues? I wanted to throw up just looking at it.

Lillianna gazed down at me expectantly. I could almost hear her voice urging me on. Telling myself she was just trying to help, I stared at the crap in my hand. *Ass Juice, cure your tummy troubles today.*

Well, here goes nothing.

"Lana,"

Oh thank God.

I placed the cup down and smiled at Parker as he entered the room.

"I can't find my keys. Do you know where I put them?"

Why would I know where he put them?

"They're on the table by the door." *Huh, guess I did.*

He smiled down at me. "Would you mind getting them for me?"

Were his legs broken? Then again, if I played gopher, I could avoid the ass juice. I glanced at the glass, then out in the hall where things smelled nice, and stood up. Gopher was definitely a better option.

I sauntered out of the room, arms swinging at my leisurely pace. No need to hurry, after all. I was halfway there, when I remembered Parker didn't drop his keys on the little black table by the door. He dropped them on the kitchen counter.

Well, crap! Back to the ass juice I guess.

I released a grumbled sigh and turned around. A kitchen had never looked more foreboding. Staring at the oak cabinets coming closer, I imagined the boogeyman hiding behind one of them. Laying in wait for me to come back and drink his putrid cup of sludge. I could see his beady eyes peeking around the corner. Sharp lips curling to bare his fangs as I came closer.

Welcome to my parlor, said the spider to the fly.

Stupid fly, walked right into that spider's house. Kind of like what I did when I agreed to Parker's dumb conditions. Was it Lillianna's cup of vomit I was afraid of? Or facing the guy I couldn't stop picturing naked? All strong and hard, with droplets rolling down his washboard abs. Trickling over each solid bump, leaving tiny little streams of goodness my tongue wanted to lap up.

"What the fuck do you think you're doing?"

My brow arched at Parker's tone. The Greek God was angry.

Lillianna almost sounded too smooth with her answer. "I don't know what you're talking about."

"What's in this drink, Mother?"

My lips curled. I doubted either of us wanted to know the answer to that one.

"It's an old family recipe."

For grossness.

"For what," Parker barked back at his mother, "Abortion?"

I froze. *What?*

"I found these in your purse."

My ears twitched at the distinct sound of a pill bottle being shaken. Nan was on enough medication–it came with age she said–that I recognized the tiny clinks ringing through the air. It made my blood run cold. Nan always claimed Lillianna Whitley was evil, but was she that evil? Would she kill her own grand-children?

"I'm trying to fix your mistake, Parker," Lillianna shrieked back. "You have no idea what this will cost our family."

"My children are not a mistake, mother."

My breath hitched as my hand landed on my stomach. My they weren't. My babies were precious and loved. Why would their own grandmother say that?

"You shouldn't be having them with *her*."

My entire body tensed as I sucked back a gasp. The way she said her... Until that moment I'd never felt different.

"There are so many other girls you could have a family with." Lillianna said. "What about Amelia Torres?"

Brandon's cousin? Of course she would suggest someone like her. I used to like Amelia.

"I'm not interested in your blue blood breeding program." Parker bit back at her.

"Sweetheart, listen to me..."

"Get out!" He yelled so loudly it made me jump.

"Parker..."

"I said get out!"

"Fine." Lillianna growled as her heels clicked off the floor, "But one day you'll thank me."

"If you come near my wife again, you won't have to worry about Preston, because I'll slit your fucking throat myself!" Parker called out as his mother stormed out of the room.

She paused long enough to glare down at me and mutter, "I hope you're happy," before she slipped out the front door.

"Are you okay?" The concern shining in Parker's eyes was almost as strong as the guilt. "I'm sorry you had to hear that. I was hoping to protect you from that part of my family."

Suddenly it all made sense. The complete one-eighty he did after our first night together. How cruel he was to me after. The asshole side of him wasn't his true colors. Parker Whitley never used me. He was trying to make me hate him. To keep me away from his mother. But that couldn't be right. Unless…

"Parker," I tipped my head, "Do you love me?"

There was no hesitation. No second where he had to think about the right response. Just one word.

"Yes."

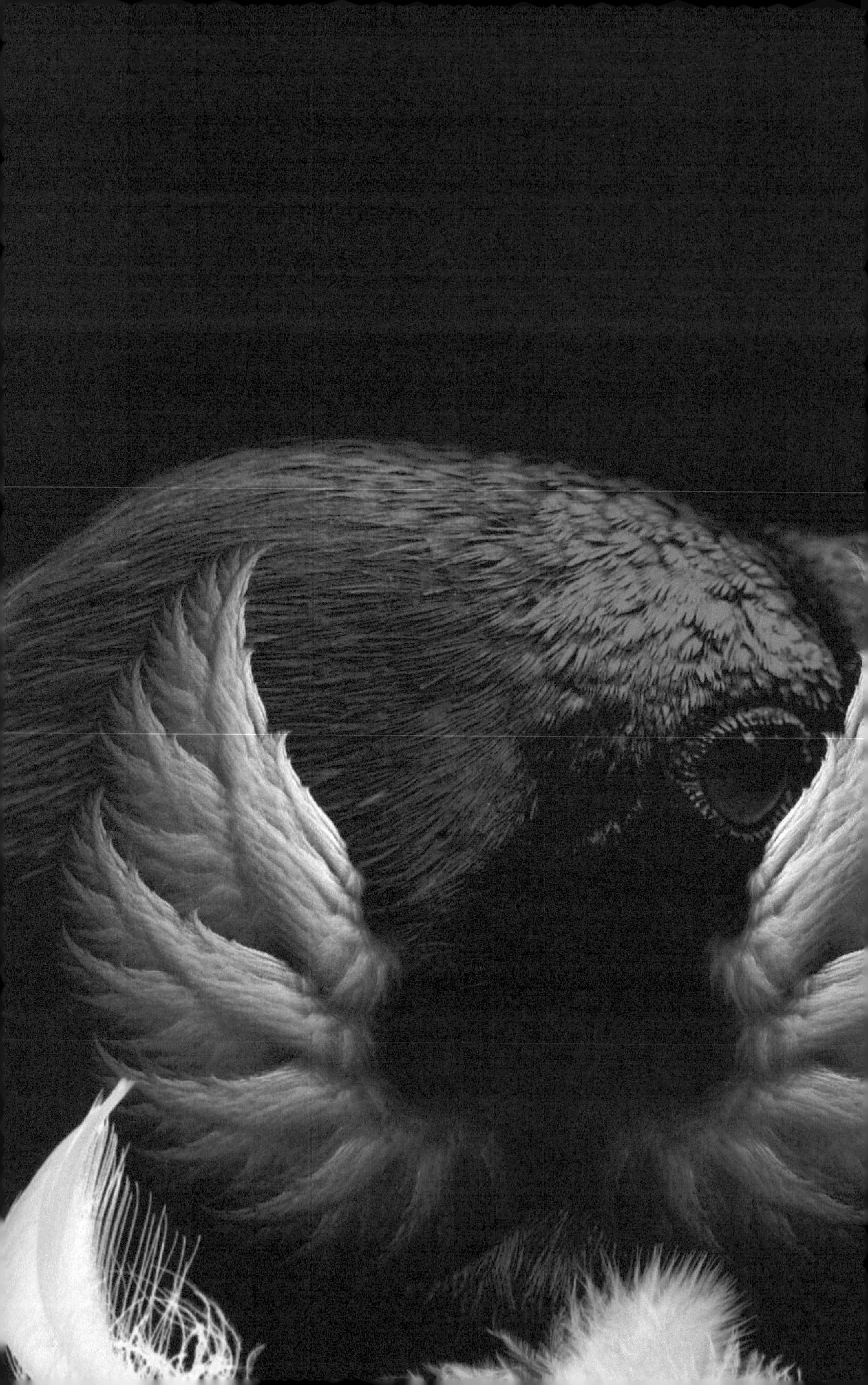

Chapter 19
Lana

I exhaled and studied myself in the mirror. The knights were all scary guys, part of their draw I suppose, but I was never really scared of Parker. I'd either admired him from afar, or hated his guts.

Now I didn't know what to think? He said yes when I asked him if he loved me. Affirmed my question with so much conviction that I couldn't doubt him. And I tried. Guys told girls lies all the time. Girls did too, except their lies were more deceptions of character than whispered promises and sweet words.

Sean told Harper and I to never believe a guy who used the L word. That they were only after one thing. Sound advice coming from a player like him. Except in this instance, one word kept ringing through my head. Wife.

Yes, Parker tricked me into marriage, but why? There was only one thing he gained from it. Me. Parker Whitley wanted me, because he loved me. That was a truly terrifying thought.

Snatching an elastic off the bathroom counter, I pulled my hair back, and then quickly let it go to fall back down in a flow of tight curls. I'd been standing in here for so long, my hair was almost dry from the shower I took.

Did I spend the time straightening my hair? Should I put on make-up? Did I pick the right pajamas? My mind was a whirlwind. I hadn't been this confused about my appearance since my first day of school. The worst part was, I didn't know why this was such a big deal. Who cared what I wore or how I looked? I was just going to bed.

With your husband...

Who loves you.

My eyes landed on the closed door. Was he out there right now, sprawled out on the bed like some perfect example of manly perfection? Nerves fluttered deep in my gut as I once again glanced at my reflection.

On the other side of the door was a smooth skinned, muscled man, and in here was just me. The tall, lanky armed girl, with a thing for Troll dolls. They were even on my pajama shirt and shorts. Smiling back at me with their crazy hair.

I'm such a child.

"Angel," Parker's voice vibrated through the door, "You okay in there?"

Parker Whitley loved me. I was so not okay.

"I'm fine." I eyed my unruly dark hair, bony hips, and protruding belly. "I'll be out in a minute."

A minute? You sure about that?

More concerned with how I looked, I didn't hear Parker walk in until his bare chest appeared in the mirror behind me.

His grey eyes skimmed over me as the corner of his mouth lifted. "You look cute."

My lip curled. Cute? I didn't want to be cute. I wanted to be hot, sexy, or beautiful. Cute was something a guy said to his kid sister.

Parker swept my hair off my shoulder and ran his fingers down the side of my neck. "You look nervous."

"Why would I be nervous?" I asked, praying my thundering pulse wouldn't give me away. Each furious pump echoed through my bones, shaking my already trembling body.

"Don't worry, baby," he purred and leaned in, grazing his lips off the shell of my ear, "I promise to take it easy on you this time."

I didn't say anything. Just stood there staring at his hooded gaze in the mirror. Watching the way he watched me. How his eyes darkened as his hands slid down my sides. The need etched across his face caused my core to clench. This shouldn't be happening.

This man had forced me to move in with him and tricked me into marriage. I should be slapping him, not enjoying the way my skin tingled.

Parker's hands skimmed over my stomach and up my shirt. My lips parted in a breathy gasp as his fingers gently tugged on my nipple, working the small nubs into hardened peaks. I should've pulled away. Put a stop to this before things got out of hand.

Instead, I melted into him. Flopping my head back on his chest. What he was doing felt so good, my body wouldn't listen to my mind.

Did I want it to?

Before I knew what was happening, Parker pulled my shirt off and latched his mouth onto my neck. Hot tongue darting out to taste every inch of skin he kissed.

Say something, Lana!

"Did you like watching me fuck Brady?"

My mouth opened with a breathy, "Yes."

Not that!

I fought hard to push back the images flooding my mind, but they kept coming. Wet, naked, muscled bodies pressed up against each other. Parker's hand firmly holding the other man, fingers digging into the back of his skull as he plowed into him.

"You're wet just thinking about it, aren't you?"

No, I thought as my thighs squeezed together.

"Mmm," Parker purred in a gravely tone that I felt deep in my core, "My dirty girl. I'm going to fuck you so good."

Why did that sound so hot coming from him?

"Parker…"

My objection was cut off when his fingers slid through the slippery mess my pussy was making and pressed down on my clit. I was seriously starting to think that small bundle of nerves was an instant shut off button.

Ding.

Your brain is now offline.

His fingers worked me, pulling and swirling my nub, drawing me closer to the edge of bliss.

Screw it. Why should I fight it? Parker made me feel good, and there was nothing wrong with that.

I had half a second of rational thought when he tore my shorts off and propped me up on the counter. Unfortunately, my moment of reality had nothing to do with what was happening.

It was stuck on the amazement of how easily he moved me. I was almost as tall as Shelby, who was not an easy person to toss around. Yet Parker lifted me as if I was a tiny little thing that weighed nothing, like Harper.

My stomach flipped at the devious grin on Parker's face. Before I could say anything, he dropped down to his knees and placed my feet on the counter. Embarrassment tore through my cheeks, heating my skin.

The most sensitive part of me was on display, and he was staring right at it. Licking his lips in a hungry way. I froze, not sure what to do as his fingers slid up my wet slit and pulled my lips apart.

"That's the prettiest pussy I've ever seen."

Was that a compliment? It felt like a compliment. Should I thank him? What came out of my mouth made me wish I had said thank you.

"You have a pretty penis."

Wow. That was a stellar response, Lana. You get the dirty talk prize.

Parker smirked up at me, increasing my mortification. "I fucking love how cute you are."

Again with cute?

I moved to get off the counter, but Parker stopped me. His fingers dug into my flesh as he held my thighs apart and leaned in. The instant his tongue slid through my slick folds, all doubt left my mind. The only thing I could concentrate on were the shivers racing across my skin. I thought his fingers felt good, but dear god...

Parker continued to eat me, causing me to white knuckle the counter as he licked me from opening to clit. Slow, even strokes that had my whole body on fire. Then his lips wrapped around my throbbing bundle of nerves and stars exploded behind my eyelids.

My moans echoed through the air, along with the inhuman noises I was making. Parker sucked and licked, drawing me into a cloud of thick ecstasy so heavy I couldn't breathe. Couldn't feel anything except his hot mouth, and the wave crashing through me.

My orgasm was just coming to an end when I felt something else. The smooth, hot head of his thick cock pressing against my opening.

"Look at me," Parker growled.

I didn't even realize my eyes were still closed until he said that. I tried to open them. Fought against the heaviness, but I couldn't do it. Because then I would see him. I'd see the adoration I could hear in his voice, and that was utterly terrifying.

"Come on, Angel." He pushed the tip of his cock in, forcing my tight walls to stretch, "Let me see those pretty eyes."

I shook my head while my hips rolled, trying to sink more of his length inside me.

Parker's hips snapped forward, causing me to cry out, and my eyes to fly open. It wasn't the sudden fullness that had my heart hammering in my chest. It was the man staring down at me. The hunger and desire shining deep inside his grey eyes. The love. I could feel every inch of him. Every song his soul sang. The anger, the need, the want. The love.

I didn't argue when his lips crashed down on mine. Didn't fight when he began to move inside me. I wrapped my arms around him and moaned every time he sunk inside me.

He growled in my mouth while digging his fingers into my ass as he used me. And I loved every minute of it. The power behind each thrust. The feeling pouring off of him into me. Nothing had ever felt so good. So perfect.

Parker stuck true to his word and took it easy on me. Sliding his hard cock in and out of me at a slow pace. I could feel everything. Every ridge of his hard length rubbed against my inner walls, filling me with need and angry desire.

I wanted his aggression. Wanted to feel the power behind his muscles. I needed to feel his dominance, because Parker was right. I was, and always had been, his.

"Harder," I moaned, looking deep into his hooded gaze. "Fuck me, Parker. Show me I'm yours."

"Fuck, baby," Parker groaned, while sliding his tongue up my neck. His finger's speared into my hair, pulling my head back with a harsh tug, "Hang on, Angel, I'm gonna pound into this pussy."

That's exactly what I did. Clung onto his shoulders as he plowed into me with so much force my body shook with each thrust. The rougher he got, the tighter the coil deep in my belly got. I felt myself floating closer to the edge. It was right there. So close I could taste it.

"Parker," I whimpered, "Please."

"You want to come, baby?"

I looked up at him and nodded, but the bastard stopped.

"Do you love me, Angel?"

I froze, inner walls clenching around his length buried inside me. How could I say that? I didn't love him, did I? Sure, I'd followed him around and admired him from afar for years. I might know that his favorite color was yellow, and he didn't like cream in his coffee, but love?

I glanced around the bathroom at the tiles and knick knacks placed everywhere. Orchids, waterfalls and sunsets. All things I liked. Even the color scheme was my favorite. Parker hand picked everything in this house for me. He stood up to his mother for me. All of it, every decision he made was for me.

"Yes," I whispered, feeling my heart swell as I met his gaze, "I love you."

Parker smiled and gave me a little thrust. Just a taste of what I needed.

"Again."

"I love you," I repeated.

Another thrust, followed by a small rotation of his hips that made me moan desperately.

"Say it again."

This time he followed his order with a hard snap. Burying his length fast and deep inside me.

"I love you, Parker," I yelled in a growl, "Now, for fuck sakes, fuck me already!"

Finally Parker picked up the pace, giving my body what it needed and throwing me back into that cloud of euphoria. My pussy clenched down on him as I screamed out my orgasm. He didn't stop. Kept fucking me with a hungry fury, heightening my pleasure filled haze until I was sure I couldn't take anymore.

"You're mine, Lana," he growled, tightening his grip in my hair until my scalp was screaming. "Every fucking inch of you belongs to me. Your body," thrust, "your mind," thrust, "and your soul."

I pulled him down to me, pressing my forehead against his and looked deep into his eyes, "I'm yours."

"Fuck," Parker growled, and thrust into me one more time.

The masculine grunt of appreciation he released as he bathed my walls with his warm release sent me right back over the edge. We stayed in the bathroom, heavy breaths mingling in the sweat filled air, and all I could think was one word. A feeling I'd never felt so deeply before.

Home.

I was finally home.

Chapter 20

Parker

"**Y**ou're in a good mood."

I smiled at Mase. Fuck yeah, I was in a good mood. My girl loved me, our babies were doing great. Everything was falling into place. My mother even came over and apologized.

That didn't mean I trusted her, but she seemed to be making a genuine effort. Which was saying a lot. Maybe there was hope for her racist ass after all? At least that's what Lana thought. I loved how she saw the good in everyone.

Mase's eyes locked on the small redhead shuffling down the halls.

Well, my angel saw the good in *almost* everyone. Mase had

amped up his torment of her best friend to a point that even Logan told him to calm the fuck down.

I lost count how many times Riley kicked him in the nuts, and Mason was probably the only person in this town that Lana genuinely hated. Can't say I blamed her. If someone was that much of a jackass to one of my friends... Let's just say he wouldn't be around anymore.

Today was apparently no exception to Mase's 'make Harper's life hell' motto. The girl didn't get within ten feet of us before he had her pinned back against the wall.

"Hey Freckles, where you going?"

"I have class," Harper whimpered and shrunk back.

Mason cocked his brow down at her and I couldn't help but wonder how hard he was right now. I'd seen the same hungry glint in my own face. The only difference was Mase's expression was also filled with unbridled hate.

"Did you pay the toll?"

Her head immediately dropped, hiding her face behind a curtain of red hair. "P-please just l-let me g-go."

I glanced at Harper's openly shaking form, and back to Mase. He was built like a brick wall, big muscles, dwarfing the timid girl. I could help her. Tell Mase to back off, but why the fuck did I care? Besides, it was kind of amusing. How long before he broke and finally took what he wanted? Now *that* was a show I wouldn't mind being around for.

"P-please." Mase mocked with a tsk. "Just when I think you can't get more pathetic. You can't even beg properly."

I cocked my head and watched two tears drop on the floor, splattering in tiny little salty pools. Was this one of those times when I had to pretend like I felt something? Logan would join in, but what would Micha do?

"W-what do you want?"

"Hmm," Mase tipped his chin and rolled his green eyes down the length of her body. "You could suck my dick."

Harper's head snapped up, big doe eyes filled with shock. It was the spark in Mase's face that had my interest peaked.

"W-w-what?" she stammered, making Mase's gaze darken.

"You heard me." He leaned in a quietly growled, "Get on your knees, Freckles."

Fuck me. Was he actually going to do this shit. Now? Here? I think I was more shocked at the fact that Harper slowly sunk down. Sliding her back against the wall as she fell to her knees. The girl was terrified of him, yet she didn't hesitate. All he had to do was bark an order and she followed. I guess fear was a powerful motivator.

"You're kidding, right?" Mase scoffed down at her. "Do you honestly think I'd let you anywhere near my dick? How desperate do you think I am?"

The tears were really falling now. Harper sniffed back a humiliated cry and wiped the wet streaks off her cheeks with the back of her hand.

"I hate you."

"Not nearly as much as I hate you," Mase snarled back.

Harper's next whisper was so quiet, I had to strain my ears to hear it. "Were you ever my friend?"

That was a mistake. Mason had Harper off the ground, with his hand around her neck, before I could blink.

"I should be asking you that." His fingers dug into her skin, tightening his grip on her windpipe. "If it takes my last breath, I'll make sure you know nothing but pain and misery."

Speaking of breaths...

"Mase, come on, man."

"Go ahead," Harper struggled to cough out her words, "You can't punish me more than I punish myself."

A dark look came over Mase's face as he leaned in and growled, "Let's test that theory, shall we."

"Mase!" I called out. Seriously, the girl was starting to turn purple. If he wanted to kill her, fine. Just don't do it in a hall full of people. "Don't you have class?"

He grumbled under his breath and dropped Harper back on the ground.

Taking one last look at the crumpled, coughing heap at his feet, Mase said, "Whatever, I'm done here anyways," and walked down the hall.

"Parker, we don't need to be here. It's too early."

I chuckled and steered Lana through the doors. My little angel didn't want to be here. Not because it was too early, but because she was starting to get self conscious. Her small belly had grown over the past few weeks into a nice bump I could put both hands on. I loved it. Watching her grow was hot as fucking hell. Lana couldn't walk past me without me accosting her.

Fuck, right now I was having a hard time keeping my hands to myself. Watching her walk into this room full of pregnant women, knowing I was the one who put those babies in her belly. Not just one, but two. How many of these other pricks did that? If she'd let me, I'd parade her around proudly, announcing how much more effective my sperm was than theirs.

I met glares with Derek, who was across the room cooing at Paisley, and smirked. *That's right, fucker. My woman is having two.*

"Can you stop smiling?" Lana growled back at me, "I'm the one that has to push two babies out."

Yeah you do.

"Have I told you how beautiful you are today?"

"Yes," she sighed, pushing her pouty lips out, "This morning before we went to school, in the storage closet this afternoon, and again on the way here."

That reminded me, I needed to get a bigger car. My truck was not a comfortable place to fuck her. Though I wouldn't mind having her legs wrapped around my head again. *I wonder if there's a closet here?*

"Oh no you don't."

"What?"

Lana grabbed my hand and pulled me deeper into the crowd of fertile couples. "I know that look."

"You weren't complaining five minutes ago."

"Exactly," she said, "It's only been five minutes."

Was there something wrong with wanting my dick forever buried in the greatest pussy ever created?

I swept her hair to the side–which she was leaving curly more often, something I liked to think she did for me–and whispered in her ear, "Tell me thinking about sneaking off into one of these rooms isn't getting you wet."

The blush in her cheek was all the answer I needed.

Unfortunately, some skinny blonde bitch walked in and started the class, ruining my fun. Since I got to sit on a mat with my girl between my legs, I couldn't complain. And I was encouraged to put my hands on her.

Every time I slipped my hand under Lana's shirt to relaxingly massage her, I snickered. Relaxed was not even close to her jumpy state. My skin would meet hers and she'd twitch. Not out of fright or nervousness. I was turning her on. All I had to do to get her motor going was to touch her.

All she had to do to get mine going was look at me. I walked around hard as hell half the day, because she breathed in my direction, so fair is fair. Two could play at that game, and this class gave me the perfect excuse to paw all over her.

As a bonus, I also got to feel my babies kicking. Every time my hand skimmed over her stomach, a tiny little bump would respond. My boy and my girl letting me know they were there.

"Men, make sure the mothers are relaxed and cared for," the instructor's arms moved through the air, mimicking a massaging motion. "Remember, everything mommy feels, the baby can feel too."

My brow rose. *Everything?*

And just like that, my dick died.

Some guy to my right piped up, throwing his hand in the air. "Um, what about sex? Does my kid know when I'm banging their mother?"

Thank fuck he asked that.

The instructor gave him a small smile, while staring at him like he was the most innocent person on the planet.

"No, when you're being intimate with each other, the baby doesn't know what you're doing. However, the endorphins released during orgasm can improve both mommy and baby's mood."

The guy beamed back at her. "So, sex is good then?"

She nodded in response.

Now that I was no longer worried that my kids were getting front row seats to a live porn show, my dick jumped back to life. *Welcome back, old friend.*

"See, I told you," I heard Derek whisper to Paisley.

It was a good thing Logan wasn't here or Lamaze class would turn into a blood bath real fucking fast. Fucking momma's boy.

We went on with class, practicing breathing exercises and various stretches. Then came the live birth video. I stared at the woman screaming in pain as her pussy was forced open to ungodly limits. It was the most disturbing thing I'd ever witnessed, and my brother was Preston. How could I do this to the woman I loved? Lana was right, I was a prick.

Lana dropped her head back on my shoulder and whispered, "I can't do that."

"Sure you can, baby," I said, even though I doubted anyone could do that and come out sane.

"No, I can't," she shook her head. "I can't do it, Parker."

Before she had a full on panic attack, I pinched her chin between my thumb and finger and forced her to look at me.

"Yes, you can." I gazed deeply into those beautiful hazel eyes and felt myself immediately calm. "You're so beautiful," I kissed her on the forehead, "and smart," my lips moved down to her cheek, "and strong," I grazed my lips off her mouth, breathing the strength she was giving me back into her. "My perfect little angel. You can do anything you put your mind to."

The woman in the video was still screaming in the background, but it didn't bother me. Staring into my angel's eyes, I knew that nothing could stop us. Apart, we were okay. We could hold our own. But together, we weren't just strong.

We were invincible.

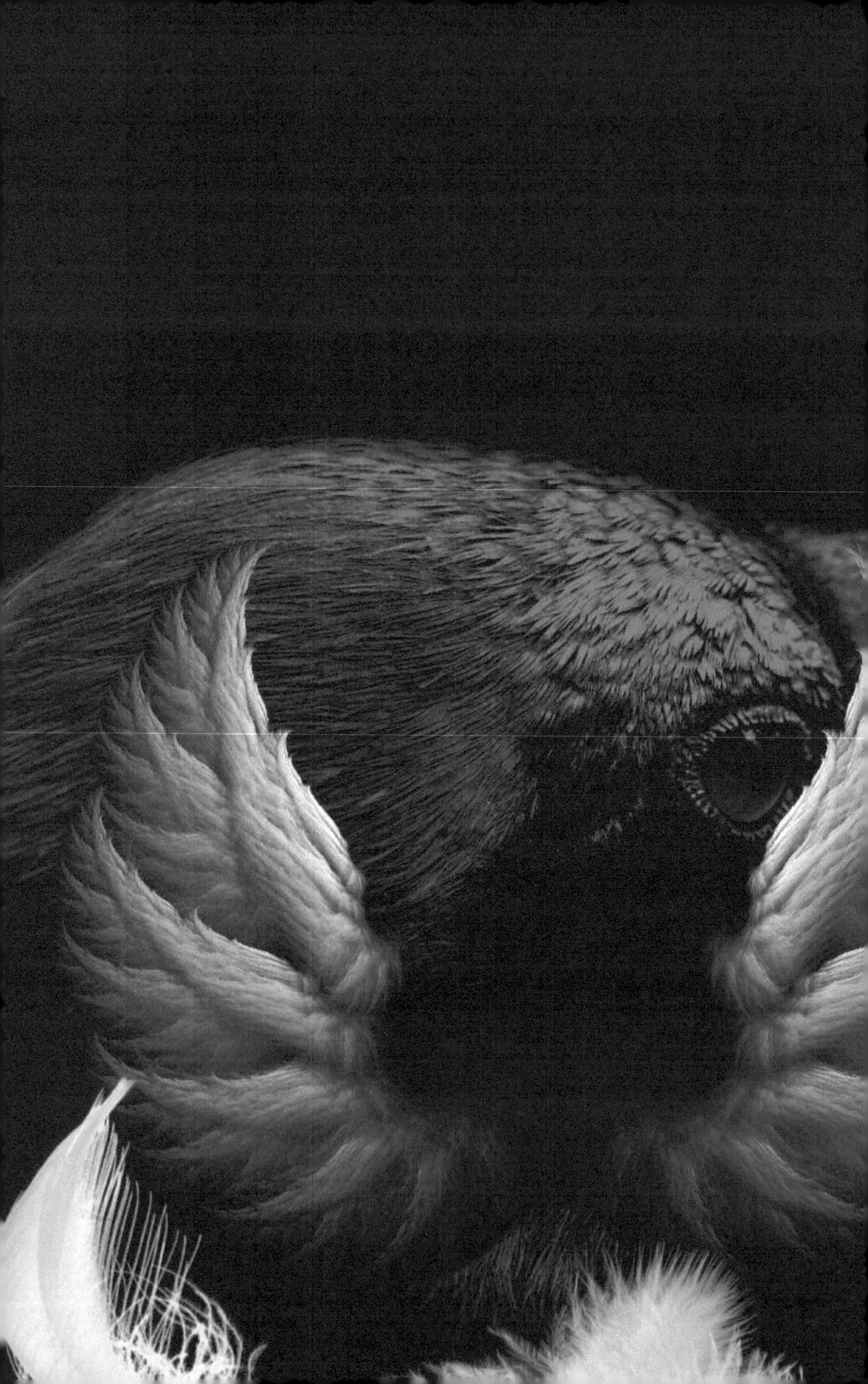

I was halfway through my first class when I got called to the office. Nerves flipped my stomach as I walked down the hall. I had a good idea why the principal wanted to see me.

Twins meant faster growth. Though the doctor did point out that because I was tall, the babies would grow up before having to push out. But there was no hiding my belly anymore.

I stared at the glass door marked office and wondered if I could claim to have a junk food addiction? *'Oh no, this isn't a baby, I just ate one too many bags of potato chips.'* *How good would potato chips be right now? Oo and French onion dip.*

Focus Lana!

These cravings were going to kill me. Last night, I ate a jar of pickles, with yogurt. Parker's lip curled as he watched me dip each one in the yogurt. At one point, I thought he might have me committed.

Hell, I wanted to have myself committed. Combining those two foods was not a normal thing to do, yet it tasted so good. And did Parker call the men in white to come put me in a straight jacket? No. He took the jar, carefully dipped each one in the creamy concoction, and fed me.

The past few weeks had been beyond anything I'd expected. I'd had my fantasies about Parker Whitley and the perfect relationship we could have, but the reality was so much better.

If my feet hurt, he massaged them. When I wanted something specific to eat, he went out and got it for me, and if I yawned, he'd cuddle close and lull me to sleep. The thing that tugged at my heart most, was the joy on his face.

Parker didn't do these things because he felt like he had to. He did it because he wanted to. The man loved taking care of me. And I loved letting him do it.

Well, most times I did. One thing I'd learned about Parker Whitley was how overbearing he could be. If he thought it should be done, there was no arguing with him. He was more stubborn than Nan.

Like the Lamaze class. I was only seventeen weeks. There was plenty of time to take it, but no. Parker had to have the information now. And that was my problem.

I'd become too comfortable. Thinking Parker would take care of everything, so that I wasn't paying attention to other things. Like Ashworth's hoity toity staff.

Having a pregnant girl walk the halls wasn't exactly great for their reputation. I glanced up at the school's motto written across the door, *'Welcome to Ashworth, the place where future leaders are born,'* and blew out a huff of air before pushing the door open.

Mrs. Grier's steely glare rolled over her square framed glasses as I entered the office. "Miss Crawford, please have a seat. We're still waiting on your grandmother."

I nodded and thickly swallowed. They'd called Nan? Well, this wasn't going to go well. Nan was probably gathering the troops, getting ready to picket outside the school. Parker's brother was a scary guy, but a bunch of angry old ladies... now, that was truly terrifying. I wouldn't be surprised if Nan's church group charged into Hell to take on the devil himself.

Speaking of terrifying...

My nose crinkled at the smirk on Mason's face. "Do you ever go to class?"

"Class is overrated." He patted the black chair next to him, which made me roll my eyes, and said, "Come join me in the row of rejects."

If there was any other option to sit, I'd have taken it. Heck, I'd have sat on the floor if it wasn't for Mrs. Grier. I didn't feel like getting in a debate with Ashworth's receptionist. I didn't even like her looking at me. That woman wasn't just a stickler for the rules, she had some freaky misbehaving radar.

The one time I'd considered cheating on a test, she'd cornered me in the hall and asked if I was prepared for my exam. Like she knew what I was thinking. Maybe Riley was right, and Mrs. Grier was a demon? I could picture her pitching something like the DMV and getting props from the devil for the idea.

Reluctantly, I carefully took the seat next to the youngest Kessler, who immediately threw his arm over my shoulders.

"So, what's Miss Goody Two-shoes doing in the bad girl's chair?"

Bad girl's chair, really?

I shrugged his arm off me and crossed mine. "I don't think we're supposed to talk to each other."

"You hear that, Edith?" Mason's lips rounded as he tsked in disapproval, "Lana here wants to follow the rules."

Mrs. Grier sighed and looked over at him. "As should you, Mr. Kessler."

A big grin spread across his face as he leaned in closer and whispered, "She wants me."

"Don't talk to me," I growled back.

Harper told me what he did to her yesterday. I was going to have a chat with Parker about that. He should've done something sooner. Then again, was it right of me to ask him to go against his friend for mine? Wasn't that the same as making him pick sides?

I hated people who did that. *I don't like him, so you can't.* Everyone should be allowed to have their own friends, and he did stop Mason when things got out of hand. I grumbled out a groan and slumped back. Since when did everything get so confusing?

My eyes slid over to Mason, sitting all proud like a peacock in his chair of punishment. Perhaps if I made an effort with Parker's friends, he would make one with mine?

"So, um… what'd you think of the game last night?" I had no idea what I was talking about, but there was always some kind of game on T.V.

Mason cocked a brow at me. "Which one?"

Crap.

"You, the uh… that one that was one."

Real smooth, Lana.

"Lana banana," his lips twisted in a smirk, "Are you attempting small talk?"

"Pfft, no."

He stifled a small snicker and nodded. "That's good, because you suck at it."

Screw making an effort.

"You know what, Mason," I huffed out, frustrated at his amusement, "Nevermind."

"No need to get your panties in a bunch," he chuckled, "All I'm saying is there are better things to chat about. Like porn."

This time my brow arched. *Seriously?* "Porn, really?"

"Porn is a sure fire way to a guy's attention."

Mrs. Grier growled from behind her desk. "That's enough talk about porn, Mr. Kessler."

"I bet she watches the freaky stuff," Mason whispered to me.

I don't think I'd ever been so happy to see Nan's pissed off expression. The curl in her lip usually meant I was in shit, though this time it wasn't directed at me. And I'd take Nan going head to head with Ashworth's receptionist, over discussing porn with Mason any day.

"You," Nan's arm flew up, finger pointed at Mrs. Grier, "Tell your boss I'm here."

Mrs. Grier's brow rose. "Pardon me?"

"You heard me!" Nan's chest puffed out as she stormed up to the stern woman's desk and slammed her hands down. "You think you can kick my girl out? I'll have twenty women storming these halls in minutes."

My face dropped in my open palm. If Nan made that threat, that meant she had the girls riled up and ready. If God was up there watching, he'd kill me now.

"If you kept a better eye on your granddaughter, then perhaps we wouldn't be having this meeting."

The lines in Nan's face deepened, intensifying her scowl.

Wrong move Mrs. Grier, it was nice knowing you.

"You listen here, you little chippy…"

Chippy? Nan really needed to learn some new insults.

Mason and I sat there watching the two older women bicker. Nan's emotions openly displayed, while Mrs. Grier remained cool as a cucumber.

Mason's eyes lit up as he enjoyed the show, I however, was pretty sure this was how I was going to die. My tombstone would read: H*ere lies Lana, she died of mortification.*

"Ah man," Mason groaned when the principal stepped out of his office, "Well, there goes my good time."

I sneered at him. "Do you always have to be a jerk?"

His answer was a single wink. Prick.

Nan's attention was instantly redirected to Mr. Sampson. I almost felt sorry for the guy. As far as principals went, he wasn't bad. Went a little too far trying to fit in with us kids, but he was nice. On a side note, it was really weird when someone close to sixty used teenage slang.

"I suppose you're the one giving my girl a hard time?"

"I assure you, the last thing I want to do is give Lana a hard time." Mr. Sampson's hand flew to his chest as he gave Nan a sympathetic look. "We just feel there are better places for your granddaughter, given her situation."

"Wait, " Mason interrupted, "So you're saying that all I have to do to get a girl kicked out of school is to knock her up?"

Mrs. Grier, Nan, Mr. Sampson, and I all stared at Mason. None of us were impressed, but it was Nan who voiced her opinion.

"Who is this fool?"

I'd complained about the prick beside me enough that Nan knew the name Mason Kessler, but she'd never met him.

My hand waved over to Mason, and back to Nan, as I spoke. "Nan, this is Mason. Mason, Nan."

This should be interesting.

Nan's eyes narrowed on Mason's cocky grin. "This is Mason?"

I nodded.

Before any of us could blink, Nan was across the room, arm swinging through the air. I watched Mason's expression morph from smug, to shocked, to confused, as her hand connected with his cheek.

"Ouch!" he cried out. "Why'd you hit me?"

"Because someone should," Nan answered, and I couldn't argue. If anyone in Ashworth needed a smack, it was Mason Kessler. "Picking on a sweet thing like Harper, you should be ashamed of yourself."

Mason grumbled under his breath and slumped back with his arms crossed. I think Mrs. Grier was a little jealous that Nan had managed to shut him up.

I'm not sure if Ashworth's principal was trying to save Mason from Nan's wrath, or if he wanted to avoid the spectators gathering in the hall, but either way, the three of us wound up in Mr. Sampson's office. Once we were alone, Nan went off.

Pacing around the room and swinging her finger through the air. Every argument Mr. Sampson made, Nan had a better one prepared. The debate kept going back and forth for so long, I was starting to get dizzy.

I tried to get a word in here or there. That wasn't happening. Every time I opened my mouth, one of them would interrupt me. Apparently my opinion didn't matter. It wasn't like this was my future they were deciding or anything. Playing on my phone seemed like a better option than getting between those two.

I was halfway through level six hundred and thirty nine in my puzzle game when the door to the office flew open. Seeing Parker there wasn't a big shocker.

Honestly, I thought he'd have shown up earlier. It was Micha, Logan and Preston standing in the doorway with him that had my mouth dropping in shock.

Mr. Sampson's eyes locked on Parker's glare. "This is a private meeting."

"Not anymore," Parker responded.

A shiver ran up my spine at the cold glint in his eyes. Parker looked downright deadly. Like he was ready to kill someone. Way too much like his brother.

Preston tipped his chin at me. "You sure you want her here for this?"

The second Parker's gaze fell on me, his face softened. "Angel, do me a favor and go sit with Mase."

I scanned the faces of the men funneling into the room and promptly got up. Whatever they had planned, I definitely didn't want any part of.

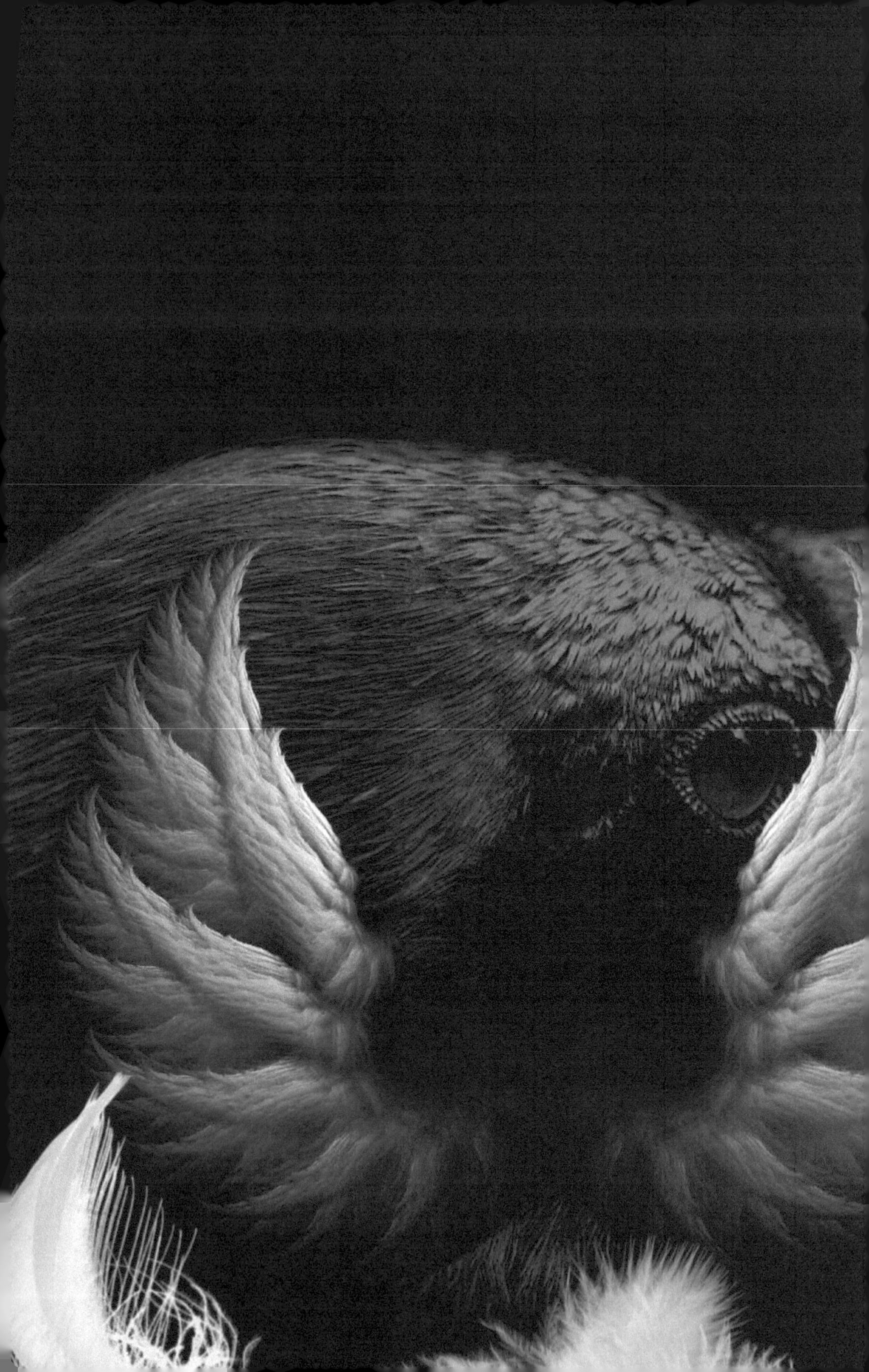

Chapter 22
Lana

$\mathcal{I}$ have no idea what Parker and his friends did, but when they came out, Mr. Sampson was suddenly kissing my ass. Asking if I needed anything to help accommodate my education through my pregnancy? And that wasn't the scary part.

That was the look Nan gave Preston while she thanked Parker. Whatever happened in that room, I highly doubted she'd be hitting him again for cussing. Was it wrong that a part of me found what they did sweet?

"He should be here soon." Harper wrung her hands nervously.

I felt for her. We'd been sitting in her kitchen for twenty minutes, waiting for Silas to show up. As suspected, her teacher paired them up. Today was the first day he could get together with her outside of school to work on their project.

"It'll be okay," I reassured her.

No matter how many times I told Harper that Silas would just want to work, she was terrified that Mason might show up with him. She was so pent up about it that when the doorbell chimed loudly, she physically jumped.

I grabbed her hand and gazed into her big doe eyes, trying to let her feed off my strength. "You've done projects with Silas before. Just concentrate on doing the work."

She sucked in a deep breath and gave me a small nod. I'd seen her do this before. It was the calm before the storm. Her body stopped trembling and she'd sit up straight, pretending she was okay.

But inside, there was a cloud of fear and sadness just waiting to burst out. If Mason stepped through that door, then the fragile dam keeping Harper together, would shatter.

Thankfully, that didn't happen. The only people Harper's maid Becca led in were Silas, and a younger boy.

"Sorry," Silas placed his hand on the boy's shoulder, "I had to bring my cousin."

I'd never met the infamous genius of the Creswell family, he spent most of his time at a special school, but the family resemblance was undeniable. They both had the same black hair and light eyes.

My heart broke at the dark circles under Finn's eyes. Everybody had heard about what happened to his parents. Their entire house had burnt down in an electrical fire, which Finn was home for.

The loss of my parents was a hole I could never fill, but I was so young when it happened. I couldn't imagine the pain Finn was going through right now. His mom and dad weren't faded images in the back of his mind.

He had memories of them. He could remember how they smelled, and sounded. What they liked to do for Christmas. For him, their deaths weren't a healed scar, they were a fresh cut wound. Still bleeding and raw.

I wanted to cry when Silas's finger tightened on his cousin's shoulder. Strictly by the books Silas had a reputation for being a grumpy, uncaring, jerk, but that single action had more emotion than any word, action, or expression. If he could, he'd take the pain for his cousin. Just like I would for Harper.

"He won't be any trouble," Silas promised when none of us answered.

"Don't worry about him." I stood up and walked over to Finn, "I'm sure we can find something to do."

Finn eyed my hand warily for a second, but when I gave him a small smile, Silas nodded and Finn took my hand. I don't know why I took him out back and led him down the small trail behind Harper's house.

The small beach below was one of the few places Harper felt safe. And I got the feeling that that was something Finn desperately needed. We followed the barely visible path down the hillside where my best friend's house sat, and quietly enjoyed the day.

It was beautiful out. The sun was shining warmly down on us as the breeze carried the salty scent of ocean air. One of those days an author would write a poem about. Just like the beach we stopped at was the perfect portrait for a painter.

Soft tan sand, and crystal clear water. Tucked inside a rocky cavern, as if God himself had carved a hole in the land. Harper and I had stumbled on this place when we were little. It was our secret getaway, complete with flower patches and fluffy green shrubs. The only other person that knew about it was Mason. The three of us used to play here.

Finn's eyes wandered over the crystal pool and up the rocky walls. "This is pretty."

"Harper and I used to come here a lot." I glanced around, smiling at the memories of my happy friend.

Finn's brows furrowed. "You don't anymore?"

"Not as much as I'd like to."

He didn't say anything, just released my hand and walked over to the water, to swirl his fingers in it.

We stayed there for awhile, me sitting on the sand as the little boy took everything in. I couldn't help but admire the curious glint in his light eyes.

He was fascinated by everything. Touching all the plants, and feeling each surface as if he was committing the sense to memory. It was amazing to watch. When he sat down beside me and rolled those light eyes to my belly, I couldn't help but smile.

"Does it hurt when you feel them?"

"No," I chuckled. "It did freak me out the first time, though."

"It did?"

"Uh huh," I nodded. "Wanna feel?"

Before Finn could answer, I placed his hand on my stomach. When the baby kicked his palm, his eyes flew open in amazement. He moved closer and stared at my stomach as he placed his other hand flattened against my shirt.

The next thing I knew, a million questions were flying out of his mouth. What's my birthing plan, will Parker be in the room, how much do I eat? I answered each one, glad that the frown on his face had disappeared, if even for a little bit.

Once his curiosity was sated, he sat back down beside me and gazed out at the water. His lips tipped down in a small frown. Whatever happy moment he had, had passed. Finn was so different from the older boys.

There was this aura of broken innocence around him that called to my protective instinct. I wanted to wrap him up in my arms and shield him from the world, because I knew the pain in his eyes all too well.

"I lost my parents too," I said, while staring out at the water with him. "They died in a plane crash when I was three."

A tear rolled down Finn's cheek. "What do you do when you miss them?"

"I try and remember the good things I have."

"I don't have any good things," he muttered, breaking my heart a little more.

"What about your cousin?" Silas seemed to love him.

"He knows too much." Finn dropped his head on his knees and sighed. "He says he doesn't look at me differently, but he does."

He knows too much? I didn't understand what he meant by that. Either way, I needed to help him. Make him see that there was good in the world. I pulled our Gramps' pocket watch, and held it up.

"My Gramps gave me this." The gold watch sparkled in the sunlight as I spoke. "He told me that anytime I felt like giving up, I should look at this and remember that time was too short to waste on sadness and misery. All that mattered in life was the memories you made with the people you loved."

I could see the wheels turning in Finn's mind as he stared at the watch in my hand.

"Here," I said, passing it to him, "You should take it."

His fingers reached out, gingerly tracing the eagle on the face. "I can't."

"Sure you can." I dropped it in his palm before he could argue and nudged him with my shoulder. "Besides, I don't need it anymore."

I had a man that loved me, and a family on the way. Parker gave me everything I needed and more. It was time for Gramps to help someone else.

THE LAST PERSON I expected to be standing outside my door when I pulled up was Luke. It felt strange to call him Mr. Lannister now.

I considered him a friend. We talked every day at school, and had recently started texting.

Parker wasn't high on it. Said he didn't like the way Luke looked at me, which was absolutely ridiculous. We were just friends. He also didn't argue our relationship too much.

My head tipped at the plant in Luke's hands. A tall leafy mini tree, with purple flowers.

He smiled when I got out of the car. "Hey, perfect timing. I was just about to ring the doorbell."

"Hi," I waved and walked over. "I'm surprised to see you here."

"It's not too weird, is it? I heard what happened in school today and wanted to make sure you were okay. And," he nodded at the plant, "It's kind of a tradition where I come from to bring friends house warming presents."

Okay, that was sweet.

"Well, thank you." I smiled up into his bright eyes and grazed my fingers over one of the leaves. "Would you like to come in?"

"I'd love to."

We walked inside and Luke handed me the plant, which looked absolutely perfect on the table by the door. I had to hand it to him, he had impeccable taste. It was simple and exquisite. I led him into the kitchen, where I poured us both a cup of lemonade, and we chatted for a bit.

I don't think Luke had made many friends in Ashen Springs, and it was nice to have a normal conversation. He was one of the few people that didn't bring up my pregnancy, or my abrupt move in with Parker. When I was with Luke, I was just Lana. And I missed being just Lana.

"I met Naomi's mom today."

"Oh God." I rolled my eyes. Mrs. Prescott was almost as bad as her daughter, and the woman had a reputation. "Please tell me she didn't hit on you."

"She didn't just hit on me, she outright offered to suck me off."

He took a sip of his lemonade and shook his head, "Right there on the field."

I watched his dark hair flop forward and thought about Naomi's mom. She was pretty, tall, and blonde like her daughter, and Luke was cute. It wouldn't be the worst girl he could have a fling with. Jasmine's mom, on the other hand…

"Did you take her up on it?"

He scowled. "God no."

"Why not? She's pretty, and you're…" I clamped my mouth shut before I said something stupid.

Luke's eyes sparkled back at me. "She's not really my type."

That was fair. As Mason would say, different strokes for different folks. That did get me thinking though. Luke Lannister had been in town for a while now, and I hadn't seen him with anyone. A guy like him should have all kinds of rumors floating around. Whispers about late night rendezvous and secret meetings, but I hadn't heard a single word in the gossip mill.

"What is your type?" I asked, genuinely curious. "Do you even have one?"

His lips tipped up as his eyes skimmed over me. "Oh, I have a type."

If I didn't know any better, I'd say he was eyeing me. But that couldn't be right. Luke Lannister was the gorgeous new staff member girls admired, and I was just a girl. And a pregnant one, at that. My stomach was getting fat and my boobs were too big. Who would want that? I had to be imagining things.

"Has anyone told you," he turned around on his stool and swept my hair behind my ear, "You have beautiful eyes."

Shocked, I pulled back a bit and thickly swallowed. Nope, not imagining things.

"Luke," I stammered, not quite sure what to say or how to react. "I… huh…"

"Tell me you haven't thought about it." His thumb grazed over my bottom lip, sending a shiver up my spine.

This is bad, Lana.

"Parker should be home any minute," was all I could think to say.

"Good," he leaned in and whispered, "I'd like to fuck him too."

Oh my god.

"Care to run that by me!" a deep voice boomed through the room.

Uh oh, hubby's home.

Chapter 23

Parker

All I could think about while stepping through that door after a tough day at practice, was holding my girl. Sucking in her sweet scent and settling back into a nice quiet night at home. Get some food, watch a flick–*Steel Magnolias*, her favorite–and have myself a little dessert.

The perfect night, with the perfect girl. And what did I find when I walked into that kitchen? Some motherfucker eyeing up my woman. Whispering shit in her ear.

I should kill him.

Had three different plans to dispose of his body before the next breath left my lips.

"Parker should be home any minute."

That's right, baby, you tell him. Poor thing didn't know what to do when shit got real with her 'friend'.

My fists balled. I'd told Lana I didn't like the way this prick looked at her. But did she listen? No. My angel, sweet little thing that she was, thought they were just friends.

Guys like Logan and Mason used the friend claim all the time. Because girls never suspected their friends. It was a good thing she had me around to protect her from fucks like Luke Lannister.

After my angel got that note, this prick was at the top of my list of suspects. Luke Lannister from Ohio. Star track runner turned assistant coach.

He'd won multiple trophies, was offered numerous scholarships, and carried both his high school and college team to championships. Exactly the kind of athlete Ashworth would recruit. Even though he was just a runner.

Pfft. Pussy.

Luke's sparkling eyes locked with mine as his lips curled and he leaned in closer to my girl.

This prick wants to die.

"Good," he said, "I'd like to fuck him too."

My brow lifted. That shit, I was not expecting. I didn't like being caught off guard. Fuck this guy.

"Care to run that by me!"

My angel squeaked and jumped back, while the smile on Luke's face spread wide.

"Parker," Lana's pretty eyes glittered with shame and fear, making me want to hurt this fucker even more. "When did you get home?"

Just in time, Angel. I got home just in time.

"Come here, Baby." I opened my arms and ushered her to me.

Lana jumped off the stool and rushed into my embrace. Keeping my eyes on the prick watching us, I leaned down and took her mouth in a deep kiss. Fuck, she tasted good. My dick sprang to life the second her tongue touched mine.

"You want to hit me right now," Luke rested his elbow on the island and tipped his head, "Don't you?"

Fuck yeah I want to hit you. Cocky, smug, fuck.

"Parker," My sweet angel's voice flowed through my ears, pulling back the red blurring my vision. "Don't," she warned, placing her palm on my cheek. "Please."

I gazed into her hazel eyes, studying the way her pupils dilated while her breath came out in short shallow gasps. Was my angel turned on? Suddenly I was eyeing the asshole sitting in my kitchen for a different reason.

After all, there were other ways to teach pricks like him a lesson. Besides, I wouldn't mind seeing what was under his jeans and shirt. Hell, I could see the outline of his cock from here.

"You're thinking about it, aren't you?" Luke rose off the stool and stalked across the room. "How good I'd feel." His hand swept down Lana's back, making her shiver in my arms. "How good she feels." His eyes rolled up to mine as he stepped in, flattening his front against my angel's back. "How good we'd feel."

Fuck. The gasp that left Lana's mouth had my dick trying to punch through the fabric of my jeans. I liked the way her feminine body looked, sandwiched between two walls of muscle. How she quietly trembled in confusion and arousal.

My hand slid down her back, grazing over Luke's hard-on, and I reached down and cupped her ass. Firm and hard, while tugging her soft body into mine.

"You want to fuck him, baby?"

"What?" Her eyes flew from me to the man behind her. "Um... I don't..."

A smirk tugged at Luke's features. I wasn't the only one getting turned on by her uncertainty. He swirled a strand of her hair between his fingers and asked, "Think she can handle it?"

My angel could handle anything. She just needed a little reassurance.

I took a step back, pulling Lana with me, and then spun her around while nodding at the other man. "Take your clothes off."

Lana's breath hitched when Luke's fingers wrapped around the hem of his shirt as he peeled the fabric over his head.

"Parker?" Her eyes snapped up to me, searching for comfort. I fucking loved the way she looked. How in her most awkward moments, she came to me.

"Shhh," I whispered, tipping her chin back to Luke. "Look at him." A shuddered gasp left her lips as Luke's fingers moved down to his belt. Deftly unbuckling the leather and allowing him to flick open the button on his jeans.

"Watch how his muscles twitch in anticipation. Feel the lust in his eyes." I pushed my hand down her skirt to finger her pussy and groaned at the wetness coating my skin. "See how hard you make him."

The other man's pants were off now, giving us a nice view of the large tent in his boxer briefs. Underneath that fabric was a nice thick shaft. Hard, and aching to go. Lana moaned out my name and dropped her head back.

I'd never make my angel do something she didn't want to do. The second I saw her face twisted in pleasure, I knew she might be hesitant, maybe a little afraid, but she wanted it as much as I did.

I gave Luke a look. The same one that all men in this position understood. A simple tip of the brow that meant it's go time. He stepped in and pressed his lips down onto hers, taking over her pleasure as I pulled off the constricting fabric of my clothes.

Once I was done, we worked on Lana. Needy hands tearing away her shirt and skirt to bare the supple flesh underneath. Soon we were three bodies pressed together in a heady cloud of heavy desire.

I grabbed the base of my cock and thrust into her from behind. Heat enveloped my shaft, sending a tingle up my spine. My angel gasped, pussy fluttering as she clung onto Luke's shoulder to steady herself.

"Fuck," I groaned, looking for a better place to do this.

I wanted to watch her touch him. See his hands and tongue slide all over her body, and that shit wasn't going to happen standing in the middle of the kitchen.

Luke must've read my mind, because he tipped his chin at the two seated lounge chairs in the corner by the back door. Within seconds we were over there. Me laying back as my girl bounced on my cock, while Luke's fingers toyed with her clit.

I watched my shaft, glistening with her juices, disappear into her tight channel, and glanced up to Luke's hand buried in her hair. My dick twitched at the way his mouth worked her. Lips swollen and wet, while their tongues tangled.

He climbed on the lounger with his, hot balls brushing against my skin as he straddled my legs with her and growled in her mouth, "You taste fucking delicious."

Fuck yeah she did. But what did he taste like?

I sat up, speared my fingers in his thick hair, and tore his mouth off hers, bringing it to mine. Lana's arm flew up, wrapping around my neck as her hips rolled.

Her other hand slid down his chest, fingers skittering across his skin and down to his cock, making Luke groan in my mouth and me to deepen the kiss. Tongues swirling and teeth clacking in a fight for male dominance neither one of us was ready to give up.

But I'd played this game before. I knew how to control, not only my woman, but a man as well. I reached down, fingering my girl's clit until she was screaming and gushing hard all over my cock. Luke barely had time to appreciate the sticky mess my girl made, before I glided my hand over the glorious firmness of his ass and pushed a finger inside.

To my surprise, he sunk into it. Pushing back when I forced in another finger while sliding his hand down my side. Had he done this before? My question was soon answered. Luke lifted Lana off my dick and shuffled up to take her place.

Her heated gaze stared down at me. Watching my eyes roll into the back of my head as he slowly sank down on my shaft, forcing my cock past his tight ring of muscles with a masculine grunt.

I fell back in the lounger, pulling my girl with me and nuzzling her neck. Her sweet scent, the salty taste of her hot skin, along with the tight grip of Luke's ass was pure ecstasy. Then the familiar sound of a foil packet being torn open peaked my ears, and Lana was pulled back, slammed hard on the other man's cock, and I damn near came.

Luke's hips rocked back and forth, fucking both Lana and I at the same time. The look on her face as her fingers dug into my skin, was better than any drug. The intoxicating blend of pleasure and confusion. The way her wet lips parted with each gasp and moan. That's all I wanted to see before I died. My girl, happy, pleasured, and carefree.

I cupped her face and pulled her down to me, enjoying the way her garbled groans warmed my face. "I love you. baby."

"I love you too," she said, placing the sweetest kiss on my lips.

I smiled up at her. My beautiful sweet angel. "Come for me."

And she did. Hard and fast. Followed by Luke, and then me.

We laid there for a bit, breaths mingling as I gently stroked my girl's back, but eventually Luke got up and gathered his clothes. Without a word, he got dressed, nodded at me, and left.

I appreciated that. His simple understanding that this was my time with my girl and his presence was interfering with that. Physical attraction was one thing. Anyone could fuck. The emotional bond I had with the woman I loved... That was sacred and deserved to be nurtured. Which was exactly what I planned to do. Every damn day of my life.

"Come on, baby," I said, scooping my angel up and carrying her up the stairs. "Let's take a bath."

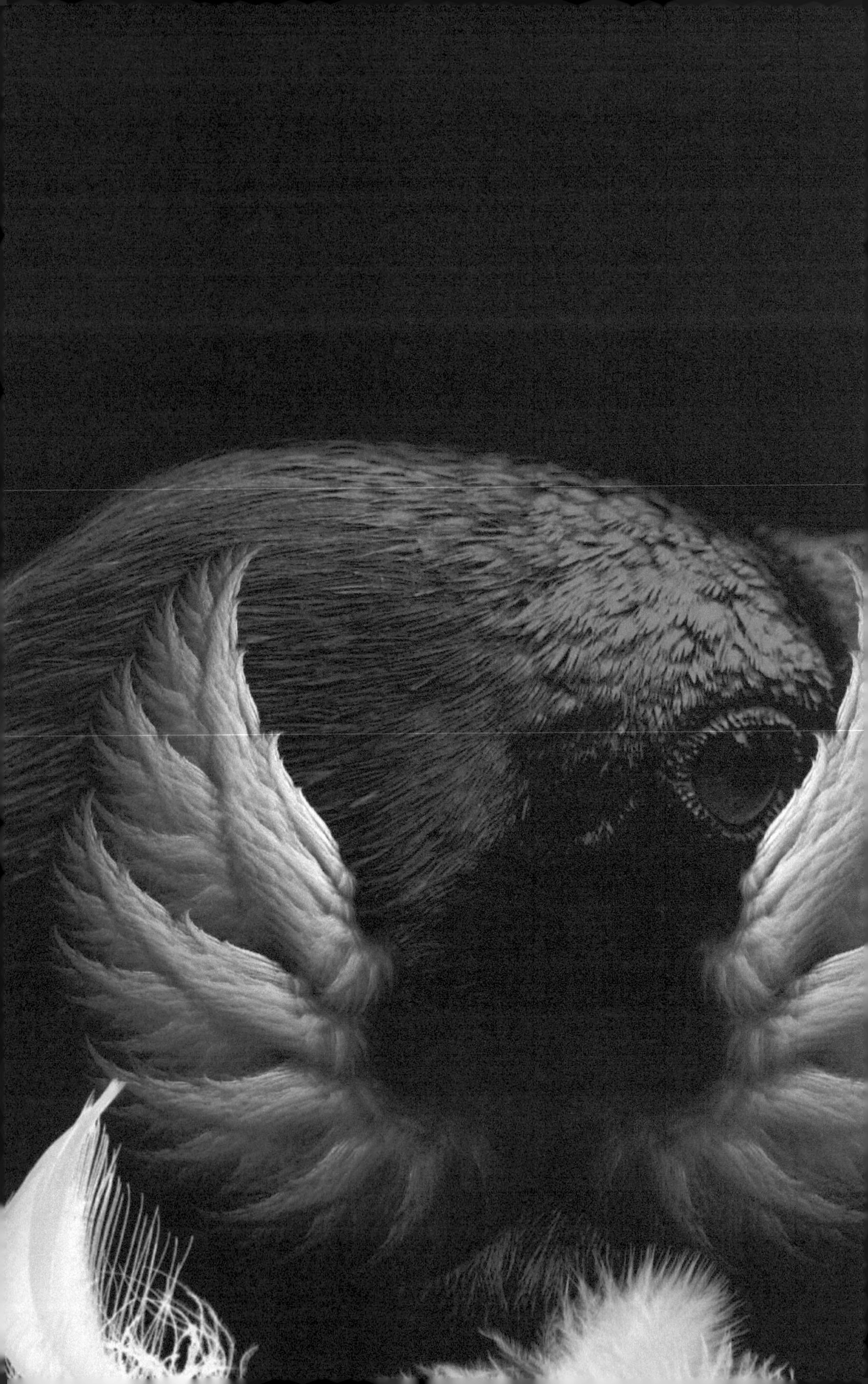

Chapter 24

Lana

I sat in the warm water, sucking in the vanilla scent of the bubbles, and tried to sort out my mind. Parker sat behind me, carefully scrubbing a loofa over my skin. Each tender stroke reminding me that I'd just had sex.

With two men. Guilt prevented me from melting back into him. I could still feel Luke's hands on me, and his thickness filling me up, while I stared into Parker's eyes.

My husband's eyes.

Did he hate me? I said I loved him, and I did. But who did that to someone they loved? He must hate me.

"I'm sorry," I muttered quietly.

"For what?"

He didn't even stop. Parker's fingers continued to glide over my skin, washing away the sweat and grime. But nothing he could do, would cleanse my soul.

"I let another man touch me."

I felt him tense and braced for the heartbreak that was sure to come.

"Baby," he pressed under my chin and tipped my head back, forcing me to meet his gaze. "I'm not mad at you."

"You're not?" My brows furrowed. Was this a trick?

"No," He snickered and kissed my forehead. "I liked watching you get fucked."

Okay, now I was really confused. Parker went off at school the other day because he thought Brandon was staring at my ass. And he was constantly badgering me about Luke's intentions, which it turned out, he was right about. Bet he wasn't going to let me live that down.

"But I thought you didn't like Luke?"

"I don't."

That made even less sense.

"So, why did you want to do that with him?"

His brow arched. "Why did you?"

Huh? Why did I? I mean, Luke was cute and all, but I'd always seen him as a friend. I think?

"I don't know," I said, trying to remember who even started that.

Was it me? Parker? Did Luke start it? He did hit on me, so that would make sense. Then again, Parker told him to take his clothes off. I can't believe he did that. *Wait... what were we talking about? Oh right, my horrible betrayal of the man I loved.*

"Okay?" My eyes narrowed skeptically.

Parker chuckled and pulled me into him. "Have I mentioned how cute you are?"

I sighed. Cute? My loving husband really needed to think of better compliments.

"Come on," Parker kissed the top of my head and got out of the tub, "We should get you dressed and tucked into bed."

I sat in the water, staring at his outstretched arm, unable to move. On his inner wrist, glaring back at me with a mocking glint, was a small black raven. I'd forgotten about Dr. Creswell and my suspicions. The whole twins thing kind of took over.

Parker cocked his head at my expression. "Something wrong?"

"No." I shook my head and accepted his help out of the tub. "Everything's peachy."

Other than you being in a secret society that probably sacrifices virgins under the moonlight, that is.

I eyed Parker, watching him carefully as he dried me off. I loved him. I really did. My heart swelled every time he looked at me. But how much did I really know about him?

"Parker, have you ever killed anyone?"

I don't know what bothered me more. The fact that he continued toweling me off, not at all disturbed by my question, or the response he gave me.

"Do you really want me to answer that?"

That was a yes.

My husband, the man I loved, and whose children I was carrying, was a killer! There was literal blood on his hands. My eyes searched his face as Parker stood up and pulled a shirt over my head. *So, why wasn't I afraid of him?*

Once I was dressed, Parker led me out of the bathroom and told me to get into bed. I slipped under the covers, thinking about Riley and Shelby. They weren't scared of their boyfriends, and Logan Hudson was definitely someone people should be wary of.

Not to mention Micha Kessler. That boy had way too much power. All he had to do was look at someone and they'd move. I'd never understood what my friends saw in them, but I was starting to understand.

It was love.

Parker threw on a pair of grey sweats and slipped into bed next to me.

"I have something for you." He pulled me into his arms and held out a small box. "Beautiful rings fit for my beautiful wife."

My hand flew over my mouth, muffling a gasp. Inside the box were two rings. One had sparkling deep sapphires decorating the petals of an orchid, and the other was a gold band of intricate stems and leaves. I gingerly reached out, carefully tracing the edges of the flower.

"Why?" Was all I could spit out.

It wasn't my birthday, and I certainly hadn't done anything to deserve such a gift.

"We are married," he pointed out. "Don't you think you should have an engagement and wedding ring?"

My hand dropped.

"I can't wear these." It was a sweet gesture but... "People are going to ask about them and wonder why we didn't have a wedding." How was I supposed to explain that?

Parker sucked in a deep breath and eyed me.

"How about this. You wear the engagement ring," he slipped the band with the orchid around my finger and added, "And we'll have a wedding after the babies are born?"

I had to admit, I liked how the ring looked on my hand, and it was a perfect fit.

"Isn't a wedding a waste of money?"

Parker barked out a laugh. To someone like him, watching what he spent wasn't exactly a necessity.

I swear to god, if he calls me cute again...

"Baby, you don't have to worry about that stuff anymore. And just so you know," he pulled me tightly into his warm embrace, "I'd spend my last cent to make you happy."

And there he goes with the sweet crap again.

"Fine," I sniffed, wiping away a tear. "I'll wear the stupid ring. But if I'm going to marry you..."

"We're already married," he pointed out.

I rolled my eyes. *Whatever. Technicality.*

"There's a few things I need to know." My gaze once again landed on the raven on his wrist, "Like what I'm marrying into."

Parker let out a long sigh. "You saw the tattoo."

So he wasn't denying it.

"Most of the rumors are bullshit."

My eyes narrowed. "But there is an Order?"

"Yes."

"And you're in it?"

"Yes," he nodded. "But you don't need to worry about that."

While my body was exhausted from our little rendezvous with Luke, I was giddy. For years I'd been searching for information. Pulling apart each piece of gossip, hoping to find an ounce of evidence, and here Parker was confirming everything I'd suspected. I wanted to know everything. Questions flew out of mouth at an uncontrollable rate.

"Who's in it? Where do you meet? Do you really sacrifice virgins?"

The next one came out before Parker could answer the previous. My mind was a jumble, picturing him and his friends chanting in dark robes next to firelight. Micha passing around a goblet of blood from their fresh sacrifice, while wolves howled in the distance. Of course, I knew that it was ridiculous. I'd paid way too close attention to way too many movies. That didn't stop my imagination.

Parker, god love him, waited patiently for my words to run out. He didn't even scoff at any of the craziness coming out of my mouth.

He simply sat back and watched my lips move with a smirk on his face. By the time I'd run out of things to say, my brain joined my body, causing me to cuddle up to Parker as a deep yawn left my mouth.

"Answer me," I grumbled, fighting to keep my eyes open.

"Shh," he hushed in my ear while pulling the blankets over us. "Sleep now."

Heaviness settled in my limbs and my eyes began to shut. "But I need to know."

"No you don't."

My lips twisted in a pout and I muttered, "Yes I do," before the sandman swept me away to dreamland.

"*I* swear to god, I'm going to kill your sister."

I couldn't help but chuckle at Lana's angry tone. Ava had gone from loving aunt, to full on obsessed stalker, calling Lana every hour to see if she'd gone into labor yet. I was excited too, and more than ready to start the next phase.

I loved how my girl looked all big and swollen with my babies, but she was grumpy as fuck and wanted this shit done with.

"Ava's just excited." I laid my hand on her leg and gave her thigh a squeeze. "She doesn't want to miss the birth."

Not that she was going to be in the room when my children came into the world. The doctor said only one person was allowed in there, and it sure as fuck wasn't going to be my sister.

"If I ever give birth," Lana grumbled, and dropped her head back.

Poor thing. We were still ten weeks out from our due date and she looked ready to pop. Which she probably was. Twins rarely came on their due date. They were usually early. Which was exactly why I had to-go bags packed into every vehicle we owned. I even made my dad and Lana's Nan put one in their trunk.

My angel's lips curled as I pulled up outside Ashworth.

"Ugh, how come you don't have to go to school."

"I'm two days away from graduation," I reminded her, "And you still have exams."

After our discussion with the principal, which was more of an argument, until Preston showed Mr. Sampson a video of his granddaughter at the playground, Ashworth had become very accommodating.

They even offered to let Lana take her final exams online. She declined, insisting she was no different than anyone else. Ever try telling a pregnant woman to calm down?

I jumped out of our new SUV–never thought I'd be driving one of those–and dashed around to help my wife get out.

"Come on, Baby," I said, holding my hand out.

Her fingers wrapped around mine as she groaned and struggled to shuffle out. I watched her nose crinkle and felt my dick jump.

Lana might not think she was sexy right now, but I though she was hot as fuck. Her skin was glowing, though she claimed it was sweat, and she smelled absolutely delicious. All I wanted to do was run my tongue all over her.

One loud oomph and a sharp tug from me and my sweet angel was on her feet.

"I hate this," she cried, tucking her face into my chest to hide her tears. "I'm so fat."

I cupped her face, turning her teary eyes up to mine while kissing her head, and cheek, and then the tip of her nose.

"You're beautiful."

This was my time to shine. The moments when I was the one thing she needed. There was nothing in this world that could compare to her gentle sighs or pretty smile. I didn't need the promised land, or a spot in paradise, because taking care of Lana was my heaven.

"Hey," Luke sauntered over and tipped his chin at the wet streak on Lana's face, "Bad day?"

I shook my head. "She's good, aren't you, baby?"

"I'm hungry," Lana grumbled in response.

I snickered at her grumpy tone. "I packed some snacks in your bag."

"Pickles?"

"Of course."

"And those granola bars I like."

I nodded. "Got those too."

"What about…"

"Don't worry," I placed my lips on her forehead and carefully passed her to Luke, "I didn't forget the blueberries."

And there it was. That happy little spark in her cheek that made my life worth living.

I leaned against the SUV and watched Luke guide her into school. A few months ago, I'd wanted to kill the asshole, and now… The three of us played a couple more times, but the more he came over, the closer we got, and physical attraction gave way to friendship. Luke was one of the few people I trusted to take care of my wife when I wasn't around. Silas was too grumpy and Mase was… well… Mase.

My phone dinged, drawing my attention from my wife's retreating form.

Mase: You coming?

Me: Don't you have exams?

Mase: Got pulled out. Order business trumps school.

I could practically see his head shake while he mocked his father's words. To say Mase liked rebelling against Lou's rules was an understatement. I think he got off on jerking his old man's chain.

Me: Why are you texting me?

Mase: Got no car remember.

Ah, yes I forgot about Lou's conditions to his youngest son getting out of rehab. No parties, no late nights, and no driving were just a few.

Me: And you need me to pick you up?

Mase: You get a gold star.

Asshole.

Me: Give me twenty to swap out the kid mobile and I'll be there.

Mase: Ten four, but hurry up. The teas getting cold.

My brows furrowed at my phone. Tea? Was Mase high again?

THIRTY MINUTES later and I was standing in Oakleigh Manor staring out at the backyard with my head cocked in confusion.

What the fuck?

My eyes wandered from the little blonde girl–who I assumed to be Shelby's sister–and over to Mase, sitting in a tiny pink chair with a big flowery hat on his head. Around the table sat various stuffed animals and a rather unamused Junior.

Each one of them had a tiny pink tea cup placed in front of them on the table and what looked like a fake scone. The little girl walked over to Mase and tipped the teapot in her hand. Whatever she said caused him to throw his head back with a loud laugh and point at a stuffed brown dog.

Seriously, what the fuck?

With a shake of my head, I made my way to the backyard. Which I immediately regretted when Junior looked at me. The kid didn't need to say anything, the warning was written all over his face. *Run man. Get the fuck out of here while you still can.*

Unfortunately, I didn't see Finn standing by the bushes, holding a tray, until he called my name.

"Parker!" he jumped up and excitedly bounded over. "Look! I'm playing butler!"

Junior's eyes met mine.

Well, you're screwed now, may as well sit the fuck down.

"That's great, Finn." I tousled his hair and eyed the pink apron neatly tied around his waist. The Kessler house hadn't seen this much pink in well... ever.

"You're just in time for tea," the little girl sang while waving at the one and only empty chair.

I glared at Mase's smirk. Why did I get the feeling he'd planned this shit?

"Thanks," I gave the girl a smile, "But Mase and I have to be going."

"You heard the girl," Mase barked back. "It's tea time. Now sit the fuck down."

Junior's dark eyes mocked me.

Told you.

I don't know how it happened, but I somehow found myself sitting at a tiny pink table with a big goofy fucker and an angry kid. The worst part was, I got a hat too.

The little girl, Mags, I'd learned, walked around pouring us tea while spinning tales of cats and dragons. Unlike her sister, Mags was a fierce little thing. Every time one of us tried to get up, she was on that shit. Harping on us and bringing out the tears.

That puffy bottom lip and puppy dog eyes made me crumple quicker than a flimsy piece of tissue paper. The military should harness that shit. That little girl's pout had the power to topple nations.

Mase and Finn seemed perfectly happy soaking in every word she said. Junior and I, though… I was pretty sure Junior was trying to plot a means of escape as well. So far I'd come up with one. Death. Either mine, or hers.

At this point, I didn't really care which. Hell, I'd jab one of the plastic forks in my own neck if it'd get this floppy straw hat off my head. I could see the gigantic blue flowers dancing in my shadow.

I'd never been so happy to see the sheriff's name pop up on my phone. I put the phone to my ear and held my finger up, silencing Mags before she could pull me back into her web.

"Hello."

"Parker," Derek's voice came across the line, "There's been an accident."

My heart stopped. "Lana?"

"No," he said, allowing me to breathe again, "Her grandmother."

That was a little better, but not much. My angel loved her Nan, and she was in no condition to have an emotional breakdown.

"Is she okay?"

Mason perked up at my question, eyes locking on mine as the smile fell off his face.

"The hospital wants to keep her for a couple of days, but she's fine. Given Lana's situation, I figured it'd be best if I called you."

"I appreciate that."

If anyone understood the instability of pregnant women, it was Derek. Paisley's due date was last week, she was on bed rest, and Logan was pacing around the house losing his damn mind. Lana's recently grumpy mood was a delight compared to the shit he had going on.

"What happened?" I asked. I needed to know how bad it was. Besides, my angel would ask questions.

She was an impatient thing and wanted all the answers right away. I told her I wasn't going to give her any information on the Order. Except for rituals like the bonding ceremony tonight, which she had to be involved in, she didn't need to know anything. That didn't stop her.

It just made her more crafty. Slipping a question into casual conversation. Half the time, I didn't realize she'd asked anything until I'd already answered. It was kind of hot, the way she could manipulate me. Probably why I bent her over every time she did it.

"She crashed her car into a tree outside of town," Derek explained. "A farmer called it in. Do you want me to contact the school?"

"No." Lana would need me to be there when she found out, and I wasn't going to let her sit alone until I got there. Even if it would only be five or ten minutes. That was too long for her to be in pain without me to comfort her.

"I'll tell her," I said.

Well, Angel, it looks like you get out of school after all.

"One more thing," Derek chimed in before I could hang up, "The backend of Gretta's car was riddle with bullet holes."

I stopped and shot Mase a glance, letting him know it was time to go. Ever since Greta heard the word 'son', she'd been acting suspicious. It was too easy to convince her to let Lana move in with me, and when we were in the principal's office, she didn't say a thing. Actually, she looked relieved when Preston threatened Mr. Sampson. I pocketed my phone and nodded at Mase to follow.

It was time to find out what Greta Crawford was hiding.

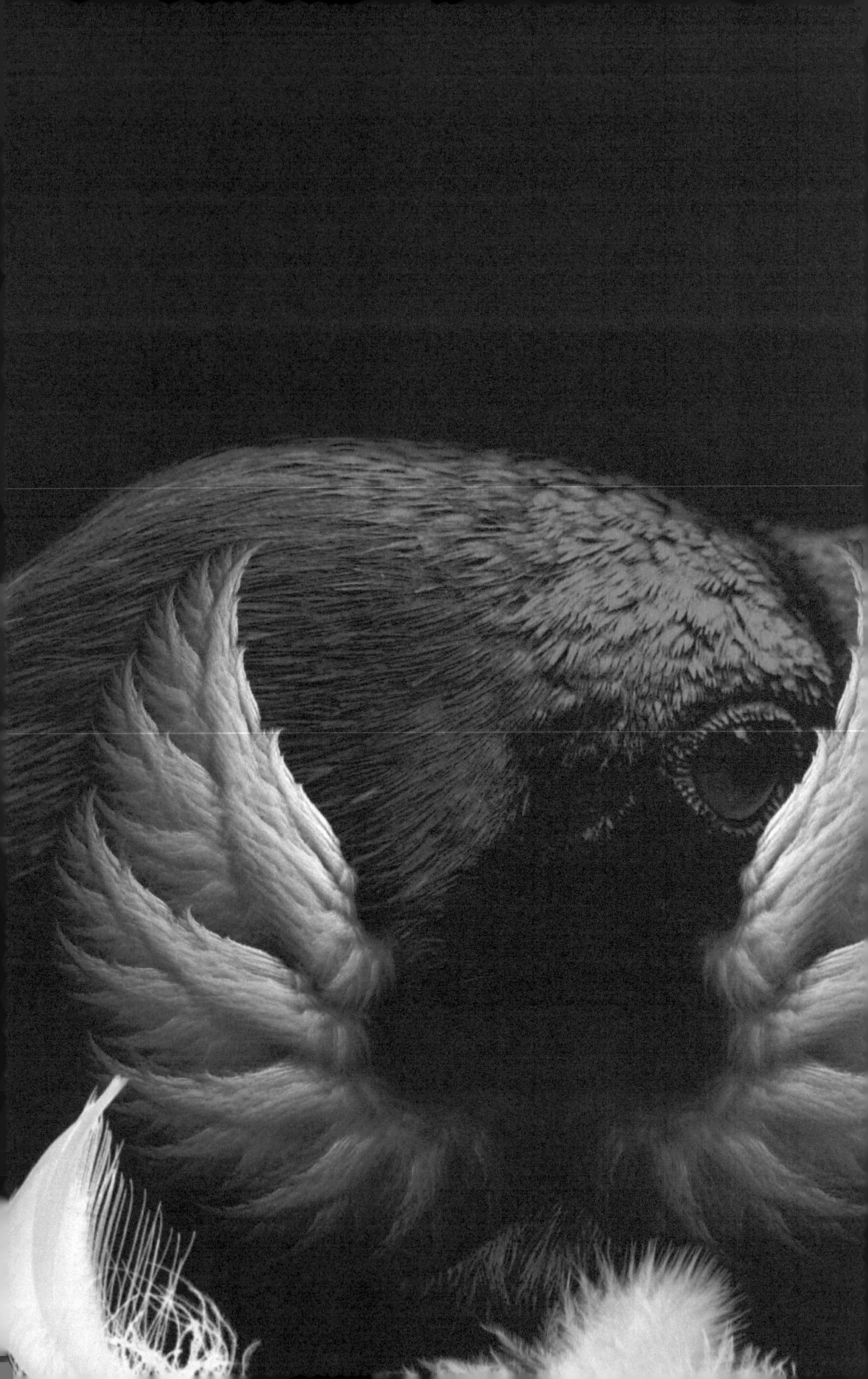

Chapter 26
Lana

Family was more than the people you were born into. It was love without bias. Knowing that no matter what you did, one person out there wouldn't judge you. For most of my life, that group was small.

Nan, Gramps, Harper and Sean. Then came Riley and Shelby. Two girls, who without knowing a thing about us, openly welcomed both Harper and myself.

Parker said I always saw the good in people, but it wasn't always that way. For years it was just Harper, Nan and I. The Mason Kessler's of the world made me leery and over protective.

I judged people as harshly as they judged me, if not more so. If someone could destroy a sweet girl like Harper, the same girl they used to claim to love, then why should I trust anyone?

It was Riley and Shelby that taught me that it was okay to stop looking over my shoulder. That no matter how many Mason

Kessler's and Naomi Prescott's were out there, I wasn't alone. They'd be right there, to move heaven and hell with me.

The daisy patches' beauty didn't come from one crooked flower with over sized petals, it came from the way the others gathered around. Holding it up high into the sun's warm rays.

That was all I could think about as Parker guided me through the hospital, with his arm protectively around me. How he was the strength holding me up. Except, if I lost Nan, there'd be nothing to hold me up into. Parker, and my friends, were my daisy patch, but Nan was my sunlight.

I clung desperately to Parker as we rounded the corner to Nan's room. The world around us stopped and every step we took thundered in my ears. Parker reached out and pushed on the door. I watched it slowly open, feeling my heart sink lower and lower. The deafening creak mingled with the beeps of the machines inside.

And then I saw her. My precious Nan, laying on a hospital bed, looking small and frail. My eyes followed the IV line running into her arm and skipped over the screen displaying her steady heartbeat.

I'd been in this situation before. Eight years ago, on the third floor, visiting someone much younger than Nan. I'd hated seeing Harper here, just like I hated seeing Nan. No one should look that helpless.

I sniffed back a sob and swept the tear off my cheek. Now wasn't the time to break down. I had to be strong for Nan. Parker's fingers tightened on my shoulder, giving me a reassuring squeeze, and the strength to take a step closer. A step is all I got.

"Good lord child, I'm not dead."

My face dropped as her brown eyes opened and rolled my way. Nan was just fine.

"You had me worried half to death."

"It was just a little fender bender." She waved her hand through the air, "Now wipe that grim look off your face."

Was it wrong to slap someone in the hospital?

"Nan," I sighed and waddled my way across the room to drop down in a chair. "You have to be more careful when you're driving."

"I'm perfectly capable of driving myself."

"Obviously not," I argued. "You crashed into the only tree on the road."

Parker crossed his arms and leaned against the doorframe. "Gotta say, Greta, that does seem awfully suspicious."

My lip curled at him. There was nothing suspicious about it. Nan was old and her eyesight was going. She probably thought a squirrel or something ran across the road. If he wanted to talk about suspicious crap, he should talk about his secret society, and the stupid ritual thing tonight. Bonding ceremony?

What kind of name was that? I had to walk down some stupid aisle and get down on my knees in front of him. How the hell was my fat ass supposed to do that? I couldn't even see my feet anymore.

I missed my feet.

"Lana."

"What?" I snarled at Nan.

"Don't you get snippy with me."

"Don't tell me what to do!"

Why was everyone always telling me what to do? The doctor was all 'don't eat this, rest as much as you can, don't take long walks.' And Parker was waiting on me hand and foot. I could take care of myself!

"Listen here, little girl," Nan sat up and arched her brow at me, "I don't care how pregnant you are, I'll still whoop you."

I blew out a huff of air, pushing my rage with it. "I'm sorry, Nan. I'm just so tired of being pregnant."

Everything hurt. I was tired all the time, and it felt like I was carrying around an extra hundred pounds. Getting comfortable was no longer an option. When I did finally settle in somewhere, the babies would start kicking. That would make anyone grumpy.

I glared down at my phone when it dinged with the twentieth text I'd gotten today. And of course, there was Parker's sister.

Parker sauntered over and knelt down in front of me.

"Don't worry, Angel," he said, running his hands over my belly in a way that helped me relax. "Before you know it, we'll be holding our babies." I smiled down at him as he leaned in and whispered, "You guys need to take it easy on your momma."

He was going to make a great father. I honestly didn't know if I could do this without him. While I was starting to hate being pregnant, motherhood terrified me. When they came out, I'd have to care for them, feed them, and teach them stuff.

What if I screwed it up? I was about to have my own kids and I'd never changed a diaper. Parker was so sure of everything that it kind of made me less afraid.

I gazed down at him and pushed my fingers through his blond locks. "I love you."

"I love you too." He beamed up at me with the proudest smile on his face.

I might've attempted to fold my oversized body and kiss him, if Nan hadn't ruined the moment by clearing her throat.

"What about me?"

I rolled my eyes. "We love you too, Nan."

"Good, because I almost died."

Groaning, I dropped my face in my palm.

The small stone building tucked away behind Oakleigh Manor was a little disappointing. My eyes ran along vines of ivy crawling across the aged walls, searching for hidden symbols or secret levers. Shouldn't the Orders uber secret ritual place be bigger, or fancier?

I wasn't expecting dungeon walls with glowing torches and obsidian ravens everywhere… Okay, maybe I was. Maybe a couple pools of blood, some naked women, and robed men chanting weird phrases? Not this simple place in the middle of a clearing surrounded by trees. The way the moonlight shone down on it was kind of cool. It gave the place an eerie kind of ambiance.

"You ready, Baby?" Parker asked, placing his hand on the small of my back.

My lip curled. "I guess."

He snickered. "I told you most of the rumors were bullshit."

That he did. But I'd been imagining their meetings and stuff my entire life. I expected… more. With a sigh, I followed Parker through the arched doorway, down a small flight of stairs and around a corner. The only thing I saw were a couple of faded etchings on the wall. One of which looked a bit like a cross. Was this a church?

We passed a wall that had an old tapestry on it of the Virgin Mary.

Oh my God, this was a church. Things just got interesting.

My giddiness levels peaked when I saw a flickering glow casting shadows on the floor next to a room where everything was covered with thick black cloth. Piles and piles of stuff wrapped up in soft fabric and chains. Sparkling heavy locks made me wish I'd watched some lockpicking videos before coming. What kind of treasures would I find?

"What's in there?"

The corner of Parker's mouth twitched in the faintest smirk. "I have no idea."

Uh huh. My gaze narrowed as I eyed him. He probably knew exactly what was in there. I bet it was secrets and stolen artifacts. What if it was something better? Like the answer to who killed JFK, or Jimmy Hoffa!

"In here," Parker said, pushing open a large wooden door.

My jaw dropped. Along the pews lining the large room were eight black metal braziers. The fire crackling in each one cast a soft glow through the metal ravens carved in the braziers' sides, making it look like birds were flying around.

Up at the altar, where a priest would normally stand, were five robed figures, three of whom I recognized to be Louis Kessler, Dr. Creswell and Parker's dad, Dean. Now this was what I was talking about!

"Do I get a robe too?"

Parker chuckled and nodded at three women standing in the back corner. "None of the wives do."

Well, damnit.

"Come on." He grabbed my hand and pulled me over to the left, where Shelby, Riley, and Logan were waiting.

I'd completely forgotten they were coming. But, I mean, could you blame me? I glanced back at the shadowy ravens flocking around the chapel and tucked away my smile. This was awesome.

"Great," Riley muttered as we joined them, "Here's the next sacrifice in our ritual line up."

My eyes went wide. Sacrifice? We weren't getting sacrificed, were we? Cause I didn't sign up for that.

"Don't listen to her, Lana," Shelby threw her arm around me and stuck her tongue out at Riley. "Rye's just grumpy."

Riley returned Shelby's comment with an eye roll.

At the same time, Logan strutted over and slapped his hand on Parker's back, then Micha joined us.

"Are you ready for this shit?" Logan teased Parker, while I eyed Micha's deep purple robes.

How come Parker didn't have robes? I wanted to see him in robes. Did the swirling gold embroidery mean anything? Maybe they were ancient spells?

Parker cocked a brow at Logan, "It's pretty standard stuff."

"You're not the one that has to fuck in front of your dad," Micha grumbled.

"What?" I looked from Micha's scowl, to the glare on Riley's face. If she'd had something sharp right then, I was pretty sure she'd stab him. "You have to do it in front of his dad?"

Even though my question was directed at Riley, it was Logan who answered.

"Not Micha's dad. Parker's," he explained, while tipping his head back at the men by the altar. "No one wants to fuck in front of Lou. Prick would take it as an opportunity to add sex therapy to his list of achievements."

"Eww," Shelby gagged, "I do not need that image of the man my mom is sleeping with."

"Exactly why I chose Dean, baby." Logan wrapped his arms around Shelby and pulled her into him. "Besides, Cherry Pie, I don't think they're doing much sleeping behind closed doors. Lou's a kinky fuck."

"Oh my god, Logan!" She smacked him in the side while Micha cracked his palm off the back of his head.

"Spying on my dad now?"

Logan's green eyes sparkled as he smirked at Micha. "Had to know if all you Kesslers were into the same sick shit."

I stood there, staring at Shelby with her arms crossed, as Logan and Micha argued about the sexual proclivities of the Kessler men, and ran through everything in my head. It took a second, but my brain slowly started to kick in.

"So... you guys have to do it in front of Parker's dad too?"

They all stopped and stared at me. Except for Riley, who

continued to glare her hatred at her boyfriend. Micha was not going to have a good night.

"You didn't tell her about that part?" Logan shook his head, "Rookie move, dude."

"What part?" I asked, looking over my shoulder at Parker.

He stiffened and glared at Logan. "Don't worry about that, Baby. We don't have to do that until after the babies are born."

I spun around and placed my hands on my hips, "Don't worry about what, Parker?"

Logan chuckled behind us. I might've slapped him, if the chapel doors hadn't burst open. Four men in robes came charging into the room, dragging the Sheriff behind them. And let me just say, I could see where Riley got her stubbornness from. Derek Adams had a bruise on his face, half his shirt was torn, and still he wasn't going quietly.

"You motherfucker!" Derek growled, throwing his fist into one man's jaw, while kicking another.

They quickly got him under control. Grabbing his limbs and holding him still as Louis Kessler marched down the aisle.

"Are we going to have this problem every time, Derek?"

Derek's answer was to spit in Mr. Kessler's face.

I didn't know where to look. My heart fluttered wildly, afraid for Riley's dad. At the same time, I could hear Riley yelling behind me, while Micha growled back. The secret society stuff was cool, but I didn't like this.

Looking up at Parker, I searched his eyes for comfort.

"Don't worry," he smiled down at me, "They won't hurt him, or her."

I didn't know if I trusted that, but I did trust Parker.

"Why don't you go get some air, and I'll come find you when things calm down."

Micha had Riley pinned up against the wall. He didn't seem to be hurting her though. He was whispering something in her ear.

Her dad, on the other hand... Once again, I looked over at the Sheriff.

"Do we need to have the cooperating conversation again, Derek?"

"Fuck you," Riley's dad snarled, "And fuck your cooperation."

Shit was about to go down. These men were ready to kill each other. Instinctively, my hands ran over my belly, shielding the babies inside.

"Air sounds like a good idea," I said to Parker, and quietly slipped out the door.

Chapter 27

Parker

My sweet Angel was having the time of her life. Hazel eyes lit up with wonder at all the shit she was seeing. And it was shit. Complete and utter bullshit. Fuck, this wasn't even the place we normally did this crap. But Lou had a valid point when he'd said Lana couldn't be trusted with locations.

My girl was sweet, and kind, and honest. She was also the kind of person that would give away something without knowing she'd given it away.

Lana was a talker, and far too innocent to keep secrets. So, Lou moved locations and said he would make it look good. Did he ever make it look good, too. The fucker played right into her fantasies. Robes and all. The braziers were a nice touch though.

And then came fucking Derek Adams, ruining my girl's good time. We all knew Riley and her dad wouldn't be cooperative, but goddamn. The guy just wouldn't quit. It took another ten minutes to calm him down enough to be let go. Even my mother left, tired of the arguments. Thank fuck Micha and Riley were up first.

Logan, Shelby and I stayed back while everyone got into place. Lou stood at one end of the aisle, with Micha in front of him, and Riley and her Dad facing them from the other end.

The point of the ritual was passing on the care of a girl to one that chose her. Daddy walks her down the aisle and gives her away. Simple, right? Not when it came to Adams. This shit was more like an intense wedding mockery.

Four of Lou's security stood by the door so Derek couldn't make a break for it, while Marco was off to the side with his hand on his holstered gun. My angel didn't need to see this.

She was stressed enough, and if one of these assholes threw her into labor, I'd have to kill a motherfucker. I don't give a shit if we had a doctor on hand.

Riley curled her lip at her dad. "Why do you have to make things difficult?"

"Difficult?" Derek's brow rose at his daughter, "They dragged me out of a hospital room where my wife is on bed rest!"

"Maybe you should've fought them harder?"

"There were four of them, Riley!"

"So? You have a gun," she snarled, "Use it."

Logan leaned over and whispered in my ear, "Ten says she slaps him."

Lou clapped, getting everyone's attention, and declared it was time to begin. I think we were all happy to get this done and over with.

His voice rang out. "Micha William Kessler. Next in line to lead the Order of Ravens and Wolves, and future King of Kings, have you made a choice for your wife and mother of your children?"

"I have," Micha nodded.

Fucker was getting off on this. His chocolate eyes were burning holes of angry lust into Riley's snarling face. I couldn't help but wonder if Logan was onto something, watching Micha fuck his girl.

I wouldn't mind seeing it, though I'd much rather fuck Micha. There was something appealing about bending one's leader over and using him like a fuck toy. Talk about a power trip.

"And who have you chosen, son."

Micha's words dripped with unbridled hunger. "Riley Marie Adams."

This was when Derek was supposed to walk his daughter down the aisle. Which he did, but only after one of the armed men behind him pressed the barrel of a gun to the back of his head.

"This is all your fault you know," Riley growled at him.

"Shut up," he snarled back and snatched her arm, "And give me your fucking arm."

She turned her head and gave him a snarky grin as they started their walk. "Chase wouldn't do this."

"Well, Chase isn't fucking here now, is he. Fucking, biker, pussy ass, bitch," Derek added in a low mutter.

Shelby walked up and placed her arm on my shoulder. "Rye's not taking this well."

I rolled my eyes her way, "Did you expect her to?"

"No," she sighed. "I don't see what the problem is? I mean, she loves him, right?"

I shrugged, "You'd know better than me."

Riley and I weren't exactly hang out buddies.

"Don't worry, Cherry Pie," Logan slapped Shelby on the ass, making her squeal, "We can show 'em how it's done."

"Oh yeah," she purred, turning around to face him.

A second later, they were gone. Probably fucking against the wall behind me. Logan wasn't exactly worried about discretion. I was much more interested in how Micha's bonding ritual was going to turn out. In a second, Riley would have to kneel and show her subservience. Somehow, I didn't think she'd be very obliging to that.

"Who gives this woman to this man?" Lou said to Derek.

He said nothing.

Lou sighed. "You may speak now, Derek."

"Oh, you want me to speak now, do you?"

"I do," Lou nodded.

"Go fuck yourself, Louis."

This time, everyone sighed. It took some doing, but after a few punches, and a couple threats, Derek finally said, "I, Derek Daniel Adams, do," with a quietly muttered, "Asshole."

And then came prying Riley's arm off her dad, which neither one of them was keen on doing. Eventually Micha had his girl, and Derek was carted off to the back. Was every step going to be this painful?

"Riley Marie Adams," Lou was no longer able to hide the frustration in his tone, "Submit to your husband, and kneel."

Riley refused, crossing her arms and eyeing him.

"Kneel, Mouse," Micha barked, loud enough that it echoed through the room.

Her lips rounded with a firm, "No."

I'd have to say yes, every step was going to be this painful. It was amusing though. Watching Micha force his girl on her knees. Listening to her muttered threats of castration when Lou recited the vows about bearing him sons. Of all the ceremonies and rituals I'd been to, this was by far the most entertaining.

When it was all done and over with, Riley stormed outside, while Micha downed a cup of what I could only assume was alcohol. I was kind of looking forward to Shelby and Logan's turn.

There was a few minute break while the next couple got ready. Since Shelby's dad was gone, Lou was giving her away, so Silas's dad had to do the ceremony. Dr. Creswell was chosen because, like his son, he had a gigantic stick shoved up his ass when it came to the rules. My father told bad dad jokes.

The girls playing the part of wives for Lana's benefit, were watching this all transpire with wide eyes. I didn't know who the fuck they were, but if I had to guess, they probably came from Lou's underground sex club.

The only actual wife here, aside from Lana, was my mother. Silas's was in New Zealand filming her next movie, and Lou didn't want Cheyenne involved. Shelby's mom was far too innocent, and since Lou wasn't having anymore kids of his own, there was no reason to include her.

Besides, it would create unwanted complications for the King of Kings. Order doctrine trumped all, even marriage. If Shelby ever tried to leave Logan, guess who he'd have to side with?

I, however, didn't give a fuck about Order doctrine. My Angel was the only thing that trumped all. The rest of these pricks could kiss my ass. And I happened to know I wasn't alone. Logan and Micha thought the same way. Either one of them would, and had killed for their girl. In their eyes, their woman came first.

I guess that was the difference between love, and an arrangement. Love could drive a man to stab his best friend. Logan was the perfect example of that. He'd pulled a gun on Micha, and he *never* threatened Micha. Speaking of Logan…

The cocky asshole was standing in his place with a stupid smile on his face, like he was king of the world. Shelby wasn't any better, staring back at him with her arm looped in Lou's and this doe eyed look on her face.

My teeth were hurting from the sweetness in the air. Somehow, the sick fucks twisted what most would perceive as a tender moment, into something sinful.

Shelby was licking her lips as Lou walked her down the aisle, while Logan's mouth curled in a wicked smirk. It felt like I was watching a fucking porn. And not a good one. One of those cheesy piles of shit that Mason kept sending to me.

With the seventies pizza man and the bikini clad housewife. At least Logan had some originality, though I could've done without the unicorn porn.

"Logan Elliot Hudson," Dr. Creswell's called out, loud enough that it made me wonder if he was trying to out do Lou, "Member of the Order of Ravens and Wolves and future King, have you chosen a wife?"

"Fuck yeah I have. Shelby Harlow Grace."

Dr. Creswell rolled his eyes. "You're supposed to wait until I ask her name."

"You're taking too long." Logan looked over at his girl coming towards him and smirked, "I'm already hard as fuck."

Silas's dad grumbled out a groan and continued. I wouldn't doubt if his foul mood had something to do with not being picked to witness the copulation. A polite person would say it was nothing against him, but I wasn't polite. Martin Creswell was a skeezy fuck that had a thing for teenage girls.

He wasn't a twisted prick, like Ryker, his age of choice was around seventeen to nineteen, which happened to be the age category our girls were in.

Shelby walked up, Lou gave her away, and she knelt down without an issue. I knew exactly what Logan was thinking as he stared down at her. I'd have the same dark glint in my eyes if Lana was kneeling in front of me.

"Hey baby," he waggled his eyebrows, "Care to help a guy out?"

I watched the rest of their ceremony, pretty sure that at any second Logan would whip his dick out and shove it in Shelby's mouth. I wouldn't complain. Don't think anyone here would, except for maybe Lou.

Though Shelby wasn't biologically his, he'd started giving her the same fatherly speeches he gave his sons. And her little sister...

She was more spoiled than Naomi. Thankfully, she didn't have the same shitty attitude as Ashworth's queen bee. Unless it came to tea parties.

My mother came back in just in time to see the end of the ceremony, when Logan scooped up his girl and promptly announced that they had to consummate right away.

Rolling her eyes at Logan, my mother gave me a smile. "Is yours next?"

"Do you care?"

"Of course I care," she tipped her pointy chin my way, "The girl is carrying my grandchildren."

Classic Lillianna Whitley.

"The girl's name is Lana, Mother."

She sneered at me. "I know that."

"You should try using it sometime," I pointed out.

She sighed and flicked her hand through the air, waving me off. At least she was calling them her grandchildren now. Some form of acknowledgment was better than abominations. I suspected Ava had something to do with that.

My sister was obsessed with her niece and nephew, and a little bit with their mother. When she found out Lana liked Troll dolls, she searched for some rare one she found online. I didn't tell Lana about the blood I had to wash off the doll. Nor did I ask my sister where she got it. Some things were better left alone.

My father walked over and slapped his hand on my shoulder. "You're up, my boy. I remember when you were still throwing dirt at girls."

Please tell me he wasn't getting sentimental.

"And now, here you are, starting a family of your own."

Fuck, he's gonna cry, isn't he?

"My boy," he wiped a tear off his cheek, "My baby. I'm so proud of you."

"Good lord, Dean," my mother snarled, "He's already married to the girl."

She was not happy about that.

My dad perked up and looked around. "Where is my lovely daughter in-law?"

"Outside," I threw my thumb at the door, "She needed some air."

"No she's not," my mother shook her head.

"What do you mean she's not?"

"I was just outside and she's not there," she explained. "I told you the girl would run."

Lana would not run. Hell, she could barely walk. If she was having reservations about this, she would've talked to me. One thing Lana Whitley was not, was a coward. She had no problem getting in my face, or anyone else's, when she needed too. Plus, her Nan was in the hospital.

I pushed past my mother and headed for the door. "I'm sure you just missed her."

"What's going on?" I heard Logan ask as I marched out of the chapel.

My mother repeated her suspicion. "The girl ran."

"She did not run," I snarled over my shoulder.

I could hear them following me. Footsteps mingled with hushed whispers, echoing off the stone walls. But I didn't care. The pit in my stomach wouldn't go away until I had my arms around my wife. Except, I couldn't find her. I must've circled the building three times calling her name, and nothing. Where the fuck was she? My pulse picked up as I circled the building again, which was when Micha came out.

"Where's Riley?" he said, scouring the area.

My father arched his brow. "What do you mean?"

"Riley came out here."

"So?" my mother piped in.

"So," Micha waved his hands through the air, "Where the fuck is she?"

Everything went quiet as Micha and I scanned the area, searching the treeline and horizon, but it was Logan's voice calling us that caused my heart to drop as Micha and I shared a fearful look.

"Over here," Logan waved, pointing at a blue shoe on the ground.

Riley's shoe!

"There's drag marks." His green eyes swung up, "I think someone took them."

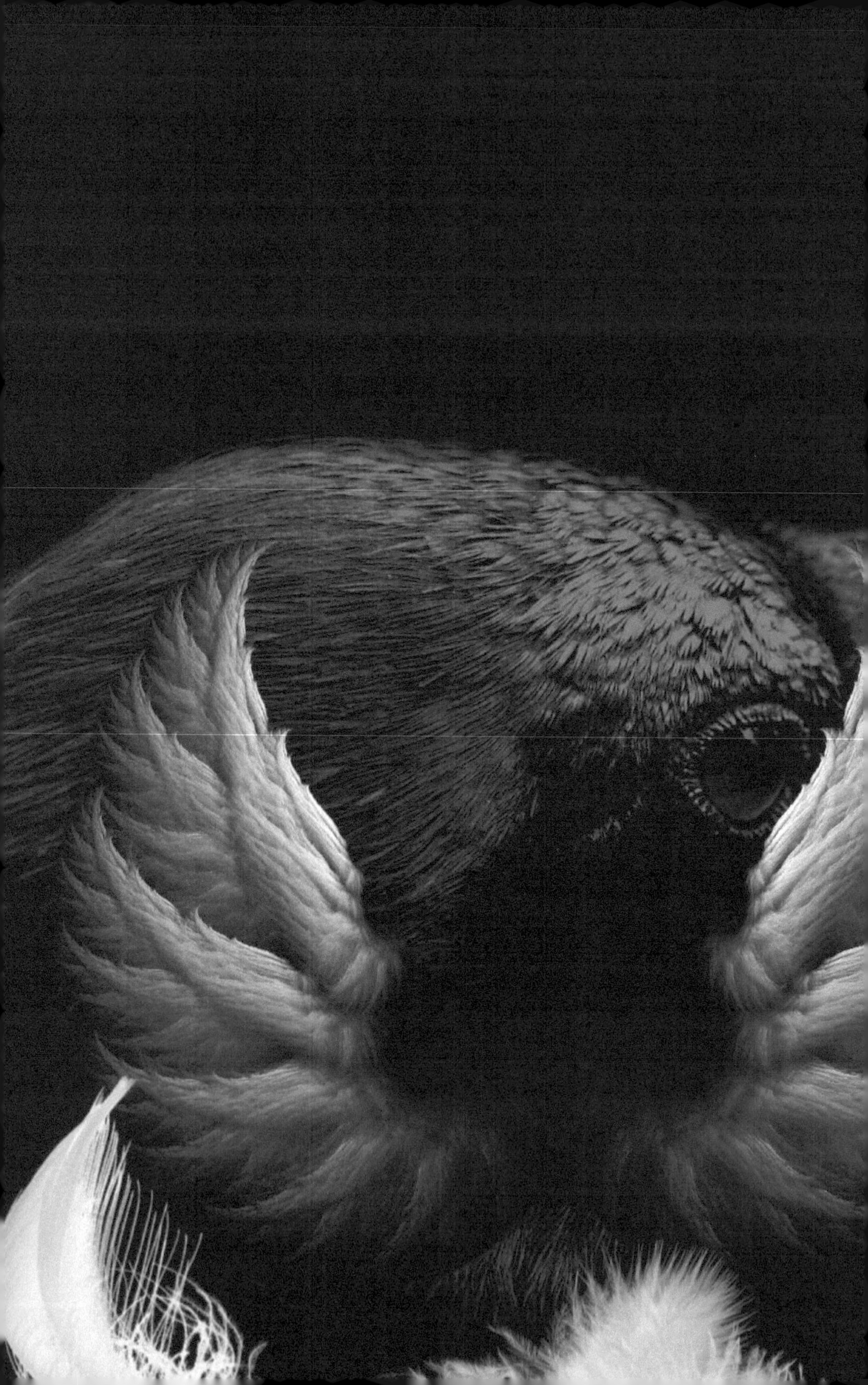

It really was beautiful out. A nice clear sky, full of twinkling stars. I inhaled the earthy scent in the air and allowed my body to relax. When Parker had told me about the ritual and what I'd have to do, I was excited. Both to be a part of something everyone whispered about, but mostly to become Parker's forever.

Yes, we were married, but this ceremony was different. It was more real than a piece of paper filed downtown. It was raw, and carnal. A true bonding, because the man I loved picked me. Out of every other girl in this town, he wanted me.

My hand pressed down on my stomach, calming the kicking inside. The babies were active today. They must be able to sense my unease. The braziers and robes were fascinating. It was the goons pushing the Sheriff around that bothered me.

He didn't want to be there, and I remembered how that felt. The frustration and anger at not being able to do anything. Yes, things turned out well, Parker and I were happy. But what if they hadn't?

I tipped my chin up and gazed up at the night sky and the bright moon shining down. A round ball of light watching the world below. Watching me. Doing nothing about the heavy weight holding me down, or the sweaty grunts assailing my ears.

'Fuck, you feel good.'

I closed my eyes and shook the image back, using the breathing techniques Mr. Kessler taught me.

"It's just a bad dream, Lana," I whispered, taking a deep breath in through my nose and releasing it from my mouth. "Nothing happened. It's all in your imagination."

"Are you alright?"

My eyes snapped open and I jumped back. Standing a few feet behind me was Lilliana. She looked different today. Less uptight, and more free. Her blonde hair was down, flowing in soft waves over her shoulders, and I think this was the first time I'd seen her in pants. They weren't jeans, but at least it wasn't her normal pencil skirt.

"I hope everything is okay." She tilted her head and gave me a smile, "I know how difficult this stage can be. You just want it over with."

She pulled out a gold case and clicked it open, to pop a cigarette in her mouth, before offering me one. I declined with a head shake. Was she being nice to me? On purpose?

"I heard your grandmother is in the hospital?"

"She was in a car accident," I nodded, "But she's fine."

More than fine. The nurses had to convince Nan it was in her best interest to stay. She would only agree if I promised to bring her some real food in the morning.

Lillianna exhaled a stream of smoke. "I'll have to send her a fruit basket."

"That would be nice."

Were things supposed to be this awkward with your mother in-law? Even the babies quieted down when she was around. It was weird, standing alone with nothing but the breeze, the crickets, and her.

I should go back inside.

"Do you have any names picked out?"

"What?"

"Names," she said, pointing the lit end of her cigarette at my belly. "I assume they will have some."

"Oh, um, yes." Parker and I'd had their names picked out for a week now, but we were keeping them secret. Though if Logan suggested Logan for a boy and Logan for a girl once more, I might tell him just so he'd shut up.

Lillianna stared at me.

I stared at her while animals called somewhere in the distance.

"Well, I should get back in there."

I moved and stepped around her, but stopped when two beams of light cut through the inky blackness. My hand moved up to shield my eyes as I watched an unfamiliar car roll down the dirt road.

Were there more people coming? Or perhaps things had gone really bad in there and they had to call in backup? A shiver ran up my spine, tensing my muscles. Was I about to see a body?

My thoughts were cut off when a bony arm wrapped around my neck and something wet was held against my face.

"I won't let you ruin everything I've worked for," Lillianna hissed in my ear.

I fought with everything I had, throwing my arms back while trying to twist away. But heaviness settled in my limbs, weighing them down as blackness seeped into my vision. The last thing I saw was Riley, running towards me with fury on her face.

I ROLLED over and smacked my lips together. Holy crap was my mouth dry. What the hell did I drink last night? Wait… My brows pulled together. I was pregnant, I couldn't drink.

"Lana…"

Was that Harper? No, it was too deep to be my best friend.

"Come on Lana, wake up."

My eyelids were too heavy, they refused to budge. I had no idea what was going on, or who was calling me. But I did know I wasn't at home. Every morning I woke up to inhale the sweet scent from the garden outside.

Right now, all I could smell was salty air, with a faint tint of fish. I stretched out on the hard bed and flopped my hand down. My confusion grew when my fingers brushed against the cool rough surface beneath me. Was I on the floor?

"Lana, please," The voice desperately cried, "Wake up."

Riley?

It all came rushing back to me then. The ritual, Lillianna, and the car.

"I won't let you taint my family."

I shot up, eyes springing open to check my belly. Relief washed over me when a hard bump jabbed me from the inside. Thank god, they were okay. My babies were safe. I didn't realize Riley was behind me until she threw her arms around my shoulders and hugged me tight.

"You're okay," she whispered into my back, "You're okay."

I took a minute to search the room, looking for some hint of familiarity. Unfortunately there wasn't much light in here. I could tell that we were about the only things in here. Our breathing echoed around my ears.

"Where are we?"

"I don't know," Riley jumped up and walked into the darkness, "But there's a metal door over here."

I think she kicked it, because the next second I was covering my ears to dampen the ringing bang vibrating through the room. What kind of metal door made that sound?

"Where's Lillianna?" I asked Riley when she came back into my sight and began inspecting the closest wall.

"You mean Parker's cunt of a mother?" her rage filled blue eyes rolled back to me, "I haven't seen her."

Why would Lillianna take Riley? What purpose did that serve, beyond attracting more attention? Lord knows what she told Parker… *Oh my god, Parker!* He must be going out of his mind right now. I had to get back to him.

Forcing my heavy body off the ground–which was not at all easy when you were over seven months pregnant with twins–I waddled over to the opposite wall. We might be trapped in here, but that didn't mean I had to be useless. If there was a way in, there had to be a way out, right?

"Lana, you shouldn't be up…"

"I'm fine."

"But…"

"Seriously, Riley," I glanced over and gave her a stern look, "I'm fine."

Her mouth pursed, but she nodded. "Okay. Look for something sharp."

"Like a weapon," I asked, gliding my hands over the wall.

"Exactly. Something I could stab these assholes with."

Assholes? "What about Lillianna?"

"Oh, she'll get hers too," Riley promised, "But right now I'm more interested in the two pricks that brought us here."

I thought back to the mystery car and didn't know what was scarier. Lillianna being bold enough to take not only me, but Riley too, while Micha and Parker were a few feet away? Or that she was prepared with backup to do it?

Nan was right, Parker's mother was evil. I felt so stupid for falling for her shit. Quietly sniffing back a shuddered gasp, I quickly brushed away the tear trickling down my face. If I had just listened to Nan…

"Don't do that," Riley placed her hand on her cocked hip, "This shit is not your fault."

I couldn't help but snicker. Leave it to Riley to give me the 'don't blame yourself' speech in the middle of a hostage situation. "You sound like you've done this before."

I was joking of course. Riley had never been kidnapped.

"Yeah, well," she returned to inspecting her wall, "Last time there was more stabby shit to use."

Or, maybe she had?

"Um… okay?" I wasn't quite sure what to say to that.

There were a million questions swimming through my head right now. Like where, when, and by who, but I suppose we had more important things to do.

My first priority was getting back into my husband's arms, and getting Riley back to Micha. On the upside, she was the Sheriff's daughter. Which meant the Ashen Springs police force was probably scouring the town right now. *If we were still even in town?*

After who knows how long, we gave up and sat by the far wall. There was absolutely nothing in this metal room. No sticks, no bars, not even a grain of sand. It was disturbingly clean. As bad as that was, Riley's plans were even worse.

Plan A consisted of her charging the first person to come through the door, while I ran. Great, if she weighed more than ninety pounds soaking wet, and if I could see my feet. Not to mention, I'd never leave her behind.

Plan B wasn't much better. That one called for me faking labor. Considering the people who took us had no problem kidnapping a pregnant woman ready to pop, I highly doubted they'd give a shit if I went into labor. Plan C was simply titled, let's wing it. Once again, I had to point out to her that speed was not my strong suit right now.

We were halfway through preparations for Plan C, which was more of an argument, when the door creaked open and we were blinded by the sudden appearance of light. I swore and threw my hand up. Riley swore too, but not because of the light.

"You son of a bitch."

I squinted and peeked over my arm at the guy smirking back at her. His brown hair flopped over a diagonal scar in his forehead. If I didn't know any better, I'd say someone had cut the letter L into his skin.

"Hey, Riley. How's the new school?" The smirk on his face grew, "Evan says the library's top notch."

I could feel the hate radiating off her as, Riley glared back at him and quietly growled, "Noah Torres."

Chapter 29

Parker

Fear was one emotion I had never understood. I knew how to fake it. Make my eyes big, put a quiver in my voice, sweat a little. That shit was easy. The comprehension of how to handle the cold shiver shooting through my veins was not.

Everyone was here, the Kings were off somewhere digging up information, and the Knights, standing in my kitchen with me, arguing over what to do.

I could see them. The wisps of smoke coming out of Logan's mouth, Micha's booming voice, and the scent of tobacco coming off my brother. All of it was there.

All of it real, but none of it broke through the spikes of panic crawling up my spine. My wife and my children were out there somewhere. Alone and scared. And I had no idea how to find them.

"Push it down." Preston dropped his elbows on the island next to me and stared out at the group arguing. "Whatever it is that's making you numb, push it back. Hold onto it in the back of your mind." He twisted his neck, locking his grey eyes with mine, "And when the time is right, use it."

"How?" I asked.

"Stop thinking about what's happening to her, and concentrate on the motherfucker that took her. Stop holding back that monster you've been hiding all these years." His fingers tightened on my shoulder as he leaned in and whispered, "It's time to let him off the leash and accept who you are, brother."

I stared at Preston, thinking about what he'd said. For so long, I fought to be normal. Played the part of good son and student, while ignoring the howling voice clawing to break free. And what for?

To lose my family. If I'd have taken Lana when I wanted to, none of this shit would be happening. I could've protected her better.

"You two care to chime in on this?" Micha growled over at us.

"Why?" Preston challenged back, "You idiots seem to be doing a good job of fucking things up."

Mason rolled his eyes, "I wouldn't say we're fucking thing up."

"You've been arguing for six hours." Preston arched a brow, "Anyone come up with a plan yet?"

They all stopped and eyed each other quietly. Of course we hadn't come up with a plan. We didn't even know where to fucking start. If they had taken one or the other, then maybe we'd have an idea. But both Lana and Riley?

Micha and I didn't have any enemies in common. Fuck, I didn't have any enemies at all. I was Ashen Springs' golden boy. Everybody loved me. Except for maybe Callaghan, and he'd never hurt Lana.

Logan ran his fingers through his hair and let out a sigh. "I'm gonna go check on Shelby."

Shelby was going out of her mind, so Logan had drugged her and put her to bed three hours ago."

"That's a good idea," Preston nodded, "I'm gonna go see if Lou's come up with anything. You idiots stay here and try not to kill each other."

"Prick," Micha grumbled as they walked out of the room.

I looked at him, understanding the fear etched in deep lines across his face. He felt just as helpless as I did. Silas and Mason sat back in their chairs, eyeing us.

They wanted to say something, I could see it. But what could they say? Silence was thick in the air. Unwavering, unnerving, and constantly reminding us that doom was on the horizon.

"Hey."

We all turned to see Luke standing in the kitchen doorway.

Luke's bright eyes only reminded me of my girl. The comfortable nights watching T.V., or playing a game. The conversations we'd had over a drink, and the fun times. As happy as I was to see him, I didn't want him here.

"Now's not a good time, Luke."

"I know," he said, which made Micha and I cock a brow.

"What do you mean, you know?"

His gaze met mine, "Lana's gone, right?"

How the fuck did he know that?

"And Riley," Micha added.

I tipped my head at the flare in Luke's nostril as his glare narrowed in on Micha. He didn't like him. No, scratch that. He fucking hated Micha. But why? I'd never seen the two of them talk, or even look at each other.

"Riley was collateral damage," Luke declared without so much as a twitch in his expression.

Micha was off his stool and across the room in half a second. I was right behind him.

"How the fuck do you know that?"

The corner of Luke's mouth lifted at Micha's question. "I know a lot of things you don't, brother."

The air in the room shifted ten degrees closer to hell as chairs screeched across the tiled floor and rage flooded Micha's eyes.

"You killed my cousin's parents!" Silas bellowed.

Luke simply lifted his gaze over Micha's shoulder and smirked. "Slit your aunt's throat myself. She bled like a stuck pig."

It was a good thing Micha grabbed him and slammed Luke back against the wall, because none of us would've had the control to not kill him. This was the prick that had handed Junior and Finn over to Ryker. Because of him, the little boy that was pumped to take on the world, was now broken.

"Give me one good reason why I shouldn't kill you?" Micha growled down at him.

"You want to find your precious Mouse, don't you?"

Micha pushed his forearm deeper into Luke's neck. "Why should I trust you?"

That was a fair question. I'd trusted Luke. A part of me still did, aching for the friendship I thought we had. Was any of it real?

"I don't give a fuck if you trust me. I didn't come here for you." Luke's eyes locked on mine. "I came for her."

Lana. He came here to save my Lana.

"Let him go, Micha."

Micha's jaw clenched and his fists balled, but he took a step back. That was when Luke pulled a folder out of his jacket and passed it to me.

"Everything you need to know is in there."

Mason and Silas took over guard duty, while Micha and I flipped through pages. Every single one was about my Lana, and not at all anything I would have expected. She wasn't a scholarship kid, her tuition was paid for in full. From an unmarked account that deposited money into Greta Crawford's account every year. Which happened to be the exact amount for tuition at Ashworth.

I had to hand it to Luke, he'd marked every dot and crossed every T. Traced the money back to an account owned by Nikolai Ivanov. The head of the U.S. chapter of the Russian Bratva.

The last pages in the folder was a letter from Nikolai's wife to Greta, and a copy of paternity papers. Lana wasn't just a girl in a small town, she was a mafia princess. Her father was Nikolai Ivanov, and his wife had been paying her Nan to keep it a secret. Guess I knew what Greta was hiding now. Surprising information to have, but…

I looked at Luke, "What does this have to do with Lana being kidnapped?"

"I gave that same file to your mother three months ago. Last I heard, she was trying to get ahold of the Italians."

My mother was involved? I should've known. *'She's not outside.'* Fucking cunt set this shit up. Played me like a fool. Just like Luke did.

"What would the Italians want with a mafia princess no one knows about?"

Micha had a good point.

"Nikolai doesn't have any other kids," Luke explained, "He can't. Which makes your son…"

"Heir to the Russian throne," I finished.

"Exactly. Kid like that is powerful to have."

There was still one thing I didn't get. "Why are you telling us this?"

If he didn't say anything, Riley and Lana would be gone, and he'd win.

"I know you don't believe me," when Luke's eyes met mine I could see the regret shining in their depths, "But I really do consider you and Lana my friends. I called it off months ago."

I know his words shouldn't mean anything to me, but they did. Yes, he lied to me, betrayed us both, but he also risked everything to come here and save her. For that, I wouldn't kill him. My mother, on the other hand…

"You hear that?" Leaning over, I nodded at Preston, who'd been watching from out in the hall. "Our mother knows where she is."

Preston cocked his brow back at me. "You know she won't survive it, right?"

"I don't care."

That was all the answer my brother needed. He pushed off the wall and marched out the door, heading off to finally live out his matricide fantasy. Ten seconds, later Lou and Derek came into the room and slapped cuffs on Luke. My guess was that Preston let them know what was going on.

Luke gave me one last look, apologizing the only way he could, before Derek hauled him away. "You're under arrest for the murder of Sebastian and Sandra Creswell."

Micha was less than impressed. "What the fuck!" he growled at his father.

"I'm sorry, son, but it's the only way I can protect you both."

"Protect us both!?" Micha roared in response. "He gave Junior and Finn to that sick fuck! He deserves to be punished."

"And he will be," Lou straightened out his suit jacket, "But not by your hand."

That was a load of crap. Lou wasn't doing this to save his illegitimate son's life. Or out of some sense of fatherly responsibility. He was doing it for one reason. Cheyenne Grace. Luke's mother. Like the rest of us, Lou would do anything for the woman he loved.

"You can't…"

"It's done, son," Lou said, cutting Micha off, after which he leaned over and rolled his dark eyes over the rest of us. "You boys will let me deal with this, understand. The mafia isn't something to be toyed with. If you go in there half cocked, you're not coming back."

If he thought I was going to sit back and do nothing, then Lou didn't know me at all.

"I mean it, Parker."

I pursed my lips and nodded. "I got it."

Go fuck yourself, Lou.

He eyed me for another second, before turning and walking away. Micha, who was pissed as fuck, followed, ranting his objections behind him.

Mason crossed his arms and shifted his gaze to Silas. "Why do I get the feeling that he's about to do something stupid. Like go pay some Russian asshole a visit?"

"Because he's got the same look you did before you hit on Ava."

As Lou said, the mafia wasn't something to be toyed with, but Lana was their princess, and my guess was that Nikolai would want to protect his heir. Miami wasn't that far.

Without a word, I spun around, slipped out the patio door, and snuck around the side of the house to my SUV. I barely got the door closed when the passenger side opened and Mase plopped down in the seat beside me.

"Oh man, there's nothing like rolling up to Nikolai Ivanov's house in the mommy wagon."

"What are you doing?"

The back door opened and Silas climbed in. "We're going with you."

"Why?" My lip curled in confusion.

"Well this one's just a moron," Silas nodded at Mase, "But Lana helped my cousin, so I kind of owe her."

"I thought you said this was stupid?"

"Oh, this is definitely stupid. Way beyond grabbing your sister's ass, but," Mase shrugged, "I just got out of rehab. Stupid's my middle name."

It took Mase two weeks to heal from that shit. There'd be no healing from what we were about to do. One of two things happened when you drove up to a mafia bosses house. You got turned away. Or you got shot.

"Last chance," I said, starting the engine.

They both said nothing. Just clicked their seatbelts on and sat back.

"Alright." I stepped on the gas and steered the SUV down the driveway.

It was time to meet my father in-law.

I leaned forward and scanned the large brick manor through the windshield. More specifically, the four armed guards by the gate. If people said *we* had money, then Nikolai owned the whole damn bank. This place put Oakleigh Manor to shame, and that was only from what I could see over the wall surrounding the property.

"Are we just going to sit here like a couple of creeps, or are we going to go over there?" Mase lifted his chin at the estate across the street, "And talk to the man?"

"And how do you propose we do that?"

Nikolai wasn't just some guy walking down the street that we were trying to sell Girl Scout cookies to. He was the damn Russian bratva boss. Don't get me wrong, the Order had power, but mafia trumped secret society. These were the guys that rained blood on the streets because they had a disagreement over territory.

They didn't just take out a traitor, they took out his family, friends, and anyone that looked at the fucker for too long. They didn't fuck around with secrets in the dark, and they sure as fuck wouldn't have a problem shooting the messenger. I wouldn't be much help to my angel if I was dead.

Silas leaned forward, propping his arms up on the back of mine and Mase's seats, and blew out a breath. "We could call him?"

"Oh sure, genius, just let me pull out my mafia phone book and look up his name." Silas and I both rolled our eyes when Mase pulled out his phone and started scrolling through contacts, muttering, "Nikolai… Nikolai… Nikolai… nope, no Nikolai. You know why? Because it's fucking mafia, dumbass." His eyes rolled back to a rather unimpressed Silas. "Get away from me with that shit."

"Well, I don't hear you coming up with any genius plans," Silas grumbled back.

Mase crossed his arms and insisted, "I'm working on it."

"Don't hurt yourself."

"Shut up, Tinkerbell. I'm trying to think."

That made me snicker a bit. Fucking Mase redoing Silas's room in princess theme. That was almost as good as the barber shop quartet that followed him around school. *Back to Nikolai…*

"Okay, we should…"

Shit, what should we do?

Whatever it was, we better do it quick, before the assholes with the AK's noticed us sitting across the street.

"Alright," Mase declared, "I got it."

Silas's scowl deepened. "He doesn't have shit."

"You underestimate me, my friend. I know exactly what to do."

I eyed the confident look on Mason's face. "And what's that?"

"Drive up there," he waved his hand at Nikolai's house, "I got the rest."

"Uh huh?" Silas hummed and sat back. "Don't listen to this fool."

I looked at Mase, and then back to Silas. Did I really want to listen to the guy that was talking to a stuffed dog yesterday? Sighing, I stared at the house. What choice did I have? I started the engine and rolled down the street.

"I hope you know what you're doing."

Mase nodded, "Of course I know what I'm doing."

Why doesn't that make me feel any better?

"He has no idea what he's doing," Silas muttered from the back.

Mase lifted his arm and waved his hand over his shoulder. "Pipe down, princess, the adults are talking."

I could feel Silas glaring at him. "I hope they fucking shoot you."

"Let's hope they don't shoot anyone," I muttered, while steering the SUV up the windy path to Nikolai's gates.

The only time I'd seen men jump to action this fast was when Ryker took Riley and Mase. Chase and his boys were on that shit. A lot like the armed men I could see behind the gate, moving into ready positions.

All it took to get everyone going was one guy on this side, blowing a whistle. The Lost Boys MC was just as organized, and Chase had been away from the club for years. Said a lot about the criminal enterprise.

The second we pulled up to the iron bar gate, a tap, tap, tap came on my window. I stared at the barrel of a 9mm knocking on the glass and up to the man in a suit peeking in at me. It wasn't just him.

There was another man on the passenger side, glaring at Mase, and one in front of the SUV watching us all. And that wasn't counting however many were on the other side of that wall. Exhaling a deep breath, I silently prayed Mase knew what he was doing, and rolled down the window.

Here lies Parker Whitley...

"I think you're lost, *mal'chik*," the man on my side said with a thick Russian accent. "You should turn 'round and go back to where you came from."

"Hey man," Mase called out, while ducking down a bit to look the Russian in the eyes, "We need to talk to the boss man."

"What do you know of boss?"

A smirk spread across Mason's face, "I know what happened to his missing shipment."

He listened to Mason Kessler.

"Ah fuck," I growled, and spit out a mouthful of blood. I'd been hit so many times that the coppery taste was lodged in my throat. "I thought you said you knew what you were doing?"

A fist cracked off Mason's jaw, jarring his chair and causing it to screech against the floor.

"We're in, aren't we?" he said through a groan.

We were in, alright. Tied to fucking chairs while four Russian pricks beat on us, demanding information. Not really the nonchalant conversation I had in mind. And we still had yet to see Nikolai.

"I told you not to listen to him."

I turned my head Silas's way and stretched my sore jaw. A trickle of blood ran down his chin from the split in his lip. We were all fucked up. My ears were ringing from being hit in the head, Silas's left eye was swollen shut, and Mase...

He looked ready to kill a motherfucker. Green eyes blazing with rage while his forearms flexed, trying to break the bonds binding them behind the chair. The only thing I could hope at this point was that he didn't break free. Then we'd all be dead, because Mase couldn't control his temper.

"You talk too much," one of the Russians stated in a flat tone.

This one I figured was the one in charge down here, since he was the only one speaking. "But you tell us nothing. I think, you have nothing to tell."

"Hey Ivan!" Mason yelled, which earned him another punch. This time in the gut. Mase hunched over as best he could and coughed out, "Get your boss down here and let's see who has something to tell."

The leader kept his icy eyes on me and tipped his head at Mase. "This one is mouthy. Perhaps I cut out his tongue?"

"You could," I growled, meeting his glare, "But what if we really do have information for your boss?"

He stared at me.

I stared at him.

Asshole Number One, who was pounding on Silas, spouted something in Russian to the leader, who barked something back. Judging by the tone in Asshole Number One's voice, and the look on his face, he wasn't too keen on the risk of pissing off Nikolai.

"You want to see boss, alright." The leader's lips twisted in a devious smirk, "I hope you have coffins picked out."

With that, he nodded at the other men and they all walked out, leaving us alone in the dank cell like room. Their absence gave me a minute to evaluate my injuries. My jaw hurt like a motherfucker, an ache was crawling up my shoulder blades, and I was pretty sure one of my ribs was broken.

Not too bad, considering. Silas wasn't too bad either. It was Mase that was fucked up. Blood poured from his nose, and I saw him spit out a tooth. Fucker couldn't keep his mouth shut, though I suppose he could take a beat down better than the rest of us. I couldn't remember a time when Mase didn't use his fists to solve an argument.

"A missing shipment?!" Silas growled loudly, "Really?"

"What? It's the mob," Mase shrugged, "There's always a missing shipment."

If I wasn't tied to the chair, I'd have kicked his ass myself.

My mouth opened, prepared to rip Mason a new one, but my words got stuck in my throat when the door opened. Assholes One, Two and Three walked in with the leader, followed by someone else.

This man had an aura of power that even I could feel. The other's dropped their eyes when he sauntered past, avoiding eye contact. His strides were long and confident as he walked into the room and stopped to stare at me.

Instead of speaking to me, he said something in Russian, which the leader answered.

My gaze wandered over the black suit jacket covering his broad shoulders, and up to the icy blue eyes with a tint of green. The slight crinkle under his eyes told me he was the right age to be Nikolai, but he was too… pretty.

"My men said you wished to speak to me?"

Well shit, guess he was Nikolai. He must've been in this country for awhile, because his English was almost perfect. I could hear the faint Russian accent behind some of his words though.

I sat up and puffed my chest out. "I have some information you might be interested in."

"I highly doubt that," Nikolai responded.

"You know," Mason piped in, making me shake my head. The asshole was going to get us killed. "You Russian's are seriously lacking in the hospitality department."

One tip of Nikolai's head, and Mase was slapped across the face. Not once did he break eye contact with me. "I'm a busy man."

Apparently patience wasn't one of his traits. "I'm here about your daughter."

"You must have mistaken me for someone else." He cocked a brow, "I can't have children."

Mase got another smack when he muttered, "Explain that to his girl."

Shut the fuck up, Mase.

"I have a paternity test that says otherwise," I said, before Asshole Number Three could clock Mase again.

Nikolai's brows knit together as he searched my face for signs of deception. Maybe this shit would work out after all, and he might actually listen to me. Until he opened his mouth.

"Kill them."

Immediately after, arms lifted, raising guns and my life flashed before my eyes. The first time I saw my angel in her red shoes. The way her face lit up when she smiled, and the pride that filled me knowing she was mine.

I'm sorry, baby.

Before bullets could riddle my body, my phone went off, and Nikolai held up his hand, stopping his men from pulling the trigger.

"*Stap,* " he ordered, and plucked my phone off the table where all of our stuff was laying. "Perhaps whoever is calling will have some answers for me." His eyes locked on mine, "Or perhaps I'll kill them too." Nikolai sauntered over to me and clicked my phone on speaker. "I'm sorry, your friend can't come to the phone right now. He's tied up at the moment."

"Nikolai?" Preston's voice rang out, "Why the fuck do you have my brother's phone."

How the hell did Preston know the Russian mob boss?

Every single man in the room dropped their armed hands, as their face's visibly paled. Someone whispered, *"d'yavol smerti,"* and Nikolai pushed down a loud swallow.

"I asked you a fucking question!" Preston barked out.

And just like that, Nikolai's whole demeanor changed. He took a few steps back and stared anxiously down at my phone. Mase, Silas and I shared a 'what the fuck' look. Seconds ago, we were looking at our own graves, and now the Russians in the room looked like the boogeyman himself was coming after them.

"I'm sorry," Nikolai stammered, "I didn't know he was your brother."

A shrill agonizing scream pierced the air, ringing out from the other end of my phone.

"You hear that Nikolai?" Preston said, making the mob boss nod, "That's my mother."

I should've felt something. A sense of loss, or sympathy for the woman that gave birth to me. But I felt nothing. My angel was god knows where because of her. The only thing I felt was satisfaction knowing that my brother wouldn't make things easy for her.

"You let my brother go, and whatever idiot friends went looking for suicide with him, or it'll be your house I visit tonight."

"Hey!" Mase called out, insulted, as Preston hung up.

Two seconds later, we were cut free from our binds and were being led through the house. I don't know what the fuck my brother had to do with him, but Nikolai was much more accommodating now.

He listened to everything I said, looked at all the information, and jumped into action, sending his people off to find information on his missing daughter. Prick even had a doctor come tend to our wounds.

"You must understand," he said while staring at a picture of Lana, "Someone like me can never be too careful."

"I get it."

The Order had enemies, sure, but nothing like Nikolai. His life was probably threatened on a daily basis. Someone like that had to be cold and callus.

He sighed and ran his fingers over Lana's smiling face. "If I'd have known about her…"

All I could think about were my wife and children. Were they hurt? Were they dead? I felt completely and utterly lost, and I couldn't imagine what Nikolai was thinking in that moment.

Learning you had a child that everyone hid from you had to hurt. Not to mention the guilt I saw etched all over his face.

"What are you going to do with your wife?"

She knew he had a child out there and said nothing.

"She's already dead," he responded as if it was a passing thought, and looked up at me. "You say she's pregnant? Are you married?"

I nodded.

"Good. I'd hate to have to kill you now."

Guess he wasn't as afraid of my brother as I thought.

The door opened and the leader, who I'd learned was called Dimitri, came in. "Luca and his men have a meet at the docks in two hours."

"Do you have a location?"

Dimitri tipped his head in affirmation.

"Get the men ready," Nikolai said, "We leave in five."

I stood up, ready to follow the Russian out the door, but stopped when I noticed Mase and Silas standing behind me. "You guys don't have to come."

This wasn't like taking on Ryker's lackeys. I was about to march into a full out mafia fight. There was a good chance I wouldn't come back.

Silas crossed his arms, while Mase arched a brow.

"We knocked on the Russian mafia's front door with you."

"Bratva," Nikolai corrected.

"Whatever," Mase grumbled, "We're not going anywhere."

My gaze shifted from one to the other. For years I'd kept myself guarded, not letting anyone in. And right now, staring at the faces of two of my friends ready to lay down their lives for me, I couldn't remember why.

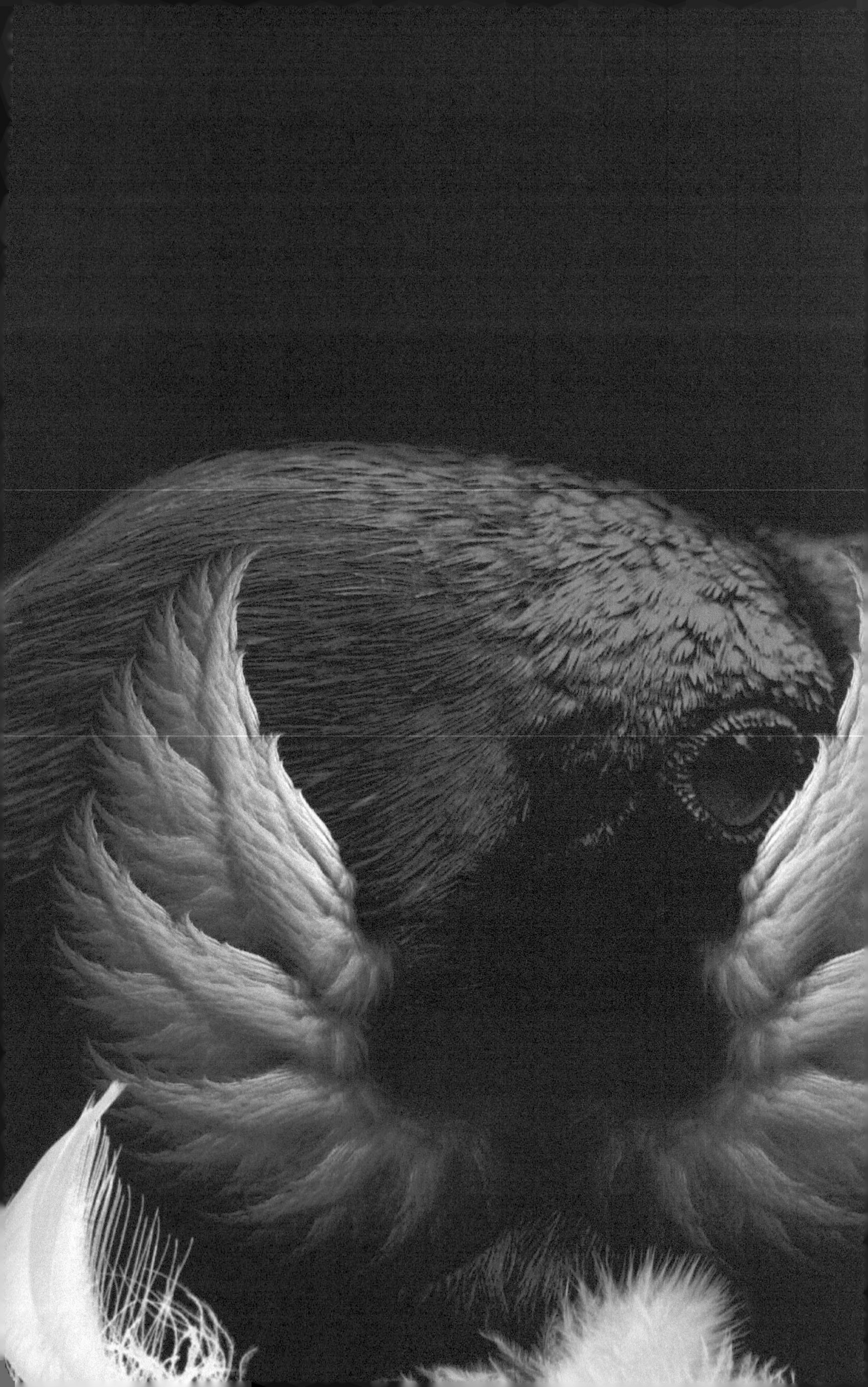

Chapter 31
Lana

I looked at Riley and the man she was glaring at, wondering if I should know who he was. Noah Torres? I hadn't heard that name before. At least, I didn't think I had. He didn't look familiar.

"Your friend seems confused," Noah's mouth lifted as he took a few steps closer. "Haven't you told her about me?"

"Sorry, rapist prick isn't high on my list of conversation topics."

My eyes flew open. Rapist? "Did he…"

"No," this time it was Riley who smirked, "He doesn't have the balls for that, do you, Noah?"

Noah's face dropped and I couldn't help but shiver. I got the feeling I was caught in the middle of some feud I knew nothing about. Not really a good place to be. A little information beyond the tension in the air would be helpful. Like, what did he have in common with Lillianna Whitley?

"Is that what this is?" Riley snarled, "Some half cocked plan for revenge?"

"Revenge?" Noah chuckled, "Oh no, that's just a bonus. My job is her."

I shuffled back when his chin pointed at me. "Me?"

"Yes you, sweetheart." Noah's gaze shifted to me. "But don't worry, I'm just the delivery boy."

Delivery boy? What did that mean? Where, or who, was he delivering me to?

Riley snickered, "Still someone else's patsy I see."

He did not like that and I really wished Riley would stop pissing him off. I looked behind Noah at the door, gauging if I could make it before he caught me.

My gigantic belly reminded me of how slow I was. I'd never make the distance, but maybe Riley could? She was small and fast. She might be able to get out and get us some help. It was a chance at least.

As if she could sense my thoughts, Riley shook her head and picked herself up off the floor.

"You want her," she said stepping in front of me, "Then you have to go through me."

Folding my arms over my stomach, I pressed my back against the wall and peeked around Riley to keep an eye on our captor. The glint in his face as he stepped forward, caused the hairs on the back of my neck to rise.

"That's what I like about you, Riley. You're the first to sacrifice yourself for someone else." Noah tipped his head as the door opened and three other men came into the room. "But this time, all you can do is watch."

The next second, all hell broke loose. All the men except Noah charged forward, lunging for my friend, and she snarled and swung back at them. I wanted to help her, but I was too afraid my babies would get hurt. I had to protect them. I had to.

Tears rolled down my cheeks as I begged them to stop and helplessly watched Riley get pinned to the ground. And still she didn't stop. She growled, and spit, bashing her head into any body part that got close enough. She was no match for three men though, and soon there was nothing she could do but lay there huffing out spent breaths.

My eyes locked on Noah, who was staring at me with a strange look on his face.

"I want you to know, this is nothing personal."

It felt pretty personal. I had no idea what was going on, or why this man was involved, but I did know, I needed to stay away from him.

Lifting myself off the ground, I slowly inched along the wall. Hoping I'd get close enough to the door before he caught me. It was still open a crack. If I could get there and scream, someone might hear me. I made it about two feet.

Noah was on me in a flash. Slamming his palm on the wall and stopping my slow escape.

"Leave her alone, asshole!" Riley screamed, and began struggling again.

"No can do," Noah's brown eyes trailed over my face, "The job's not done."

I sucked back a gasp and waited as dread settled in my gut, pumping panicked spikes through my system. Time literally slowed down, voices drowned out, and all I could smell was the minty scent of Noah's breath.

I whimpered and shrunk back when his fingers wrapped around the back of my neck and he pulled me in closer. His hard body pressed against mine, ear grazing off the shell of my ear.

"Lillianna says hi" he whispered, and threw his fist into my stomach.

Pain folded me in half as my knees gave out and I crumpled to the floor. Riley was screaming, and Noah was grunting as he continued his assault on my belly. I tried to protect them. Curled my body around my babies and shielded them with my arms. It didn't matter what happened to me.

I could take each hit, every spike of pain, as long as my babies were okay. But no matter how hard I tried I could stop him, I couldn't shelter my stomach from his strikes. My arms weren't large enough to shelter my whole belly.

When it finally stopped, my entire body ached, tears streamed down my face, and it hurt to breathe.

Noah smirked and hissed down at me. "You shouldn't step in gardens you don't' belong in."

"You're a lot of thing Noah Torres," Riley once again tried to lunge at my attacker. "But I never took you for a racist asshole."

"Racist?" Noah threw his head back and laughed. "You really are stupid. This has nothing to do with race. It's all about the power and money baby. The original plan was for a Torres Whitley alliance, then you came."

He swung his foot kicking me again. The hot slices of agony wracking through my body wouldn't let my brain work long enough to wrap around what he was saying.

"Just imagine what my family could do with a seat to the king-dom?" He hit me again, this time in the head.

I was too afraid to move and look up at the man panting down at me, so I played dead. Tucked my head into my curled body and let my chin quiver. I could hear Riley's sobs.

They called to me, tugging at my heart and making me want to reassure her. But my body seized as my stomach clamped down hard and a gush of wetness soaked through my pants.

"Feel that?" Noah crouched down and swept my hair off my sweat soaked forehead, "That's your babies coming. And do you know what I'm going to do when they get here?"

My stomach cramped, causing me to cry out as a searing burn raced through my system.

"I'm going to take them out that door and throw them in the ocean. Ashen Springs doesn't belong to The Order. It belongs to us. Why do you think Lillianna married that dumb fuck Dean?"

Unable to force my aching limbs to do anything else, I whimpered and shook my head. I was going to die and my babies were going to die because their grandmother wanted more than what she already had. I could live with someone hating me because of the way I looked. But this… this was worse.

"You sick fuck!" Riley screamed, "I'll kill you!"

"I'm sorry," Noah sighed, and brushed his thumb along my jawbone. "I've been paid a lot of money to make sure your babies don't survive."

Nan was wrong. Good didn't triumph over evil. Lillianna won. This time when the contraction came, I surrendered to the pain. Letting blackness bleed into my mind. I'd failed. There was no point in fighting anymore. My babies innocent souls were being traded for nothing more than simple greed.

The last thing I heard before falling into oblivion, was Riley's desperate screams, mingling with echoing pops.

"It's time to wake up, Angel."

Parker was calling me, but I couldn't see him. There was nothing around me but darkness.

"Parker!" I called out desperately, searching for his comforting arms. "Where are you?"

"I'm right here, Angel."

I could feel his fingers grazing over my skin and his hot breath warming my cheek. But where was he?

"I'm right here, baby, open your eyes."

I felt myself floating up, pulled by his voice. Drawn into a world more substantial than the one I was trapped in. Cool air tickled my arms as the soft beep of something mechanical filled my ears. My eyes fluttered open, clearing the haze fogging my mind. The first thing I saw was a pair of grey eyes staring down at me. Parker's eyes!

Wait…

I twisted my head, looking around the room. White walls, beeping machines, along with a clean floor. I was in a hospital room! Laying on a soft bed with an IV in my arm. But where was Noah? And Riley.

"But…" I turned back to Parker, "How?"

"Don't worry about that." He smiled down at me and pressed his lips to my forehead. "Would you like to meet our children?"

Oh my god! The babies!

My heart picked up it's pace, thundering in my chest. "They're okay?"

"They're perfect," Parker beamed down at me. "Just like their momma."

Relief unlike I'd ever felt washed over me. It felt like I was taking my first breath, but I needed to see them. I wouldn't be able to relax until I held them and kissed their tiny heads. "Where are they?"

"In the nursery," Parker strode across the room to grab a wheel-chair. "Come on, I'll take you to see them. There is something you should know."

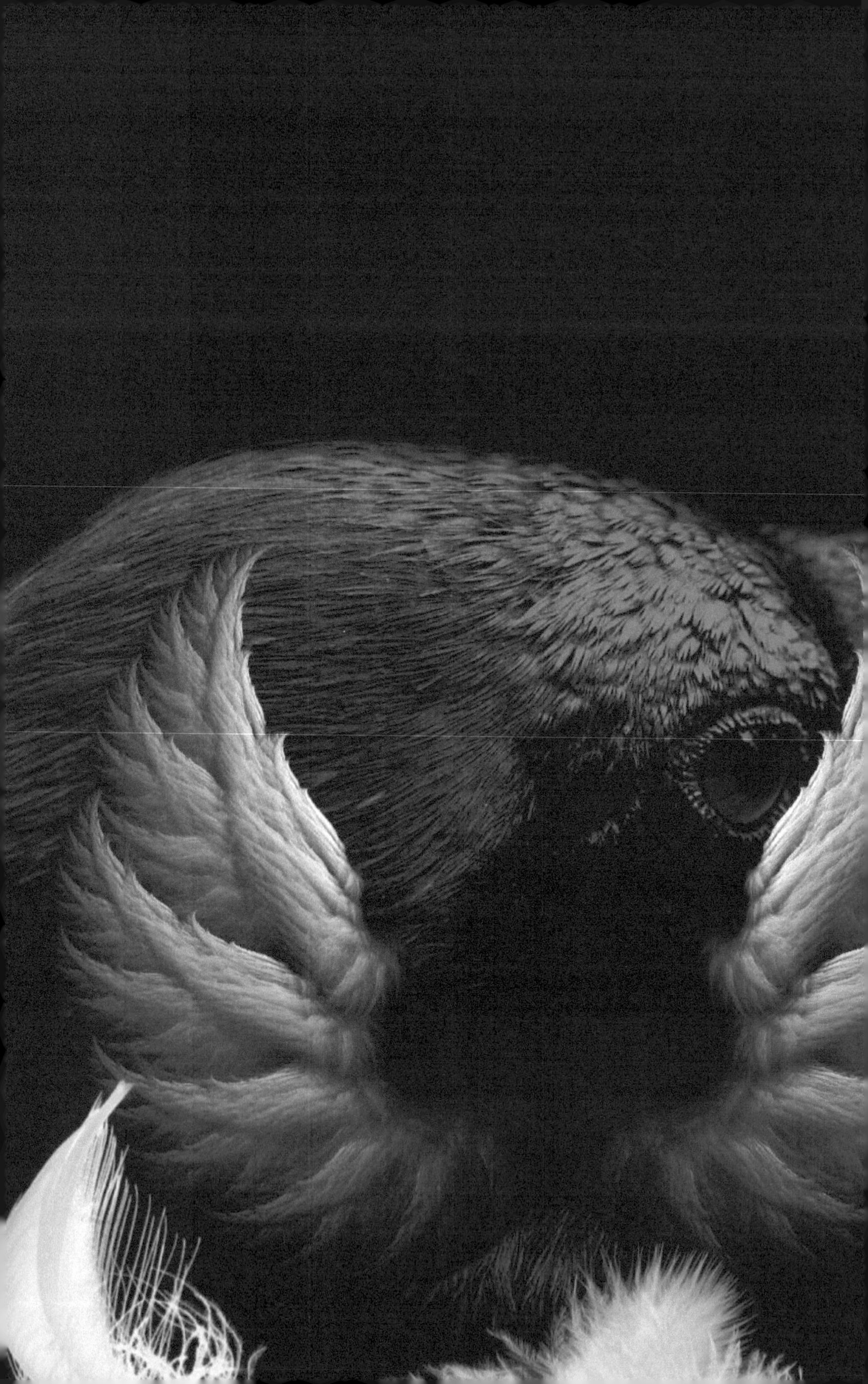

Chapter 32
Lana

Parker was right, our babies were perfect. He had me worried when he said there was something I should know, and when I found out our daughter was blind, I couldn't help but blame myself. But it turned out to be genetic.

Something my child had inherited from my father's side. A father who happened to be alive, and the head of the Russian mob! It was a lot to take in.

After I talked to Nan and met Nikolai, I realized that my father knew as much about me as I did of him. I didn't blame him for it. Nan thought she was protecting me by hiding me. I didn't blame her, either. No one could use me against Nikolai if they didn't know I existed.

Nan did what she had to, to keep me safe. Just like I was doing for my children, by accepting Nikolai's men into my house. No mother should have to worry about armed protection for their son. Unless that son was the heir to the bratva throne.

"Nan, stop hogging the babies."

She scrunched her nose at me. She had our son, Weston, in one arm and our daughter, Winslow, in the other. Meanwhile, poor Ava was bouncing back and forth, waiting for her turn.

"They're my grandchildren," Nan argued.

"They're my niece and nephew," Ava challenged back. "Come on, give me one."

I couldn't help but chuckle as Nan hesitantly handed Weston to his aunt.

Our babies were so beautiful, I couldn't stop looking at them. They were so different for twins, yet so similar. Weston Sampson Whitley – Sampson was our way of combining Silas and Mason, as they did help rescue Riley and I – had my dark hair, with his father's grey eyes. His complexion was darker as well, but more olive looking than bronze, like me.

His sister, Winslow Greta Whitley, was the opposite. She had my eyes with a light dusting of her father's sandy-blonde hair, and a creamy light complexion. Lillianna would be proud of her.

A lot had happened in the past week. Too much love for my son and daughter was a good problem to have. Though I couldn't blame Nan and Ava for fighting over them.

Parker assured me that I wouldn't have to worry about his mother anymore. I didn't ask why, or what happened to her, because I didn't want to know. Nor did I want to know about the man who'd beaten me. Riley was fine, my babies were fine, and that was all that mattered. It was time to move on to the next phase of our lives.

"Is my sister hogging the kids again?" Parker chuckled and strutted into the room with a big bouquet of orchids and lilies.

I had six others just like it. One for every day I'd been here.

"No," I smiled at him and happily accepted his kiss, "It was Nan this time."

Nan curled her lip at me as she softly cradled Winslow.

Everybody had come to see the babies. I think the first time I'd seen Micha smile was when Winslow grabbed his finger. He promptly wiped it off his face when he saw me gawking. Logan had started to instruct my son on proper pick-up lines.

Which, according to him, Weston was never to use on Logan's new baby sister Tristan, or else. Riley agreed. Shelby was all about the babies right now. I think it terrified Logan, because anytime she'd mention their future kids, he'd pull her out of the room.

Silas and Mason had been by a couple of times. Silas brought his cousin, Finn, who asked me a million questions, and Mason brought Shelby's sister and set up a tea party to have with Winslow. And then there was Preston...

He'd hold his niece and do a bit of the typical baby cooing, but when it came to his nephew, he'd glare down at the baby in his arms. The weird part was, I swear Weston glared back at him.

"Well," Parker said, looking at Nan and Ava, "You two can leave."

"Hey!" they both cried out in unison.

"Nope. don't care," Parker shook his head and scooped the babies out of their arms, "I want to spend time with my family, get out."

Nan huffed, but obliged, gathering her purse and kissing my cheek before she walked out. Ava was a little harder to shoo away. She argued and stamped her foot a couple times before she eventually gave in, promising she'd be back tomorrow. Which I didn't doubt.

Ava Whitely sure loved those babies, which was a little scary. Chuckling to myself, I watched her shake her blonde head, stick her chin up in the air, and prance out.

"You didn't have to tell them to leave."

Parker placed the twins in their bassinet and nodded at the door. "Someone else is waiting to see you."

I looked at the door in time to see Harper come in. My heart lifted as she threw her arms around me. She was gone on a trip with her dad and I hadn't seen her in two weeks. And after what Parker told me about Luke, I really needed to. Her gentle smile and warm gaze reminded me what true friendship felt like. Yes, I had Riley and Shelby, but Harper was my person, and she always would be.

I tucked my face into her neck and sobbed, "I missed you."

"I missed you too," she sobbed back. "I can't believe you had the babies."

"I can't believe it either."

We sat there for awhile, catching up on everything. Well, I didn't tell her about the kidnapping and beating. There was no need to worry Harper when everything was dealt with. I did tell her about my father though.

I hated keeping secrets from her, and Nikolai was making an effort, so he was probably going to be in my life from now on. Plus, it was kind of hard to hide the armed guard.

The whole mafia thing gave Harper another reason to be jumpy.. though she did seem extra twitchy today. Maybe it was because Sean had graduated and would be going off to college soon? Graduation was something else I'd missed. I wanted to watch Parker get his diploma, but he didn't even go.

Stubborn jerk wouldn't leave my side. Just like he refused to go to college until I could. Bastard used the 'our family has to stick together' excuse on me.

I don't know how long Harper and I chatted. Time seemed to just pass by as we cooed over the twins and chatted away. Before we knew it, Harper's dad was walking into the room.

"Hey Pumpkin, you ready?"

Harper was standing over the bassinet staring down at the twins. "Look at how cute they are."

Ned Callaghan nodded a greeting at Parker, and strode across the room to peek in on the sleeping infants. My blood turned to ice cold when his lips curved up, baring a gold tooth.

"Remember to keep your mouth shut, Doll." The ogre smiled down at me, moonlight glinting off his gold tooth. "No one would believe you anyway."

Oh my god!

"Aw," Ned cooed at my kids as I fought to pull in a breath. "Look at their cute little faces."

I could feel his hands on me as clear as if it was happening now. His fingers digging into my skin as he held me down and used me hard.

"Baby," Parker's brows knit together with the concern on his face. "Are you okay?"

I wanted to tell him. My mouth even opened to do so, but I couldn't choke out the words. I just kept staring at Harper standing next to her dad. She tucked a lock of hair behind her ear and smiled. A big, genuine, smile like she used to. Before her mother ran off and Mason started tormenting her. Ned was all Harper had. How could I take that away from her?

"Lana," Parker called out with a little more urgency.

I swallowed down my pain and forced a smile on my face. "I'm fine."

Apparently he didn't believe me. "Are you sure?"

Looking over at Ned with his hand on Harper's shoulder, I nodded. "Yeah, I'm just a little tired."

Truth was, I wasn't sure if I'd ever sleep again.

THREE MONTHS LATER:

I drove down the dirt road, winding around a clutch of trees leading to the basement. Every day for the past three months I'd been here paying a visit to the asshole that had beaten my wife. Today was the day I was going to end it.

There was something I had to do first, though. Someone else who deserved to carve a pound of flesh out of Noah Torres's hide.

Riley was sitting on the back of her car, looking rather unamused when I pulled up.

"What am I doing here, Parker?"

I gave her a glance and headed for the middle of the clearing. "Did you tell Micha you were coming?"

He'd lose his shit if he found out about this. Lana told me what

Riley did for her. How she fought multiple men to protect her. Someone should return the favor.

"No, I didn't tell him," she grumbled, "And what's with all the cloak and dagger stuff?"

Instead of answering her, I stepped on a rock to my left. Riley's eyes went wide as a slab of dirt slid out of the way, revealing a set of stone stairs.

I walked down a few steps and paused to glance back at her. "You coming?"

It was probably sheer morbid curiosity that made her follow. Either way, she came down the steps, going where I led. I made it a point to stay away from the branding room, since that was where Ryker had held her and Mase.

Plus, she was unconscious when they dragged her out here. The last thing I needed to explain to Micha was why his girlfriend had watched the basement burn.

Once we got to the right door, I stopped and looked her square in the eyes.

"Before we go in here, I want you to know, that you don't have to do anything you don't want to." Her brow rose as I continued, "But whatever happens in this room, will stay between you and me."

"Alright?" she stated, with a lip curl.

I sensed she had a question, but the second I opened the door they were lost. Riley was too busy eyeing the bruised body tied to a slab.

Noah rolled his face our way and groaned, "Just kill me already."

The dry blood coating his skin made me smile.

"Parker, what's this?"

A way for Riley to gain her power back, that's what this was. She'd lost it twice now. Once, when Ryker took her, and again with this prick. I couldn't bring Ryker back from the dead, but lucky for her, this asshole was still alive.

"Revenge," I stated, holding out a knife for her.

"What am I supposed to do with this?"

"Whatever you want."

She eyed the blade carefully. "What if I don't want to do anything?"

"Then don't do anything," I shrugged.

It didn't matter to me what she did. The opportunity was out there if she wanted it. After a few minutes of thought, she gingerly took the weapon from my hand and walked over to Noah. He might've gotten away with a couple of minor slaps–the girl didn't seem that into it–if he hadn't opened his mouth.

"Come to thank me for the show?"

Smooth move dumbass. Never taunt a chick with a knife.

Riley *lost* it. She went off, slapping and punching her frustration out on his already beaten body. I let her have her fun. Let her vent her rage on him, until she slammed the knife down into his nuts. That's when I grabbed her.

"Okay, that's enough."

"Let me go," she snarled, swinging her fists back at me. "He needs to hurt."

I grabbed her face in my hands and forced her burning glare on me. "You need to leave now, before you do something you can't come back from."

Hurting someone was a lot different than taking their life.

Realization flooded into her face as her assault ceased.

"You're right," she sighed, taking one last look at Noah, "I should go."

I let her go and walked over to Noah, pulling out the blade she'd stuck in.

"Parker," Riley called from the doorway, "Thank you."

I gave her a nod in response. Once Riley was gone, I slid the blade across Noah's neck and watched him bleed out.

"Do we have to?" my angel whined.

"Yes, baby," I nodded, "We have to."

"It's just… weird."

Lana and I finally completed the bonding ceremony the day before, but still had to do the coupling, which she was not looking forward to. I tried to make it as comfortable on her as I could. I picked Lou to watch us. She was officially his patient, and seemed to like him the best. Besides for my dad, who she claimed was a worse option than asking her own dad to watch.

She stamped her foot and popped her bottom lip out.

"Why don't you have a nap?" I smirked, and kissed the top of her head, "And I'll take the twins for a walk?"

Like any new mother, my Angel was tired. Lack of sleep, and three o'clock feedings would do that. So, I tried to help any way I could. Not to mention, I loved spending time with my kids.

After tucking Lana into bed, I headed for the nursery. I found Preston inside the room, staring at my son. Since Nikolai's men were here keeping guard, he'd been around a lot.

"What are you doing?"

"Your baby stinks."

"So, change him."

Preston's eyes narrowed on my son, watching him from his crib. "No, that's what he wants me to do."

I shook my head and sighed.

A few minutes later, I had the babies all snug in their stroller and was walking down the sidewalk. I couldn't help but notice how nice it was out. The perfect day. The sun was shining, my family was happy, and I got to end the prick who'd hurt my wife.

Things couldn't get much better than this. At least, that was what I thought, until I saw Mase and Silas standing outside Silas's house, watching the neighbors move in.

"Hey, check it out," Mase said when he saw me walking up, "This this the greatest shit I've seen."

Judging by the twinkle in Mase's eyes, and the scowl on Silas's face, I'd have to say his best friend didn't agree.

"You don't have to live next to the Manson family."

Okay, that made me look. Down the street sat a large moving truck that men were carrying boxes and furniture out of. Nothing too unusual or upsetting there. The five half-naked little boys running around screaming bloody murder, however... Now that made me chuckle.

"Oh look," I teased the grumpy asshole to my left, "It's your dream neighbors."

"Go fuck yourself," Silas grumbled back. "They're on your street too, asshole."

"Yeah, but I'm way down there," I tipped my head back down the road.

"You missed the best part." Mason could barely hold back his laughter, "They led a camel to the back."

My brow rose. "A camel?"

"Not just any camel," he sang with a raised finger, "A camel with an eye patch."

A camel with an eye patch? Uh huh?

I was about to ask if he was high again when a cooing whistle assailed my ears. We all turned to see a peacock. Tailfeathers spread out in all their majestic glory as it pranced back and forth in front of Mason, moving it's neck while calling out a song.

Well, you don't see that everyday.

Mase cocked a brow and leaned over. "Is there a peacock flirting with me, or am I still in rehab?"

Not quite believing what I was seeing, my gaze shifted from the bird to Mase, and back again. The bird lifted its feet in a proud march and bent over, shaking its ass and tail.

I'd seen girls hit on Mason, and a couple of guys, but this was a first.

Mase waved his hands at the peacock, "Go away, bird."

It responded by clucking out a shrill coo and shuffling closer.

"Any of you fuckers know how to turn down a peacock?" Mason asked, while keeping his eyes on his unwanted admirer.

"Shoot it," Silas suggested. "I got a gun in the house."

"I can't shoot it?!"

Silas cocked a brow at Mase, "Why not?"

"Dude," I don't think I'd ever seen Mase look more insulted, "It's a bird."

"Exactly. Bird is good eating."

Mase's mouth dropped. "You can't eat it. You wouldn't eat someone's dog!"

"If it was running around unattended I would."

And by unattended, Silas meant wandering around making noise and screwing up his hyper organized life.

"Bloody hell, Roger," a girl yelled while running up to grab the bird's leash. Yup, the peacock had a leash. Along with a tiny pink collar. "I'm sorry about that, he's used to having room to run."

The girl was British, the accent was a dead give away. She wasn't bad to look at, either. A tiny thing, with platinum blonde hair and dark, almost black eyes. Mase seemed to notice her looks too, because he immediately perked up, plastering a charming smile on his face.

"Hey," he stepped forward and held out his hand, "I'm Mason."

She accepted his hand with a smile. "Star."

"Star isn't a name," Silas barked out, making both Mase and I arch a brow, "It's a thing."

Normally, he was a pretty quiet guy. Didn't speak unless he had to. It was completely out of character for him to snap at someone like that. Unless it was Mase, of course. Even more interesting was the deep red flush that flooded the girl's face when she looked at him.

"The grumpy fucker here," Mason threw his arm around Silas and flashed him a smile, "Is Silas."

Star walked over and held out her hand, "It's nice to meet you."

Silas took one look at her outstretched hand, and promptly turned around and walked into the house, slamming the door behind him.

"Well, he's a bit of a cunt, isn't he?" Star muttered.

Mason and I were both staring at Silas's door. While I was confused as to what the grumpy prick had up his ass this time, there was a sly grin on Mason's face.

"You have no idea," he sang as the grin grew.

And just like that, Mason Kessler had a new goal in life.

EIGHT MONTHS AGO:

Somewhere else in a small room where quiet beeps filled the air...
    "Doctor, we have a pulse."

Hey, Jackass

What the fuck Mason? Am I not good enough to talk to in person? I see you every day in school and do you even say hi? No, you run away and avoid me. And now, you're writing me a letter like everything is fine. Alright, fine. You want me to write a letter and pretend everything is normal. Here you go, Jackass!

Everything here is pretty good, (as you know). Logan and I have a new sister, Lana has the cutest twins, and Paisley is beyond happy. Seriously, I think she might need some help. No one should smile ALL THE TIME. I guess the only thing I can complain about is this prick who's been avoiding me. Now, now, don't worry. I know you want to shed some tears for my misfortune, but I've got it handled. See, I'm going to HUNT down the asshole and corner him in a room until he talks to me. And he WILL talk to me, because I've got steel toed boot I'll kick him in the balls with if he doesn't.

Anyways, I hope everything is going good with you and you're getting lots of exercise, because you never know when you'll have to run.

Hugs and kisses,
Your imminent
death.

Ten years ago:

My nose crinkled as my dad hugged my mom and kissed her cheek. Adults were so gross. They were always holding hands and stuff. Didn't they see the cooler of snacks was beside them?

I wanted a snack, but I wasn't going to go over there. Then my mom would kiss my cheek. Eww. She'd been all lovey since she got back from making her movie.

I'd watched the last movie she made. My dad said I couldn't watch this one, though, cause I was too young. I was always too young. When I got bigger, I was going to watch all the movies and do the other things I wasn't allowed to, and no one could stop me.

"Silas! Put those down." My dad waved his finger at the feathers in my hand, "They're dirty."

"Stop it, Martin. They're just feathers." My mom reached up and touched my dad's cheek. "Let Silas have his fun."

Yeah, let me have my fun.

I wouldn't say that out loud, or else I'd lose my game. Or worse...I'd get the belt.

"Do you know how many diseases birds carry?" My dad's firm eyes swung my way. "Put them down, now."

With a sigh, I opened my hand and let the feathers flutter to the ground.

It took me forever to collect those. When I grew up, I was going to have all the feathers, too. I'd sprinkle them on my furniture so when my dad came over, he'd have to sit on them.

My dad's brow rose when I just stood there glaring at him. "Go play."

Those were my feathers. I frowned and crossed my arms.

"We can go home if you want."

Instead of arguing, I stomped my way back over to the sandbox, where Mason and Harper were playing with my cousin, Finn. It took all morning for Mom and me to convince my dad to come to Cherry Lake, and we'd just gotten here. I didn't want to go home. Why were adults so bossy?

My lip curled at Mason's mom. She was still standing on the docks, staring out at the water. She was so weird.

The lake was busy today. Kids were everywhere while the adults laid around. Even Logan was here, and he never came to Cherry Lake. Everyone was happy, except Mason's mom. She was just standing there by the water. Not moving, or sticking her foot in it, or anything.

"Why is she doing that?"

"I don't know. Maybe she's trying to find that mermaid guy...." *Mason's head tipped up as he squinted against the sun, "what was his name?"*

"King Triton?"

I rolled my eyes at Harper's answer. "Did you guys watch that movie again?"

Every time I went over to Mason's house and Harper was there, that movie was playing in the background. He said it was because Harper liked it, but I think he liked the mermaid's red hair.

It wasn't even close to the same red as Harper's hair. Hers was darker, and it shone in the sun and bounced when she ran. It was also really soft when I pulled it.

Harper's brother ran by, yelling, "I got it!"

Clutched tightly in his raised fist was a swimsuit top, flapping around like a flag behind him as he ran. Actually...it would make a good flag, and we needed one for the sandcastle. Maybe Sean would drop it?

That idea got squashed when his mom ran after him. "Sean Douglas Callaghan, you get your ass back here right now!"

I'm not sure who's suit Sean had snatched, but their mom didn't seem happy about it. Oh well, I had other things to worry about.

Like my cousin.

"No, Finn." I sprang across the sandbox and grabbed the rock out of

his hand before he could stick it in his mouth. "Why do babies have to eat everything?"

"Oral exploration is a key development stage for kids Finn's age."

We all cocked our heads at my dad's answer.

"What's that mean?" Harper whispered.

"Don't ask," I warned her. "Then he'll explain it."

LUKE

For more Luke Lannister check out Vivian Murdoch's Bastard's Bride

Ashley Hardesty here's your answer

Thank for reading Scartissue.

If you enjoyed this book please consider leaving a review. Reviews are always much appreciated by authors.

If you'd like to be among the first to know about new releases and get an inside look into my world join my Facebook group T.L. Hodel's Murder Of Ravens.

Look for more books in The Order Of Ravens and Wolves.

Next book in the series Accident-Prone

Also by T.L. Hodel

The Order Of Ravens And Wolves:
Aftereffect
Scartissue
Happenstance
Accident-Prone
Relapse
Panic-Button (coming soon)

Deviant House:
Innocence
Innocence corrupted (coming soon)

The Lost Souls:
Adversaries
Frenemies

Brothers Of Shadow And Death:
Backfire
Backstab (coming soon)

The Seven Sins Series:
Pride

The Buchanan Brothers
Twisted Abel
Twisting Tallon (Coming soon)

ABOUT THE AUTHOR

T.L. Hodel is a Canadian author, poet and artist. Through coming up from a difficult childhood she exceled at writing, having her first poem published in junior high. When not writing she occupies herself with numerous crafts, hobbies and is an avid gamer and horror movie fan. She lives in Calgary with her kids and cat, (who is a complete asshat), and may have a slight weakness for true crime shows.

Connect with T.L. Hodel online:
www.facebook.com/groups/272402970612789/?ref=share
www.instagram.com/tarahodel
www.facebook.com/Author-TL-Hodel-102923044775313/